SAPPHIRE

Sapphire
By
Paul Anthony

Published by
Paul Anthony Associates UK
http://paul-anthony.org/

By the same author

~

The 'Boyd' Crime Thriller Series...
The Fragile Peace
Bushfire
The Legacy of the Ninth
Bell, Book, and Candle
Threat Level One
White Eagle
The Sultans and the Crucifix
Thimbles

*

The 'Davies King' Crime Thriller Series...
The Conchenta Conundrum.
Moonlight Shadows
Behead the Serpent
Breakwater

*

In the Thriller and Suspense Series...
Nebulous
Septimus
Sapphire

*

By the same author

~

In Autobiography, true crime, and nonfiction...
Authorship Demystified
Strike! Strike! Strike!
Scougal

*

In Poetry and Anthologies...
Sunset
Scribbles with Chocolate
Uncuffed
Coptales
Chiari Warriors

*

In Children's book (with Meg Johnston) ...
Monsters, Gnomes and Fairies (In My Garden)

~

GLOSSARY
of basic surveillance terms

~

Boss car	= The leader of a surveillance team
Commentary	= Talk on the wireless network
Trafford	= Manchester Police Surveillance Squad
Eyeball	= The officer watching the target
Handler	= The detective meeting an informant.
Medway	= Kent Constabulary Surveillance Team
Mersey	= Merseyside Serious Crime Squad
Net	= The surveillance wireless network
Reciprocal	= Returning the same route
Red Alpha	= Maguire's Surveillance Team
Sabre Team	= Metropolitan Police Armed unit
Sierra	= Suspect
Skiddaw	= Cumbria Surveillance Squad
Strike!	= Detain and arrest
London Bridge	= Security Service Surveillance Branch
Tail End Charlie	= The last vehicle in the convoy
Tango	= Surveillance Target
Trigger	= Firearms Incident
Victor	= Vehicle

~

1

The Mountains of Mourne
County Down, Northern Ireland
One Sunday morning, some years ago

The mountains of Mourne run down to the sea, or so it is said.

Actually, the mountains of Mourne slope down to the Irish Sea from Northern Ireland's highest mountain which is Slieve Donard. The summit stands at 2,790 feet above sea level and dominates the granite mountain range in County Down. It is an area of outstanding natural beauty.

The Mourne Wall was built between 1904 and 1922 and connects fifteen summits to enclose the catchment basin of the Silent Valley and Ben Crom reservoirs. To the south-west of the Silent Valley reservoir lies a village supporting a population of fewer than 200 people. Known as Atticall, the source of the Kilkeel River is found just south of this village, and, from this location, the land sweeps downwards to a plain where the larger town of Kilkeel is situated. The Kilkeel River is a narrow stream that winds its way from its source near Atticall to the harbour at Kilkeel and the Irish Sea.

Kilkeel has a population of about 7,000 people and traces its origins back to the 11th century. It is the most southerly port in Northern Ireland. The town is the home of the Irish Fishing Fleet which boasts the largest armada of seagoing trawlers based in Northern Ireland. The fleet operates out of Kilkeel harbour and fishes the Irish Sea. They land their catch on the west coast of England at various ports stretching from Fleetwood in Lancashire to Silloth in Cumbria.

On this day, a fishing vessel left Kilkeel harbour when the day was moving towards night. It by-passed the Isle of Man and headed directly to the port of Whitehaven.

The journey from Kilkeel harbour to Whitehaven port took over three hours due to adverse weather conditions and a desire from the trawler's captain to deliberately steer well clear of other ships in its immediate area. Every blip on the radar screen had to be evaluated, assessed, and challenged. Eventually, in the early hours of Sunday morning, the vessel put into Whitehaven harbour and began to unload its catch.

Below deck, a man called Ricky paid the captain a substantial cash sum for the ride, shook hands, and made his way topside where he stood close to a deckhand whom he knew as Sean McArdle.

Gesturing for Ricky to remain exactly where he was, Sean laid a metal gangplank from ship to shore and then stepped onto Whitehaven's quayside.

Looking towards the town, Sean swivelled his head towards Ricky and said, 'Now, Ricky! Quickly! Before they come. Sometimes there's only one. Other times two or three. Don't hang about! You should be safe at this time of night. Good luck!'

Hauling a canvas rucksack over his shoulder, Ricky stepped onto dry land, murmured, 'Thank you,' to Sean, and then growled, 'Now forget my name.'

Sean frowned, shook his head, and then watched Ricky step briskly into the town centre.

Ten minutes later, with the edifice of the Beacon Museum gazing down on the harbour, a grey saloon car drove onto the dock. The male occupant got out of the vehicle and approached Sean saying, 'Special Branch! I'd like to speak to the captain. Security check! Usual procedure!'

'Of course,' replied Sean in a twisted Irish accent. 'Sure, I remember you from last month, so I do. How are you, my friend?'

'Well, thank you. Sean McArdle, isn't it?'

'That's me.'

'Any problems on your voyage from Northern Ireland?'

'That'll be a no sir, so it will. Sure, it's a bit windy out there but no harm done Just a bad day for fishing, so we decided to dock until the weather improved. We'll not be leaving the boat.'

The Special Branch officer nodded his understanding and then glanced towards the captain emerging from the lower deck.

'Sure, it's you again,' greeted the captain with a chuckle. 'Nothing to report, but would you be liking to take a wee drop of Bushmills before you move on.'

'Aye,' replied the detective. 'But only if you can tell me all the latest news from Kilkeel.'

'So, I can,' replied the captain. 'Sean! Fasten down the boat tight for the night. With luck, the weather will be better tomorrow. We'll fish towards Fleetwood if we have to.'

'Aye! Aye! Captain,' replied Sean.

As the Special Branch officer boarded the vessel, Ricky made the taxi rank in the town, negotiated a journey to Carlisle, and took a seat in the rear of the vehicle.

Next to him lay a rucksack containing two kilos of 'once cut' heroin with a street value of at least £120,000 based on multiple 'cuts' at the street dealer level. The product had originated in Colombia, had been shipped across the Atlantic to Dublin in Southern Ireland, and had then been cut in a warehouse rented for the operation from a hundred kilos to smaller more manageable packages for an overabundance of dealers in the distribution chain.

'Come far?' inquired the taxi driver trying to establish a conversation.

'Far enough,' came Ricky's reply. 'I'm tired. Sorry, but I'll take a nap if you don't mind.'

'No problem,' replied the taxi driver as he gunned the car towards the A595 and Cumbria's only city.

Ricky lay back, closed his eyes, knew his adrenalin was at an all-time level, but also knew he had to leave the taxi driver with no memories of the passenger with a rucksack who embarked upon a journey from Whitehaven to Carlisle.

An hour and a half later, the taxi drew into the city centre and the taxi driver shouted, 'Sorry to wake you. I didn't realise you were fast asleep. Whereabouts?'

'The railway station please,' replied Ricky. 'I've got a train to catch.'

The taxi pulled into Court Square where the driver pointed at the meter. Ricky paid the driver in cash, gathered his rucksack, and got out of the vehicle. The taxi took off and headed towards West Cumbria.

Checking the time on the station clock, Ricky walked away from the railway station and headed for the bus station half a mile away. It was just another ruse employed by Ricky. If anything went wrong, the taxi driver might remember a youth who said he was catching a train at Carlisle railway station. The police would spend time going through CCTV footage at the railway station when he had travelled onwards by bus.

Taking a seat at the rear of the coach, Ricky placed the rucksack at his feet, wrapped his foot into one of the handles as a precautionary measure against theft, and gazed out of the window.

The coach set off with Ricky taking in the sights of the city as he sped south through the night.

Back in Kilkeel, Sean McArdle's father reflected on the day and wondered how his son had made out on the fishing trip to Whitehaven. Word in the harbour was that the weather was bad, and the fleet had put into England's west coast until the morning when it was hoped the weather would improve. McArdle's only interest in the fishing fleet was his son who worked as a deckhand on one of the vessels. For himself, he was the town's main drugs dealer. He poured himself a large beer from a can, savoured the drink, and counted the money he had made that day.

Turning to his wife, McArdle said, 'Do you know something?'

'What?'

'That Englishman!'

'What about him?'

'I never got his name.'

'Ronnie!'

'Robbie?' argued the dealer.

'He paid!' replied the wife. 'Young Sean will know him by now anyway. Does it matter?'

'Suppose not. The less we know the better. Just one of many but he was very uptight.'

'What do you mean by uptight?'

'Very security conscious! Determined not to get caught! He spent more time looking around than checking the goods. Anyway, I need to make a note for when he comes again. Ronnie! Yes, I'll call him Ronnie, so I will.'

The dealer's wife chuckled and said, 'Well, that's the first one you let go without getting his name. Idiot! Still, you can write him up as a man of mystery, so you can.'

'The man of mystery,' nodded the dealer. 'Aye! Mister Nameless? I'd say the name he gave us was false anyway.'

The waves pounded the walls of Kilkeel harbour when the drug dealer and his wife turned off the light and went to bed.

~

2

The City
Some years later.
Night

Carlisle's town hall clock began to strike four in the morning when Chris Cobb placed his left foot on the lowest pipe clip and heaved himself off the ground and into the climb. His right foot immediately moved slightly higher up the ageing wall as he sought purchase in the space that separated the brickwork.

The mortar cracked and crumbled when Cobb pushed himself upwards using the strength of his lower limbs, the agility of a cat, and the cunning of a fox.

Grasping the cast iron drainpipe with his gloved hands, Cobb gently tugged the metal, confirmed it was strong enough to take his weight, and then surged upwards digging his toes into the concave mortar joints that were a feature of the old building. Reaching another clip around the drainpipe, Cobb tested its reliability once more and then stubbed his toes into the mortar joints before climbing towards the guttering that bordered the roof of the jewellers.

Striking four, the Town Hall clock looked out upon the stocky figure of a young man who threw a leg over the guttering before heaving himself onto the lowest part of the roof.

Adopting a crouched position, Cobb looked directly towards the face of the clock, chuckled, and quietly remarked, 'Beat you by half a second, but only just.'

Cobb angled his body towards the pitched roof, retained his balance with an outstretched hand that trickled along the timeworn roof tiles, and made his way to the glass skylight.

Removing a short jemmy hooked to his trouser belt, Cobb forced the latch, opened the aperture, and peered into the shop's attic. A black void met Cobb's eyes and initially prevented him from going over the edge and into the depths of the attic.

There was a rustle of clothing when Cobb fumbled for a pen torch and then shone it downwards trying to unmask the shadows lurking below.

Cobb made out a table, four chairs, a cabinet, and a dozen shelves that carried cardboard boxes.

Are the contents of those boxes the jewellery that I'm after, thought Cobb as he leaned down into the attic space to enjoy a better view.

Dropping down to floor level, Cobb pulled open a drawer, rifled a velvet-covered gift box, and removed a diamond and sapphire necklace. He stuffed the necklace inside his jacket and opened the container next to it. The box was empty, so was the next.

In a corner to his left, at the height of the attic's ceiling, a red light began to flash. Cobb realised his actions had activated a movement sensor which had set off a silent alarm.

Three minutes thought Cobb. Three minutes in which to retrace my steps, climb down the drainpipe, and get away before the police arrive. Maybe longer if they are busy.

Calmly, he climbed onto the table and heaved himself back onto the roof before making his way to the corner of the building. Cobb bent down, saw where the guttering met the pipe and began his descent to the ground.

In a monitoring station in Manchester, a light flashed on a computer console and relayed to the operator that a burglar alarm had been activated at Baxter's Jewellers in Carlisle.

The operator lifted her telephone and immediately connected with Cumbria Police in their Headquarters in Penrith.

Moments later, the police control room at Carlisle was notified and responded on the radio with, 'Baxter's jewellers,

English Street. Silent alarm sounding! No sirens, no lights. All city centre units attend. Crime car! Are you available?'

The city crime car that night was manned by Detective Constable Les Maguire, a twenty-five year old local man of medium build with a reputation for being a good thief-taker despite only serving five years in the job. Prior to joining the police, Maguire had worked as double-glazing salesman for a company based in the city. The hours proved long and unsociable. Wages were flat and depended on commission to achieve a good income. Maguire realised that the career path was restricted to the point that it was almost non-existent. A single man, he'd not yet found the girl of his dreams but was hoping he would find her one day. A keen sportsman, Maguire enjoyed running in the winter and playing tennis in the summer. With carefully combed long dark brown hair that rested on his ears and spread towards his collar, Maguire wore his usual black leather blazer, dark jeans, and a blue roll-neck sweater. He was accompanied by an older and more experienced partner in Detective Constable Stan Holland. Stan was also casually dressed. He had recently celebrated his thirtieth birthday although he looked closer to forty than thirty and featured a timeworn face that supported such a theory. Happily married, Stan and his wife were the proud parents of a boy and a girl who had recently started primary school. Unlike Maguire, Stan had joined the police shortly after leaving college and was intent on a successful career. They both knew the city centre well.

Stan lifted the car's radio telephone and replied, 'Crime car attending. Estimated time of arrival is one minute.'

Maguire swung the steering wheel into a gentle arc as they negotiated a long sweeping bend, drove past the old law courts, and entered English Street.

'Drop me here,' suggested Stan. 'I'll take the back. You take the front.'

'Will do,' replied Maguire as he brought the squad car to a standstill. 'Uniform are on their way, but it looks like we're here first.'

Stan Holland was out of the car and running towards one of the many lanes that connected English Street to Blackfriars Street. The city centre was a labyrinth of interconnecting lanes and alleyways that peppered the area, made it a burglar's paradise, and was a maze of hidden niches and doorways that served the criminals well when the hunt was underway.

Maguire hit the accelerator hard, drove another hundred yards, and slammed on the anchors.

Out of the car, he ran to the front door of the jeweller's, shone his torch inside the shop, tried the front door, and then radioed, 'Maguire at scene! All correct at the front!'

'Holland at the rear! All correct!' radioed Stan as the two detectives made a cursory examination of the shop. 'Control! Make a cordon at one-quarter of a mile please.'

'Will do,' from Control who immediately began redeploying officers to various locations to cover possible escape routes.

Two signed police cars arrived, followed closely by a couple of foot patrol officers who radioed for the keyholder to attend and check the premises.

'Basement or roof?' inquired an exceptionally tall uniform Sergeant.

'One or the other,' replied Maguire.

'Or neither if it's a false alarm,' argued Stan. 'These electronic alarms don't always work properly.'

Five minutes later, with the jeweller's still surrounded, the owner of the shop, a Mr Baxter, arrived with a bunch of keys, opened the front door, switched off the alarm, and closed the front door behind him. The police began to search the building.

Watching the police activity from above, Chris Cobb realised a detective had beaten him into the rear lane and the back entrance to the jewellers. Halfway down the drainpipe, he'd heard Stan Holland running down the lane and immediately scampered back to the rooftop. Remaining on the roof, he clambered across a row of air conditioning and heating units that straddled the lane and gave access to the roof of the neighbouring premises.

'I must improve,' he whispered to himself. 'Now can I get across there or not?'

Curling his fingers around the end of the furthest air unit, Cobb pulled himself onto the roof of the newsagents next door. Crouching low, he gradually made his way to the roof of the next building which was a chemist. The two buildings were separated by a narrow lane.

Studying the void, Cobb took a couple of steps back and then leapt across to the roof of the chemist where he landed awkwardly and fell backwards. Grabbing the guttering, he eventually pulled himself up onto the roof and rolled over to get his breath back. Above him, the night clouds masked the moonlight that might have betrayed his presence as he shook his head and wondered how lives were allocated to a cat.

Mr Baxter lit up his shop on every level to help the police search the premises. Yet there was a lack of passion in the search because the officers were used to finding a door panel kicked through, a window smashed, or a jemmy used to force an obvious point of entry at ground level. The consensus was that it was a false alarm that may have been accidently set off by a fault in the electrical circuit, or perhaps a drop in the temperature. There were many theories as to why burglar alarms sometimes went off for no apparent reason.

The determined Maguire negotiated the staircase until he reached the top landing, could see nothing amiss and turned to the owner asking, 'Where would your alarm circuit be broken if someone had broken in up here?'

'The only place you haven't covered is the system in the loft. If the beam is broken there it would tell me that the skylight has been forced. There are no windows in the attic area, by the way. We use it as an extra storeroom. There's nothing of value there.'

'I'll look if you don't mind,' replied Maguire. 'It'll only take a minute, if you don't mind?'

'Thank you,' came the reply. 'The door should be unlocked.'

Maguire turned the handle, entered the room, and immediately felt a draft from above. He shone his torch and took in the heavens above, a skylight that had been forced, and a collection of broken glass and debris littering the floor.

'It's a break,' remarked Maguire flashing his torch into all four corners to ensure that he was alone in the room. 'Stan,' he radioed. 'It's a roof job. Widen the cordon. Our man could still be in the area. I'm going up top.'

'All received,' replied Stan who set about reorganising a search pattern in the city centre.

'Mr Baxter! Have you got a ladder I could borrow?' inquired Maguire.

'No!' replied Baxter. 'Just a three-step footstool but it does me, so it's bound to be enough to get you there.'

The footstool arrived. Maguire manipulated it into position, climbed to the top, and then heaved himself through the gap and onto the rooftop where he flashed his torch and searched the area.

Three buildings away, Chris Cobb was on his hands and knees peering over a low parapet that encircled the pitched roof of a café. Cautiously, he sneaked a view over the parapet and watched Maguire checking the area with a torch.

Step by step, Maguire covered the roof but there was no sign of the offender and he returned to the skylight.

'The skylight has been forced,' radioed Maguire. 'I have a jemmy mark at the point of entry. There's no trace of the offender on the rooftop. Hold the cordon.'

'Will do,' came the reply. 'Scenes of crime examiner requested.'

'Noted,' from the control room radio operator.

'Everything okay down there?' asked Maguire.

'I've just remembered something,' replied the owner. 'I picked out a diamond and sapphire necklace from the stock for my wife. I put it up here out of the way and where I know she wouldn't see it. The box is empty and thrown on the floor. The necklace is gone.'

'I'm sorry to hear that. Mr Baxter. Anything else!' voiced Maguire.

'No! Just the necklace. All one thousand pounds worth of it.'

'I'll be down shortly,' revealed Maguire. 'I'll check on the roof first just in case the thief dropped it. If you have a catalogue with a photograph of the necklace it would be useful.'

'Yes! I have it somewhere. I'll get it for you.'

Retracing his steps, Maguire swept his torch around the roof area looking for the necklace that might have been dropped by the burglar. Nothing came to light, so he revisited the edge of the jeweller's roof, knelt, and noticed a scuff mark on the guttering. He leaned forward and realised there was access from a drainpipe that reached up from ground level. Shining his torch onto the ground, Maguire noticed a scattering of loose mortar that had gathered at the drain.

Climbing up or climbing down, he wondered before radioing Stan Holland with, 'Stan! Halfway down the back lane, you'll see loose brickwork on the ground. What do you think? I reckon he's climbed up the drainpipe from there.'

At ground level, Stan examined the location and replied, 'I'm with you on that one, Les. There's loose mortar up the wall where someone has dug his toes into the space between the bricks, kicked out the mortar, and got onto the roof via the pipe. This is where the scenes of crime examiner should be. Footprints, fingerprints, material trace marks! Who knows what they might find!'

'Burglary and theft,' suggested Maguire. 'Mr Baxter tells me he's short of a diamond and sapphire necklace worth one thousand pounds. It was for his wife's birthday.'

'Well, that's something else to go on. Stolen property! Good! Come on down before you fall,' proposed Stan. 'Or do you want the Fire and Rescue Service to attend with a turntable ladder? Is he still up there?'

Cobb remained glued to a rooftop four buildings away suddenly aware of police below surrounding the area, worried that he might be discovered.

Maguire stood up and looked across the rooftops from left to right. The darkness of the night did not help, and his torch, charged with a fading battery, was no more than a warning of his presence.

Another decision to make, thought Maguire. Fire Service turntable ladder or not?

Checking the time on the Town Hall clock, Maguire considered the matter for a moment and then replied, 'I'd say he was off the roof and gone before we arrived. There's no trace up here. Hold the cordon for half an hour, search the surrounding lanes, and then we'll resume patrol. I have the owner here. I'll do the paperwork. Is that okay with you?'

'Yes! I've got that,' replied Stan. 'I'll do a search in the immediate area down here and then resume patrol. Shout when you're finished. I'll pick you up.'

Maguire switched off his torch, retreated to the skylight, and made his way into the attic room and then the main body of the jeweller's.

'Mr Baxter, I'd like a statement from you, please,' ventured Maguire. 'When was the jeweller's secured. Who secured it? Point of entry! Stuff like that.'

'No problem,' replied Baxter. 'Come to the office and we'll sort that out. I have a photo of the stolen necklace for you, but I need to get back to bed as soon as possible and before the morning.'

'I understand that. Are you sure nothing else has been stolen?'

'Nothing else! I'd hazard a guess that the burglar realised he'd broken the beam and scarpered before it sounded in the control centre in Manchester.'

'Just what I was thinking,' replied Maguire listening to his radio. 'The scene of crime examiner has just arrived. He can do the necessary while we're doing a statement. Come on.'

As the bureaucracy around crime reporting and criminal investigations took over, a crime scene examiner arrived, was briefed by Maguire, and began his inspection as the cordon held its position and Stan Holland continued searching the area.

High on the rooftops, Cobb began to feel the cold when he decided to remain exactly where he was and cuddle into the brickwork. He held the diamond and sapphire necklace up to the moonlight and marvelled at its brilliance before returning his plunder to an inside pocket. Tugging his coat tightly to his chest, Cobb turned the collar up and huddled as close as possible to the wall parapet and bided his time.

Maguire's pen scrawled across a statement form. The scene of crime examiner took an imprint of a jemmy on the skylight and then dusted down looking for fingerprints. Stan Holland exhausted his search of the surrounding area. The cordon was lifted, and the police resumed patrol.

The town hall clock was just leaving five when Maguire shook hands with the owner of the jeweller's shop, bid farewell, and made his way into the main street to be picked up by Stan Holland.

Simultaneously, Chris Cobb hid the jemmy inside his trouser belt at the small of his back and pocketed his gloves. He threw a leg over the parapet, connected with the pipe clip, and began a hurried descent from the roof. As soon as his feet touched the ground, he flattened out his collar, unbuttoned his jacket, and casually made his way down the lane into the adjoining street.

Placing one hand in his pocket, Cobb began quietly whistling to his heart's content. He was brimming with self-confidence and strutted down the street like a peacock.

It didn't take Cobb long to realise he wasn't the only one in the city centre. The Royal Mail night train had just pulled into the city's railway station. A dozen night sorters had disembarked and were headed towards their lodgings. Tired, but cheerful and chatty, they huddled together in small groups as they headed for a day in bed before returning to the station for the next leg of the mail train journey later that day.

The city was slowly beginning to come to life and welcome the new day. A milk float appeared in an adjoining street and the clink of milk bottles could be heard in amongst the chatter of the Royal Mail workers.

And taxis. There was always a taxi plying for hire in the city centre, touring the streets, looking for a pickup from a nightclub or on their way for an early morning pick up.

Carlisle, like so many cities, enjoyed a thriving night economy that gradually merged with the daytime marketplace when night clouds tumbled asunder and dawn eventually broke over the rooftops, church spires, and castle battlements. Such events were almost seamless, but the streets were never short of footfall at any time of day or night.

Stan Holland negotiated the traffic lights and cruised towards Baxter's jewellers looking for his partner.

Maguire waited at the bottom of St Cuthbert's Lane as a stockily built young man in his late teens approached. The detective noticed that the youth had jet-black curly hair and a rounded nondescript face. He wore a three-quarter-length black coat, dark jeans, and an open-necked grey shirt as well as trainers. It was Chris Cobb and Maguire decided to question him as to where he had been that night.

Cobb walked down the lane with a blue hue of light behind him. The colouring of the night sky was caused by the old-fashioned lighting units that lit up the lane and reflected the buildings and night sky that were endemic in the lane at certain times of the night. It was a popular place for photographers and often appeared in several magazines. The location was on the edge of the city's historic quarter.

Glancing at the boarded-up windows, the unevenly paved alley, and the drainpipes dropping from the shop roofs to the ground, Cobb then turned the collar of his coat up. His heartbeat went into overdrive when he realised Maguire was studying him with interest. He continued walking towards Maguire deliberately adopting the centre of the dimly lit lane, but the cockiness in his walk had gone and his nerves were jingling. Conscious of the numerous drainpipes running from roof to ground amidst the shops that sported metal gratings to protect the windows, Cobb forced a faint smile and bid, 'Good morning.'

'On your way to way to work, are we?' inquired Maguire gesturing the man to stop with an outstretched arm.

'Yes, I am,' replied Cobb. 'Why? What's it to you?'

Producing his warrant card, Maguire replied, 'I'm a detective investigating crime in the area. That's all. I wondered who you were and what you were doing at this time of night?'

'Early shift at the biscuit factory in Caldewgate, boss,' lied Cobb quickly. 'What's happened?'

'A factory worker?' queried Maguire.

'Cracker packer,' chuckled Cobb. 'Best crackers money can buy! A detective? Wow! I've never met a detective before. Anyone hurt then?'

'No, no-one hurt,' replied Maguire. 'And your name is?'

'Christopher Cobb, cracker packer of this parish!'

'A religious man are we?' ventured Maguire. 'Or just good humoured?'

'Just a joke,' replied Cobb. 'Sorry, pal.'

Maguire looked deeply into Cobb's eyes, saw Stan approaching in the crime car, and replied, 'Okay! Thank you, Mister Cobb. You'd best be off. I wouldn't want to keep you late for work.'

'Okay,' smiled Cobb. 'See you later. Good luck, Mister Detective. By the way, nice jacket! Looks like leather!'

'It is. Have a good day.'

'I'll try,' replied Cobb.

Taking a deep breath, Cobb began whistling again. Casually walking along the street, he wanted to set off running as fast as he could but thought better of it.

Cool, he thought. Stay cool and relax. But a score of worries invaded his brain. Would the detective check out what he'd said? Would he remember him again? And if he decided to ask him another question right now, should he turn and answer or run for his life?

Maguire watched him go, took little interest in the Royal Mail workers, and slid into the passenger seat of Stan's motor.

'Problems?' ventured Stan Holland.

'No, not really,' replied Maguire. 'I just thought I'd have a word, but he seemed okay.'

'He seemed okay!' challenged Stan. 'What the hell is that supposed to mean? Why did you stop him?'

'He was in the right place at the wrong time.'

'Did you search him?'

'No!'

'You idiot! Why not?' probed Stan. 'That could be the man we're looking for.'

'I should have,' nodded Maguire. 'But it just didn't feel right. He was on his way to work.'

'You mean he told you he was on his way to work, but I bet you didn't check that out, did you?'

'No,' admitted Maguire.

'Did you ask for identification or did you take him at face value?'

'I didn't push him. No!'

'He could have been the King of Timbuctoo for all you know,' proposed Stan. 'Les, you really need to get to grips with the job. You can't live halfway all the time. It's all the way or no way.'

'Sorry! I'll try to do better next time.'

'Don't worry,' ventured Stan. 'It's too late now. He's gone. If he is the guilty party, he'll come again. Meanwhile, we've had two cars stolen from Upperby and found burnt out in Melbourne Park, Botcherby, three domestics, and a smash and grab at a newsagent's in Harraby.'

'Oh! You have been busy, Stan. Where next?'

'I think we'll cruise the Upperby area. It's worth a shot. There's a car thief up there somewhere.'

'Do you want me to drive, Stan?'

'No! I want you to listen and learn. How long have you been a detective?' inquired Stan Holland.

'Six months!' replied Maguire. 'Or is it nine? I'm off to detective training school in Wakefield soon.'

'Good!' nodded Stan as he drove off. 'The DI must think you're made of the right stuff. Between you and I, let me tell you something.'

'About the DI?'

'No! About you,' challenged Stan. 'At the detective training school, you'll do an initial course lasting ten weeks. They'll teach you criminal law and relevant practices and procedures, but they won't teach you that if you've got a gut feeling about someone then follow it up and check them out properly. If you go and check him again now and he's okay, he might shout harassment and he'd be right. Remember, Les. You need to interact with people correctly. When an opportunity presents itself, take it and do the job properly. Understand?'

'That's me told,' replied Maguire. 'Thanks, Stan or rather, understood, sir!'

'Call me, Stan!'

'Call me, Maguire!'

'Okay, Maguire! Don't be an amateur.'

'I'll try.'

'Actually, Les,' revealed Stan. 'Call me coach. Are you training this afternoon?'

'Yes,' nodded Maguire. 'Bring the bike. I'm going for the hill again.'

'In that case you do need a coach,' replied Stan. 'Come on. Let's go.'

Chris Cobb made Castle Street, glanced behind, and then took a short cut through the cathedral grounds towards his flat in the Shaddongate area of the city. The lodgings were close to the biscuit factory, probably as close as he would ever be to the biscuit factory at any time in his life.

Taking deep breaths, Cobb's right hand went to a silver chain around his neck. The chain carried two silver ingots and a St Christopher pendant. It was his comforter: a personal piece of jewellery that he'd been given by his recently departed uncle when he was younger. Just holding it and running his fingers around the silver cord was enough to unwind and free himself from the thought of being arrested.

Breathing out, relaxed, more confident than ever before, Chris Cobb realised he'd just learnt how a smile and a friendly response could get you out of trouble with the police. Smoothing the chain with his fingers, he lengthened his stride as he crossed the bridge over the River Caldew.

That afternoon, Maguire dressed in his track suit and running shoes, left his flat, and began his training run through the housing estate. He teamed up with Stan Holliday who was sat astride his bicycle waiting for the off-duty detective.

'Good sleep?' inquired Stan.

'Great!'

'Good! I want you at the top of the hill in twenty-seven minutes. Ready?'

'I'm ready, coach,' replied Maguire.

Activating his stopwatch, Stan shouted, 'Go!'

Maguire strode out with Stan riding the bike beside him giving him timings and instructions.

'Easy pace! Shorten those steps for the hill.'

Nodding, Maguire gritted his teeth when the going got tough and he felt the pressure on his thighs.

'Increase the tempo,' ordered Stan. 'Shorter steps, lean into it slightly, power on.'

Maguire nodded in agreement as he reached the halfway mark.

'Fourteen minutes!' from Stan. 'Steady as she goes. Drive it now. All to go for. Drive those legs.'

Yet despite the best of intentions, Maguire ran out of steam and sank to his knees. He was totally spent!

'I can't make it,' revealed Maguire. 'It's too steep.'

'It's a three-mile ascent,' replied Stan. 'Not easy!'

'Am I a born failure?' inquired Maguire.

'Possibly!' declared Stan. 'We'll try again later in the week. Jog back. Nice and easy. Get the miles in those legs of yours. Lengthen out on the straight. Come on.'

'Thanks, coach,' nodded Maguire as he eventually found his feet. He took in a lungful of air and began a slow descent as Stan turned the bike around and cruised down the hill ahead of him.

~

3

Two nights later
Carlisle City Centre.

Cobb stalked the city centre lanes and alleyways before finally arriving in English Street once more. Hesitating at the end of the lane, he took stock of the thoroughfare. The town hall clock approached three in the morning, but it was mid-week, and the streets were dead. Not a soul moved other than a black cat roaming the streets in search of prey. Or was it just a bored cat enjoying a starlit night?

Taking a backward step into the dimly lit lane, Cobb donned his gloves, turned, climbed eight feet above the ground via a convenient drainpipe, and then reached across to a fire escape ladder that serviced a five-storey bank. Grabbing the bottom rung, Cobb felt the ladder gently swing into an upright position thus allowing him to quickly climb to the third storey. Standing on the ladder, he directly faced a wooden sash window that was part of Manuel's discount jewellery store.

Composing himself, taking deep breaths, Cobb removed the jemmy from his belt and forced the window open.

Within seconds, he was inside the building, listening for an alarm, and looking for a tell-tale light that might indicate a security beam of some kind.

It's a storeroom again, he thought. Amateur! Will I ever learn? I should have checked the place out properly. Should I go down a level or what?

No matter how calm he tried to remain, Cobb felt the adrenalin rising within him and decided to search the storeroom. He approached a chest of drawers. Sliding the bottom drawer out, he rummaged inside and found several wristwatches which he pocketed. Then he moved a drawer higher, slid it out to rest on the bottom drawer, and repeated his search. He recognised the cheap costume jewellery and stuffed a dozen packets into his inside coat pocket before withdrawing the top drawer where he found a collection of gold and silver necklaces. Gathering them together, he pocketed them too and then stood up to examine the rest of the room.

Empty boxes, he thought as he rifled more drawers and searched through the contents of a shelf. Not a bad haul but it's time to go. Time is always a factor. You get too greedy and steal more, stay longer, and then get caught. In and out in five minutes. No more and no less. Goodbye!

Retreating, Cobb balanced on the window ledge and reached out for the fire escape ladder. Missing the rungs altogether, he almost stumbled headlong to the ground but quickly snatched the upright of the ladder and manhandled himself back to the ledge.

Cobb's pulse surged upwards when he realised how stupid he had been.

This time, calmer and more determined, he reached for the fire escape ladder again, grasped it with his free hand, and pulled it towards him.

Moments later, he was on the ground with his gloves and jemmy safe and his loot stashed inside his clothing. Heading down the lane, he glanced over his shoulder, saw a blue light rotating from the corner of the building, and realised he'd somehow activated the burglar alarm. Annoyed that an alarm system had again beaten him somehow, he shook his head and bit his lip in anger.

Retracing his steps, Cobb ignored the main street and headed into the lane system as fast as he could. The sound of police sirens invaded his ears as the enemy rushed to the scene to try and catch the crook bang to rights.

Cobb's feet crossed West Walls, headed down Sallyport steps, and hurried through a car park towards the railway line. Racing towards a wall at full speed, he launched himself from the ground, grasped the top, and pulled himself onto and then over the wall. Dropping to the ground, Cobb glanced to his left to see a goods train heading north out of the station on its journey to Glasgow.

Flattening his back against the wall, Cobb narrowly missed being wiped out by the train.

Cobb held his breath, waited for the diesel train to pass him, and then set off in pursuit of the last wagon. Sprinting hard, he caught up with the train and threw himself across the rear buffers, clambered into a comfortable and safe position, and then watched Carlisle railway station disappear from view as the train accelerated and ran parallel to the River Caldew on its journey north.

Suddenly, he realised that the train's vibration was working the stolen jewellery out of his clothing. He rammed his spoils deeper inside and clung on tight. What happens next, he wondered. Nothing is going right today.

The goods train gathered speed as it travelled out of the city and towards the Scottish border. Cobb would ride the train until they reached Gretna when the speed reduced sufficiently enough for him to jump from the buffers and roll onto the ground. Bruised and sore, it was mid-morning before he hitchhiked back to Carlisle. He was richer in one way, yet felt he was a failure in others.

Back at the scene of the crime, uniform officers were first to arrive in response to the burglar alarm. Upon arrival, the point of entry was quickly established, and a cordon was organised to detain the offender. A dog handler attended and, with the owner of the premises, a Mr Rex Manuel, they commenced a search of the interior of the building. The bird had flown.

Stan Holliday and Les Maguire arrived midway through proceedings and began the detective work. They examined the fire escape ladder and then made their way into the building working from the ground up until they reached the storeroom which had been ransacked.

'Anything stolen, Rex?' probed Maguire.

'Rings, watches, and assorted jewellery,' replied the owner who was a debonair gentleman in his Sixties. Despite the time of day, Rex was smartly dressed in a dark suit, white shirt, and black bowtie. 'No cash was taken and whoever it was doesn't appear to have been anywhere other than this room,' he explained. 'I will not countenance such behaviour and intend to write to the Chief Constable, the council, and our local MP about this unwanted intrusion. It should not be allowed to happen these days.'

'I agree, but to keep it simple,' suggested Maguire. 'The offender climbed the fire escape ladder, broke in through the second-floor window, searched everywhere, and stole what he found. Is that correct?'

'That's how I see it,' replied Rex. 'I've had smash and grabs before but that's the first time I've experienced a proper burglary. You're looking for a young man who is ultra-fit and strong. The window is about twelve feet from the ground, maybe more? I don't know. I'm no expert. That's not an easy ladder to climb and it's not the work of a drunken opportunist. I'm furious. Furious, I tell you.'

'I'm sorry to hear that, sir. What value are we talking about?' inquired Stan.

'I'll need to check the books, but I'd say it was no more than fifteen hundred pounds of mixed jewellery.'

'Are you sure of that?'

'Pretty close! The uniform boys told me to make a list for you. It'll be ready soon. The articles stolen were shop-soiled. It was stuff that wasn't selling so we take it out of the showroom and sell it back to the reps who we deal with or traders looking for a sell on that will show them a profit.'

'I see, thanks,' replied Stan.

Maguire gazed out of the window and realised how high up they were. Peering out he looked down to the ground, glanced at the fire escape, and said, 'Whoever managed to do that is a good climber because that route is much harder than it looks.'

'There's half a dozen climbing jobs on the books this year. All undetected. I wonder if it's the same offender as the last jeweller's,' proposed Stan.

'You mean you don't know?' remarked an astonished Rex. 'I thought detectives were supposed to keep their finger on the local underworld?'

'Possibly,' remarked Maguire. 'What's this?'

Kneeling, Maguire pointed to a silver chain on the floor next to the open sash window. He shuffled the chain into an envelope and turned to Rex with, 'Two silver ingots and a Saint Christopher pendant. Looks like he didn't get away with everything, Rex.'

Studying the chain, the jeweller took a close look and said, 'Not one of mine. Where was it exactly?'

'On the floor by the window,' replied Maguire. 'Are you sure it's not yours?'

'Well, it's not clean. It's discoloured and that tells me it's been worn by someone.'

'It might be shop-soiled then?'

'It's not new, definitely second hand. I suppose it could be one of ours. I'm not sure. You know what it's like. This is a dumping ground for us. Downstairs we have single items of jewellery each valued between one thousand and five thousand pounds. Upstairs we keep stuff we can't sell that's ready to return. We're just a normal high street shop. Not Fort Knox. All I can say is, I'm not sure.'

'Do you sell chains with two ingots and a pendant on?' probed Stan.

'Not as a single article. No!' replied Rex.

'This is three pieces of jewellery on one chain so it's more likely to have been accidently left by the offender as opposed to being a piece of yours that's been dropped on the floor?' suggested Stan. 'Unless it was put together as a display.'

'If it were ours, it would have been in one of the drawers that the burglar rifled,' offered Rex.

'DNA?' probed Maguire. 'It looks to me as if the chain might belong to the offender.'

'Possible,' replied Stan. 'Keep it in the envelope and ask the scenes of crime man to get it tested for DNA.'

'Will that identify the burglar?' inquired Rex.

'Only if he has a criminal record and is on the DNA database,' replied Stan. 'If he's not, the DNA sequence will be kept on record and if a match comes to light in the future it will tie him to this scene.'

'Sounds good,' suggested Rex.

'Interesting,' ventured Maguire. 'I'll do just that but there's a couple of things that occur to me, Stan.'

'Such as?'

'Did the thief act alone? Where will he fence the stolen goods?'

'Well, that's exactly what you can do tomorrow, Maguire. Visit all the second-hand shops and circulate some photographs of the stolen property.'

'Ahh!' remarked Maguire. 'That'll teach me. Okay! Rex, have you any photographs of what has been stolen?'

'I can give you copies of the rep's catalogues. You'll find some of the gear in there.'

'Let's make a start,' proposed Maguire.

'You do that,' said Stan. 'I'll see the DI and ask him to authorise a plan I have in mind.'

'A plan!' queried Maguire. 'Oh yes! Great idea! You can't beat a plan.'

In the days that followed, Maguire toured the local second-hand shops with photographs of the stolen property whilst an examination of the silver chain resulted in traces of DNA. There was no match on the national database which suggested the burglar had no criminal record.

Meanwhile, Cobb returned home to his flat in the city, hid his spoils, and planned his next burglary. He spent the next few days wandering the city centre visiting selected premises, noting alarm systems, and sometimes watching when certain shops were opened and closed. He was determined to improve his skills. Quite determined. It didn't take him long to work out what kind of burglar alarms were in use at certain shops. Cobb was becoming more professional in his approach and planning.

One lunch break, Maguire touched base with Stan Holliday who had news for him.

'We're on,' revealed Stan. 'The DI agrees. Twelve-hour shifts as from tomorrow night.'

'Jeans and tee-shirts?'

'That's what we'd decided, isn't it, Maguire?'

'Yes, it was.'

'Don't forget. Bring a flask tomorrow night.'

A week later, Cobb ambled into the English Street area once again. It was well after midnight and the streets were quiet enough for him to carry out his next job.

Cautiously, he took time to check out his surroundings, strolled past the entrance to a lane once more, and then loitered at the corner of Devonshire Street near its junction with Friars Court. Several taxis and private cars drove by before there was a lull in the traffic at which point Cobb melted into the shadows of Friars Court.

In a high rise building close by, a plainclothes police surveillance officer radioed, 'I have a suspicious movement. The subject is black on black and has now moved into Friars Court. He should appear in Lowther Street in a few minutes.'

'Roger! Black trousers black top!' from another surveillance officer. 'Male, I presume?'

'Yes! Yes!' on the net.

Branching off into Old Post Office Court, Cobb took a close look at the building which was a two-storey second-hand shop selling antique jewellery, collectable stamps, and coins. On the wall above the front door, an alarm box was visible, but Cobb knew it was only connected to the front door and ground floor window because of the pattern of the wiring he had observed during an earlier visit. A study of the second floor had revealed no such wiring of any kind. He donned a pair of skin-tight leather gloves and glanced around to make sure he was alone.

Cobb knew he was on a winner if he could make the flat rooftop and either force the skylight or drop in through the second-floor window.

Grasping a drainpipe at the corner of the building, Cobb quickly climbed onto the flat roof. He found the skylight in the centre of the roof and glanced around. It was then that he realised the roof was bordered by a low parapet that overlooked the guttering which ran around three sides of the roof. There was no fourth side since it abutted onto a higher wall that was part of a retail unit. A fixed fire escape ladder graced the wall and gave access to every building on that side of English Street, Bank Street, Lowther Street and Friars Court. But Cobb's interest tonight extended no further than the second-hand shop since the goods inside were easy to transport, easy to sell, easy to hide, and much more accessible than other targets in the area.

Cobb had learnt that there was no point in stealing goods from an expensive designer clothes shop if you couldn't carry them away quickly and sell them rapidly. His growing criminal contacts wanted easy to sell goods, and he wanted easy to carry plunder. The second-hand shop remained his target.

One thing left, he thought as he checked the roof for wiring and then ran his fingers gently around the rim of the skylight. Again, he felt for a tell-tale wire that might indicate a hidden alarm system. There was nothing there other than part of the wooden skylight frame that crumpled in his fingers. The wood was rotten. There was no motion sensor or wiring to find.

I don't even need the jemmy, he chuckled as his fingers selected the weakened area and prised open the skylight.

In an observation post in a high-rise building in Lowther Street, a police surveillance officer radioed, 'No sign of the subject egressing from Friar's Court into Lowther Street.'

'Give him a couple of minutes,' radioed Maguire. 'Then we'll go in. There's a pub down there. Maybe he's going to a lock-in.'

'The publican left thirty minutes ago,' came the reply. 'I believe the premises are closed.'

'Understood,' replied Maguire. 'Stan!'

'I'll walk in from Lowther Street,' revealed Stan Holliday. 'You take the Friars Court route. Control! We'll check him out.'

'Understood!' from Maguire.

'Roger that!' from Control.

As Les Maguire and Stan Holliday made their way gradually to the area under surveillance, Cobb dropped into the second-floor area of the building, opened a door, walked down the staircase, and entered the shop area. He knew there would be no alarm sounding because the system only covered the front door and window. Safe, he began robbing items from the display.

Maguire turned into Friars Court about the same time as Stan Holland did from the opposite direction.

A jemmy lightly applied to force a glass cabinet open resulted in Cobb's ability to reach in and select a stack of old jewellery, wristwatches, pocket watches, and fob watches. Removing two plastic bags from behind the counter, he filled both bags, added some collectable coins, and then inspected the stamp display.

Maguire hugged the nearside wall of Friars Court, did not use a torch, and then moved into Old Post Office Court where there was only one shop. Meanwhile, Stan made his way down Friars Court from the opposite direction checking property as he closed with Maguire.

Cobb's handful of collectable and valuable stamps ended up stuffed inside his pockets. He glanced outside and saw a shadow fall across the dim light of a lamp standard situated at the end of the lane. He froze.

Approaching the shop, Maguire saw that the front window was intact. He tried the door handle. The premises were secure. On looking down the lane towards Lowther Street, he watched Stan Holliday doing the exact same thing. Maguire stepped back and peered towards the roof. In so doing, he again broke the beam of light from the old lamp standard and saw his shadow cast against the brick wall.

Holding his breath, Cobb felt the adrenalin rising inside his body. He took a step forward so that he could get a better look outside.

Maguire saw movement inside the shop. Snatching a torch from his belt, he shone it directly into the shop.

Caught in the beam, Cobb was momentarily blinded. A hand flew to his cover his eyes. His feet stepped backwards and tripped over a metal waste bin. Lying on his back, caught in Maguire's torchlight, he was lit up like a Christmas tree.

Maguire rushed to the door, grabbed the door handle, and pulled.

The door held.

Cobb was on his feet. He crashed into a display cabinet. Glass exploded and spilt onto the floor. Ignoring the danger, Cobb raced up the staircase into the upper level of the shop.

'Thieves on,' screamed Maguire on the radio. 'Old Post Office! Burglary in progress. Assistance required!'

'Roger!' from Control. 'All units, city centre Old Post Office Court. Burglary in progress. Officer at scene requires assistance. Surveillance team! Copy!'

The wireless filled with replies and positional movements with Stan now running to help Maguire radioing, 'Suspect is black on black. Close the lanes. Cordons!'

Oblivious to the police response, Cobb reached the second floor, mounted the table, and pulled himself onto the flat roof.

At ground level, Maguire rattled the front door again, stood well back and then shone his torch on the roof. He lit Cobb up like a beacon, repositioned a dustbin, and stepped away.

Turning, Cobb shinned up the fire escape ladder having decided to escape via the rooftops.

Maguire ran towards the dustbin, jumped onto the top, and launched himself towards the roof. Seconds later, he crashed to the ground and rolled over in abject failure.

Reaching the top rung of the fire escape ladder, Cobb glanced over his shoulder and then dragged himself onto the city rooftops.

Determined to catch his man, Maguire abandoned the climb to the roof, raced at the front door of the shop, and shoulder-charged the entrance taking the door from its hinges in the process. Within a heartbeat, his torch lit the way forward and he was through the inner door and rushing up the staircase shouting, 'Stand still! Police!'

'What the hell are you doing?' yelled Stan on reaching the shop door.

Cobb was on the rooftops, gingerly making his way across the roof of the chemists, searching for the route across a bank, and in his element. Only the occasional glance over his shoulder betrayed the nervousness gnawing at his body. But he was determined to escape.

Maguire found the fire escape ladder and quickly climbed it, rung by rung.

Dropping one of the plastic bags that held his booty, Cobb paused, recovered the bag, and then continued his bid for freedom.

'On the rooftops,' radioed Maguire nervously. 'Making for Bank Street maybe Lowther Street. I don't know. Ground cordons all around please.'

'Get off the roof, Maguire,' radioed Stan. 'You'll hurt yourself.'

'Is the suspect in sight?' from Control.

'Vaguely,' replied Maguire trying to listen to the radio as well watch his feet. 'Black on black has thirty yards and two rooftops on me.'

The police radio filled the airwaves until a surveillance officer broke in with, 'I'm in Bank Street on a third-floor observations point. Suspect is on the roof above the clothing shop heading towards Lowther Street.'

'Roger!' from Maguire. 'In pursuit!'

'Oh, shit!' mouthed Stan. 'Somebody is going to get hurt. Get off the bloody rooftops.'

On the rooftops, two men ran across an expanse of corrugated metal sheeting that had been laid as a temporary repair during the refurbishment of property owned by an insurance company. Any pretence of a silent getaway was lost in the loud clanking noise when the hound chased the fox towards a perimeter of doom.

There was no going back.

Cobb reached the end of the building, glanced behind to see Maguire closing with him, and tottered on the edge of the temporary roof repair.

'Don't come any closer,' shouted Cobb. 'I'll take you with me.'

Maguire slid to a halt yards from his prey and replied, 'Easy now! You're not going anywhere, and neither am I. You can come quietly, stay here for the night, or jump. It doesn't matter to me but if you jump then you'll probably kill yourself and my pals down there will be scraping you up from the footpath for the rest of the night. Is it worth it for breaking into a shop?'

'You would never have caught me if hadn't been for this death trap of a roof repair.'

'Stand still,' ordered Maguire. With his arm outstretched, Maguire offered a handcuff to Cobb and suggested, 'Here! Put this on and I'll pull you to safety.'

Ignoring his adversary, Cobb turned and began to tip-toe along the perimeter of the repair. Despite wobbling on the ill-fitting corrugated sheets, he eventually found a gap, saw a route to another part of the roof, and jumped across the divide. Luckily, his fingers found purchase and he dragged himself onto a stretch of concrete. On his feet, running along the flat roof, he made his way to the corner of Bank Street and then turned to run along the roof of a tailor's shop. Glancing below, he could see police in uniform gathering in Lowther Street. The street was alive with blue lights flashing.

Shaking his head in disbelief, Maguire took one look at the pathway Cobb had followed and then retraced his steps.

Still determined to escape, Cobb was like a rabbit in a car's headlights because there was no way out and confusion dominated his thinking. Reaching the corner of Friars Court, he jumped another rampart on the roof, realised there was a travel agent's below him and made for Old Post Office Court and the place where it had all started.

Stan Holliday heard the commotion on the roof. Figuring it was Maguire and the burglar clambering across rooftops, he began to keep in line with the noise from above and stalked the lane parallel to the footsteps on the roof.

Meanwhile, Maguire stood on the roof by the fire escape ladder at Old Post Office Court and waited for Cobb to come into view.

Peering cautiously to the ground, Cobb realised there were no uniforms to be seen. Potentially, he was home free if he could get back to the second-hand shop and a way out of his self-made enigma.

I'm young, fit, agile, and uncatchable once I get on the ground, thought Cobb.

Maguire saw Cobb coming, ducked down behind the parapet, and waited.

Scanning the rooftops, Cobb saw nothing of the man who had been chasing him minutes earlier. He made the fire escape ladder and threw a leg over the side and onto the first rung.

Springing from his crouched position, Maguire took Cobb to the ground with the sheer force of his body hurling through the air at speed. The two men rolled over on the roof, swopped punches, and fought each other like cat and dog before Maguire spun Cobb onto his stomach and heard the snap when his handcuffs finally secured the burglar.

'You, young man, are under arrest,' remarked Maguire as he wiped the blood from his nose and then cautioned him.

A bundle of plunder escaped Cobb's clothing when Maguire dragged him into an upright position.

Maguire looked Cobb up and down and noted a slim young man who stood about five feet nine inches tall. He wore a black three-quarter-length coat, a grey tee-shirt, and dark blue denim jeans. His jet-black hair was cut short but matched his image perfectly.

'Good God!' wheezed Maguire. 'How old are you?'

'Nothing to say!' replied Cobb.

'Name?'

'Nothing to say!'

'Address?'

'Nothing to say!'

'Age?'

'Nothing to say!'

Dragging Cobb into the light, Maguire took another look at his prisoner and said, 'We've met somewhere before. Your face is familiar.'

'Nothing to say!'

'Later maybe,' replied Maguire before radioing, 'One detained on the rooftop of the attacked premises in Old Post Office Court. Prisoner handcuffed but can I have some assistance on the roof, please? We need to get off safely.'

There was a loud cheer on the airwaves when the arrest was announced followed by the re-deployment of various officers to the arrest scene and elsewhere.

The job of policing never stopped. It was one job after another. There was the quiet of the night followed by dawn and then, later in the day, twilight. But the city never slept. For now, this chase was over.

Stan was first to climb the ladder to help Maguire and opened with, 'Well done! Good job you opened the door downstairs for me, Les. You couldn't have got it any wider.'

'Ah!' replied Maguire. 'Over exuberance on my part, Stan.'

'I'm sure the police authority will pay for it in the circumstances,' chuckled Maguire's colleague. 'Who have we here?'

There was no reply from Cobb. Just a look of contempt as he stared at both men.

'I'll have to search you,' revealed Maguire who began rummaging through Cobb's pockets.

Finding an assortment of watches and jewellery, Maguire then discovered a driving licence which he studied before handing it to Stan.

'Christopher Cobb! Nineteen years old!' voiced Stan. 'You look about fourteen. Have you been in trouble before?'

Cobb relented slightly by shaking his head. 'No!'

'Sure?' probed Stan.

'Never been caught before,' laughed Cobb suddenly.

'You are our drainpipe man,' ventured Maguire. 'Not the first job you've done, is it?'

'Who me?' chuckled Cobb suddenly cocky and alive. 'You've nothing on me. You just got lucky this time.'

Nodding, pursing his lips, Maguire produced a silver chain from his pocket and said, 'You dropped this last time out.'

A look of shock flashed across Cobb's face. Had his hands been free, they would have rushed to his neck because he recognised it immediately.

'Never seen it before,' lied Cobb.

'In which case, the DNA traces that we found on this silver chain will not match your DNA when we test it,' proposed Maguire.

'DNA?' queried Cobb. 'What's that?'

'Better than fingerprints,' revealed Maguire. 'Come on! It's time we took you to the nick.'

The two detectives carefully guided their prisoner down from the roof and escorted him to the police station where he was booked in, searched, and then placed in a cell. Revisiting the shop, they interviewed the owner, made a list of property that had been stolen and recovered from either the roof or Cobb, and carried out a further examination of the crime scene.

Returning to the cell block, the detectives took Cobb to the charge office where a DNA sample was taken from him under the provisions of the Criminal Justice Act 2003, which authorises the police to take and retain a DNA sample of any person arrested for any recordable offence.

Meanwhile, a police search unit entered Cobb's home address and returned a negative search report. No suspected items of stolen jewellery were recovered during the operation.

Shortly thereafter, Stan Holliday accompanied Maguire to an interview room where the duty solicitor was ready and able to represent Cobb.

'I confirm that I am James Harkness,' said the solicitor introducing himself to the two detectives. 'And I represent my client Christopher Cobb with whom I have enjoyed a structured, private, and confidential conversation. My client agrees to being interviewed by yourselves.'

'Thank you for that,' nodded Stan. 'I am Detective Constable Stanley Holliday, and this is the officer in the case, and the arresting officer, Detective Constable Les Maguire.'

Once the preliminaries were over, Maguire informed Cobb that he was questioning him with regards to the burglary and theft of jewellery, coins, and stamps to the value of £1,525 from premises in Old Post Office Court.

The interview wore on before Maguire asked, 'You were arrested on the roof of a shop. What were you doing on the roof?'

'You know what I was doing on the roof. Running away from you. That's why you arrested me. No comment.'

'I didn't arrest you for running away,' challenged Maguire. 'I arrested you for breaking into the shop. You were on the roof of a shop that had been burgled and were in possession of property stolen from that shop I saw you in my torch beam on the floor of the shop that you had burgled and before I caught you on the roof.'

'Okay! No comment though. Write that down.'

'Have you been on any other shop roofs lately?' inquired Maguire.

'No!'

Maguire produced the silver chain and said, 'Is this yours?'

Cobb did not reply.

'I found it inside the Rex Manuel jewellery shop that has been burgled recently,' explained Maguire. 'Whoever burgled Manuel's climbed into the premises and probably accidently dropped the chain on the shop floor.'

'No comment.'

'I think the chain may have snagged on something during the time they were entering or leaving the shop by a window that had been forced.'

'No comment.'

'I believe it fell from the wearer's neck without them realising they had lost it. If the DNA taken from you matches the DNA on the chain, I will have to ask you again if it's yours.'

Physically disturbed, Cobb took a moment to think things through. He knew he had mastered the drainpipes, parapets, and skylights, but he'd never been interviewed at length by the police before and didn't quite know how to reply.

Cobb looked at his solicitor who nodded and suggested, 'No reply.'

'Yes,' replied Cobb in answer to Maguire's question. 'I mean no comment. Write it down. No reply! It's not mine.'

Harkness closed his eyes for a moment and quietly shook his head.

'I recall stopping to question you one morning shortly after a burglary had occurred in the city centre,' revealed Maguire. 'You told me you were on your way to the biscuit factory to start work. Do you remember that morning?'

'No!'

'My colleague, who is sitting next to me, also remembers seeing you that morning. We both identify you as the one I stopped that morning. I let you go but my colleague picked me up in a car moments later and recalls seeing you.'

'That is correct,' added Stan. 'You are the man Maguire stopped shortly after a rooftop burglary at Baxter's jewellers.'

'No comment,' replied Cobb.

'You told me that morning that you were on your way to work. Enquiries reveal you are not employed by the biscuit factory and are not, and never have been, on their payroll. Do you agree that you do not work at the biscuit factory?'

'Nothing to say,' from Cobb.

Maguire continued with, 'This silver chain was recovered from Rex Manuel's. I believe it is yours and suggest there may be a DNA match.'

'No reply! No comment!'

Cobb then leaned over to his solicitor, cupped his hand, and had a private conversation with him.

The solicitor then addressed Maguire with, 'May we have a private moment, please. My client wishes to discuss DNA.'

'Of course,' replied Maguire. 'For your information, if a person wore this silver chain and its attachment, it's likely that traces of sweat, skin, and human hair may well be present on the chain. I believe that such traces will match the bodily elements of Mr Cobb.'

The two detectives left the room but about ten minutes later James Harkness stepped into the corridor and said, 'My client wishes to speak to you now.'

Stan and Maguire re-entered the interview room and continued their quest.

'Do you wish to speak to me?' inquired Maguire.

'It was me,' replied Cobb. 'I did it. That's my chain. My uncle gave it to me years ago. I want it back.'

'I'm sorry,' explained Maguire. 'But I need to secure this chain because it is an exhibit in the case against you and I can't return it to you until after the matter is completed.'

'I want it back.'

'You can have it back when the matter is finalised and not before.'

'It's important to me. I must have that necklace.'

'I'm sorry,' replied Maguire. 'That's not possible now.'

Cobb glanced at Harkness who said, 'The officer is correct. He's not depriving you of the chain forever, Chris. It is being kept for evidential purposes and if your DNA is on the chain it will be produced in court as evidence against you.'

Nodding, Cobb replied, 'Okay!'

Harkness then said, 'Remember my advice, Chris. If it is your chain and you are responsible, then the best course of action may be to tell the truth now. If you decide to constantly deny the matter, and are subsequently convicted, then you may find the court is not at all lenient with you when you appear before them. As I said, it is your decision.'

Folding his arms, Cobb visibly slumped in his chair before responding with, 'Okay! I'm the drainpipe climber that did some jewellers and stuff. Can I have a cup of tea and I'll tell you the truth.'

'Of course, you can,' replied Maguire glancing at Stan. 'Where is the stolen property?'

'Tea!'

Moving away from the table, Stan nodded at Maguire and left the room.

'The tea is on its way,' suggested Maguire. 'Do you find it easy to climb drainpipes?'

'Sometimes.'

'Which is the easiest drainpipe that you've climbed?'

'None of them was easy,' replied Cobb. 'It's the skylights that were the best. Most of them are made of wood which is rotting. You can almost break some of them up with your bare hands.'

'And then climb into the premises via the skylight and from the roof,' suggested Maguire.

'Yes, that's right. Most of them are wooden but I found a few that were made of plastic. UVPC or something. Metal even!'

'UPVC,' corrected Maguire.

'Is it? Whatever! You know what I mean.'

'How many premises have you burgled by climbing onto the roof, forcing the skylight, or a handy window, and then entering to steal items that you wanted?'

'I'd say a dozen,' admitted Cobb glancing at his solicitor.

Harkness nodded and gestured for Cobb to continue.

'Maybe more. Not sure!'

'And how many did you steal from?' inquired Maguire.

'All of them.'

'What did you steal?' probed Maguire.

'Mainly costume jewellery. Cheap stuff usually, but I got a few good necklaces, watches, things like that.'

'Did you ever steal any cash?'

'A few quid from the till now and again but most of the shops I did had empty tills or just a couple of quid. The float! Hardly worth the trouble.'

'Where is the property now?'

'I got rid,' replied Cobb.

'Where to?' probed Maguire.

'I can't remember,' replied Cobb shuffling in his chair.

'You look quite nervous suddenly,' remarked Maguire.

'I'm okay,' replied Cobb. 'Just need a cup of tea.'

'The tea will be along shortly, Chris,' remarked Maguire. 'Did you keep what you stole?'

Cobb stared at his solicitor who offered the words, 'You have my advice, Mr Cobb.'

'Later maybe. No! I can't say. No comment!'

'What can't you say?' probed Maguire.

'The property! I haven't got it anymore.'

'Did you sell it?'

'Yes!'

'To whom did you sell the property?'

'I can't say,' replied Cobb shuffling back and forward in his feet once more.

'Why not?' queried Maguire. 'You seem unwilling to talk about it. Are you frightened or just refusing to tell us because you've hidden the property somewhere and don't want us to know?'

'Look, can I just tell you about the roof jobs for now?'

'Can you confirm that the silver chain I showed you earlier is your property?'

'Yes, it's mine.'

'Do you recall dropping it at the scene of a break-in?'

'No! It must have snagged somewhere as you said. It's mine though.'

There was a gentle tap on the interview room door before Stan entered with a tray and then began pouring tea out for everyone.

'Thank you,' replied Maguire. 'Would you like to make a statement?'

'Yes! Can you write it for me?'

'If you wish unless you would rather write it.'

'You write it. I'll tell you what to put,' replied Cobb.

'And I'll advise you on the words to use,' added Harkness. 'Please proceed, officer.'

'Yes, I will,' replied Maguire taking a statement form from his briefcase. 'But can I suggest that if you are going to tell the truth and the whole truth, as advised by your solicitor, then you might wish to include the whereabouts of the property and details of whom you sold it to?'

Cobb pursed his lips and shook his head before launching into his sorry tale of criminality. Within the hour, he had detailed the burglary of twelve properties in the city. On each occasion, jewellery had been stolen as well as cash, bric-a-brac, coins, stamps, watches, necklaces, bracelets, and various chains. He refused to say what he had done with the stolen property.

The interview ended with Cobb's signed confession and a handshake with his solicitor.

Escorting Cobb back to his cell, Maguire said, 'Thank you for that, Chris. You'll probably be charged with a couple of those offences and the others will be taken into consideration or lie on the file. Do you know what that means?'

'Yes! My solicitor told me.'

'Okay! By the way, do you have a job to go to or anyone that needs to know you are here?'

'No! No job. I wasn't particularly good at school and haven't been able to get a job. And I don't need to tell anyone I'm here. The custody sergeant has already asked me that.'

'Fine, that's alright then. Despite what you previously told me I see you have a record for petty crime. Have you been in a cell before?'

'Yes, once or twice.'

Maguire unlocked the cell and said, 'Well, here you go again. It's a habit you need to break at your age.'

'Shoplifting four times,' replied Cobb. 'Jewellers' shops.'

'Two convictions as a juvenile and two as an adult,' remarked Maguire. 'And you're only nineteen. Not good for a man of your age.'

'Twenty soon and my solicitor thinks I'll get probation.'

'You've had it before and it didn't work,' replied Maguire. 'And it's the court's decision, not his.'

'What do you think I'll get?'

'Not sure,' replied Maguire. 'It's up to the court. Your problem is that I reckon, altogether, you stole about seven thousand pounds worth of property from twelve different break-ins. You refuse to say what you did with it and that means the victims have lost out. We recovered £1,525 worth of stolen goods. All of it from the Old Post Office Court job. There's about £6,000 worth unaccounted for and that's down to you. The court might not like that.'

'Tough!' chuckled Cobb.

'Admitting what you did with the property and telling us where you sold it might result in recovery and that would look better in court,' suggested Maguire. 'It's not my place to give you legal advice but you might like to think about what I've said to you or contact your solicitor for another meeting. It's only a 'phone call and I'll arrange that for you if you want.'

'Thank you.'

'You see, Chris,' continued Maguire. 'My job is to catch crooks and place them before the court. What the court does with people who appear before them is up to them. I'm not judge and jury. Never will be, but that's the way it is.'

'I'm not sure what to do,' replied Cobb.

'Most people admit who they sold the gear to,' suggested Maguire. 'Although a good few tell us it was sold at a market or in pubs and clubs to people they didn't know.'

'Yes! I remember now. I think that's where the stuff went.'

'I think you are telling lies again,' proposed Maguire. 'If I were the court I'd smile politely to your face, know you were making it up, and probably decide that it was just another lie. That kind of information doesn't get you anywhere.'

'How do I get probation, a suspended sentence, or a lower than normal jail sentence?'

'Tell me where the stolen property is,' replied Maguire. 'It's as simple as that. The court is likely to take a completely different view if you give information that leads to the recovery of other people's property.'

Cobb turned away from Maguire and stared at the grey walls that offered a grim welcome to the incoming guest.

Maguire held the cell door open as Cobb took a step inside. A tear seemed to form at the corner of his eye, but he quickly wiped it from his face and replied, 'I can't tell you. I'll be done over and thrown in the river.'

'What! For a couple of thousand quid's worth of cheap jewellery. Ring another bell. I didn't hear that one.'

'It's true,' voiced Cobb. 'It's too dangerous for me. I can't tell you.'

'Why not?'

'You don't want to know. You can't help me, Mister Detective.'

'That's what you called me when we first met.'

'I know.'

'Can I help you?' pleaded Maguire.

Cobb stared at the four walls again, dropped his head, and replied, 'No! There's no way you can help me. I'm in too deep.'

'What about your solicitor?'

'What about him?' queried Cobb. 'He's a suit and I don't trust him.'

'Why not?' probed Maguire.

'I'm just a client in the cells,' replied Cobb. 'He gets them every day. Apart from that, he can't help me, and I wouldn't trust him. I'll do the time. I have no choice.'

Looking deep into Maguire's eyes, Cobb stared at Maguire for what seemed an eternity before repeating, 'I have no choice, Mister Detective.'

Maguire returned the long stare, guided Cobb into the depths of the cell, and said, 'Am I talking to someone who might be a great drainpipe climber, but hasn't a clue how to answer questions when interviewed by the police? Are you trying to con me into something that doesn't exist? Or are you really in trouble?'

'No! I'll only be in trouble if I tell you the truth. You can't help me.'

'I might be able to if you come clean with me.'

'I don't think so,' replied Cobb.

'You mentioned an uncle,' remarked Maguire. 'Presumably, you have a family. Could they help?'

A look of dread momentarily filled Cobb's face as he quickly looked away.

'It's just that you've mentioned your uncle a couple of times since we met,' continued Maguire. 'He gave you the silver chain, didn't he?'

'Yes! Mum and Dad were killed in a car crash. I survived. He brought me up, but he's not around anymore.'

'He died too?' queried Maguire.

'Yes, but not before landing me with a problem,' explained Cobb.

'What do you mean?' probed Maguire.

'None of your business,' argued Cobb.

'You're probably right,' agreed Maguire. 'It isn't my business, but you mentioned it. I was just interested, that's all. You've been on probation before so the Probation Service must have your family on record. It's things like that they put to the court so that magistrates and judges know what kind of person they are dealing with.'

'Never done me any good,' contended Cobb.

'Your uncle! What was his name?' inquired Maguire.

'You don't want to know,' replied Cobb.

'Actually, I do.'

'My uncle was called Elias Benjamin Lee. Have you ever heard of him?'

'A traveller?' suggested Maguire. 'A Romani! A member of the travelling community.'

'You mean a gipsy,' replied Cobb. 'A well-known one at that.'

'Famous,' remarked Maguire in a jocular manner. 'In his day, he was an arch-criminal and prominent...'

Maguire stalled.

'Go on,' urged Cobb.

'Prominent gangster,' concluded Maguire.

'That's the man,' confessed Cobb. 'A gangster!'

'But he's dead,' contended Maguire. 'I don't understand how your dead uncle can influence you so much.'

'The gang! His gang! He's gone but they own me now.'

'Own you? What do you mean?'

'He brought me up to be a traveller like him. That's why he gave me the chain with St Christopher on. It was something he gave me when he took me with him on his jaunts.'

'Is the silver chain stolen property?' queried Maguire.

'I don't know. I knew better than to ask. It could be part of the Crown Jewels for all I know. He could have got it from anywhere. He had more contacts than you could ever imagine. From Ireland to Indonesia and everywhere in between.'

'Are you telling me that you couldn't even trust him when he gave you a gift?' voiced Maguire.

'No way,' snapped Cobb. 'It might not even be silver for all I know.'

'Oh, it's silver alright,' replied Maguire. 'I can see the hallmarks.'

'Can I have it back?' pleaded Cobb. 'I've got so used to wearing it. It's part of me now.'

'Eventually,' replied Maguire. 'You know why.'

'Okay! Look, his life wasn't for me, Les. I didn't want to live in the back of a caravan going back and forward from Musselburgh in Scotland to Dale Farm in Southend, and every traveller's site in between. It's not what I wanted out of life. Anyway, the travellers called me a gorger which says it all.'

'Excuse my ignorance, Chris, but what does that mean?' inquired Maguire.

'A gorger!' chuckled Cobb. 'It's a person who doesn't belong to the community and is not a gipsy.'

'But your uncle still looked after you.'

'He did but my Mum and Dad didn't bring me up like that. I wanted out so I got out. Or at least I tried.'

'Did you like your uncle?'

'I did once.'

'He's had a profound effect on your upbringing by the sound of it. Yet I don't understand how his gang owns you when he's not around anymore and you're a gorger. Why do they still use someone who is not part of their lifestyle?'

'Things have moved on. They're not all gorgers now. It all began a couple of years ago.'

'How?' probed Maguire.

'I couldn't get a job. Not a proper job. I've no qualifications. Nothing at school. I could run faster, jump further, jump higher, and throw further than anyone else in the class but I couldn't count, couldn't write a letter, and couldn't pass an exam. Then my parents were killed, and I was left to fend for myself until Uncle Elias came along.'

'Let me think,' remarked Maguire. 'Your uncle didn't teach you how to read and write but he did show you how to burgle and steal? Is that what you mean?' asked Maguire.

Cobb withdrew into himself for a while.

'Did he take the stolen property from you and sell it on to his contacts?' demanded Maguire. 'Was he your fence, Chris?'

Cobb looked up at Maguire and stared directly into his face.

'Chris?' insisted Maguire. 'That's it, isn't it?' suggested Maguire. 'Your uncle died but you had nowhere to go so things carried on the same way. Did his mates take over from him?'

'Does it matter, Les? The property has gone now. I can't get it back.'

'What else have you done for this gang?'

'Nothing.'

'There's just two of us here, Chris. I'm not writing down what you say, and this conversation is strictly private. What else have you done for this gang?'

Turmoil in Cobb's mind forced him to say, 'I can't trust you.'

'You don't trust your solicitor either,' replied Maguire. 'But you need to start at some point if you want to change things around.'

'Les!' shouted Chris suddenly. 'They wanted me to collect stuff and then deliver it elsewhere?'

'Okay! Okay!' soothed Maguire. 'Settle down. No one is going to hurt you. I'm trying to find out the truth so that I can help you. There's no need to shout at me. I'm not shouting at you and I'm not threatening you in any way.'

Cobb nodded.

'Drugs?'

'Yes,' admitted Cobb.

'Anything else?'

'Funny money!'

'Do you mean counterfeit notes, Chris?' inquired Maguire.

'Yes. I wouldn't do it at first. They wanted me to go to places like Liverpool, Manchester, and Birmingham and then bring it back here or take it over to Newcastle.'

'Did you carry or receive money?'

'No, I had nothing to do with the money. They just wanted me to be a runner. They threatened me and I gave in to them. I know how these people work. They wouldn't hesitate to do me over and throw me in the river if I didn't do as they asked. They are all bullies and gangsters.'

'What else have you done for them?'

'I once drove a tractor to a garage. They hooked it up to a cash machine and we dragged it away. We dumped the tractor and I drove them back in a borrowed van.'

'They must trust you then?'

'I think they do,' explained Cobb. 'I suppose I went from being bullied to just accepting things the way they were.'

'Why didn't you tell us that during the interview we had with you?'

'I'll do the time.'

'Did you tell your solicitor what you've just told me?'

'You must be joking. No way! He knows most of the crooks in the town. I'll do the time, Les. I can't prove any of what I've said without getting myself into more trouble than I'm already in. I might not know much about DNA and UPVC but I sure as hell know those remnants of my uncle's gang will take me with them if they can. After all, I could have said nothing from the beginning and then ran away from them on day one, but I didn't. I'm as much to blame in some ways. I didn't appreciate what I was getting into. And yes, I enjoyed climbing drainpipes and smashing my way through skylights. Sure, as hell I did. It gave me a buzz like you'd never understand. I'm as guilty as hell, Les, even if my uncle's mob have driven me into doing stuff for them that would get me a whole lot more than a few months in the pokey.'

'Why have you gone from Mister Detective to Les?' snapped Maguire.

'Because I think you're trying to help me and can't.'

'I understand,' replied Maguire.

'I want out, Les. I can't go on like this.'

'It's your call,' suggested Maguire. 'You can work with me, see your solicitor again, and make a new statement. If the court accepts you were bullied into committing these burglaries, then they might deal with you without giving you a custodial sentence. It's up to them but you might be free to go.'

Cobb listened intently.

'Or you can do whatever time is coming to you. It's your choice, Chris.'

Nodding, Cobb replied, 'I'll do the time, Les. I want to live, and these guys are just the type who would kill me if they had to.'

'Seriously? They'd kill you! Are you sure?'

'Oh yes! No doubt in my mind. They're a brutal lot when they want to be.'

'What are they up to that is so damn serious that they'd kill one of their own?'

'This and that!' frowned Cobb. 'I've told you enough already. I'm not telling you anymore.'

'So be it,' replied Maguire reluctantly. 'Look me up when you get out, Chris. I might be able to help you.'

'I'll think about it,' replied Cobb. 'But I doubt it.'

Reaching the door, Maguire glanced back and remarked, 'No! I mean it, Chris. Look me up when you get out. Detective Constable Les Maguire! Don't forget the name. I might be able to help you provided you can help me.'

'You'll remember me?' probed Cobb.

'We don't get many drainpipe men,' chuckled Maguire. 'I'll remember you.'

Maguire closed the cell door on a frightened and confused young man who had lost his way in life and seemed to have sold his soul into a life of criminality that he did not anticipate.

Strolling down the cell corridor thoughtfully, Maguire wondered if he'd just been told a pack of lies, an elaborate tale that had been exaggerated for his benefit, or was it just a plea for some kind of lenience that Cobb thought the detective could arrange?

Maguire reached the custody office and hung the cell keys on the hook before returning to the office.

Meeting up at the hill climb, Maguire was warming up when Stan arrived on his new bike.

The coach clicked the stopwatch, shouted, 'This time you follow me. Understood?'

'Okay!' replied Maguire. 'I'm ready.'

'Stick close to my rear wheel,' ordered Stan. 'Go!'

The two men set off. The pacemaker on the bike hammered into the three-mile ascent with Maguire adopting the powerful short steps method of hill running. They were around the bend and halfway up the hill with Stan in the lowest gear on his bike still shouting Maguire on with 'Fourteen minutes again. Power, Maguire! Power!'

Another bend appeared, was conquered by the slimline Maguire in his tracksuit bottoms and vest, was rounded, beaten, and left behind as the summit came into view.

Again, it was too much for the determined Maguire who collapsed in a heap on the tarmac with oodles of sweat rolling out of his skin and his chest heaving for all it was worth.

'You okay?' probed Stan.

'Never felt better, coach,' chuckled Maguire. 'I failed again. Is it a mental thing or is it the incapable me?'

'You've lost weight,' replied Stan. 'But you're improving. Just don't collapse next time. When it gets to you try cutting back and slowing down for half a minute, no more, then change gear back to normal. That short respite might be enough to get you the top in one go.'

'Okay, thanks, coach.'

Weeks later, Stan Holliday and Les Maguire, both suited and booted, stood at the back of the courtroom when Cobb appeared before the magistrates and pleaded guilty to three offences of burglary and theft. Other offences were taken into consideration and Cobb's solicitor rose to speak on his behalf.

Turning his head, Cobb stared at Maguire who merely returned a look of absent emotion.

The case was outlined to the magistrate's and the story of Cobb's criminality was told. Cobb was sentenced to nine months imprisonment. He knew the prison system would release him when he had served seven months, provided he kept his nose clean. During the trial, no order for compensation was forthcoming, and no mention of either his uncle or the crime gang was made.

Taking it on the chin, it was as if Cobb expected the length of sentence as he stood impassively, offered no regret of remorse, and turned to go when the officer standing next to him touched his arm and gestured for him to take the stairs to the cell area.

Cobb stared directly into Maguire's eyes.

Maguire returned a thumbs-up as his head slanted slightly and his eyes conveyed a question to the man who was on his way to HMP Durham.

In a split second, Cobb returned a thumbs up and disappeared below stairs into the cells.

'What the hell was all that about?' whispered Stan Holliday.

'An agreement to meet in the future,' replied Maguire.

'I sure as hell hope you know what you're getting into, Maguire,' remarked Stan. 'Cobb's connections are a keg of gunpowder waiting to be lit.'

'I know,' revealed Maguire. 'I have a target in mind.'

'Who?' demanded Stan.

'The remnants of a gang once controlled by Elias Benjamin Lee!' replied Maguire.

'Well good luck with that one,' chuckled Stan. 'It's called Bennie's gang now. That's quite deliberate because there's no one involved called Bennie in it. I've heard they just want the police to chase around looking for someone called Bennie who doesn't exist. The gang is a bunch of target criminals working in the North West. I'll tell you now, they won't be easy to catch. They've got the Regional Crime Squad onto the gang, but they don't seem to be able to break them down.'

'We'll see,' replied Maguire. 'None of them is easy to catch, but I'll be back from detective training school by then, Stan. We'll see. Oh, yes, we'll see.'

'See?' queried Stan. 'This gang you are taking on has a reputation for excessive violence, Maguire. It's not just a bunch of crooks from a council estate intent on what they can knock off from the local off-licence. They've got a finger in every pie going.'

'Which pies?' inquired Maguire.

'Counterfeit money! Drugs! Armed robberies! Organised shoplifting! High-end luxury car thefts! Antiques! You name it and they're into it.'

'I thought there was only about a dozen of them,' proposed Maguire.

'There's at least a dozen of them,' replied Stan. 'Probably more, you'd have to be on the squad to know that.'

'Or in the gang,' ventured Maguire.

'Yeah, that's true,' nodded Stan. 'In the gang, I never thought of that.'

A gavel rapped on the clerk to the magistrate's table and the next case was announced.

The door closed behind the two detectives when they melted into the public arena outside the courtroom.

~

4

Eight months later
The CID Office.

The clutter of paperwork on Maguire's desk held testament to the undue amount of investigations allotted to the detective. There seemed to be an ever-increasing pile of documents that were constantly multiplying.

Sitting opposite, Stan Holland, Maguire threw a digestive biscuit across the desk and shouted, 'Catch this, Stan. No dunking!'

Stan's fingers grasped the item in mid-air and promptly dipped one locally manufactured digestive biscuit into a deep brown sea of coffee.

'Well caught!' chuckled Maguire. 'You got a fraud enquiry on Johnson's cleaners?'

'Not so much a fraud as a book of cheques stolen from a daytime sneak-in burglary. Why do you ask?'

'Because the DS had just allocated me this.' Maguire held up a crime report and continued with, 'One stolen cheque from that book duly signed and presented for payment to an off licence in town last night, presumably by the thief. I think you should carry the crime. It's connected to the sneak in, isn't it?'

'Pass it over,' replied Stan. 'It's my crime. An off licence! Any CCTV?'

'I need a break,' replied Maguire. 'My eyes are rolling from the paper system. Statements, crime reports, messages, circulations, There's no end to it all. How about we take a walk around there after coffee and look?'

'You're on,' replied Stan taking a drink from his mug. 'Sounds like the suspect could be local.'

A 'phone on Maguire's desk rang and he quickly answered it with, 'C I D! Maguire!'

'Les!' from the 'phone.

Moving documents around on the desk, Maguire replied, 'Detective Constable Maguire! Can I help?'

'Les! It's me. You said to look you up.'

'Who?' inquired Maguire. 'Who's speaking?'

'The drainpipe man!'

Holding the 'phone for a moment, Maguire thought back to a magistrate's court and a young man receiving a prison sentence.

'Say again!' remarked Maguire.

'Cobb! Chris Cobb!'

Sliding paperwork and a mug of coffee to one side, Maguire took a deep breath and said, 'You're out!'

'Been out a week,' replied Cobb. 'I'm in a hostel for the homeless.'

'Are you in trouble?'

'Someone wants me to be,' declared Cobb.

'And you've no escape route?'

'Just the man on the 'phone I'm talking to.'

'Are you free now?' inquired Maguire.

'Yes! Until tonight. I need to be in by eight because that's when they lock the doors.'

'Do you know the park where the castle is?'

'Yes!'

'I'll meet you there in thirty minutes,' said Maguire. 'Make for the statue in the middle of the park. I'll see you there.'

'Will do!'

'When you see me, I'll walk right past you without so much as a smile. Just follow me until it's safe to talk and there's no one else around. Understood?'

'Yes!'

The conversation died and Maguire returned the 'phone to its cradle.

'Problem?' queried Stan.

'Not sure, Stan. Cancel our walk to Johnsons. You'll have to go yourself. I need to see someone.'

'Anyone I know?'

'I'll tell you later,' revealed Maguire putting his jacket on. 'I'm not sure which way this one will go.'

'If the DI asks where you are, what should I tell him?' inquired Stan.

'Tell him I'm meeting someone.'

'Who?' probed Stan.

'Sapphire!' explained Maguire. 'Tell him I'm meeting Sapphire, Stan.'

'I've not heard that one before.'

'Well, neither have I actually, but all being well someone we know might need a new name.'

Maguire grabbed a set of car keys as he vacated the office and headed for his meeting.

'Sapphire?' puzzled Stan. 'Jewels and gems, I wonder.'

Parking a safe distance from the castle, Maguire entered the park on foot and casually made his way towards the statue of Queen Victoria. The old stonework dominated the centre of a large lawned area that was surrounded by benches which were occupied by people out enjoying the fine weather.

For a moment, the detective wondered if the meeting that was about to take place would be safe. Or was he being lured into a trap by a crook he had imprisoned who was now intent on getting revenge? Maybe he should have asked Stan to along and watch his back.

Selecting one of the tarmac pathways that crisscrossed the lawn, Maguire noted the presence of Chris Cobb sat on one of the benches. Ignoring Cobb, the detective strolled past the statue towards the river.

Once on the path by the riverbank, Maguire slowed and waited for Cobb to catch him.

Dressed in a dark three-quarter-length coat and denim jeans, Cobb approached as Maguire glanced over his shoulder, smiled, and said, 'Follow me.'

Where's he taking me, thought Cobb. It's ages since I last saw this man. Has he changed? Can I trust him? Maybe I shouldn't have made that 'phone call.

Stepping from the pathway, Maguire selected a track which ran parallel to the River Eden. Broad enough for two people, Maguire offered a handshake that was accepted and began with, 'Long time, no see. How are you, Chris?'

'Fine,' replied Cobb uneasily. 'Good to see you too.'

'Hard time or easy?' inquired Maguire looking around the immediate area.

'Harder than I thought in some ways. I've had it up to here with evil thuggery and prison guards who look the other way, but it's over now and I'm never going back.'

'Good,' offered Maguire.

'Are we okay to talk here?' asked Cobb.

'Ten minutes!' replied Maguire firmly. 'That's how long it will take us to reach a fork in the pathway. I'll take the left fork. You take the right and walk away. No handshake. No waves. We're covered here because of the trees on the riverbank, but in a few hundred yards the trees will have gone, and we'll be more visible. Okay with that?'

'Yes,' replied Cobb glancing over his shoulder. Feeling slightly more comfortable, he added, 'I'm okay with that.'

'What's the problem?' inquired Maguire. 'Speak quickly if you need to.'

'Bennie's gang! They want me to drive for them. It's a post office job. I don't know the full details yet. Anyway, I told them I'd do it.'

'Have you driven for them before in jobs like that?'

'Just the tractor and the cash machine I told you about, and the deliveries. The drugs and dud money.'

'What else do you know about the job?'

'That's all now. I'm their second choice. The usual driver got six months last week for drunk driving.'

'Second choice! Does that bother you?'

'Not one little bit,' replied Cobb. 'I'll get the nod to meet them somewhere and the job will probably go down that day.'

'When do you think that will happen?'

'Usually within a couple of days,' revealed Cobb. 'They don't hang about once they're on the boil.'

'Do they have a third-choice driver?'

'Probably, but I don't know who that would be.'

'Do you think they still trust you?'

'Yes, I'd say so,' revealed Cobb. 'I've been to prison. I'm one of the team now. That's the way they look at it. A nine-month sentence seems to be a promotion in their eyes.'

'How many are there in the gang?' probed Maguire.

'Forty or fifty, something like that.'

'That many!' gasped Maguire. 'Do you know who the leader is?'

'Wayne!'

'Wayne who?' ventured Maguire.

'That's all I know. He's called Wayne.'

'Come on, Chris,' challenged Maguire. 'You must know more than that. Say it like it is or don't say anything. I've no time for playing games. What's his full name and age, for example? Where does he live? What's he been inside for?'

'I don't know,' replied Cobb. 'Honestly! Wayne is a bit of a mystery man as far as I can see.'

'In what way?' inquired Maguire.

'He never goes on a job,' declared Cobb. 'I think he does all the planning and handles all the proceeds. Money, jewellery, whatever it is.'

'How do you know that?' probed Maguire.

Cobb walked on before replying, 'I don't. I'm just guessing because I've never met him. What else would such a man do? It's all a mystery to me.'

'And me,' replied Maguire.

'Sorry, but that's all I know about him.'

'But he does exist?' suggested Maguire.

'Yes, of course, why?' asked Cobb.

'Because people call it Benny's gang after your uncle, but he died a while back. I was wondering if Wayne was just a name made up. A red herring? Something to make detectives run around looking for a man that doesn't exist.'

'Why would they do that?'

'To make us waste our time,' replied Maguire.

'Oh! Oh! I never thought of that,' voiced Cobb.

'They tell people like you that the gang leader is someone called Wayne,' explained Maguire. 'They do that so that if you ever break down during an interview with the police, you'll tell them the leader is a man called Wayne. The police then charge around the countryside looking for a man that doesn't exist. The gang get to know who the police are looking for and realise the people they've mentioned the name Wayne to are probably informants. You're burnt, in trouble, and of no use to either the gang or me. That's why I need to know that Wayne exists, and you're not being tested by the gang.'

'Ah! I see,' nodded Cobb. 'Now you're making sense. Did you stop to think that I might have lulled you here to give you a tip-off about something when all I was planning was to give you a good bashing? After all, you're the man who got me nine months in a prison cell.'

Maguire glared at Cobb but did not reply.

'So, you've no sense of humour,' smiled Cobb. 'I was just testing you, Les. Not to worry.'

'If there was a test, you'd fail,' growled a discontented Maguire.

'Well, Les, I can tell you for definite that Wayne exists. I've heard others talk about him for a year or two. He's well and truly in charge and there's a few quite frightened of him.'

'Okay! You once told me that you didn't do very well at school,' remarked Maguire.

'I didn't. Me and school just didn't get along.'

'Have you got a good memory?'

'I suppose so. I don't know.'

'What's a red herring?' queried Maguire.

'Something that doesn't exist,' replied Cobb. 'Why?'

'In my world, that might be you,' revealed Maguire. 'I'll explain shortly. Tell me, can you memorise things?'

'Why?'

'Because you're no good to me if you can't remember things about the gang, what they tell you to do, and who tells you. Does that make sense?'

'I think so.'

'You need to be good in the memory stakes if both of us are to succeed.'

'I'll try my best,' promised Cobb.

'Okay,' nodded Maguire. 'I want you to listen every time the name Wayne is mentioned. I want to know everything about him. I want every scrap of information you hear. Is that understood?'

'Yes! You want to know everything about the boss. I get that.'

'Good!' smiled Maguire. 'Now can you remember a mobile telephone number?'

'Yes. I reckon I could. Why?'

'Chris, I don't want you to ring the CID office anymore,' directed Maguire. 'I don't want anyone to know about you. I want you to be that red herring and cease to exist in the office. Anyone might answer the 'phone and if you're going to work for me, I need to keep you safe. That means you only talk to me and no-one else.'

'Like an informant?'

'That's what you would be,' confirmed Maguire. 'Officially, Chris, you would become a registered informant. Someone legally described as a covert human intelligence source.'

'Shit! What a mouthful! I suppose it legally recognises me as a human. I think.'

'Yes, it does,' chuckled Maguire. 'Just! It's a bit technical for some, but basically, there are things I have to legally do if you become an informant.'

'Like pay me?' beamed Cobb.

'Register you with my big boss,' explained Maguire. 'You'd never meet him, but he'd see the paperwork I give him, and he'd make sure that I was looking after you.'

'Do you trust him?' probed Cobb.

'Yes!'

Cobb nodded as they walked on. The trickle of the river could be heard nearby.

'Do you want to be paid?' inquired Maguire.

'Not really! I'm not bothered. I want to be free. I want them off my back so I can do something positive with my life.'

'Good!' replied Maguire.

'But a little money now and again would be good for me because I'm not working. I've no savings, no pensions, and no prospects.'

'And you need a new pair of jeans, a pair of trainers, and a new coat.' remarked Maguire.

Cobb looked down at his trainers, saw how the sole had finally detached itself from the rest of the shoe, and replied, 'Yeah! I suppose I do. That's what you get for climbing in the wrong gear.'

'I'd no idea,' frowned Maguire.

'Could you pay me?' inquired Cobb.

'Upon results only,' replied Maguire. 'And I don't want you involved in this job that you're on about.'

The two men walked on in silence as the breeze changed to a wind and a cold gust whistled across the Eden and caused ripples on the surface. In the distance, a fisherman stood waist-high in the river and cast his line into the water in search of prey.

'Do you know what I mean by the term informant, Chris?'

'Yeah! Snitch!'

'Snitch! Snout! Stoolie! Sneak! Nark!' added Maguire. 'And worse! If you are ever found out, you will be regarded as the lowest of the low. Total and utter scum. Sorry, but you should know what might lie ahead if it all goes wrong.'

'But only if they find out about me,' replied Cobb.

'Exactly!' agreed Maguire.

'So, if we're careful, that won't happen,' suggested Cobb.

'It's as complicated or as easy as you want it to be,' proposed Maguire. 'It would be your job to give me information. It's my job to protect you from being found out.'

'Sounds complicated,' replied Cobb.

'It is,' nodded Maguire. 'But we can make it easy.'

They walked on.

Maguire glanced at Cobb and realised his protege was thinking things through, deciding on whether he was on board or not.

Cobb glanced back, looked away, and dug his hands deep into his pockets as the two men realised that a decision made today might impact on both lives in the years ahead.

'Do I get out of the gang eventually?' inquired Cobb.

'You could move three hundred miles away, but I suspect they'd still come after you because you know too much about their operation,' declared Maguire. 'Can you work for us? If we can break the gang up it will open an escape path for you, and you might just get out safely without any problem.'

'Without any problem?' challenged Cobb.

'All being well,' ventured Maguire.

'I want you to arrest the entire gang on the same day,' ventured Cobb. 'That's the only way I can get out and make a run for it knowing that I've got a chance of changing my life. Can you do that for me? Arrest them all at the same time?'

'Right now, I've nothing to arrest any of them for, Chris,' replied Maguire. 'And that's a tall order from someone who hasn't even decided if they're on board yet. But it would be a good thing to do even if it started as near impossible.'

Nothing was said between the two until the fork in the pathway appeared and Cobb replied, 'Informant it is then. But only until I can get out safely.'

'Agreed! Here, read this,' replied Maguire.

A business card was handed over and Maguire said, 'Memorise the number. When you ring it, I will be the only person who answers it.'

Cobb took the card, studied the content, and then closed his eyes before returning the card and repeating the number out loud.

'Good lad!' remarked Maguire.

'It would be easier to keep the card,' suggested Cobb.

'And dangerous if you were found in possession of it,' replied Maguire. 'From this moment on, I need you to trust me, Chris. Every step of the way. If I ask you to remember telephone numbers and stuff like that, it's for your own good.'

'I see what you mean,' nodded Cobb.

'Now that you know the number, ring me when you know what the job is about,' instructed Maguire. 'Which post office? Where? When? How many involved? The works! I want to know everything you know. Is that understood?'

'Yes, then what?' probed Cobb.

'I'll tell you what to do when I know what the score is,' explained Maguire. 'One more thing.'

'Go on.'

'If you ask the wrong question or too many questions, someone might get suspicious,' explained Maguire. 'That's usually how things start to go wrong.'

'So, what do you want me to do?'

'Listen mainly,' replied Maguire. 'Don't go diving in and asking who Wayne is for example. They'll be wary of you from the word go. No, just easy does it. Listen out, get a little more friendly to the ones running the show and see what develops.'

'I can do that,' replied Cobb.

'Next time you're in a pub,' proposed Maguire. 'I want you to take a beermat home with you. Tear a piece off and when you close the door whenever you leave the flat push the card into the bottom of the door jamb so that when someone opens the door, the card will fall out. Can you do that for me?'

'I get it,' nodded Cobb. 'That way I'll know if anyone has been inside whilst I was out.'

'That's right,' confirmed Maguire. 'If they get suspicious one of the gang might turn your drum over. They'll be looking for a telephone number, extra cash, anything that might rumble our relationship. Are you with me?'

'Oh, yes. I think I'm going to be ahead of you soon.'

'Keep on your guard, that's all,' added Maguire.

They arrived at the fork in the pathway and took their separate ways as Cobb broke into a gentle jog and Maguire took the long route back to his car.

As Cobb disappeared into the distance, Maguire asked himself if was being set up by someone he could trust? He doesn't want money, but he hasn't got any. Is he playing me for a fool or what? I just don't know.

Padding along the track at a jogger's speed, Cobb wondered how much money he would be paid and whether he could trust Maguire to keep him safe from the gang.

~

5

Three days later
North Cumbria

The call had been made and the team had been briefed.

A succession of vans and saloon cars followed each other out of the back yard of the police compound and headed towards the premises where an armed robbery was scheduled to take place.

On reaching Wetheral, on the outskirts of the city, the team split up and took up positions surrounding the village post office.

Parts of the team moved to the rear of the target premises and parked unobtrusively in the car park of the local medical practice. Others occupied hotel car parks in the immediate vicinity whilst several plainclothes officers congregated in the area.

A woman pushing a pram stopped near a bench, tended to a baby inside the pram, and then took a seat where she gently rocked the pram. A man walking a dog on a leash strolled by, nodded at the lady with the pram, and slowly dragged the zip down an inch or so on his anorak.

Halfway down the green, a couple met a man in a suit outside a bungalow displaying a 'For Sale' sign. The estate agent removed a key from his pocket, unlocked the front door, and gestured for his guests to enter first.

Moments later, Maguire, the estate agent, removed his suit jacket, gestured a welcome to the couple, and then engaged the radio.

'Team Alpha in position,' radioed Maguire. 'Alpha is the forward control point! I have control! Please acknowledge.'

The airwaves were crammed for a moment as various undercover units checked in and reported their positions.

Inside the post office, an elderly man wearing dark spectacles, a wig, and a bulky jacket, stood in a room behind the counter watching the postmaster going about his business.

A reflection from a mirror reminded Stan Holliday that his disguise was probably the best on show that day.

Stan adjusted his earpiece and cradled a side by side double-barrelled shotgun as he watched proceedings inside the premises and listened to the ongoing commentary outside.

When the airwaves went quiet, Stan engaged his throat mic and said, 'Ground Zero reports all correct! No change!'

'I have that,' replied Maguire.

On the village green, the sun was shining, the dog walkers were in abundance, and a wireless recording was triggered to deliver the sound of a baby crying in a pram.

In an empty house boasting a 'For Sale' sign, Maguire turned to the couple he had recently admitted and asked, 'I'm DC Maguire. I presume you are from the Regional Crime Squad. We've not met before.'

'DC Jenna Thomlinson and DS Larry Coulthard,' replied the lady as she scanned the area with a pair of binoculars. 'Who's the DI in charge?'

'Greg Archer,' replied Maguire.

'Where is he?' queried Larry.

'Walking the dog!' replied Maguire.

'He should be in here,' suggested Larry frowning. 'The DI should be in control.'

'Well, today, he's out there and I'm in control here. I wouldn't get in his way if I were you,' replied Maguire suddenly aware he was in the presence of critics rather than supporters. 'Our DI has a reputation of not suffering fools gladly and, believe me, he'll be first through the door if the job goes down.'

'We heard an informant was involved,' remarked Larry.

'Did you?' queried Maguire. 'Whoever told you that?'

'My brother,' replied Larry. 'Brian! He's in the force too.'

'I've never heard of him,' offered Maguire. 'But then I'm new to the game with not many years in. Should I know your brother? Is he a detective too?'

'It doesn't matter,' replied Larry. 'We get to know all about stuff like this. If the DI is on the ground, then that tells me he's running the informant and he's going to let one of the crooks run away and get off scot-free. Now tell me I'm wrong, DC Maguire because I know more about these capers than you could ever imagine.'

'Funny that!' ventured Maguire. 'I can tell you the information came from an anonymous telephone call. Weren't you at the briefing Detective Inspector Greg Archer gave?'

'Yes! Yes, of course!' replied Larry. 'I've been chasing this gang for three years and want to know who is close enough to these scumbags to be able to make a 'phone call that moves half the squad from Lancashire to the middle of nowhere.'

'I've never been to Scotland before,' chuckled Jenna.

'You didn't quite make it,' replied Maguire.

'Two things will happen today, DC Maguire,' suggested an increasingly aggressive Larry. 'Nothing will happen, or the job will go down and one of the robbers will walk away untouched. A tenner says your poor DI Greg Armer might…'

'Archer!' corrected Maguire. 'Greg Archer!'

'Archer!' Yeah, Archer!' admitted Larry. 'A tenner says your snout makes a runner, gets clean away, and your poor DI gets a smack in the face from his informant so that it looks good.'

'That's the Lancashire trick is it?' challenged Maguire.

'Ah! Do me a favour,' remarked Larry. 'We're not stupid.'

'Good! Pleased to hear it,' replied Maguire. 'Now, if you don't mind, the DI will take control when he's ready and not before. He's callsign Majestic, by the way. One of you upstairs in the bedroom with the binoculars, please, and the other on the computer system here. I want every vehicle passing through the village checked as to ownership and whether it's stolen, hired, or of interest. Is that not too much trouble?'

'Really?'

'Yes, really!' replied Maguire. 'As I said, I'm in control.'

There was no reply from the two detectives, merely an unspoken acquiescence as they went about their business.

Annoyed, Maguire shook his head and studied the immediate area referred to on the radio as the plot. From his position, he took in the post office, the green, the medical practice, and several hotel car parks sprinkled with squad cars and undercover personnel,

In the city, an ambulance drove into a parking bay at the rear of the Accident and Emergency Department and discharged its latest patient. The paramedics removed the patient from the vehicle, placed him on a trolley, and pushed him into the medical reception area where he was seen by a member of the triage team.

'A head injury, you say,' queried the medic.

'Yes!' came the reply. 'And my eyes seem a little fuzzy.'

The medic interviewed his patient, examined the man's cranial area, checked his eyes with the appropriate instrumentation, and then said, 'Any pain at all?'

'Like a really bad headache,' voiced the young man. 'Like I said, I came a cropper from the ladder cleaning the gutters out and when I hit the ground everything went blank.'

'We'll start with an X-ray,' declared the medic.

'Will I be here long?' inquired the patient.

'That depends on what we find,' replied the medic. 'But I'll need some personal details. You weren't going anywhere important, were you?'

'No, not at all.'

'Good! Now then, sir, your name? Your full name please.'

'Cobb!' replied the patient. 'Christopher Cobb.'

Back in the village, the minutes had grown into hours and the team were getting restless. A succession of false alarms, the arrival of badly parked vehicles, and an influx of walkers heading for the riverbank had given way to a period of comparative inactivity.

Maguire yawned, poured a drink from a flask, and continued his watch from the Forward Control Point.

A dark grey van drove through the village and maintained its route to the motorway.

'Did you get that one?' inquired Maguire.

'No!' replied Jenna. 'The number plate was muddied up and unreadable. It's gone now anyway.'

'You got that grey van, Larry?' asked Maguire.

'Straight through the village. It didn't stop,' replied Larry watching the route with his binoculars.

Fifteen minutes later, Maguire radioed, 'Ground Zero! Status report!'

'No change!' replied Stan. 'All quiet.'

'Looks like a wasted day,' suggested Jenna. 'Unless you want to submit a report indicating we've seen two untaxed cars pass through the village, and the bus service is running five minutes late. Is it always so quiet in Scotland?'

'You're still in England,' snapped Maguire. 'Cumbria to be precise.'

The grey van reappeared and moved into the plot causing Maguire to remark, 'Larry! That van is back. Can you make the number plate out?'

'Stand by!'

Focusing his binoculars, Maguire zoomed in on the front passenger compartment as Larry read out the registration number and added, 'That's what I see but the number plate is muddied. Does it come back as a grey Transit, Jenna?'

'Wait one!'

Jenna interrogated the computer as Maguire radioed, 'All units! One possible on the plot. A grey Transit van containing three male occupants in the front passenger area. Stand by!'

The grey Transit turned right at the green, faltered opposite the post office, and then drove towards a nearby hotel situated close to the riverbank.

'If you got the number right, Larry,' revealed Jenna. 'It's a blue Ford Escort.'

Engaging the binoculars again, Larry replied, 'Well the number given is the number I see even if it is clogged with mud.'

'Are the front and sides of the van muddied over?' probed Maguire.

'No! Just the number plate,' from Larry.

Selecting the wireless handset again, Maguire radioed, 'All call signs. The grey van on the plot is designated Victor One. It appears to be on false plates.'

'Majestic has that,' replied DI Archer. 'Who has an eyeball on Victor One?'

'I do,' replied a lady rocking a pram on the green. 'Victor One is turning around in a hotel car park. Wait one...'

The airwaves went silent.

'Victor One is approaching Ground Zero.'

'I have that,' interjected Stan Holland.

'Alpha has control,' radioed Maguire. 'All callsigns move into your predetermined positions.'

Gradually, slowly, without fuss or panic, various bodies emerged from their hideaways and began walking towards the post office. They could be seen entering the medical practice where they watched from the windows. Another entered a telephone box and lifted the telephone handset. A dog walker turned around and strolled towards the post office but only to pause and tend to his dog. A woman on a bench leaned into a pram, switched off an audio recording, and took hold of a handgun.

'Victor One is on the plot,' radioed Maguire. 'It's a stop, stop, stop outside the target premises. All callsigns stand by.'

DI Archer tied the dog to a lamppost by the leash and unzipped his anorak further before radioing, 'This is Majestic. I have control. I say again, this is Majestic, I have control. I have an eyeball on Ground Zero. Hold all positions and wait. I say again, wait.'

The airwaves remained quiet as the undercover team held their positions and tried to contain their impatience.

'What's he waiting for?' remarked Jenna.

'Evidence!' replied Maguire. 'Right now, we've got a Transit van on dodgy plates and nothing else.'

'Sorry,' voiced Jenna. 'I know that but there's too many of the public around.'

'Let's see what happens,' replied Maguire.

The two passengers in the front of the van got out, looked around, and strolled to the rear of the van as the DI radioed descriptions of the suspects and then added, 'Majestic has the eyeball. They're at the rear of the van. The driver remains in situ. The engine is still running.'

One of the gang opened the rear doors wide and reached inside. He removed two sawn-off shotguns from a holdall on the floor area, slung the holdall over his shoulder, handed one of the weapons to his accomplice, and took another look around the immediate area.

Kneeling, tending to a dog, the DI quietly radioed, 'Majestic has an eyeball and calls Trigger. I say again, Trigger! Trigger! Trigger! Two sawn-off shotguns. Mobiles stand by to lockdown. This is Majestic, I have control. Alert status one!'

A car engine fired on a car park at the medical practice. Another ignition burst into life two hundred yards away on a hotel car park.

Adrenalin surged through the bloodstream and pulses increased as the situation reached fever pitch. The team knew that 'Trigger' meant the situation had evolved into an armed incident.

Inside the post office, Stan Holland emerged from the room behind the counter, ushered the only two customers into safety and took the postmaster's position behind the counter saying, 'Stay in the room as discussed.'

The postmaster nodded in agreement and locked the door behind him.

Stan laid the shotgun on a ledge beneath the counter and waited. Through the front window, he could see two men approaching the front door. One of them had a holdall slung over his shoulder.

'This is Majestic, I have control,' filled the airwaves. 'Stand by! Stand by! Stand by!'

The hand of an armed criminal reached out and casually pushed the front door of the post office open, looked in, saw a newspaper rack, a display of confectionery, soft toys, birthday cards, a lottery terminal, and an elderly man standing behind the counter. The post office appeared to be otherwise empty.

A second armed robber joined his partner.

They took a step into the building.

'Strike! Strike! Strike!' radioed Majestic as the undercover team began to run towards the post office with their firearms drawn.

Simultaneously, three mobiles set off at breakneck speed and roared into the main street. There was a screech of tyres and the sudden snatch of a handbrake before the vehicles slewed across the highway and boxed in a grey Transit van and its perplexed driver.

Seconds later, a woman who had sat with a pram on the green most of the day, thrust a handgun through the driver's open window and shouted, 'Freeze! Armed police! Don't even breath!'

The driver's mouth flapped open and the female detective reached in and grabbed the ignition keys adding, 'Hands! Let me see your hands! In the air now!'

Terrified, with the barrel of the gun inches from his forehead, the driver slowly raised his hands towards the roof of the van.

A drop of pure perspiration trickled down his cheek, curled around the curve of his chin, and hung like a teardrop waiting to crash to the ground.

It was at that moment that the female detective looked down and saw a handgun resting on the driver's lap.

Inside the building, the two robbers levelled their shotguns and screamed, 'The money! Hand over the money!'

Stan held his hands high.

They rushed towards the counter. One of the robbers raised his shotgun to shoulder height and pointed the weapon at Stan Holliday. The other tucked his shotgun into the side and drew nearer to the counter.

'Now! Money!'

A holdall was thrown towards Stan and landed on the counter before him.

'My hands,' stuttered Stan in a deliberate show of weakness. 'My hands. Can I put them down?'

'Just get the bloody cash out of the safe and then the till,' shouted one of the robbers.

Turning slightly, Stan lowered his hands and said, 'The Till! I'll get the till first.'

'Just do it,' screamed the robber.

Outside, the hornets had gathered around the nest and succeeded in encircling the post office. Every entrance and exit were covered by armed officers. The sound of sirens gradually filled the air

There was a quiet controlled thud when the van driver was pulled from the cab and landed roughly on the pavement. A snap of the handcuffs and the seizure of a handgun married the first arrest.

Maguire held his position, watched proceedings evolve, and interrupted the constabulary radio system with, 'This is Alpha, the Forward Control Point, Wetheral Post Office, North Cumbria. Operation Ground Zero is now a trigger operation. Trigger incident! Undercovers engaging!'

The Force radio system went into overdrive as Headquarters responded by diverting several uniform units to the scene.

At Ground Zero, DI Greg Archer bolstered his bulletproof vest by utilising a full-length ballistic shield delivered to him by a mobile unit. He held it high before him as he took his first step into the building and proclaimed, 'This is the police. Put your weapons down and your hands up!'

Startled, the robbers swivelled around to see a curved structure gradually approaching them. The grey armour-plated full-length ballistic shield incorporated an armoured viewing point through which the DI reconnoitred the scene ahead of him.

Coming into the robber's view, two more individuals appeared behind DI Archer. Each carried an identical shield. An impregnable barrier had been formed at the main entrance of the post office.

The men from Bennie's gang immediately swung around intending to push Stan out of the way and rush to the rear exit.

In the mini-second of turning, Stan's hands crashed down from on high, grasped a side by side shotgun from the shelf below the counter, and raised it to a firing position with the words, 'Armed police! You are surrounded! Drop your weapons!'

A two-second delay in the mind of a criminal thinking, 'should I or should I not,' was enough for the police. Several plainclothes detectives carrying ballistic shields rushed in from behind Stan and dominated the space.

'Down!' ordered Stan waving his shotgun slightly from side to side. 'Put the weapons down.'

The two robbers had no time to answer when they found themselves abruptly taken to the ground following the deployment of batons to the back of the knee.

The gang fell. They were outnumbered ten to one. The gang's weapons fell. They had been thwarted by a better armed and more organised gang.

There was a rush to secure the robbers and take them into custody.

Placing his shield to one side, DI Archer ordered, 'Get them handcuffed, arrested, and searched on site. I want the exhibit officer and the tactical officer to come through and secure the scene. Bag and tag the weapons and recover all ammunition. Three officers to each prisoner no-one leaves the scene with a prisoner unless they have an armed escort. Years in the catching is not going to be spoilt by minutes of incompetence. Expedite!'

Nods of agreement followed as the team followed orders.

Approaching Stan, the DI asked, 'You okay, Stan?'

Opening his jacket wide, Stan revealed a heavy-duty bulletproof vest and replied, 'Hot! Just hot, boss! Remind me not to wear one of these things again. It's an iron corset, for God's sake.'

The DI chuckled and said, 'Well, I think a pint or two at the club tonight might just go down a treat.'

'I'll be there,' replied Stan.

As the prisoners were taken to waiting police vehicles, the DI engaged his radio with, 'This is Majestic. I have control. The trigger is closed. I say again the trigger is down. Let the log record three arrests. No shots fired. Crime scene management now in progress.'

Acknowledgements followed and a short time later, as the DI strolled outside, he radioed, 'This is Majestic. I relinquish control. Alpha now has command. Well done everyone. Debrief in four hours.'

Acknowledgements followed before Maguire replied, 'Alpha now has control. The following officers will secure witness statements and relevant crime scene evidence…'

Maguire read out a pre-determined list of names as Larry and Jenna gathered their kit and made ready to leave the premises.

Half an hour later, DI Greg Archer, a tall former Scots Guard, walked into Maguire's environment and said, 'Have the others gone?'

', Guvnor,' replied Maguire. 'They're packing up the kit and on their way to the nick for the debrief. Oh, how happy are they? I've never seen such sulks before.'

'Really?' queried the DI. 'That's interesting and you need to bear that in mind.'

'Yes! Really!' suggested Maguire. 'Their boss will be at you for details of the informant first thing in the morning. They are upset they had to come to Scotland to arrest the main members of Bennie's gang.'

'This is Cumbria. We're not in Scotland,' voiced a confused DI.'

'You and I know that but I'm not sure our colleagues do. Strange pair! I'd say a little jealousy is afoot,' proposed Maguire.

'Any other problems?' probed the DI.

'The informant,' replied Maguire.

'An anonymous 'phone call,' replied the DI. 'And as for anyone else wanting to dig deeper, it will remain an anonymous 'phone call. We have a recording to deliver to the court if needs be.'

'Good! That was the best idea I've heard in a long time. A confidential 'phone line that recalls incoming calls.'

'Maguire, one day you will realise that being a boss is about having good ideas and sitting down at the desk and putting them into action.'

'I know,' replied Maguire. 'I like to see my bosses on the ground, not behind a desk.'

'Well, if you ever become Chief Constable – which I doubt – you'll discover that the Chief can't be on the ground twenty-four-seven, if at all.'

'Less than five years' service, not yet made double figures,' ventured Maguire. 'My knowledge of bosses extends to Sergeant and Inspector, Guvnor. The Sergeant is the Commander, and the Inspector is the King. Never met anyone higher since the day I joined.'

'You might one day,' revealed the DI. 'By the way, how did you come to pick Sapphire as a codename for your source.'

'The source has blue eyes, Guvnor,' replied a straight-faced Maguire.

Nodding, accepting the remark, DI Archer continued, 'And how did you secure your source during this operation?'

'You don't need to know, Guvnor,' replied Maguire. 'It's what you told me when I declared my source as Sapphire, and you authorised his use. You advised me that I should remove him from any crime that he reports is about to happen and secure his ongoing safety. I did what you told me. How I did it is something you don't need to know.'

The DI studied Maguire with unwavering eyes, considered the situation, and replied, 'Benny's gang is known to be ten, maybe twelve leaders, at the most. We took three out today. Nine left!'

'Anyone called Wayne?' inquired Maguire.

'No! They're all known, previous convictions, records as long as your arm. The gang leader isn't amongst this trio, Maguire.'

'Better luck next time then,' remarked Maguire. 'I've searched all our criminal records, downloaded scores of possible suspects for enquiry, checked hundreds of leads, and I'm no nearer to identifying Wayne than the day we first started.'

'Crack on, Maguire. Fingers crossed,' replied DI Archer. 'Here's the deal.'

There was a pause before Maguire replied, 'I'm listening.'

'The paperwork for Sapphire is done. He will be run by you and I have authorised his use. It's all been a bit of a rush, given the timescales involved, but everything is now validated and signed off by the Chief of Detectives,' revealed DI Archer. 'There's one thing you need to know.'

'What's that, Guvnor?'

'Thirty years of experience tells me it will all fall if the security of the source does not become paramount. Sometimes you have to step outside the box and make things happen. If you genuinely believe in what you do, and what you stand for, you must sometimes walk a tightrope. If your balance goes awry, it's easy to fall off. When you run an informant it's easy to do all the wrong things and get into trouble yourself. This is your first informant, I believe?'

'Yes,' confirmed Maguire. 'That's right.'

'Not to worry,' nodded the DI. 'We'll talk further tomorrow about running informants. My office ten in the morning.'

'Ten! Okay, Guvnor.'

'Is your man good to go, Maguire? I mean, is he in it for the long haul?'

'Yes! I have complete assurance in him,' replied Maguire. 'I intend to make it happen.'

'That's your first mistake,' replied the DI. 'If you don't run the source properly, it will bite the hand that feeds it. Never place complete assurance in your source.'

'Oh!' exclaimed a shocked Maguire.

'Do you understand what I'm saying, Maguire?'

'Yes!'

'Good! I'm sending you on a course. It's about running informants. You learn most about these things when you are doing it, but an initial course in London for a week will knock you into shape and switch you on.'

'Wow! Thank you.'

DI Greg Archer stepped away to the door and said, 'Great work, Maguire.'

'Thank you, Guvnor.'

'With his hand on the doorknob, the DI turned and queried, 'Why Accident and Emergency, Maguire?'

Stunned, Maguire did not explain.

Tapping his nose with an index finger, DI Archer remarked, 'Good luck. Don't ask. You don't need to know. And by the way, don't ever use that ruse again, Maguire. Never a hospital. They're busy enough as it is.'

'Right! Okay!' agreed Maguire. 'I just thought...'

'I know what you thought,' interjected the DI. 'I am a reader of minds. Just think of a better place next time.'

Greg Archer close the door behind him saying, 'Ten in the morning. Don't be late.'

Was that a good guess or did he know the truth about what happened to Chris Cobb, thought Maguire?

He hadn't told anyone of his plan other than Cobb, and that was simple. On the day of the robbery admit yourself to the local hospital with a head injury and stay there for the duration. That will force the gang to either abandon the robbery or select option three as the driver. They must have activated choice three, thought Maguire. But how did the DI know that? Maybe he has an iron in the fire too.

Maguire packed up, closed the Forward Control Point down, and walked to his car.

Answering his mobile, the detective said, 'Maguire!'

''It's me. I'm out.'

'And they're in,' replied Maguire. 'All three. Any problems at your end?'

'None at all. I told them I was on my way to the hospital and they enlisted the other driver I mentioned. I'm clear and I'm in demand now apparently.'

'Keep your nose clean,' ordered Maguire. 'Don't get involved and lose your 'phone for at least a month.'

'What if I've got something for you?' inquired Cobb.

'Only in an emergency,' declared Maguire. 'It won't take them long to work out someone is talking. Stay away from me and stay safe. It's as easy as that. Let them run around and chase each other for a few weeks. They've nothing on you. Don't give them anything. Don't contact me unless you are in personal danger. Okay?'

Maguire fired the car engine and drove away.

Operation Ground Force concluded.

That afternoon a grey saloon car driven by a male, who was accompanied by his wife, set off from a detached bungalow on the outskirts of Oxenholme, near Kendal. The vehicle made its way to Windermere.

Stopping in the car park near Windermere Railway Station, the woman made her way to a nearby bank where she deposited a large amount of cash into an account.

On leaving the bank, she entered a café close to the railway station and had coffee with her husband before returning to Oxenholme in the car.

As the couple entered the A591 bound for home, a high-powered black motorcycle moved into a line of traffic behind them and journeyed in the same direction. As the bike negotiated the highway towards Staveley two saloon cars moved into position and followed the motorcycle.

At the summit of a hill, Stan leaned against a gate post where he had parked his bike and watched Maguire clamber over the imaginary finishing line at walking pace.

'Thirty-two minutes,' announced Stan.

'I made it to the top though,' enthused Maguire.

'You made it most of the way running and then took a breather.'

'You said to. Remember?' challenged Maguire.

'True! But keep running. Don't stop to walk. You're disqualified. See you tomorrow.'

Maguire shook his head when Stan pedalled down the hill shouting, 'Stretch them.'

~

6

The Crematorium
Carlisle
Forty-Eight Four Hours later

There was never a nice day at the City Crematorium. It didn't matter whether or not the sun shone, or it rained. It was always a sad day. Today, the sun was shining.

Maguire waited in the car park for the cortege to arrive and then got out of his vehicle and strolled behind the queue of mourners waiting to enter the building. His dark suit and black tie blended well with the colours of the day.

As the funeral service got underway, Maguire sidestepped proceedings and casually walked towards the adjoining cemetery which was no more than a hundred yards away. Carrying a bouquet, he walked through a break in the hedgerow that took him from the crematorium area into the vast cemetery that lay before him. On meeting the tarmac area, he turned right and began to tread the broad path that bordered the cemetery.

Here and there, several parked cars littered the pathway where the occupants had stopped to lay a wreath or tend to a graveside. The serenity of the area bore testament to the peace of mind that the mourners sought.

Reaching the end of the path, Maguire turned to his left and then followed the route which took him back into the heart of the cemetery.

Following a circular route, his actions were deliberate. Maguire was looking for someone and, from the highest point of the cemetery, he could see the vast burial ground stretching out into the distance. The gradual downhill stroll allowed him to check out the cars and people who were in the area, who was doing what, where, and why.

Cobb, he thought. Where are you?

On approaching the long line of white war graves, Maguire caught sight of Cobb kneeling beside one of the graves and watched him lay a bunch of flowers beside the headstone.

Maguire paused for a moment, allowed a red salon car to drive past him towards the entrance, and then continued his tour.

Stepping from the tarmac path, Maguire felt the gravel beneath his feet as he headed towards a wooded area where only a few graves were surrounded by the tall trees that dominated the city's cemetery. The gravestones had seen better days, were weather-beaten, and in places, the wording could not be seen for the fingers of moss that were creeping across them.

Kneeling, Maguire placed a bouquet on the grave and then began cleaning the gravestone.

Cobb glanced at the detective, tidied the war grave, and then joined Maguire in the wooded area.

Maguire glanced up and asked, 'Are you good to go?'

Cobb declared, 'I'm as clean as a whistle. No problems.'

'Good,' replied Maguire. 'Does anyone know you are here?'

'No! I wasn't followed either. I've been careful like you told me to be.'

'The grave,' gestured Maguire. 'Why that one?'

'Oh, that wasn't part of the act,' revealed Cobb. 'It was my grandfather's resting place.'

'I'm sorry,' explained Maguire. 'I didn't know.'

'And your flowers?' probed Cobb.

'Similar,' voiced Maguire declining to elaborate.

The two men stood quietly for a while lost in their thoughts before Maguire took a step away and said, 'I'm sorry you had to ring me. What happened?'

'They smashed the door down at six o'clock in the morning,' explained Cobb.

'Six in the morning!' from an astonished Maguire.

'Not even the birds were awake,' frowned Cobb. 'They dragged me from my bed, filled the bath with cold water, and then tried to drown me in it. Oh boy! I thought I was done for, Les. No escape! No explanation! Just almost drowned.'

'Who were they? Did you know them?'

'Jawbone Jones! Smudger Murray and Tiny Philpotts. They're all gang members who have been in since the start, Les.'

'I see, thank you,' replied Maguire. 'I know the names.'

'Good!' said Cobb.

'How did you stop them from drowning you?' ventured Maguire.

'It didn't dawn on me until later, but I don't think they ever intended to drown me to start with,' explained Cobb. 'They hit me, tried to get me to admit I was the snout, then stuck my head in the toilet and kept flushing it until I broke down.'

Perturbed, Maguire rasped, 'You broke down!'

'No! Not that way, Les. I broke into tears, threw myself on the floor and cried. I cried so much they lifted me and handed me a towel to dry myself with.'

'Did you tell them you were the snout?' challenged Maguire.

'No way,' snapped Cobb. 'I played the hero and told them it wasn't me, couldn't have been me because I wasn't there, and then volunteered that I'd try and find out who it was for them.'

'You bloody idiot,' exploded Maguire. 'I told you to listen and report, not volunteer yourself into a gang punishment society. What the hell have you done?'

'Calm down! Calm down, Les,' soothed Cobb. 'They don't want me. It worked out alright. Anyway, I've since heard half a dozen gang members got turned over the same way. They didn't know who it was, so they turned everyone over just as a warning. They use violence on everyone because it's all they know.'

'I don't get that,' replied Maguire. 'You might not have been at the post office, but you knew about the job. There can't have been that many who knew about it.'

'They think their 'phones are bugged,' declared Cobb.

'What?' exclaimed Maguire.

'In amongst the bruises, beatings, and tears, I told them I'd been a loyal gang member for years. I reminded them that I'd served time when I could have spilt the beans and walked away a free man. Then I suggested they wouldn't find a snout in the gang. Oh boy, did they laugh?'

'I bet they did,' remarked Maguire.

'No! I told them they wouldn't find a snout in the gang because it was the police who were onto them,' explained Cobb. 'I told them their 'phones must be bugged. It's the most likely way the police got onto them.'

'Are you telling me they bought that?' queried Maguire.

'Not right away but they sat me down, made some calls, and then told me it was okay. I should keep my nose clean and stay out of trouble.'

Maguire studied Cobb's face trying to work out if he was telling the truth or not.

'Do you remember, Les?'

'Remember what?' probed Maguire.

'That time you nicked me, and I told you the gang ruled my life.'

'In the cell block at the police station. Yes, I remember. Why?'

'You told me that if I told the court I'd been bullied and harassed into a life of crime that I'd probably walk out a free man or have to serve what they call a non-custodial sentence. Well, I didn't, did I? I did the time like I said I would, and they know I could have rolled over that day. I'm safe, Les. They don't think it's me that's the snout.'

A dark saloon car cruised down the narrow pathway amongst the gravestones and caused the two men to fall silent. Gradually, the car disappeared, and Maguire shook his head in disbelief.

'That makes sense, but we didn't plan for that to happen.'

'Well, it did, Les. Believe me, it did.'

'Are they completely clueless?' asked Maguire.

'No! Not at all,' replied Cobb. 'I think they have got away with things for so long that they think they're impregnable.'

'How do you mean?'

'When they started, a few of them got nicked in the early days,' explained Cobb. 'Smudger and Tiny have both done time for assault and thieving. When they got out, they got better. The gang picked people they could rely on more, bullied others into a life of fear, beat the crap out of some of them, and eventually thought they were uncatchable. I know some people who they've threatened with red hot pokers and one guy I know was held upside down from the castle battlements as a punishment for nicking twenty quid from a delivery run.'

Maguire's eyes penetrated Cobb's brain.

'Come on, Les,' Cobb responded. 'These lot started as amateurs but look at them now. It's years since those three were nicked. The gang has done so many jobs since and they've walked away every time. They're so arrogant that the thought of them being infiltrated by a snout just doesn't wash with them. They're beyond capture, Les.'

'Not anymore, Chris. Are you sure you're safe?' challenged Maguire.

'I feel safe. I didn't get the impression they were coming back to beat me up again if that's what you mean.'

'Was the boss mentioned? Wayne?' probed Maguire.

'Nope, but I bet he was behind the idea of turning a few of us over.'

'You mentioned Jawbone Jones, Smudger Murray and Tiny Philpotts. Would you describe them as the main players?'

'Jawbones is pretty high up,' replied Cobb. 'Smudger and Tiny are just foot soldiers.'

'Did those three turn the others over?'

'I suppose so.'

'Who ordered them to do that?' probed Maguire.

'Bobby Nelson, I'd guess. I'm not that sure, to be honest. Wayne? Hey, I don't know.'

'Who would you describe as the main players now, Chris? The ones who are involved in the drugs and all the other stuff going on.'

'How long have you got?'

'I have an idea who we're after. I want to hear your version,' voiced Maguire.

'Bobby Nelson seems to be the main man next to Wayne. It's a long time ago but I once heard someone say that Wayne had a fancy for Bobby's sister.'

'What's her name, Chris?'

'I've no idea. I don't even know if it's true or not. It's just a bit of gossip I heard one day. Mind you, thinking about it, I've never met his sister and never heard of her since.'

'Okay, thank you, I'll bear that in mind,' replied Maguire. 'Who else in the gang do you know about? Convince me you're telling the truth and not making it all up.'

Cobb frowned but replied, 'Jeffrey Jackson, Bill Ashworth, Jed Atkinson, and Colin McArdle. Colin has family in Ireland. I've heard him described as the Irish connection. They would be my main men and I'd add Jawbones to the list because he's eaten some of them alive to get where he is. They're the ones who seem to run everything, but they've all got mates, runners, drivers, backup men, and so on. It's a proper gang, Les. Not just a bunch of bruisers on a housing estate.'

'Any police mentioned?'

'Bent cops?' queried Cobb. 'Is that what you mean?'

'Why not?' queried Maguire. 'Heard anything?'

'Not a peep,' replied Cobb. 'I might be wrong, but these people hate the police.'

'Yeah, I know,' revealed Maguire. 'But you still didn't mention the leader.'

'Wayne!'

'That's him,' ventured Maguire.

'I suppose he's the banker,' replied Cobb. 'I can't get near him.'

'Okay,' considered Maguire. 'We'll keep on with what we've got and see how it goes.'

'I've got something for you,' offered Cobb.

'Since when?'

'They want me to drive for them again. Runner, rider, delivery man, whatever you want to call it.'

'Running drugs from one place to another?'

'Yes! It might be a test, but I'll give it a go,' revealed Cobb. 'Jawbones put it to me before they left. I said yes. The delivery route is something I've known about for a while. I don't think it will have changed much since the last time I did it. The gang's network won't have changed much either. Probably bigger than my last involvement. It might be a good time to take that side of the gang's money down. I'll think about things.'

'Drugs!' remarked Maguire. 'If the whole gang is involved in some way or other, then a chain of command might be apparent. If there is such a formal unspoken structure, then we might be able to untangle it to the extent that we can think about taking the whole gang down at the same time. What do you think of that, Chris?'

'Easier said than done, Les,' replied Cobb. 'As you once told me. Mind you, I'm all in on that one. It'll take time, but I'd be well out of it if the gang collapsed.'

'Someone will tell me it's not possible, but if we sit down and unpick the threads, we might make progress,' ventured Maguire.

'I told you once that I'd driven for them. Nothing has changed. The drivers drive, the runners run, the suppliers supply. The only thing that has changed is the customers and the pubs and clubs they use.'

'What's the difference between a runner, a rider, and a supplier in your eyes?' queried Maguire. 'These terms are often used and can be quite confusing because different people see things in various ways. What do they mean to you?'

'They're all similar in a way,' replied Cobb. 'They're all associated with the gang. That's why the gang might be about a dozen but could easily be a hundred dependant on what you want to see it as. I see less than a dozen, but I also see the others who come and go and never really know who they are working for.'

'Go on,' enthused Maguire. 'A runner?'

'A runner is someone who travels from A to B to collect drugs and deliver them. A rider is a person who protects the runner on the journey. He might be armed if it's a big consignment. Gun! Knife! Knuckleduster! Baseball bat! It all depends, I suppose. The delivery man is the money man because they often deliver hard cash from one kingpin to another. These kingpins have bank accounts, Les, but the buyer on the street doesn't pay by credit card. They pay by cash. The delivery man delivers to the boss who banks the money. That's how this gang works.'

'How far can you take me?' queried Maguire. 'Local, regional, or national?'

'I can't take you all the way, but I can see how you could lead yourself to a port where the stuff first comes into the country. Someone does the import-export side of things.'

Maguire stepped away for a moment or so, glanced at Cobb, and suggested, 'Wayne?'

'Could be,' replied Cobb.

'International?' queried Maguire.

'It comes in from somewhere,' admitted Cobb. 'All you need to do is follow the runners and riders.'

'If it were that easy,' mused Maguire. 'You're upset at being done over, aren't you?'

'I told you. I want out. I'll do whatever it takes to dismantle Benny's gang although it's Wayne's gang now.'

'Seems that way,' agreed Maguire.

Cobb continued with, 'You'll need to do it slowly though because when I walk away, this gang isn't going to exist, and I won't be Chris Cobb anymore. I want the works, Les. I want a new life and a new name.'

'I know you do.'

'Do I get paid for the last job?'

'Yes!' revealed Maguire. 'The money will be put into a bank account in your name. I'll have papers for you to sign next time we meet.'

'And if I change my name?'

'Then we'll change the account. You'll still get what's owed to you.'

'No cash now then?'

Maguire handed two twenty-pound notes over and said, 'Beer money to be going on with, I don't want you to flash money about, Chris. You're not rich and you' haven't got a rich uncle who has just died and left you a sizeable inheritance. If gang members give you money to spend then that's all you do spend. Don't do anything that might lead them to believe you're on the take.'

'When do I get my bank account?'

'When we're done,' replied Maguire. 'What's in the account will be transferred to you and the account will then be closed.'

'So, I have to trust you all that time?'

'Yes,' replied Maguire. 'But then I have to trust you too.'

'Okay,' nodded Chris. 'This drugs network, how long have you got? Can we meet somewhere else? There's a lot to tell you.'

'Let me get this right,' proposed Maguire. 'Jawbones has you lined up for a drugs run but you've not done it yet?'

'Correct!'

'Okay! I'm off on holiday for a week. I won't be around. When I get back, I want you to ring me on Tuesday morning and we'll arrange to meet. I need you for a full day, maybe two, so make sure you're not tied up all week. Meanwhile, just play along with the gang and see where you go. Understood?'

'Fine,' replied Cobb. 'I'll make some notes.'

Maguire stared at Cobb.

'In my head,' replied Cobb. 'In my head, Les. I've got a good memory now.'

'Good man,' nodded Maguire. 'In your head, it is. I'll be in touch as discussed. Now I'm going to leave you and walk away. Give me five minutes before you follow on.'

Cobb nodded agreement as Maguire closed the meeting and took a circuitous route back to the car park.

On returning to his vehicle, Maguire reached inside his coat pocket, removed a tape recorder, and switched it to the 'off' position.

In the days that followed, Maguire documented his meeting with Sapphire, submitted the paperwork to the authorising officer: Greg Archer, and then headed off to a training school in London for a week's crash course in his current line of work, its regulations and protocols, and the product informants delivered.

He trained every night at the college running track. Tired of being a failure, he was determined to win, untiring in his desire to make a name for himself.

Whilst he was away, DI Greg Archer submitted his retirement papers, took the holiday entitlement he was due, and vacated the CID office. Retiring staff always led to gossip, speculation, and staff movements. Who is getting that job was the most common question when someone retired or left for pastures new? Greg Archer's retirement was no exception.

The popular DC Stan Holliday was promoted Detective Sergeant in the CID. The team were delighted because they knew he was such an experienced and knowledgeable man. And he was famous for keeping everyone in check using a quiet professional manner. There was a raft of transfers and promotions on the card, but an empty chair at the DI's desk was there for all to see, and the incoming boss wasn't known to the current crop.

As predicted, Maguire returned from his course in London bursting with new ideas, more aware than ever before about the mistakes he had made, and ready to push on with the Cobb relationship.

Maguire took the call from Cobb, made the arrangements, and booked himself out of town for two days with the officer in charge of the local CID: Detective Sergeant Stan Holliday.

There was an unspoken loyalty between Maguire and Holliday, Stan Holliday was the only officer who could identify Sapphire as Maguire's source. The only officer who had ever seen the source close on the streets. Cobb was never spoken of between the two men, but the growing respect between had been born out of loyalty, honour, and discretion. Perhaps there was a hint of an experienced coach and an aspiring athlete in play. Whatever that relationship was, it was cemented when Stan informed Maguire that the Head of CID had appointed him as Maguire's supervisor in respect of the Sapphire operation.

Paying cash for his ticket, Maguire strolled onto the platform, waited for the train to arrive, and selected a seat to the nearside of the rear carriage. With a lurch, the train set off and soon left the station behind. The carriage was barely full, occupied only by day-trippers, and filled Maguire's requirements exactly.

Five minutes later, the train drew up beside a platform at the next station. Maguire looked out of the nearside window and studied the crowd waiting to board the train. Picking out Cobb, he observed the people around him, how they acted, how they reacted to Cobb's movement's, and where they went. Cobb selected a carriage in the centre of five carriages and boarded the train.

It wasn't long before the rear carriage door opened, and Cobb appeared walking down the aisle towards Maguire. Ignoring the detective, he took a seat halfway down the carriage on the offside, unfolded the local newspaper, and began to read.

Tilting his head slightly to the offside, Maguire looked along the aisle of the carriage but couldn't see anyone else remotely connected to Cobb.

Maguire yawned, allowed his foot to nudge the holdall on the floor, and waited for the train to pull away. Twenty minutes later, the train pulled into another railway station.

Alighting from the train last, Maguire followed Cobb along the platform, through the main entrance, and across the road into a nearby hotel.

Both men took a lift to the top floor, strolled along the corridor, and entered room 511 at Maguire's behest.

Minutes later, Maguire shook hands with Cobb and gestured him to take a seat.

'Tea or coffee?' queried Maguire.

'Lager!' replied Cobb.

'Later,' chuckled Maguire. 'Business first. Any problems?'

'None and I'll have a coffee! And you, Les, is everything okay with your side of things?'

'I'm fine, thanks,' replied Maguire. 'I hope you don't mind but I brought a tape recorder so that I don't miss anything.'

Maguire unzipped the holdall and removed the device from the bag. He plugged it into a socket, switched it on, and said, 'Just let it run. I'll take what I need from it later. I just need you to tell me everything you know about the gang's drugs network. I'm going to listen mostly, I hope, and you're going to talk until you've nothing left. Okay?'

'Sounds good!' replied Cobb. 'Where do I speak into?'

'No need to hold the microphone,' explained Maguire. 'It will pick us both up wherever we are in the room. We'll take a break whenever you want one and I'll switch the machine off. Don't look upon the recorder as your enemy. Look upon it as your friend. Are you okay to continue?'

'Where do you want me to start?' inquired Cobb.

'Right at the beginning,' suggested Maguire. 'Everything you know about the drugs network. How does it work? Who are the main players? Where is it situated? Where is it strong? Where is it weak? What kind of drugs? Prices! Weights! Packaging! Runners and riders. Drivers! Cars! Hired, borrowed, or stolen! You wanted to tell me about the network, well, here's your chance. Take as long as you want. We'll eat later, have a few pints, talk football, and then wrap it up and go home. If it's too much, we'll stop over and start again tomorrow morning. The room is booked.'

Nodding, Cobb stepped to the window, moved the curtain slightly with his hand and asked, 'Where are we exactly?'

'Scotland!' replied Maguire. 'Bonny Scotland!'

Later that night, nimble fingers set aside a small screwdriver and worked free the panel clips that were fixed to one side of a bath. Beneath the bath lay a cavity big enough in which to stash the banknotes carefully arranged inside a clear plastic bag.

A hand lifted the bag, weighed it carefully, and then shoved it into the space behind the bath panel.

There was a soft 'clip' when the bath panel was refitted and tapped gently into place.

The self-appointed fitter pocketed his screwdriver and returned to the lounge where he poured himself a large glass of whisky and settled down for the night. Switching the television on, he selected a news channel and watched a short report regarding several arrests that had been made earlier that week following a post office raid in Wetheral, Cumbria.

Chuckling, he shook his head as he watched a senior policeman tell the audience of the day's events.

Elsewhere, a man dressed in gardening gear strolled into a greenhouse and removed a wad of cash from his jeans pocket. Kneeling, he placed a roll of banknotes into a clear plastic bag and then rearranged a collection of plant pots hiding the cash between the pots. Eventually, he tidied away the loose soil that had fallen onto the floor and placed the pots in a corner with other bits and pieces normally found in any greenhouse anywhere in the land.

Standing back, the gardener studied the corner where he had hidden his stash and then retired to his nearby home.

~

7

The CID Office
Eight weeks later

The new DI had arrived, and he was proving to be about as popular as a snowstorm on a beach. According to newly transferred Detective Inspector Colin Coulthard, he had been moved from another division to increase his experience of operations within the force area.

There were no ifs, ands, or buts with the new DI. Standing at five feet eight inches tall, at a stretch, he was always immaculately dressed and often wore a dark pinstripe suit, pristine white shirt, and colourful tie. The model was always finished off with a handkerchief in the breast pocket that matched his tie. His highly polished black shoes cloaked a pair of size nine feet and he enjoyed a straight back and good posture when walking. His problem was that none of the detectives in the office wanted to walk with him because they didn't believe a word of what he had told them.

No one knew why he'd been moved to their neck of the woods.

'What have we done to deserve this?'

'Why us?'

'If Headquarters have moved Coulthard here to develop his career then God help us. Is that the best they can do?'

What's the real story, they all asked?

In the space of fewer than two months, the CID office had gone from a close-knit hub of hustle, bustle, and excitement, to a vacuum of hurrying and scurrying out of the office for any reason that came to mind.

No-one wanted to work with the new DI. There were too many unsavoury rumours going around about him. From gambling to womanising, from bullying juniors to flattering superiors, there were so many rumours that the truth had been buried in a deep well of mystery.

Plants! Colin Coulthard loved his plants, watered them sparsely every day, cleansed their leaves where appropriate, and kept a tiny trowel and small watering can on the windowsill so that he could tend to his hobby whenever he wished. It was often said that there were days when he only spoke to the plants and no one else.

DI Coulthard was watering a selection of plants that adorned his windowsill when he heard footsteps in the corridor. Setting his watering can to one side, he smoothed his pinstripe suit, squared his tie, and shouted, 'Maguire!'

Locked inside a busy mind, the detective ignored the shout and walked into the main office.

'Maguire!' yelled DI Coulthard. 'Get in here. Now!'

Suddenly alert, Maguire realised his name had been called. Spinning on his heel, he entered the DI's office and offered, 'Inspector!'

'Good God, man,' bellowed Coulthard. 'Are you deaf?'

'No! Just busy!'

'No! Just busy, sir,' corrected Coulthard.

'Inspector,' offered Maguire. 'You wanted me. How can I help you?'

'Take a seat. We need to talk.'

'Thank you,' replied Maguire pulling a chair closer to the DI's desk.

The telephone rang and was answered curtly by Coulthard who listened for a moment before replying, 'Ring me back later.' He replaced the 'phone and voiced, 'Sapphire! I want to know all about Sapphire.'

'I do not have the relevant file, Inspector,' replied Maguire.

'I know that, Maguire,' replied Coulthard hastily. 'I'm in charge now and I want to know who Sapphire is.'

'Source protection, Inspector! You know I can't tell you,' replied Maguire. 'It's pretty standard. I'm surprised you asked but there is an authorising officer, and a supervisory officer has been appointed to oversee things.'

'The previous DI knew who it was,' remarked Coulthard.

Maguire faltered for a moment, realised Coulthard did not know of Stan Holliday's involvement in Sapphire, and replied, 'Yes, but that's because he was in the chair at the time. DI Archer was a great source of advice and help to me. He was aware of the situation from an early stage and validated the recruitment and accompanying paperwork.'

'Yes, I know,' replied Coulthard. 'But that doesn't answer my question.'

'Then I'm sorry but I have been instructed to follow the procedure. Accordingly, Inspector, DI Greg Archer authorised the informant and Detective Chief Superintendent Elliott validated the use of the informant. The source was recruited and recorded in accordance with the current protocols and the product therefrom has been delivered in intelligence reports which are open to all officers subject to their level of access to the intelligence system.'

'A fine speech, Maguire,' glowered the DI. 'Did you learn those words parrot-fashion?'

'Perhaps! I don't know but it is my job to secure my source lawfully and appropriately and use that resource within the current guidelines.'

'You will tell me, Maguire, or I will make your life a misery. I've been sent here because I'm destined for higher office. You will tell me from the beginning who Sapphire is and then we shall go and see him. You will introduce me to him, and I will help you run him. Understood?'

'I didn't say the source was a male, Inspector.'

'Don't get smart with me, Maguire. Who is he?' rasped Coulthard.

'I'm afraid I can't tell you,' ventured Maguire. 'You don't need to know, and I don't have to tell you unless you think I'm doing something wrong, or to be precise, that I'm unlawfully using the source. If that is the case, Inspector, the procedures are such that you should suspend me from duty and inform the Chief of Detectives of any malpractice that I am alleged to be involved in so that an investigation can be launched.'

Maguire reached for a glass intending to help himself to water from a jug.

'Who said you could have a drink?' challenged Coulthard.

'Sorry,' replied Maguire replacing the glass. 'My mouth is dry.'

'I bet it is,' snapped Coulthard. 'You keep forgetting the word sir!'

'I prefer to use the term Inspector. Sir is merely an indication of respect.'

There was a long period of silence between the two before it was broken by Coulthard who declared, 'You're a clever arse, aren't you, Maguire? A real clever arse! What's his name?'

'I refuse to tell you, Inspector.'

Coulthard leaned towards Maguire and bellowed, 'You are therefore disobeying a lawful order, Maguire. I'll ask you again and remind you of the disciplinary proceedings that may follow if you fail to obey a lawful order. Who is Sapphire?'

Maguire took a deep breath and replied, 'Your order is not lawful since I have been instructed by the Chief of Detectives that if I am ever asked such a question by an officer of higher rank than myself then I must immediately refer that person to the Chief of Detectives so that the said officer may be given advice accordingly.'

'That doesn't wash with me,' snarled Coulthard. 'And you speak like a textbook.'

'I choose to speak like a textbook to you on this occasion because that is what the Chief of Detectives instructed me to learn and to act upon,' ventured Maguire. 'With respect, Inspector, is there anything else I can help you with today?'

'Who the hell is this Chief of Detectives, Maguire? This isn't America. It's the Detective Chief Superintendent, for God's sake.'

'When the Detective Chief Superintendent is not available due to annual leave or sickness then the correct rank I am required to refer to is whoever is declared by the postholder to be the next highest available rank in CID: The Chief of Detectives.

Coulthard sat down, relaxed somewhat, and replied, 'You will tell me, Maguire. One day you will tell me because you will be tired of me breathing down your neck and I will be Chief of Detectives.'

'I've had people breathing down my back since I joined the job, Inspector. I tend to ignore them, do things my way, and just quietly get on with it.'

'Get out, Maguire. Get out!'

'Thank you! Have a nice day.'

Standing up, Maguire made for the doorway.

'Maguire!' growled Coulthard. 'I'm watching you. I'm waiting for one mistake, just one tiny little mistake, and your head will roll.'

Maguire held the door handle, paused, and asked, 'Why is that?'

'Close the door,' instructed the DI trying a new tack.

Maguire did as he was bid and turned to face the DI.

'You're noted for being a pretty quiet unobtrusive individual, Maguire. Yes, you've got the manners of a sharp talking Brillo pad salesman with that abrasive attitude, but I'll forgive you for that today. You keep yourself to yourself and do the job better than most of those who shout and bawl and tell the world how good they are.'

'Thank you!'

'You don't gamble. You don't drink. You don't chase women. You don't even like fast cars. What is it with you, Maguire?'

'You don't know me, Inspector,' suggested Maguire. 'You only think you know me because you've read my file and you've listened to people talking about me. But the reality is that you don't know me and never will. Furthermore, we've never had more than a two-minute conversation with each other since the day you arrived. To be honest, you give me the impression that you have absolutely no interest in me.'

'Maybe!' growled Coulthard. 'It puzzles me that a nonentity like yourself can successfully penetrate one of the most prolific crime gangs in the region. What's your secret? Ah! Don't tell me. I don't need you to throw the textbook at me again. I'm tired of your textbook speeches.'

'Good! I learnt them for just such an occasion.'

'I can see from the paperwork that you've got your finger on the pulse of the drug supply coming into Kendal. How did you do that?'

Maguire did not reply.

'Or need I ask around to find out more?'

Again, Maguire remained silent.

Standing, Coulthard strolled to the front of his desk and parked himself on the corner directly in front of Maguire before saying, 'You've got one of the most important snouts in the whole damn force, Maguire. You've locked it up so tight that no-one has a clue who it is. It's the secret that no one talks about because they don't know about it. Even those that think something is afoot are put off the scent with a bundle of intelligence reports that are good, bad and indifferent, and so complicated that you'd need to be a magician to work out the origin. To succeed like that, you must be good at lying, cheating, denying, and disregarding every rule in the book.'

'Now you're making things up,' proposed Maguire. 'There is no book and I'm just following Greg Archer's advice.'

'You're selling yourself short again, Maguire. Now listen, I want to know who it is so that I can help you. You're close to falling from that tightrope you need to walk on when you're dealing with criminals the way you do. You're only going to fall one way. I want to know because I want to be able to help you.'

Staring at the DI, Maguire replied, 'Firstly, it is right to say that after some weeks of responding to intelligence from Sapphire we have manoeuvred ourselves into a position that suggests we have a good knowledge of what's going on in the drugs world in Kendal. Secondly, Inspector, the truth of the matter is that you want to know who Sapphire is because you want to resurrect your career and claim the glory that can come from a whole series of operations currently in the planning stage. Sorry, but Sapphire isn't for sale. Now, if you excuse me, I have an appointment with Detective Chief Superintendent Elliott at Headquarters to discuss a recent intelligence report.'

'I can break you, Maguire,' threatened Coulthard.

'I don't see how,' replied Maguire. 'Have a nice day.'

Maguire closed the door behind him.

Seething, Coulthard returned to his seat, drummed his fingers on the desk, and then lifted the 'phone. He dialled a number, waited, and eventually said, 'Larry! I'm glad I caught you in. You do remember Maguire, don't you? Yes, that's the one. Wetheral post office! A right clever arse and he is running the informant that you thought Greg Archer was running. We need to meet.'

That afternoon, Maguire parked his squad car at police headquarters and made his way to the Detective Chief Superintendent's office. The actual Chief of Detectives was ultimately responsible for all crime enquiries in the force area. Whether it was fraud, theft, cybercrime, sex offences, robberies, or criminal intelligence, the buck stopped with Alexander George Elliott, who was affectionately known by the rank and file as 'Alexander the Great.' Elliott was also responsible for all staffing posts, training courses, promotions, secondments, and development pathways in respect of officers under his command.

In his mid-Fifties, Elliott was a man of stocky build. He carried a slight paunch that rested on his trouser belt and wore a light grey suit to hide it. His attire complimented a receding hairline and a grey shallow moustache. He was leafing through a travel magazine when his secretary announced Maguire's arrival.

Moments later, with a clear desk, other than a telephone, Elliott beckoned Maguire to take a seat and said, 'Good journey, Les?'

'No, problem, sir,' replied Maguire. 'Parking in headquarters was the hardest.'

Elliott chuckled and said, 'You can say that again. It's a nightmare at five o'clock.'

'I believe so,' returned Maguire. 'You wanted to see me, sir.'

Withdrawing a buff folder from a desk at his side, the Chief Superintendent leafed through the papers and selected one to concentrate upon.

'Sapphire, sir,' ventured Maguire. 'Something I've done wrong?'

'Sapphire?' queried Elliott. 'Oh no, we'll come to that shortly. No, you applied for a vacancy as a detective constable in the National Crime Squad in London. Are you still interested?'

'Yes, I am,' replied Maguire. 'Very much so.'

'Then I'm pleased to inform you that I have recommended you for that position and, subject to the usual vetting procedure, you'll be seconded to the National Crime Squad in the next few months. You'll essentially be working out of the Finchley office where you will find other officers from other forces and organisations. Do you understand this, young man?'

'Yes, sir,' replied an elated Maguire. 'I read everything they sent me. I understand the secondment. What can I say? I'm over the moon. I didn't think I was good enough. London! Wow!'

'I think you'll find the job is in London and everywhere else, Les,' remarked Chief Superintendent Elliott. 'An old friend of mine is the Commander in charge. His name is James Harkness and I recommended you personally to him.'

'I don't know what to say,' replied Maguire.

'Then don't say anything,' suggested Elliott. 'But here's a tip for you. Commander Harkness is a wily old bird. You'll

110

go down there and expect to find a leader who is all fire and brimstone. You'll find a quiet reserved gentleman who is a legend in his lifetime. A proper thief taker with more cards up his sleeve than I'd care to mention. Don't ever play poker with him. But I'll leave that for you to discover. Meanwhile, congratulations.'

Elliott stood up and shook hands with Maguire who replied, 'Thank you, sir, but there's still the vetting procedure to pass.'

'I know you, young man,' replied Elliott. 'Never heard much about you until the Sapphire file landed on my desk but I know all I need to know about you now. Do you think I sit here reading travel brochures all day, Maguire? Do they nickname me Alexander the Great or Alexander the Incompetent? Don't answer that! I prefer the former to the latter although that's not a lot to match if the truth is known.'

'I'll bet it is,' offered Maguire.

'A word in your shell-like, Maguire, when people love you, they will say you are great. Upset them and they'll call you incompetent. Now then, don't you worry about the vetting system. I would not have recommended you if I'd thought you would fail it, and I know exactly what kind of detective they are looking for. I've done my homework and I trust you will not let me down. You fit the bill for the National Crime Squad, young man.'

'Wow!' ventured Maguire. 'A day of two halves.'

'Two halves?' queried Elliott. 'What's happened?'

There was a pause before Maguire reluctantly replied, 'Nothing! Just busy, you know what it's like.'

'I know what it's like here, but not where you are,' explained Elliott. 'The look on your face tells me something is wrong, Les. What's going on?'

'Nothing I can't handle, sir.'

'Too slow, Maguire. Too slow,' berated Elliott. 'Does this involve Sapphire?'

Maguire did not reply.

'Because if it does, I want to know. I approved Greg Archer's report and authorised him to work with you concerning Sapphire. Stan Holliday is now your supervisor relevant to that operation, but if you have a problem I want to know.'

'Just a slight problem, sir,' replied Maguire. 'My DI wanted to know who Sapphire was and I referred him to you as per the procedures you explained to me. I expect he'll 'phone you at some stage to discuss the matter.'

'Coulthard?' queried the Chief Superintendent.

'DI Coulthard, sir! Yes, not a problem.'

'Oh, he's a problem alright,' snapped Elliott smoothing his thin moustache. 'I take it you know why he was transferred to you?'

'No! None of us do,' ventured Maguire. 'It's all a bit hush-hush if you see what I mean.'

Elliott returned Maguire's paperwork to his desk drawer, leaned back in his chair, and said, 'I see. Hush-hush, is it? The jungle drums missed out on this one then. Tell me he wants to help you run Sapphire.'

Shuffling his feet for a moment, Maguire eventually replied, 'You must have a fly on the wall, sir. That's exactly what he wants.'

'And you said?'

'I told him Sapphire wasn't for sale.'

'Good!' replied Elliott. 'DI Coulthard has a bad habit of looking into everyone's business so that he can jump onto the best bus going and take everyone for a ride. Between you and I, he's living on borrowed time.'

'Can I ask why he was transferred, sir?'

'Of course, you can, Maguire, but you won't get an answer from me. Try the Professional Standards Department although I'd say you'll get the same reply. It's their problem, not mine. If it becomes my problem, you'll know about it.'

Maguire nodded his understanding.

Staring at Maguire, the Detective Chief Superintendent began drumming his fingers on the desk before stating, 'The

National Crime Squad! The six current Regional Crime Squads will be merged with parts of Her Majesty's Customs and Excise along with the National Criminal Intelligence Service. The unit will be responsible for matters relevant to national and transnational organised and major crimes. They want new blood and your Cumbria's contribution to the future. Let's hope it works out for you and everyone involved. Out with the old and in with new, they tell me.'

'I see,' replied Maguire. 'I think,'

'Les,' advised Elliott. 'It's a place where secrets are going to be buried under the carpet and hidden beneath the wallpaper. Maybe we need to think of it that way.'

'I'm not following you. What do you mean, sir?' inquired Maguire.

'You'll see. Meanwhile, Detective Inspector Coulthard! I'm told he has a bad habit of bullying,' revealed Elliott. 'Would you agree?'

'So far, yes,' replied Maguire. 'Although I've only had one proper conversation with him.'

'Rumours tell me he's a bullying womaniser who needs to wise up quickly, but then I don't listen to rumours. I don't expect you do either.'

'No, of course not,' replied Maguire as a thin smile appeared at the corner of his cheeks.

'Put it this way, Les,' explained Elliott. 'He wouldn't pass the vetting procedure, and neither would his brother, Larry Coulthard.'

'Larry Coulthard,' queried Maguire. 'Where have I heard that name before?'

'The North West Regional Crime Squad!' replied Elliott. 'Surveillance?'

Maguire racked his brains for a while before eventually concluding that he knew the man.

'Got him! The very first armed robbery from Sapphire. Wetheral Post Office! I didn't take to him, but then I don't think he took to me either.'

'He's been sniffing around the intelligence system trying to find out who Sapphire is,' revealed Elliott. 'That's not illegal but it sure as hell isn't right either.'

'We could do without that, sir,' suggested Maguire.

'Agreed! The next phase of the Sapphire operation would be to involve the North West Regional Crime Squad in surveillance, but I've decided that's not going to happen. There's too much going on in the background that I can't tell you about, but you'll know in due course. Meanwhile, I'm going to second you to the Force Surveillance Squad until your papers and start date come through from London. You'll be working with Jim Latimer. We don't have a Serious Crime Squad. The Force budget won't stretch that far, but as far as I'm concerned, it's the nearest thing we've got to it. He's the DI and he has my utmost support. If he needs to cross borders, then he will but we'll be keeping things undercover and out of the way of the Coulthards until Professional Standards have concluded their investigation.'

'Investigation!' queried Maguire. 'I didn't realise the Coulthards were under investigation, sir.'

'Can you keep a secret, Maguire?'

'Yes, I think so.'

'Good!' replied Elliott. 'You've managed to keep Sapphire under wraps and your new job in London will have more secrets attached to it than you could ever imagine. I can advise you to keep the two Coulthard men out of the picture until the investigation is completed. Both of them are in hot water. It's only a question of time until things are wrapped up. That's all I'm saying, and I don't expect you to repeat it. After all, you've got a whole new set of secrets to learn about in the next twelve months. Meanwhile, push on with Sapphire and let's get this gang banged up. Okay?'

'Of course, sir,' replied Maguire. 'I must have misheard everything you recently said to me about the Coulthards.'

'Good! You're learning. Tell me this, what happens to Sapphire when you move to London? You can't take him with you, Les. The reason I ask is that I'd like to enquire as to how

Sapphire would feel if he had a handler other than yourself? As you know, it's quite regular for long term valuable sources to be introduced to the next handler when the previous handler moves on.'

Maguire nodded his understanding and replied, 'If we can take the rest of the gang down, Sapphire walks away with a good bank book and the chance of a new life. If the gang doesn't go down, he'll struggle and to be honest, I don't think he'll want to know us anymore after all I've promised him.'

'And your gut feeling?'

'I'm working on something for him,' revealed Maguire. 'I know now that I should never have promised him anything from the very beginning because I had no way of knowing what the outcome might be. It's been a severe learning curve for me. That said, I can't criticise his work for us. No, sir. All being well when I go Sapphire will disappear into the woodwork as well.'

'I see. We'll discuss that further in due course, Les. We need to do right by him if possible. Now then, DI Latimer will be joining us shortly.' Elliott checked his wristwatch and continued, 'You will need to take Jim Latimer into your confidence at some stage, Les. He will be in operational control and the chances of him encountering Sapphire are likely. He's not stupid and he's one of the finest detectives we've got. If I can trust him, so can you.'

'Yes, I see,' replied Maguire. 'Understood, sir.'

Elliott continued, 'In respect of your report about the planned drugs operation. I agree with you about the switch and the divide and conquer plan. What a cracking idea, but I reckon we need to tweak the job as follows…'

The afternoon wore on with Maguire, Elliott, and Jim Latimer, all contributing to an operation which was designed to deliver a major blow to the drugs network and bring down the remainder of Wayne's gang.

But nothing is as simple as it seems and what you plan does not always work out the way you wanted it to.

That night, Colin Coulthard took advantage of the dark badly lit street in Carlisle where a row of terraced houses graced the area. On reaching the last house in the street, number thirty-six, Colin removed an envelope from an inside pocket and posted it through the letterbox.

There was a movement at the window and the curtain fluttered slightly but no-one came to the door.

It was just as he expected. Turning, Colin turned his collar up, retraced his steps, and walked in and out of the shadows as the moonlight danced behind the clouds in the sky causing patterns on the pavement.

Laced with a score or more of parked vehicles, the darkness of the narrow street did much to deny the caller's identity, but then there was only one house with one number at the end of the street. The family therein were well known in their field of activity.

Many miles away, a man known to some as Wayne, stood on the clifftop and looked out across the sea. The sky was a myriad of stars, an enigma of hidden planets, far off solar systems, and a complete mystery.

'Do you like what you see, Veronique?'

'Mais oui! I do,' replied the young French lady holding Wayne's hand. 'Très beau! Incredibly beautiful, my love.'

'At this time of night, it is beyond comparison,' replied Wayne. 'Here! Stand closer. I'd like to take a selfie of us before the sun goes down completely.'

Veronique shuffled closer as Wayne manipulated his mobile 'phone, positioned themselves in a good light, and took a photograph of them both.

'Not bad,' remarked Wayne checking the product. 'It will look good by the time I've edited it and got it printed. Just another memory for us both, Veronique.'

'It's getting late and I'm a little chilly from the wind,' smiled Veronique. 'What time is it?'

Checking his diamond-studded Rolex wristwatch, Wayne replied, 'Time for home and a late-night dip in the pool.'

'Too cold,' she replied. 'Chilly!'

'It's a breeze,' laughed Wayne. 'But it's time for home as you say. Manuel will need picking up from the airport tomorrow and I don't want to be late for him.'

'He is an important man, I believe,' suggested the woman.

'Without Manuel, we cannot make these things happen, Veronique,' explained Wayne. 'We wouldn't be able to hide the proceeds effectively. He is what I would call my unofficial Director of Finance.'

'Will he need to see the books that you keep if he a director?' ventured Veronique.

'No! They are not those kind of books,' explained Wayne. 'They are notes, codes and listings relevant to bank accounts and safety deposit boxes. Only your brother knows about them and they are safely hidden away. Manuel needs to know about other things just as I need to clear up a few points with him before the big one goes ahead.'

'Big one?' queried Veronique.

'Or shall I say the biggest shipment yet,' suggested Wayne. 'It is not for the faint-hearted.'

'Or for the cold,' chuckled Veronique. 'That is the wind, not a breeze.'

'Life is a breeze,' replied Wayne. 'If you make it so. Manuel will make it so. Come on!'

The couple turned, strolled hand in hand to a nearby car park, kissed, and then parted.

'I'll drive,' revealed Wayne.

'Of course, you will.'

Wayne unlocked the doors of the bright red Ferrari two-seater, climbed in, and fired the engine as Veronique joined him in the passenger seat.

Moments later, the engine roared like no other as Wayne worked through the gears and headed for his villa in the countryside.

~

8

Two weeks later.
The Forward Control Point.
Kendal

Detective Inspector Jim Latimer was a proportionately built man in his forties. In the office, he would be suited and booted looking as smart as a new pin, but today he was in an empty baker's shop with Maguire, and he was in jeans and a tee-shirt drinking tea from a flask and eating chicken salad sandwiches. It was said that he had a thing about them.

The unplanned event was called 'eating on the hoof' and took place anywhere at any time dependant on the availability of food. Today, eating on the hoof took place between bouts of surveillance on the target premises. The surveillance weapons in use were an array of high-powered binoculars that were hidden behind a veil of thin lace curtains. A positive sighting of one of the many suspects entering or leaving the target premises could be confirmed by reference to three dozen photographs pinned to a wall at the back of the room. Each image carried a name and a codename ranging from Tango Zero One to Tango Three Six. These codenames were how the various persons of interest would be referred to on the radio. The photographs had also been compiled into a wallet size album to be used for instant reference by surveillance officers engaged in the operation.

There were photographs of Jawbone Jones, Smudger Murray, Tiny Philpotts, Jeffrey Jackson, Bill Ashworth, Colin McArdle, Jed Atkinson, and Bobby Nelson who were earmarked Tango Zero One through to Tango Zero Eight. The remainder of the photographs were either suspects, unknown persons or innocent parties that were dominant enough in the Saloon to feature in the unfolding mystery of who was who.

A blank space occupied part of the wall where the words Tango Zero Zero were written. The code was attributed to Wayne, of which hardly anything was known, and there was no photograph. He was the man the detectives wanted, but he was nowhere to be seen.

Maguire observed a surveillance photograph of Cobb and noted that the codename Sierra Two Four had been allocated to him. The operation so far had not identified the informant as one of the main players.

The two detectives took to each other instantly. Maguire looked upon the older DI as a good teacher he could learn from whilst Latimer considered Maguire to be a youngster willing to listen and eager to succeed. At least there was a starting point in their working relationship. How it would end might be another story.

Latimer and Maguire were on the second floor of a shop that had been deserted, abandoned, and unused by its owners for the best part of twelve months. A 'For Sale' sign jutted out from above the main doorway, but despite numerous visits from interested parties, the property remained empty and wasted away in what was now the entertainment and leisure area of the town. The hinge on the sign was rusting and often grated when the wind caught the sign and swung it back and forward. Furthermore, the paintwork on the shop front was flaking off and leaving unsightly patches on the façade.

Close to the River Kent and a roundabout that led to half a dozen arterial roads out of the town, the abandoned bakery had proved the ideal choice for an observation post in the long term surveillance schedule that was part of the overall plan.

The operation was in its second week, was already returning valuable intelligence, and the airwaves were often filled with the movements of 'Tangos'.

Maguire and the team had occupied the building since the beginning of the operation and their presence was still undetected. The baker's shop was directly opposite the front entrance to the public house that was the main target of the activity. Nicknamed 'The Saloon', the licensed premises was situated in the centre of town, sported one large bar, a collection of pool tables, amusement machines, darts boards, and all the usual paraphernalia associated with a thriving venue in a big town centre. The sizeable building stretched almost fifty yards along the street and was fitted with various booths that enjoyed a window view onto the adjoining highway.

Scores of innocent people visited the premises every day. Some played pool, darts, dominoes, or crib. Others listened to music and socialised with their friends. Between them, they hadn't a clue what was going on in the corner booth that was always occupied by middle-aged men who seemed to keep themselves to themselves.

They must be alright, it was said. Rooney, the licensee, ran around after them like a man possessed. Still, the pub had the best door staff in town. There was never any trouble in the Saloon.

The Saloon was the centre of the town's drugs industry where the dominant suppliers met with their runners and riders and passed on instructions to collect and deliver the product to recognised street dealers. This is where the business took place. It was a hub of illegal activity that overtly occupied a building in the centre of town, and only chosen runners and riders were in the know.

Jim Latimer's binoculars were set up on tripods in various areas and were all focused on the Saloon. Each device was linked to real-time video recording and there was a direct covert link to the town's CCTV system. In addition, Latimer controlled an encrypted wireless system that was connected to each member of the surveillance team at his disposal. To the casual onlooker, it was two men watching a pub. To the professional surveillance officer, it was a handsfree complex surveillance system capable of relaying 'live' intelligence to the rest of the team at the push of a button. And the communication system was a powerful 'state of the art' encrypted system that, if necessary, extended its reach to surrounding counties and beyond.

Sapphire was the source of intelligence. Cobb had gone into precise detail with Maguire some weeks earlier when they had visited Scotland together. It was there that Cobb had detailed the network, how it worked, who was in the network, and how the drugs were distributed locally.

Simply put, Cobb had told Maguire that the Saloon was the centre of the drugs supply in the south of the county. Whoever was bringing illegal drugs into the county worked through the two main drug suppliers in the town: Jawbone Jones and Bobby Nelson.

Neither boasted a string of criminal convictions although they both had a record of minor crime from their teenage years. Neither man trusted the other completely since they had grown up in separate parts of town with different ideas and varying degrees of dependency. Jones had strolled through school without much success and was the more violent of the two. He had made his way in the drugs world by physically beating the living daylights out of the opposition. The mere threat from Jawbone was now enough for others to back off and not to tread on his patch. Starting his career as a street dealer, he'd worked his way up the ladder by buying at the lowest price and selling at the highest price possible. When supply exceeded demanded, he'd used threats of violence, blackmail, and dishonesty to maintain high prices whilst subduing and removing the other dealers around him. Jawbone Jones had inadvertently climbed to the top of the tree in the area by identifying other dealers in the neighbourhood and beating them at their own game. He found out where they stashed their drugs, and hid their money, and thought nothing of breaking in and stealing that which belonged to the opposition. Then one day, he realised he'd reached the top of the tree. He'd worn out the street dealers or converted them to his way of thinking, and then joined Wayne's gang more years ago than he cared to remember. He'd never used drugs, other than cannabis many years ago. He was clean and untouched even when stopped and searched on numerous occasions by police who did not know his true position in the league table.

Conversely, Bobby Nelson was more astute, mature, and brainier. What he lacked in strength and physique, he made up for in cunning and intellect. He'd done well at school, made the sixth form, and then opted for a foray into the drugs world when his parents died and left him a sizeable inheritance. Nelson had gone in big, initially bought the product at a higher than normal price, learnt of his mistakes, and then grown in wisdom. Step by step, he'd played one dealer off against the other learning who could supply the most at the best price. Bobby Nelson became a businessman overnight and was soon recruited into Wayne's organisation because of how he conducted his business.

That said, there were occasions when it could be argued that neither of them was the sharpest tool in the box. Realistically, they were typical of suppliers up and down the country who plied their evil trade by either forcing and manipulating others into a life of crime or by investing in a 'hands-free' business. Chris Cobb was one such victim but not the only victim to have succumbed to their ways.

Nelson and Jones had several things in common. They both knew Cobb. They were both chieftains in the local drugs world, and they both worked to the orders of a man called Wayne who commanded them all and was involved in the importation of drugs into the country. Their problem was, they knew nothing about Wayne's operation outside the county other than he was always armed and often surrounded by armed bodyguards whenever he travelled.

If Jones and Nelson had a weakness, it was that they had reached the top of the local charts with minimal experience of police involvement over recent years. They'd been lucky. Jawbone's victims were not the kind that ran to the police to report being assaulted because they wouldn't tell where their drug stash was or identify who their main supplier was. Nelson's money trail led back to his parents' inheritance and he was an accomplished accountant who had learned some of the basic arts of money laundering. Both hoodlums oozed confidence in public but occasionally portrayed an air of arrogance that often hid a silent complacency that the detectives hoped to exploit.

It was one thing for the police to gather gossip, titbits, anonymous 'phone calls, and informant's tips over the years. It was quite another to develop such so-called intelligence into a file of evidence that would stand up in court and get a result. Intelligence was a form of secondary evidence that was rarely produced in court as the main contender. Hands-on evidence, original documents, and validated videos and photographs, plus admissions, recorded interviews and the actual proven fact was considered primary evidence. It was primary evidence that the police lacked.

Now in their forties, Nelson and Jones rarely got their hands dirty. They spent their time facilitating the importation of drugs into the county from places like Liverpool, Manchester, Preston, and Birmingham via the good offices of Wayne.

The drugs were collected from the suppliers in these principle towns and then conveyed to the Saloon where, at pre-determined times, local runners and riders would turn up and collect their share of the product for distribution down to street level throughout the county.

There was no drug use taking place in the Saloon. It was clean although occasionally boasted the odd unsavoury character. The Saloon was a meeting place, a delivery and collection hub, a place where friendships were of no concern to the participants and the décor was no more than a convenient façade for the events taking place. It was a place where quiet words over a pint in a booth in the corner led to the next consignment, the transfer of hard cash, and the promise of more business in the months ahead. All this took place in the quiet secure confines of a public place that the gang controlled to the point where everyone who entered the place was scrutinised and watched over as appropriate. There were no large consignments to worry about. Wayne's end of the business had already ensured that every package was portable, easy to carry, and capable of being quickly disposed of if need be. All the gang did was provide a haven.

It was Wayne who ran the show in many ways, and his dominance concerning procedure was such that if a courier were detected carrying drugs then only a small amount of the total importation would be jeopardised. He theorised that the loss of a huge consignment would be a major blow to the business. Alternatively, splitting a huge consignment into dozens of smaller ones meant that the business would not be jeopardised if such a consignment were intercepted. To lose a little was preferred to losing a lot, and the route back to him was as complicated as Spaghetti Junction on the M6 motorway.

Even though Wayne was still an unknown mystery, Maguire had deduced that he was streetwise, more than an administrator running a criminal enterprise from afar, and a man who had handpicked donkeys to carry the merchandise whilst recruiting lions to put fear into those he sought to oppress.

The problem was, thought Maguire, Wayne who? What was his last name?

The Saloon was full of runners and riders responding to those with all the connections, and the local kingpins had a reputation for coming down hard on anyone who stepped out of line.

The police operation was painfully simple. Watch, record, analyse and, where appropriate, identify and house the suspects. Gathering intelligence was the aim of the surveillance operation. Who drove what? Where did they live? Who are their closest friends? How do they dress? Bank? Drink? Eat? Places frequented? The list was as long as you needed it to be. The problem for Maguire and Latimer was that they were inundated with suspects, and many of them were innocent.

'It's time to put two men in,' suggested a dominantly speaking Jim. 'Barney and Rod! They'll be clean. No radios! We don't want them going in there first time around and getting searched by some gang bodyguard that we're not aware of and knackering the job just like that. No, I've instructed them to get in early, play the labourer looking for work card, and spend the day hitting pool balls across the table whilst quietly drinking for England and keeping their eyes open as to who is who and what's going on. We need to sort the wheat from the chaff. I want to know who uses that pub as a hub for the drugs business. Some people are going in there and are oblivious to what is happening around them. If we can identify those that aren't of interest to us, then that will leave the way clear to concentrate on the real targets. Everything! If they sell pickled eggs with a pint I want to know where from.'

'And what they taste like,' suggested Maguire.

Jim threw an icy glare at Maguire before continuing, 'I also want to know how close to the gang Rooney, the publican, is. Is he under their thumb or not?'

'Barney and Rod?' queried Maguire. 'Bad decision, Jim. They'll be to cart home of they're in there all day.'

Jim held his breath, laughed out loud, and said, 'I'm not sure if it's a challenge for them or a joy. Either way, it will be a nice change for them both.'

'Would it not be easier to put a camera into the building?' suggested Maguire. 'Or drop some recording devices? You know, bug the spot?'

'Definitely,' replied Jim. 'But I don't think the publican is fully onside and what we have learnt so far is that a team of cleaners turn out every morning and tidy the place up. It's too much to risk deploying a one-time listening device and a covert static camera in the hope they aren't found. No! There is a way to improve things and we will even if it means doing it the hard way and the safe way. It might take time'

'Okay!' replied Maguire. 'That makes sense. We're in it for the long haul when all is said and done.'

'Sure, the pub has no record of drug-taking inside, but I'll eat a horse's hat if he doesn't know he's turning a blind eye to the suppliers coming and going,' proposed Jim.

'He could be getting a cut,' proposed Maguire.

'I'm sure he is. I'll make a note to spin his bank account before we do the strike.'

'They're all drinking in there,' ventured Maguire. 'The place is rammed all morning and afternoon. Most of the business throughout the day is the runners and riders arranging collections or deliveries. I bet he doesn't have a blind eye on the till. He'll be making a fortune.'

'My men have been instructed to watch him,' replied Jim. 'Who knows, they might lock him into the supply network. Let's see how they do. By the way, Maguire, are you sure your man isn't on the plot?'

'My man on the plot?' puzzled Maguire. 'Absolutely no way, Jim. He's miles away.'

'Good! That's one problem I can forget about then,' chuckled Jim. 'I haven't got him on camera then. Not so far.'

Jim winked knowingly at Maguire who sneaked a view through the binoculars and saw Cobb walk through the front door of the Saloon.

'Oh yes,' replied Maguire. 'Sapphire is nowhere near the business end of this lot.'

'Of course not,' chuckled Jim. 'Just let me know when the switch is done, Les.'

'I will. You'll be the first to know,' replied Maguire.

'Does he have a Tango number?' probed Jim with a sly smile.

Maguire deliberately checked the images on the wall and replied, 'She's not there.'

'Funny that,' replied Jim. 'They're all males.'

Maguire grinned and said, 'When you need to know....'

'You'll tell me,' proposed Jim. 'We'll cross that bridge when we come to it. Just don't fall off the tightrope, Les. If your man is taken down in the operation, it will be your problem. Not mine. Because I'm not putting my hand in the till for you and neither will Alexander the Great. Sorry!'

'Don't be sorry,' replied Maguire. 'My man is clean.'

'Good! Now I know he's a man,' chuckled Jim. 'Stay with me, Maguire.'

Cobb closed the front door of the Saloon as Maguire swept the street with his hands-free binoculars to make sure he wasn't been followed.

Inside the pub, Rod and Barney had acquired a pool table, set up the balls, chalked the cues, and captured an upright bar table that boasted a circular top capable of holding two pints of cheap lager, two mobile 'phones, a pornographic magazine, and a scarf that hung loosely from the table and drooped towards the floor in a 'couldn't care less attitude'. Both in their early thirties, they were unshaven, long-haired, and the epitome of two men looking for work. Rod wore jeans that looked as if they hadn't been washed for a month and Barney wore a denim jacket that had lost all its buttons. But they could both play pool and talk for England.

There was a wholesome clack of phenolic resin when two pool balls collided causing one to ricochet into an empty pocket and the other to finally come to rest close to the cushion.

Rod smiled, chalked the end of his cue, and said, 'I'm hot today, Barney. Unbeatable!'

Bending down, Rod took sight of his next shot along an imaginary line on the table and played another shot. As the ball casually rolled towards another empty pocket, Rod followed the line of the ball as he allowed his eyes to take in four men sitting in a corner booth.

'Unbeatable is not the word,' laughed Barney. 'Come on, drink up. Another lager?'

'Please,' replied Rod. 'A tenner on the game?'

'No! A fiver will do,' chuckled Barney placing a five-pound note on the edge of the table.

Close by, but out of earshot, George Rooney served a tray of drinks to the four men sat in a corner booth. He placed the tray in the centre of the table and dispensed the drinks from there.

Jawbone Jones was the main man at the table. Well over six feet tall, he was broad and barrel-chested with arms like tree trunks and a jawbone that stuck out from his face like a pier jutting into the North Sea. He sat opposite the other top dealer in town who was the ginger-haired Bobby Nelson. Wearing a rusty coloured bandana as a necktie, Nelson wore an orange coloured short-sleeved shirt and denim jeans. Of slighter build than Jones, Nelson habitually sported a three-day growth of hair around his face. The look was complemented by long flowing ginger hair that swept down his neck and tied in a ponytail. In addition, Nelson was proud of his heavily tattooed arms which were quite muscular yet somewhat out of kilter with the rest of his frame.

Both men enjoyed those hardened features across the facial area where a gnarled appearance only added to the swarthy complexion seen in both males.

Sitting with the two head honchos of the town's drugs world, were Smudger Murray and Tiny Philpotts. Younger than Nelson and Jones, Smudger and Tiny were the deputies sitting with their sheriffs and learning the rules of the game. It was almost as if they were kingpins in waiting as they often imitated Jones and Nelson and sought the prestige that they could see but could not yet fully enjoy. Both men had large muscular arms and broad shoulders, whether the brain was as awesome was a matter of conjecture.

Smudger and Tiny both wore good quality leather jackets and suffered a bad case of wearing too much bling. Heavy chains around the neck, gold bracelets, and London Bridge rings were the order of the day and indicated that they were somewhat ahead of their peer group in the environment in which they lived.

Tiny reached across the table and swopped a lager for a bitter saying, 'George, for a publican you have a memory like a sieve. I'm a bitter man. I don't drink larger. Only women drink larger.'

'In that case, we're three females and you're going to get bounced through that door soon,' threatened Jawbone. 'Shut up and enjoy your pint. We've business to do.'

Nodding, Tiny, who was neither tall nor small, shrunk into his seat and took a sip of beer.

Another clack sounded from the pool table as the two players jockeyed for position and chalked their cues.

'Who are they?' asked Jawbone. 'The new men playing pool. Locals?'

'Labourers apparently,' replied Rooney. 'Looking for work.'

'They're not looking for work in here,' suggested Jawbone. 'Keep an eye on them, George. There's a good lad.'

'I will,' replied Rooney. 'They were half pissed when they came in, Jawbone, so I wouldn't worry if I were you. They're not locals, just drifters. One of them said they were from Carlisle looking for work.'

'Did he indeed! Did you believe him?' probed Jawbone.

'Do me a favour, I run a bar, not Question Time. There are plenty of labourers knocking around town looking for work. It's boom time with new housing estates and the same with roads. I've told them to stick around and sign up with Paddy on Saturday morning. Cash only for wages. You know what I mean.'

'I like to know about everyone in here,' replied Jawbone. 'Put these drinks on the tab and keep an eye on those two plonkers. Best not make a habit of trusting strangers, George. If they start asking you or anyone else questions, I want to know. Understood?'

The publican nodded, finished placing the drinks on the table, and withdrew.

'Settle down, Jawbone,' voiced Nelson. 'You've been watching too many gangster films again. They're a couple of benefit cheats chasing the dole queue. That's all.'

'How do you know that?'

'Take a good look at them,' suggested Nelson. 'They look like something the cat dragged in. Leave it alone.'

'One of us has to watch our backs,' chided Jawbone. 'If I left it all to you three, we'd have been finished years ago.'

'Well, we're not finished and we're doing very well, thank you,' replied Nelson. 'You got any gear on you?'

'Of course, not. What do you take me for?'

'Good!' voiced Nelson. 'Just checking! And you guys, Tiny? Smudger?'

Both men shook their heads.

'Then keep it that way and let the others get their hands dirty,' advised Nelson. 'You do the footwork, Jawbone, I'll do the thinking and I'm telling you not to worry about two casual drifters wandering into town.'

'Yeah! Yeah! Yeah!' replied Jawbone. 'Heard it! Done it! Bought the tee-shirt and I don't need advice from you. One day a man is a drifter, the next he's looking at you down the barrel of a sawn-off shotgun robbing you of your business. I know it because I've done it. Keep your eyes on the runners and riders, Bobby. I'll look after the infiltrators and security.'

'I asked you if your hands were clean,' growled Nelson.

'My hands are clean,' voiced Jawbone. 'That reminds me, who's that at the bar? I can't see him properly from where I'm sat.'

'Cobb!' responded Nelson. 'He'll be with us shortly. He's just getting a drink. Now, will you settle down?'

'Do you trust him?' queried Jawbone.

'Never let us down yet and he's done his time. Doesn't that count?' voiced Nelson.

'I don't trust anyone,' revealed Jawbone. 'We never bottomed out the Wetheral job. Remember?'

'He reckoned our home 'phones were bugged. So, what did we do?' questioned Nelson.

'Stopped using them and bought mobiles,' replied Jawbone. 'And I've never let mine out of my sight since. I change the sim card every week. I'm not stupid and we will never be caught by the police bugging our phones. Impossible when we're changing sim cards every week.'

'Me too,' responded Tiny. 'My exact thoughts, Jawbone.'

'And me,' imitated Smudger. 'My mobile is always in my back pocket. Never use a landline anymore. Great invention but they've taken a long time to catch on.'

'They're just a couple of years old,' explained Nelson. 'One day everyone will have one.'

Jawbone ignored Nelson and stared disapprovingly at Smudger and Tiny for a moment before glancing towards the bar.

'He's got a drink but he's not joining us,' revealed Nelson.

'Stay here,' murmured Jawbone. 'I'll have a word with him. Something might be wrong.'

As soon as Jawbone stood and approached the bar, George Rooney dropped a cleaning cloth and moved to serve Jawbone. Simultaneously, two pool players swung around the table following the balls and taking the lines for the next shot as they followed the activities of one of their targets.

There was a thud against the cushion when a red ball jettisoned violently into a vacant pocket.

Bobby Nelson heard the slam, glanced at the players, and then took a drink.

Jawbone gestured Rooney to back off as he sidled next to Cobb and said, 'Everything okay?'

'Fine!' replied Cobb. 'You ready for a drink?'

'No, thanks. I already got one. Why didn't you come over and join us? We're expecting you and there's business to sort.'

'I know,' replied Cobb. 'I just wanted a private word, that's all.'

Jawbone nodded to Cobb to step away from the bar area before venturing, 'What's the problem?'

'How are you getting on with Bobby?' queried Cobb.

'As usual,' remarked Jawbone. 'Why?'

'You know my feelings,' remarked Cobb. 'You blamed some of us for the cock-up at Wetheral and I told you it was the police bugging your 'phones.'

'Yeah! So what?'

'Have you forgotten that I also told you that I thought Bobby Nelson might be the source?'

Jawbone guided Cobb by the arm further from the bar and said, 'What's going on? What have you heard?'

'Nothing! Forget what I said,' replied Cobb. 'I'm way out of line and it's been playing on my mind. That's all, Jawbone. Maybe I just need to relax more. Here, let me get you a double or something. What's your poison?'

'Forget the drink! What's been playing on your mind?' persisted Jawbone.

'Like I said,' offered Cobb. 'Forget it!'

Snatching Cobb's jacket, Jawbone lifted him an inch from the ground, pushed him into a vacant booth, and growled, 'If you've heard something, I want to know. What is it that's going on in that tiny little mind of yours?'

'I got you some sim cards,' revealed Cobb.

'We'll come to that later,' rasped Jawbone. 'Now tell me what the hell is going on or I'll squash your head into little pieces and put it through the mincer.'

'Bobby Nelson!' proposed Cobb trying to wriggle free. 'It's so bloody obvious, isn't it? He's the man. It has to be him.'

'How!' challenged Jawbone strengthening his grip. The muscles in his arms gave life to the tattoo of an anchor on both forearms. He thrust Cobb further into the booth and scowled, 'Tell me what's going on. I don't understand.'

Sweating now, Cobb ventured, 'You blamed me for the Wetheral job, then you blamed a few others, then you blamed everyone else. Didn't it occur to you that the man you were with – Bobby Nelson – was just egging you on and pushing you into suspecting every Tom, Dick and Harry in the gang?'

'Why should he do that?' probed a puzzled Jawbone.

'Because he wants the business to himself. That's why. He wants you out. That's why he's slowly turning everyone against you. For God's sake, it's obvious to me,' explained Cobb. 'Don't you know? Can't you see it? Why hasn't anyone told you? He's going around whispering to people that if they've been threatened or beaten up by Jawbone Jones then it's nothing to do with him. It's you that's stepped out of line.

Not him. Bobby Nelson is plotting to bring you down, Jawbone. He wants full control not half a share.'

Jawbone gently lowered Cobb to the ground and shook his head saying, 'No! No, it can't be.'

'For all I know this man Wayne might even be involved. I mean, what do I know about Wayne? I'll tell you. Nothing! I don't know anything about Wayne, but I can tell you that the drugs racket is all about money and he's involved somewhere along the line. We all know that. Does anyone give a damn about people who get hurt if they're in the way of the money wagon? No!'

'Wayne? I don't understand,' replied a confused Jawbone. 'What does it mean?'

'I told you,' replied Cobb. 'I'm way out of line but I had to get it off my chest. Forget it. Forget I even brought the subject up. I'm not even here. I've had too much to drink. My fault. I didn't say what I just said, okay?'

Jawbone stared at Cobb and then glanced across his shoulder towards the corner booth.

'Crazy fool! You've not had a drink,' observed Jawbone releasing Cobb from his grip.

'My uncle,' remarked Cobb. 'Uncle Benny told me to look out for people. He taught me to watch out for things. He'd have wanted you at the helm with him. I know that. He's gone now. Dead and buried, but I learnt a lot from him about people. Who to trust, who to distrust? He taught me how to read people, what was in their mind, what they were doing behind your back. That's what Uncle Benny taught me. You make your mind up, Jawbone. I'll leave it like that.'

'Okay! I'll think about it,' voiced an uneasy Jawbone.

'How did you get to where you are today?' quizzed Cobb.

'By getting rid of the opposition,' replied Jawbone.

'Exactly!' voiced Cobb. 'I'm with you, Jawbone. I'll listen out for you, but don't say I didn't warn you.'

A veil of hesitancy crept over Jawbone's face as he weighed Cobb's words. In all his days, he'd never given a thought to another member of the gang being clever enough or strong enough to usurp his position never mind displace him.

'I'll kill him,' rasped Jawbone. 'I'll snap him in two and feed him to the dogs.'

'No! Never!' advised Cobb. 'You need to play him at his own game.'

'How?' inquired Jawbone.

'Turn the tables,' proposed Cobb. 'The sim cards! Let's do the sim cards.'

Confused, stunned by Cobb's words, Jawbone's inferior intelligence finally accepted a way out of the current impasse, and he responded by placing an arm around Cobb's shoulder.

'Yes! The sim cards! You got them,' nodded Jawbone.

'Come on,' replied Cobb. 'We're in this together.'

The two men strolled over to the corner booth and sat down opposite Bobby Nelson.

'You two okay?' inquired Bobby fiddling with the front of his necktie. 'You've been ages.'

'I've been showing him these,' offered Cobb who slid a plastic bag across the table. 'Jawbone was just making sure they were kosher. Sim cards! I did as I was told and bought new sim cards for the mobiles.'

Tiny reached out to grab the bag but felt a sharp rap on the knuckles from Nelson.

'Who told you to get these?' asked Nelson.

'Jawbone!' replied Cobb. 'He told me to get some more because you were running out of them. I got a hundred for you. I did what I was told. I always do, Bobby.'

'Who did you get them from?' inquired Nelson.

'Last time I was over the North East I got some from a couple of different outlets I know about. That's all you need to know.'

'All I need to know?' queried Nelson. 'Who the hell do you think you're talking to?'

'Easy, Bobby,' interjected Jawbone. 'He's on our side.'

A look of unease seeped into the booth until Cobb offered, 'Jawbone told me to be secure or he'd turn me over again. I've still got the bruises from last time. Do you want to see them?'

Smudger chuckled and said, 'I think I gave you some of them.'

'Me too,' added Tiny proudly.

'Why a hundred?' probed Nelson.

'There was no point in raising suspicions with anyone,' argued Cobb. 'A couple here and a couple there don't bat an eyelid. Buy a hundred in one spot from a trusted source and the job is done. I know some of you might not like me but then what makes you think I like you? We're all in this together and I'm buying stuff to protect me as well as you. We're all out to make money without getting caught. Five years or so at this lark and I'll be off. I'll be living a life in the sun somewhere surrounded by gorgeous looking chicks, the best wines in the house, maybe a beer two, and a pad next to the beach. Do I look stupid? Do I look like a clown? I've been inside once before. I'm not going back. I got a good deal.'

'No! You could have gone to Carlisle, Workington or Barrow,' suggested Nelson. 'But you went to the North East. Why?'

'I didn't go to the North East to buy sim cards,' stated Cobb. 'I bought them there because I happened to be doing a delivery for you over there and knew someone who could produce the goods. Do you think my source just does sim cards? Business! Do you know what I mean? Now if there's no business for me today and you don't want these, I'll sell them elsewhere.'

Cobb reached across to retrieve the cards when Nelson stopped him with, 'Just checking, Chris. Take it easy, man. Relax.'

'I am relaxed,' replied Cobb. With his hand still firmly on the bag containing the sim cards, Cobb asked, 'Do you want them or not?'

'We'll take them,' declared Jawbone. 'We need them. There's eight of us in the mainframe. Split them up. Me, Bobby, Smudger. Tiny, Jeff, Bill, Colin, and Jed. I want ten in my pocket, split the rest and then we'll get them again.'

'No! There's eight of you now,' grunted Cobb. 'Make it nine. I want in on the action. I've earned it. By God, I've earned it. I could have sold you all down the river once, but no. Do you remember or have you forgotten? I decided to stay with you and keep my mouth shut whatever it took. That's not because I like you. It's because you need me, and I need the money. I want the money. Goddamn it, man! I need the cash. I want that crinkly stuff in my back pocket! Now tell me you're not in this for the money. Go on! Anyone!'

There was a look like a snowstorm that swept around the faces gathered at the table before Bobby Nelson recognised there was no challenge. He replied, 'Agreed! Welcome to the top table. Do you need hard cash for these, Chris?'

'Not if you have work for me today, no.'

'We've plenty of work. Sit down,' ordered Nelson. 'We'll get around to it soon.'

'New 'phone numbers?' queried Smudger.

'Aye, new numbers?' confirmed Tiny. 'Same network?'

'That's the way it is,' confirmed Jawbone. 'Each sim card gives you a new telephone number although, for our purposes, we're sticking with the same provider. At least we know the network is good in this area. Change every few days and don't touch a landline. Just presume the landline bugged and the mobiles are clean. That's the way it is.'

'Understood!' replied Smudger a microsecond before Tiny Philpotts imitated him.

'Did you get them from someone you know?' asked Smudger.

Pausing for a moment, Cobb looked into Smudger's face and eventually replied, 'They're clean. Use them.'

With the sim cards removed from Cobb's bag, Nelson slid the back from his mobile 'phone and inserted a new card.

Rod and Barney ended their game and approached the bar where Rod asked for two sets of darts and more drinks. Duly served by a young barmaid, Rod placed the darts on the bar and began a conversation with her.

Meanwhile, Barney clasped Rod on the back and said, 'I'm going on the machines for a while. Wish me luck.'

Rod nodded and Barney removed some pound coins from his pocket. Once the two men had repositioned themselves, Barney began feeding the slot machine as he chased the jackpot and weighed everyone up in the bar. It didn't take them long to work out who the innocent parties were and who was of interest to the ongoing investigation. The photographs on the bakery wall were about to be updated.

The barmaid burst into laughter when Rod told a joke and then bought her a drink.

In the Forward Control Point across the street, a mobile 'phone resting on a table next to Jim Latimer came to life. A shudder of sudden power surged through the gadget and an advanced technological extraction device plugged into a socket shone a green light and began to purr softly.

'The switch has been made,' revealed Maguire. 'We're up and running.'

Jim stepped towards a bank of eight mobiles and watched as one by one four came to life.

'We certainly are,' confirmed Jim. 'With thanks to Sapphire, some of the gang are now arming themselves with a new batch of sim cards. Look!'

More 'phones lit up as Maguire approached and offered, 'Jawbone, Bobby Nelson, Smudger and Tiny have all fit new sim cards.'

'Anyone else you know?' asked Jim.

Ignoring the question, Maguire replied, 'There's only four of the gang in there now. I reckon the others will follow within twenty-four hours, don't you?'

'All being well,' confirmed Jim. 'I love this little machine, Les. It will download all the numbers they ring, all the texts they send, and a lot more. We'll get the product tomorrow, but by then I'll have moved this lot to the office, and we'll put two on the 'phones permanently. One to listen in real-time, the other to download and print out the product for analysis.'

'Brilliant,' suggested Maguire. 'It's all coming together nicely.'

'And it can all fall just as quickly. I'll need to speak to Alexander the Great about staffing levels,' revealed Jim. 'Leave it with me.'

Half an hour later, Jim Latimer gestured to Maguire and said, 'Tripod three. Your man is looking up.'

Maguire engaged the relevant binoculars and saw Cobb leaving the Saloon by the front door. As Cobb left, he looked towards the upper windows of the bakery and peered deeply into the premises.

Cobb nodded to an unseen face.

'My man?' replied Maguire. 'How do you work that out?'

'Come on, Les. I've been on these binoculars for days on end. He's Mister Mystery because he's not a target. He's a regular. I'm not stupid and neither are you. We can soon clarify his position when Barney and Rod join us later. They'll have recognised Nelson, Jones, Smudger and Philpotts whilst they were in there. Or are you suggesting that your source handed the sim cards over remotely and never contacted the four targets? Have a look on the wall behind you. Is your man a Tango? No! It's time to level up, Les. Your man wants an urgent meet. I can tell. Go!'

Maguire engaged the binoculars and replied, 'The boss told me I would have to tell you one day. He also told me that I had to trust you because he did. Keep it quiet, please, Jim.'

'Trust me,' replied the DI. 'Do you think you're the only one in Cumbria police with an informant? Do me a favour, Les, and grow up. Things are good but you need to broaden your attitude to covert criminal investigation. It's what a lot of detectives do. Some are great investigators that will turn a haystack over and find that needle. Others are brilliant interviewers who are like a dog with a bone when they finally get to grips with the crook on the other side of the desk. And some are gifted with an ability to read crooks, find their weak spot, and turn them into informants. Which one are you?'

Open-mouthed, Maguire couldn't offer a good response.

'Now go whilst he thinks it's safe,' suggested Jim.

Maguire was out of the door, down the stairs, and out of the back door in a flash. Finding himself in the bakery's rear yard, he unlocked the door which led into a lane that wandered around several premises and provided a delivery route for the retailers owning property in the area. Locking the door behind him, he adopted a steady walking place. Appearing at the end of the lane, he stood in open view for a couple of minutes before making his way towards the car park next to the River Kent.

Cobb was onto him within seconds and casually followed Maguire who turned a corner, stepped into a shop, and watched Cobb walk past as he browsed the products on display.

Satisfied Cobb was not being followed, Maguire left the shop and followed Cobb who walked through the car park and onto the riverbank.

Five minutes later, the two men met beneath a large oak tree that had branches leaning heavily towards the ground.

'What's the matter?' asked Maguire.

'My flat has been searched. What's going on? I thought you told me I was safe.'

'What do you mean? What happened?' inquired Maguire.

'You told me ages ago to put a beermat into the bottom of the door jamb every time I went out,' explained Cobb. 'I did that yesterday but when I got back home the card had fallen to the ground and someone had searched the spot.'

'Ransacked?' queried Maguire.

'No way,' snapped Cobb. 'I was in the Saloon all day so I'm quite sure it wasn't Jawbone and the gang. Most of them were busy doing deliveries or sorting out business in the bar. No, Les! This was someone else.'

'Are you sure the flat was searched?'

'Oh, yes. Whoever did it wasn't particularly brilliant, but I know they rummaged through the drawers, checked the wardrobe, and I presume had a good look around.'

'Was anything moved?' challenged Maguire. 'I need to know why you are so sure you were burgled. The beermat might have easily fallen because it's worn and torn.'

'I change the beermat regularly because they get droopy after a while and I have found them on the floor before. That said, this time someone used a key or something to get in. A pair of shoes in the wardrobe had been moved and put back in the wrong place. One of my old anorak pockets had its flap turned inside out and one of the bedside drawers hadn't been replaced properly. I'm not making this up, Les. Someone turned the flat over.'

'Anything stolen?' asked Maguire.

'Not a thing,' remarked Cobb becoming agitated. 'They were looking for money, weren't they, Les? Just like you said. Well, they didn't find any because there's none to find. And they didn't find a book or a note with your telephone number on because it's in my head, not written down in a diary. There's nothing in here to incriminate me. I did just like you said.'

'Okay! Okay! Settle down,' advised Maguire. 'Definitely not the gang, you reckon?'

'No way and definitely not the gang after today's meeting.'

'Oh, sounds interesting,' ventured Maguire. 'First things first! It's tempting to put a forensic man into the flat and see if there are any fingerprints or anything we can use. How do you feel about that?'

'The whole apartment block would know I'd been burgled,' replied Cobb. 'And if the gang heard of any connection with the police it might spoil years of work. No! I'm not up for that. We're too close. Come on, you only tell me what you want me to know. Who else could it be?'

Maguire rubbed his forehead before replying, 'A rival gang. I have someone in mind but, as you say. I only tell you things that I want you to know. Give me time. I've my own ideas. You'll have to trust me, Chris.'

'Again?'

'I'm afraid so.'

'Really?'

'Wait one,' replied Maguire. 'I need to make a call. Don't go anywhere.'

Maguire connected his mobile to Detective Chief Superintendent Elliott, updated the boss on the current security position regarding Sapphire, and threw Cobb's burglary problem at Elliott.

'I'm sending you an app,' replied Elliott, who then divulged confidential information to Maguire. 'The icon is titled Family Pets. You do love cats and dogs, don't you, Maguire? You do now if anyone asks. Use it as discussed. It's a one-use application because thereafter it will self-destruct. I kid you not. It has a three-minute life. No more. Use it well and get back to me with the result. Don't discuss this app with anyone. Understood?'

'Yes, sir,' replied Maguire thinking, what the hell is all this about.

Minutes later, the app appeared on Maguire's phone.

'Do you know anyone by the name of Coulthard?' probed Maguire.

'Coulthard?' queried Cobb who delved into his mind before replying, 'Coulthard! No! Should I?'

'Leave it with me,' replied Maguire. 'Just remember the name and let me know right away if anyone with that name turns up on the doorstep. Okay?'

Cobb exhaled, studied Maguire, and replied, 'For the last time, I'll trust you. I have to, I don't have any other choice.'

'We've still a long way to go, Chris,' ventured Maguire. 'Tell me about today.'

Exhaling again, Cobb shook his head, and replied, 'I made the switch. They've got the new sim cards. Here, I brought you this little lot.'

Cobb handed a plastic shopping bag over which Maguire opened, peered into, and declared, 'What the hell have you got there?'

'A slice of heroin and a couple of rocks of crack cocaine. That's what I pulled from the last consignment I delivered to Newcastle. I thought you might want to test the stuff and make sure I'm delivering drugs for them and not lookalikes. I'm sure it's kosher, but I want to be completely sure they trust me enough with the real thing. Otherwise, they're testing me like you told me once.'

'What weight is this little lot?'

'A gram, knocking on the door of two. I just lifted it. I didn't weigh it.'

'They won't miss it then?'

'Snow off the dyke,' replied Cobb.

'They must trust you if they're using your sim cards,' proposed Maguire. 'Otherwise, they wouldn't have taken them from you.'

'I hope so. The switch went well,' revealed Cobb. 'It was easier than I thought and one of your better ideas. They've no idea you've cloned their cards. They took the old sim cards out of their mobiles and I collected them for binning. You're the bin, not the one in the corner of the gents. You'll find the old cards in a matchbox at the bottom of the bag.'

'Where do they think the gang is now?' inquired Maguire.

'Ditching the cards in the river,' replied Cobb. 'Which is why I'm going back emptyhanded. Take the drugs and check them for me. If it's not heroin and crack cocaine, then get back to me pronto because it means they're taking me for a ride. Now, Les, tell me one thing. How the hell do you clone a sim card?'

'I can't tell you,' declared Maguire.

'Because you don't trust me?'

'Of course, I do,' laughed Maguire. 'It's just not that easy.'

'You just make two sim cards look the same, don't you?' proposed Cobb.

'Not quite,' replied Maguire turning towards the car park. He scanned the area for the unwanted whilst explaining, 'Every mobile has what they call an International Mobile Subscriber Identity. It's like a fingerprint because every 'phone has a unique number. You connect the sim card to the computer and copy it onto another one.'

'You make it sound easy,' suggested Cobb.

'It's not but then I'm not telling you the whole story, Chris. We don't want you trying this at home, do we?'

'Do both phones end up with the same number,' inquired Cobb.

'The cloned card has the phone number. The copy has no number but is in our possession,' explained Maguire. 'That's all you need to know.'

'It must have taken you ages to clone all those cards,' ventured Cobb.

'Long enough,' replied Maguire. 'Who's in there now?'

'Bobby Nelson, Jawbone, Tiny and Smudger!' voiced Cobb. 'I'd best get back. There's a lot of movement taking place this week. A big consignment apparently.'

'What do you mean by a big consignment?' probed Maguire.

'Everyone's on it, that's all I know,' replied Cobb.

'Including you?'

'Yeah!' I got Scotland. Glasgow and Edinburgh to be precise.'

'Collect or deliver?' inquired Maguire.

'Deliver! It's a solo run and I think it might be counterfeit notes as a taster for a new customer. That's what the conversation was about. I don't suppose there's a lot to carry. I reckon it's the first delivery to somewhere up there. I've no address yet. That'll probably come on the 'phone once I get to Glasgow. It's a new thing. You go from A to B and then they 'phone you and tell you to go to C. They like to keep the information tight. It's the only thing they're any good at.'

'Why did they pick you for that one?' ventured Maguire.

'They didn't,' replied Cobb. 'It was mentioned, and I snaffled it. I said I needed a break and a different route.'

'Why do they suddenly love you?' challenged Maguire.

'You told me to try and play Jawbone and Bobby off against each other, so I did,' explained Cobb. 'I told Jawbone that Bobby was going around telling everyone that if they'd been threatened or beaten up by Jawbone then it was nothing to do with him.'

'Did he believe that?'

'Put it this way, Les, he's not that bright and stood in my corner when I dished the sim cards out. He's suddenly realised Bobby might be trying to get rid of him. You wanted me to divide. Can you conquer?'

'I'll try,' nodded Maguire. 'It looks like Jawbone has opened a door for you and Bobby Nelson hasn't realised.'

'Jawbone isn't the sharpest tool in the box,' remarked Cobb. 'And Bobby hasn't got that much street sense once you get to know him better. He's an admin man, not a street man. The thing is, Les, I've been around so long that I've become part of the furniture. They love me!'

'Well, someone has to,' laughed Maguire. 'Long enough! Time to get back, Chris. Let's not upset things by being away too long.'

'I'm gone. I'll be in touch.'

'Wait one!' ordered Maguire. 'The fallen beermat! I'll be at your place in two hours. Open the door, leave the flat, and wait for me outside.'

'No way!' rumbled Cobb. 'I don't want you anywhere near my flat. The neighbours never miss a trick.'

'Expect a gas leak,' replied Maguire. 'And allow him in.'

Cobb spun on his heel and set off in the same direction, cut across a pedestrian bridge over the river, and quickly headed back towards the Saloon.

Holding a plastic shopping bag containing a gram of heroin, a couple of crack cocaine rocks, and a matchbox full of used sim cards, Maguire watched Cobb's progress before returning to the bakery.

How deep is this quagmire, thought Maguire?

Me, thought Maguire. Suddenly I'm in possession of class A drugs and I'm wondering what that course they sent me on was all about. That tightrope they told me about is feeling a bit slack, and I'm breaking the law. If I get stopped and searched now, who will support me and who will crucify me? I'm tired of reading about politicians arguing for and against a protective law for the police and intelligence services when things move to the wild side. Should I call it a day and stay legal and ditch these drugs in the river or should I allow Sapphire to penetrate the target by his illegal actions which I condone and am an ancillary to? How do I find out if these components are heroin or cocaine when there is no clear path, at my level, to ascertain whether that can be done? Even if I bundle and submit these drugs to Forensics for examination, how do I substantiate my submission to an independent agency outside the police service? How can I protect a valuable source when the bureaucratic system hasn't a clue about covert criminal investigations that sometimes play a crucial part in everyday policing? I think I'm beginning to learn more on the street than I ever learnt in the classroom.

Walking quietly along the path next to the River Kent, Maguire took time out and weighed the good and the bad that lay before him. A step in one direction might happen today. Another step would take him in another direction.

Decision made!

A short time later, Maguire handed the old sim cards to Jim Latimer with a suggestion that they are examined in the extraction device used for such technical enquiries. There was untold intelligence waiting therein to be discovered. He also declared the drugs for examination. Maguire was certain they would prove to be heroin and crack cocaine but was unsure that his report titled 'Found on a riverbank' was sufficient to bypass the forensic gatekeeper.

'Could be a busy few days if there's a big consignment due in,' ventured Jim.

'You'll not agree with me,' replied Maguire. 'But I think we should let it ride.'

'Let it ride?' challenged Jim. 'Why? This is what the job is about.'

'True!' admitted Maguire. 'But there are too many bodies still to account for. Too many gang members that are on the loose and not showing in the game. Let's get behind them. Let them run. See where they go and then take all of them down on the same day.'

'Not possible,' argued Jim. 'Insufficient staff.'

'At the moment, yes,' challenged Maguire. 'If we make the case, then we have got a strong argument to take it further.'

'Anything else?' inquired Jim.

'I need to talk to Detective Chief Superintendent Elliott as soon as possible.'

'He'll take some convincing. We're not a money machine and you're talking about potentially deploying hundreds of officers to sort out a fairly local problem.'

'Regional,' added Maguire. 'Trust me.'

'Convince me,' argued Jim.

'Run those old sim cards through the system,' suggested Maguire. 'Penny to a pound says there's a trace to Wayne. If there's a link to Wayne, then there's a route to the importation market. If we can prove that, then we're halfway there with enough evidence to jack up the operation.'

'You don't give in, do you, Maguire?'

'It's like you said. This is what the job is about, but there's something else I need to see the boss about.'

'Is there a problem with Sapphire?'

'Possibly,' replied Maguire.

'What's happened?'

'His flat has been broken into.'

'Tell him to report it to the police. Anything stolen?'

'No! I don't think it's quite like that, Jim. I reckon someone is onto him and it might be one of ours.'

Jim Latimer stroked his chin thoughtfully before replying, 'I hope you're not thinking what I'm thinking. I'll make the arrangements. You need the Pets app.'

'Pets App! What do you mean?' queried Maguire. 'I've no time for purring cats and yappy dogs.'

'Oh, nothing much,' replied Jim. 'Ever tried reptiles?'

Stepping away from the tripods, the binoculars, the sim cards, photographs, and everything else in that makeshift control room, Jim hit the digits on his 'phone and got through to Detective Chief Superintendent Elliott.

The call was extensive. Various problems were quickly addressed by Alexander the Great. The Pets app was forwarded directly to Maguire's mobile. It was little wonder Mr Elliott was respected by all. He always found a way out even when there wasn't one.

Jim Latimer began packing up for the day as Rod and Barney staggered through the front door of the Saloon and out into the street.

'Here come Rod and Barney,' voiced Maguire looking through binoculars. 'They're walking into town.'

'Good! One of the team will pick them up soon,' revealed Jim.

'You're not convinced,' proposed Maguire. 'What did Alexander the Great think, or is a lowlife like me not allowed to ask?'

'No! He's not convinced the operation should be upgraded,' replied Jim. 'This man Wayne might not even exist for all we know, and you want to suspend a massive strike into the local drugs world just to satisfy your ego. There's not enough evidence, Les. It's all intelligence.'

'Tell me what he said,' implored Maguire.

Jim Latimer smiled and replied, 'I thought you'd never ask. His message was simple. We've got twenty-four hours to produce the evidence that might change the situation into a major crime scene. As for Cobb's burglary, Mr Elliott has sent you a text message and the app. Follow the instructions to the letter.'

'What the hell does that mean?' lied Maguire.

'I've no idea,' lied Jim. 'But that's what he said.'

'Did he mention anyone by the name of Coulthard?' probed Maguire.

Jim Latimer did not reply immediately. Rather, he stared at Maguire and asked, 'I can read your face, Les. I expect you can read mine too. Why don't we give each other a breather and start telling the truth? We were thrown into the same bath together. That doesn't mean we have to splash water at each other all day. We need to start trusting each other.'

'Mr Elliott told me this might happen,' replied Maguire. 'I'm sorry I splashed. Maybe we need to chuck some water out of the bath.'

'I agree! Do you know what I know?' probed Jim.

'I've no idea,' replied Maguire. 'I'll just add the term under investigation.'

Nodding, Jim Latimer replied, 'He told you, didn't he? The boss told you about the Coulthard enquiry.'

'Maybe!' replied Maguire. 'To be honest, he didn't tell me much at all. What do you know about the Coulthards, Jim?'

'Watch this space,' ventured the DI. 'It's all going down soon. That's all I can say.'

'Are you involved in the enquiry?' questioned Maguire.

'I was, or to be more accurate, we were involved in some surveillance work. Things happened and the Detective Chief Superintendent took over the investigation. That's all I can tell you,' explained Jim.

'I see.'

'You think the Coulthard brothers broke into Sapphire's flat, don't you?'

'I'm not sure,' replied Maguire. 'I've no evidence, not even intelligence.'

'Then stand back and give Mr Elliott room,' suggested Jim. 'He's on the case.'

'Whatever it is,' remarked Maguire.

'Yes, whatever it is,' agreed Jim. 'And talking about intelligence, let's sort these sim cards out. The boss will update us when he wants to and not before. Right now, we don't need to know.'

'Okay! Show me how this device works,' ventured Maguire. 'Either Jawbone Jones or Bobby Nelson must have had contact with Wayne.'

'It would be good if that were right,' proposed Jim. 'Here, watch this.'

For the next fifteen minutes, Jim Latimer instructed Maguire in the use of an extraction device that interfaced with a stack of old sim cards that Cobb had delivered from the gang's possession. As the day moved on, the gear was moved quietly from the bakery to a secure office in the local police station where Maguire worked through the night to achieve his objective. With no one around, Maguire read Elliott's text message, downloaded an app to his mobile, and made plans for the rest of the night.

Shortly after midnight, Maguire took a break and dressed in a fluorescent jacket and works trousers. A panel on the back of the jacket revealed the words, 'GAS EMERGENCY.'

Knocking on the door of Cobb's flat, Maguire walked in and held his forefinger to his lips thereby signalling Cobb to remain silent. He activated his mobile and stood in the middle of the room. Gradually, he turned and pointed his mobile at all four corners, every electrical device in the apartment, and then included the lightbulbs and electric sockets that were situated in the room. He checked the Pets app on his 'phone and told Cobb, 'The flat is clean. You may have been burgled but no one has bugged you. There are no covert listening devices in this room. Relax, Chris. Use the beermats again. Okay?

'If that's what you recommend,' replied Cobb.

Maguire shrugged his shoulders as he closed the door behind him and nodded at an elderly woman who appeared in the communal hallway.

'No problem' remarked Maguire with an embracing grin. 'Everything is fine. You are safe now. The leak has been repaired. Have a good day, madam.'

Returning to the office, drinking copious amounts of black coffee, Maguire worked away at the extraction device for the rest of the night. In the back of his mind, however, he wanted to know about the investigation into Colin Coulthard and Larry Coulthard.

Why was the Chief of Detectives investigating two detectives?

~

9

Later that week
Dawn
Garstang, Lancashire.

Lying on the River Wyre, River Calder and the Lancaster Canal, the market town of Garstang is situated close to the A6 road, the M6 motorway, and the West Coast Main Line, between Lancaster and Preston. It lies on the eastern edge of the Fylde, and the Forest of Bowland is not far to the east. The town is overlooked by the ruined remains of Greenhalgh Castle, which is often called Garstang Castle and is situated about ten miles north of Preston.

A dark saloon car turned off the A6 and journeyed to one of the more prestigious housing estates in the town. Arriving in a cul-de-sac, the vehicle pulled into the driveway whilst two following police vans parked close by.

Two men emerged from the lead car and walked the path to the front door whereupon the taller of the two pressed the doorbell and waited.

When Larry Coulthard opened the door to Detective Superintendent Martin Norris of Lancashire Constabulary he initially smiled, but then realised that the Head of Professional Standards seemed to be in no mood for jocularity.

'Detective Constable Larry Coulthard?' questioned the Superintendent.

'You know it is,' replied Larry. 'What's going on?'

Gesturing to the man standing next to him, Superintendent Norris said, 'This is Detective Sergeant Stan Holliday of Cumbria Constabulary. Cumbria Police are leading an investigation that we are assisting with. We have a warrant to search your premises, Mr Coulthard.'

'What? A warrant! What the hell!'

'May we come in and commence our search, or are you going to be confrontational?'

'No! I mean let me see the search warrant,' challenged Larry.

'We're looking for the proceeds of crime, Mr Coulthard,' explained the Superintendent as he retained the warrant and clutched it tight. 'And I have to inform you that I am arresting you on suspicion of conspiring to attempt to pervert the course of justice.'

As the arresting officer cautioned Larry, a woman appeared in the hallway and shouted, 'Who are these men? What's going on? Larry!'

'We're police officers,' explained Stan to the woman. 'Mrs Coulthard presumably?'

'Yes! Who are you?' replied Mrs Coulthard.

Larry stepped backwards into the lounge as Stan ignored the question, stepped outside, and gestured towards a couple of police vans that began to trundle towards the detached bungalow.

Picking a telephone up, Larry began to hit the digits but was immediately stymied when Superintendent Norris hit the cradle and said, 'I'm afraid that I cannot allow you to obstruct me in the execution of my duties at this stage. A search of the premises, outhouses, and your vehicle will be made and, thereafter, you will be taken to Kendal police station where a Custody Sergeant will be appraised of the reason for your arrest and will offer you particular rights under the Police and Criminal Evidence Act. One of those rights involves your right to legal representation. Right now, I advise you to co-operate and remain seated whilst my officers carry out their duties.'

'No way!' screamed Larry. 'I'll make my call.'

Bending down, Stan Holliday ripped a telephone cable from the socket, held it up, and said, 'I don't think so.'

Aghast, Larry stood open-mouthed when Norris handed a document to him and said, 'This is a copy of the search warrant duly accredited by me. Keep it and show it to your solicitor if you decide you need one.'

Larry reached out for the document, then ducked beneath Norris's outstretched arm and made a run for it. He sideswiped Stan and was halfway down the hallway when he grabbed a set of car keys from a table and bolted for the driveway.

Responding quickly, Stan Holliday regained his balance and set off after Larry. In the process, he overturned a table laden with potted plants and barged into the front door causing it to bang heavily against the door jamb.

Unlocking his car, Larry jumped into the driver's seat and fired the engine. A glance in his mirror alerted him to the fact that his unwelcome visitors had blocked him in. He was stranded. Snatching reverse gear, he began to manoeuvre the vehicle around the squad car and onto the lawn.

Intent on preventing escape, the driver of a signed police van drove his vehicle onto the pavement to close a gap.

At that precise moment, Stan smashed a solid steel baton into the driver's door window.

The explosion of glass showered Larry Coulthard.

Stan reached into the vehicle, removed the ignition keys, and said, 'Like the boss said, you're under arrest and you're not going anywhere.'

Pulling the door open, Stan grabbed Larry's hand and secured one of his hands with handcuffs before dragging him completely from the vehicle and taking him to the ground to handcuff him behind his back.

Moments later, a uniform search team entered the premises and began searching for more evidence whilst Stan bundled the prisoner into a waiting van.

Simultaneously, in Oxenholme, near Kendal, South Cumbria, Detective Chief Superintendent Alexander George Elliott, affectionately known to his detectives as Alexander the Great, in the company of Detective Inspector Jim Latimer of the Force Surveillance Squad, rattled on the door of Larry's brother – one Detective Inspector Colin Coulthard – and served upon him a search warrant.

Where Garstang is formerly recognised as a village because it has a church in the form of Saint Thomas's church, as well as two Methodist churches, Oxenholme is recognised geographically as a hamlet because it does not support a church. Named after a cow farm in the 1880s, the hamlet is pronounced Oxen-Home but has always been spelt Oxenholme.

Such matters were irrelevant to Colin Coulthard who was initially compliant from the start and stood back and said nothing.

'This is a copy of the search warrant,' revealed Elliott. 'We're looking for the proceeds of crime, Colin. Have you anything to say to this?'

Coulthard remained silent despite his wife joining him and staring her husband in the face.

'What have you done?' asked Mrs Coulthard. 'What are they looking for?'

Shaking his head, Coulthard stepped into the lounge and with an air of typical arrogance finally said, 'I've no idea, my dear. I think someone has made a big mistake. Ring Larry for me and then ring our solicitor. I'll need to sue the police for harassment, I suspect. See to it, please.'

'We'll get you a solicitor later of you need one,' explained Elliott. 'Right now, your brother is currently being taken into custody in Garstang, and I am obliged to inform you that you too are being arrested on suspicion of conspiring to attempt to pervert the course of justice.'

Elliott began delivering the formal caution to his prisoner.

'Really,' laughed Coulthard smugly. 'Is something missing from the property store at the nick? Go on. Tell me some cash is missing and the last DI has blamed me for taking it.'

Ignoring Elliott, Coulthard picked up a newspaper, sat down on the sofa, and turned the first page. Deliberately, he used the newspaper to hide from Elliott as he tried to maintain that aura of aloofness for which he was famous.

'You don't seem to understand,' proposed Elliott. 'We've been onto you for some months, Colin. It's all fallen apart.'

'What has?' inquired Mrs Coulthard.

'On your feet, Colin,' ordered Elliott. 'We'll discuss this further at Kendal police station.'

'Colin! What's going on?' challenged Mrs Coulthard.

Shaking the newspaper angrily, Coulthard made no reply.

Behind the headlines, Coulthard's ego began to fracture when his brain deduced that his racket might have been rumbled.

'Get your coat on,' ordered Elliott. 'You've been in cahoots with some of the county's top criminals over the last few months. We know what you been up to. I'll put it like this, Colin. We know that when you were stationed at Carlisle you were the DI on the CID. Your brother was a Lancashire detective in the Regional Crime Squad. Neither one of you have ever run a registered informant in your entire careers.'

With a noticeably shaky voice, Coulthard confronted Elliott with, 'Do you intend to insult my integrity all day?'

'The jitters!' chuckled Elliott. 'I detect you've got the jitters.'

'It's the only thing you'll ever detect,' replied a nervous Coulthard.

'I think not,' ventured Elliott. 'We know you and your brother worked together to identify informants ran by Cumbria Police, Lancashire Police, and the Number One Regional Crime Squad based in Salford, Manchester. You then named those informants to criminals who were working in organised crime in exchange for money. You're nicked, pal.'

The newspaper lowered from the sofa to the carpeted floor when Detective Inspector Colin Coulthard eventually realised the game was up and turned a whiter shade of pale.

'Oh, yes, we know, don't we, Jim?' remarked Elliott. 'Colin! You do know that Jim Latimer oversees our surveillance squad, don't you?'

Elliott let the words sink in before continuing, 'Of course, you do, Colin. It's just that you forgot that he's not the only one on the squad capable of following you and your brother around for weeks on end noting who you've been talking too and what you've been saying.'

Colin Coulthard stood up, looked at his wife, and said, 'I was just trying to help Larry out.'

'Take him away, Jim,' ordered Chief Superintendent Elliott. 'We'll continue this conversation down at the police station.'

As Jim Latimer escorted a handcuffed Colin Coulthard to a waiting police car, Elliott beckoned in a search team, turned to Coulthard's wife, and said, 'Shall I put the kettle on? I'm sure this has been a complete shock to you, Mrs Coulthard. Mary, isn't it?'

'Yes, yes, of course! But I want to see Colin.'

'And there's no reason why you should not once we've had a chat,' revealed Elliott. 'That depends on what you say.'

'What do you mean?'

'You see, Mary, I believe that you are fully aware of what has been going on and I need to ask you some questions.'

'Such as?'

'I am aware that you opened a joint bank account in the name of your husband and brother-in-law. You are Mary Amanda Coulthard, are you not?'

'Yes, you know that already.'

'The account was opened some months ago at a bank in Windermere. You were under surveillance at the time you opened that account. Your husband had driven you there from your home here in Oxenholme and waited for you whilst you opened the account. You then went for coffee in a café close to the railway station. Can you confirm that for me?'

'Yes! Yes, if you say so.'

'It's not what I say, Mrs Coulthard. It's what you did,' proposed Elliott. 'Do you admit opening such an account?'

'Yes,' replied an adamant Mrs Coulthard.

'Do you admit banking large amounts of cash into that account on behalf of your husband and your brother-in-law?'

Sinking onto the middle of the sofa, Mrs Mary Amanda Coulthard hugged a cushion to her chest, then buried her face in it for a few seconds, and eventually emerged in tears with the words, 'Am I a witness or a suspect?'

'Did you know where your husband and brother-in-law had acquired that money?'

'No! Not really. I just thought it was odd.'

'The account holds close to one hundred thousand pounds. Did you know that?'

Mary Coulthard did not reply.

'According to the bank's records, on each occasion that money was deposited into that account, you made the deposit. Indeed, Mary, I suggest you knew the money was the proceeds of crime at the very least?'

Nodding, weeping, Mary said, 'Larry told me it was squad expenses to start with. Colin laughed at that and told him to be careful with his expense claims. Then the money surged in. We had cash all over the house. It was everywhere. He hid it behind the panels in the bath to start with, then a couple of boxes under the lagging in the loft. All notes, fives, tens, twenties.'

'Loft insulation?'

'What else could it be,' replied Mary. 'Colin wondered if they would come and steal it back.'

'Who is they?' challenged Elliott.

Mary Coulthard allowed her head to fall and replied, 'The whole thing was ridiculous! I think they started in the hope that they might make a few extra quid. There was always something wrong with it. I just never knew the whole story, just that it was corrupt. Bribery or something like that. They weren't bribing good people. It was the scum of the earth that they were bribing or whatever they were doing. Hey! We got away with it. How did you find out?'

Elliott smiled, cautioned Mary, and then announced, 'I am arresting you on suspicion of conspiring to attempt to pervert the course of justice.'

'I've nothing to say,' replied Mary.

Chief Superintendent Elliott withdrew, turned to other officers who had entered the room, and instructed, 'Take her to the cells. She is under arrest. Tell the video officer to join me. I want a recording of the search. Thank you.'

Mary was taken into custody and the search warrant was executed.

By late afternoon, the searches were finished, and all three prisoners had been interviewed by Detective Chief Superintendent Elliott and Detective Sergeant Stan Holliday. Money was recovered from the Garstang house where Larry had secreted one thousand pounds behind the bath panels in their bathroom. Similarly, money from a greenhouse at Colin's was recovered hidden inside several potted plants. In both cases, cash had been placed in plastic bags to preserve them from any damp.

Whilst there was nothing particularly wrong about hiding money in your house, Elliott presumed the cash was being held there only until the suspects got together and arranged another drive to the bank in Windermere. He further believed that the cash was so hidden because the two corrupt detectives feared that the crooks, they had initially received the money, from may well break in and steal it back. To substantiate this line of thought, details of telephone numbers and addresses relevant to known criminals were found in diaries and notebooks belonging to Larry and Colin Coulthard. Added to Jim Latimer's surveillance evidence, Elliott's team was gradually proving that Larry and Colin had identified various informants in the pay of detectives from Cumbria, Lancashire, and the Regional Crime Squad. In their position as prominent detectives, the Coulthards had obtained such information initially by encouraging junior officers, like Maguire, into declaring the identities of their informants in exchange for support in their careers. Soon realising that not everyone wanted to play that game, the Coulthards gradually became more subtle and removed confidential folders from unlocked files and insecure cabinets in the possession of senior officers. They discovered who the informants were, and crucially found out which criminals, gangs, and associates, they were targeting. Armed with such knowledge, the two detectives then covertly approached the named targets and offered them such information in exchange for cash. Initially, such approaches were made by a note shoved through a letterbox, or by a veiled telephone message, and then finally by a direct invitation to meet.

Put simply, in exchange for cash, the crooks were told an informant was working against them. They were then played along and encouraged to pay more and more money to the corrupt detectives to learn who that informant might be. The detectives got richer and the crooks got poorer but much wiser.

Things began to go awry for the police when they realised that the long-term strategy of surveillance operations against key targets was no longer working. Weeks of failed operations, tip-offs about crimes that were supposed to occur but didn't, and a marked lack of success in comparison with previous years led Chief Superintendent Elliott to suspect there was a leak in the department. Someone somewhere was talking out of turn.

Initially, the offices of the Chief of Detectives were examined for any technical devices that may have been planted by the other side. Had the crooks bugged them came to mind. Eventually, new informants were recruited and learnt what the police didn't want to know. There was a leak, and it was somewhere amongst the detectives.

The entire saga had gone on undetected for over eighteen months.

But on this day the Coulthards admitted responsibility as the weight of evidence continued to grow against them when the Professional Standards Department also stepped in and began interviewing younger officers who realised they had been the earliest of Coulthard's targets in months gone by.

Charges against the three prisoners were expected by the end of the day.

Eager to exploit a system designed to regulate and protect informants, the Coulthards were brought down by several regulated and properly registered, informants.

Chief Superintendent Alexander George Elliott had earned his nickname yet again. He made a call to Jim Latimer and updated him on the situation with regards to the Coulthard arrests.

'Maguire will ask me if the Coulthards are responsible for breaking into Sapphire's flat, sir. Can we prove that? What shall I tell him?'

'Tell him the truth,' replied Elliott. 'We don't know at present, but I'm sure they did. We've found details of Cobb's name and address in Colin Coulthard's notebook.'

'So, Cobb was on the list,' ventured Jim. 'That would make you think that he was considered a criminal worth tapping up for money, or someone they suspected was an informant. Which?'

'The latter, I suspect, Jim,' replied Elliott. 'Either way, our surveillance squad didn't tie Cobb to the Coulthard's, and Cobb has never said that he's been challenged directly by the Coulthards. I'd say he was still in the clear. I've discussed it with Stan who has gone through all Maguire's reports and we both agree. We think he's still clean. You're clear to go. Move to the next phase as planned.'

'Great! We'll do just that,' replied Jim. 'By the way, you wanted a result regarding checking the old sim cards. Maguire has traced a call to a man called Ricky. The call was made over twelve months ago from Bobby Nelson's mobile to one Richard Arthur Wayne of Crosby, Merseyside who is the subscriber to the mobile phone.'

'Is he known to us?' probed Elliott.

'No criminal record that we are aware of,' revealed Jim.

'But Wayne is his middle name,' proposed Elliott. 'We've always suspected it was his first name. Damn it! Are we stupid or what?'

'We could be wrong about where his name lies,' responded Jim. 'No disrespect, boss, but everyone calls you George, not Alexander. Wayne could be a first, middle or last name when you think about it. We're just so used to thinking that names are a surname we've accidentally radicalised ourselves into either ignorance or incompetence.'

'Fair point,' chuckled Elliott. 'It's an old contact though. Twelve months ago? Tell me Merseyside Police have a file on the man!'

'Not a lot,' voiced Jim. 'Their Serious Crime Squad have traces on a man of the same name having loose connections to some of their local targets but nothing conclusive.'

'What have they got?' queried Elliott. 'For example, do they have a photograph or a vehicle trace?'

'No! Neither! I asked if they did and they told me they have a couple of intelligence reports from staff who have been watching local targets in clubs, pubs, bars, and cafes over the years. The name comes up as being someone who seems to go to the same places but doesn't have any known concrete associations with them. In the criminal sense if you see what I mean? He just seems to drift in and out of the plot but doesn't have an important part to play.'

'Understood,' replied Elliott. 'Another mystery man to put in the back of the mind. By the way, I'm promoting Maguire to temporary sergeant for the duration of the operation.'

'May I ask why? He's hardly qualified,' questioned Jim.

'He's earned it so far and the truth is that we've got two sergeants in the pub drinking for England and I don't want to change them. They've identified every member of the gang as we know it locally and this led to each one being photographed and profiled to the point that we're getting closer to the hit. More importantly, they've ruled out scores of possible suspects, tied the licensee to the gang, and given us a stack of car numbers we've matched to the suspects. All our Tangos are now matched to a vehicle. As for themselves, they're now as common as tables and chairs in the pub. I'm not changing that relationship. It works.'

'Costing us a fortune in beer money and expenses, boss. I hate to tell you what the expense forms will be this month.'

'Don't!' snapped Elliott. 'If we can burst this one wide open, it will be worth every penny.

'And if it doesn't?'

'The Chief Constable will have my guts for garters, and I'll be in charge of parking cones for the rest of my career. By the way if the surveillance is blown then you'll be with me.'

'In that case, we still need to bottom out Wayne,' suggested Jim.

'Yes, we do! Press on and keep in touch. Early start?'

'When the Saloon opens,' replied Jim. 'I'll keep you posted.'

~

10

A Week Later
The M6 Forton Services
Southbound Carriageway

'Red Alpha One I have the eyeball. The target vehicle is southbound, seven zero miles per hour in the offside lane of three just approaching Forton Service area,' radioed Maguire. 'I'll peel off. Back up come through.'

'Back up making ground,' came the reply on the net.

Watching the car ahead of him, Maguire was conscious that it was being driven by Jawbone Jones with Colin McArdle sat in the front passenger seat. Although he was a good fifty yards behind the target, driving his Mazda CX 5, Maguire had an unrestricted view of the road ahead and knew it was time to hand over the lead position in the surveillance convoy. The service area was an obvious location to rotate the convoy and give it a new leader.

'Three hundred yards to the turnoff, stand by,' radioed Maguire.

The two men in the target vehicle were deep in conversation. Maguire watched their heads swivel towards each other, and then back to the road, as they conversed.

I wonder what they are talking about, thought Maguire.

'Two hundred yards! Stand by!'

The talking heads continued to swivel

'One hundred yards. No deviation from the target. Red Alpha One is peeling off. Down to you back-up,' radioed Maguire using his covert mouthpiece.'

'Back up coming through,' voiced Danny in his Ford Focus.

The target was a dark blue Volvo estate that had left Kendal earlier in the morning and had made good progress south. They seemed unaware they were being followed by Maguire's hastily put together surveillance squad.

Maguire activated his nearside indicator and reduced speed. Glancing in the mirror, he saw Danny gaining ground in the Ford and knew the squad was about to change positions. Danny would take the eyeball and have the lead view on the target.

Moving slightly to the nearside, Maguire guided his vehicle onto the slip road as Danny moved closer. The plan was simple. Maguire would leave the motorway, drive gradually through the service area, and then join the carriageway once more. Except this time, he would be at the rear of the convoy and, if necessary, would allow the others to overtake him if they were too strung out. It was a fact that if the target drove at seventy miles an hour then Tail End Charlie, the last vehicle in the convoy, would probably have to drive the fastest once the changes had occurred to catch and then keep up with the faster moving vehicles ahead.

As the Volvo neared a parallel line with the bottom of the slip road, Jawbone suddenly slammed on the brakes, simultaneously wrenched the handbrake, and slewed the vehicle from the motorway towards the service area. Sliding broadside, the Volvo lurched over all three lanes of the carriageway, crossed the hatch markings that were there to separate traffic lanes from the slip road, tore up a section of grass, and then clipped the kerb as Jawbone managed to eventually place the Volvo on the slip road.

Maguire's heart rate hit an all-time high for the day as he watched the split-second manoeuvre. He eased off the accelerator to avoid a collision causing Danny to pull out into the middle lane and overtake Maguire's Mazda. Trying to control the surge in adrenalin rushing through his body, Maguire rolled the window down and took a deep breath. He'd never been in danger, but had he been closer, the Volvo would have taken him out.

'Straight through!' yelled Danny on the radio, almost panicking. 'Loss of eyeball. I'm straight through.'

Calmly, Maguire engaged his radio and said, 'Red Alpha One has the eyeball. The target is off, off, off the motorway and into the service area at Forton. I'm right up behind the target. 'Bernie! Where are you?'

'Bernie is your new back up,' replied the driver of a light blue Renault. 'I'm making ground. Stand by!'

'I'm running at three,' radioed Peter in his grey Audi. 'That looked like a deliberate movement from the target designed to see if he was being followed. Bernie, plot to the exit area of the services. Maguire, park up and walk away. Danny, continue to the next turn off and wait there. I'm plotting to the service area. Team adopt the hard shoulder and await developments.'

When seen from above, Bernie went to an area close to the exit road from the services to the motorway and Danny drove straight on. Maguire narrowly missed a collision with the target and when Jawbone took a right into the parking area Maguire took a left. Meanwhile, Peter casually accelerated intending to take up a watch on the target. The rest of the six-vehicle single-crewed convoy, which consisted of Carol and Angela, pulled onto the hard shoulder, and stopped.

They were being tested, and no one liked to be tested on a busy motorway.

Maguire cruised into a vacant space on the car park some fifty yards from the target vehicle which was still in his view. Peter followed suit but stopped close to the car park's fuel pumps.

Meanwhile, Jawbone parked his motor, opened the door, and ran into the service area. His passenger, Colin, casually followed, paused at a newspaper stand at the entrance to the services, and then eventually made his way into the café area.

On the net, Maguire reported, 'Tango Zero Six is Colin McArdle. Same age as Jawbone, six-foot-tall, muscular build, bird tattoos on knuckles of both hands, and wearing dark blue denim jeans and jacket. Looks like a black crew neck tee shirt from where I'm standing. Black slip-on shoes. I understand he has a soft Northern Irish accent as well. Information only. Stand by for movements!'

Sauntering into the services, Maguire found the shop and perused the goods on display whilst Peter watched the target vehicle and stated, 'Les, it's an ideal opportunity. What do you think?'

'Proceed with caution. I'll give you a safety countdown from ten if required.'

'Please!' replied Peter.

'All units, I have control,' radioed Maguire. 'Both targets are inside the services. Temporary loss of eyeball. I have the egress to the target vehicle covered. Stand by for insertion.'

Peter opened the boot of his vehicle, removed something from the boot, pocketed it, and then strolled casually towards the Volvo. As he got closer, Peter engaged his throat mic and radioed, 'Closing on the target. Twenty yards.'

'Ten...' replied Maguire. 'No movement from the Tangos.'

Inside the services, Maguire moved slightly and saw Colin sat a table with a drink and Jawbone emerging from the gents' toilet.

Chuckling, Maguire realised someone had needed the bathroom urgently. They weren't being tested. A call of nature was in play.

'Nine!' radioed Maguire. 'I have an eyeball on both Tangos now sat together in the café.

'On target,' radioed Peter. 'Fifteen yards.'

'Still nine!' radioed Maguire. 'No movement here.'

Peter closed with the card and radioed, 'Five yards.'

'Still nine!' replied Maguire. 'All clear.'

Bending down at the front of the vehicle, Peter removed an electronic tracking device from an inside pocket, attached it to the underside of the Volvo, and then walked away.

Returning to his vehicle, Peter radioed, 'Tracker fitted. Test please.'

'Angela?' queried Maguire.

'Angela is at four receiving tracker signal,' came the reply. 'All correct.'

'Thank you,' from Maguire. 'Carol?'

'Carol at Tail End Charlie receiving.'

'Come through and take a break,' radioed Maguire. 'Tango Zero One and Tango Zero Six are in the café area sitting by the window at the third table on the right as you enter. They might be meeting a third party who has not yet arrived. Cover proceedings please.'

'Roger! Coming through the convoy,' replied Carol.

As Maguire fathomed out where everyone was, he decided to top up his food store situated in the Mazda's glove compartment. He presumed it might be a long journey. In quick time, Maguire selected several chocolate bars, some Kendal Mint Cake, three chicken and salad sandwiches, and a couple of cold drinks from the shop. Snatching a hot coffee from a vending machine, he paid cash at the till, shoved his provisions into a plastic bag, and walked into the amusement area near the entrance. Maguire slotted a coin into a pinball machine and began to play. From this position, he covered the café entrance whilst taking refreshment and blending into the scenery.

A short time later, Carol parked her white Berlingo van, entered the services, totally ignored Maguire, and joined the queue in the café area. Five minutes later she sat two tables away from Jones and McArdle and Maguire had reclaimed his vehicle.

The longer the two targets sat and talked, the surer Maguire became that they had taken a natural break despite the last second deviation from the carriageway onto the slip road.

As the motorway grew busier with traffic, Colin McArdle and Jawbone Jones vacated their table and headed back to the car park. In deep conversation, they often laughed at what the other said, and seemed oblivious to the surveillance team. There was no indication they were on the lookout for followers.

'Carol with the eyeball. Tangos Zero One and Six are out of the café. No meeting with a third party observed.

They're at the exit. Stand by! Crossing the car park. Approaching their vehicle.'

'Got that,' cut in Maguire. 'The tracker is deployed. All units, the tracker is deployed. Carol! Peel off!'

As a tall dark-haired surveillance officer rearranged her leather shoulder bag, she deviated from a normal route and entered a vacant 'phone booth to ostensibly make a telephone call.

Maguire stood his ground whilst Peter quickly snatched a cold drink in the shop and a bar of chocolate. It was another 'eating on the hoof' day.

'They're in the vehicle,' radioed Maguire as he eventually emerged from the services. 'Ignition! Manoeuvring! They're off. Angela?'

'Red Alpha Five has the target vehicle on the tracker screen,' radioed Angela from her black BMW. 'Stand by.'

The screen in Angela's car burst into life and revealed a tiny white dot on a map. She reached forward, adjusted the device, and enlarged the dot whilst reducing the scope of the map.

'We're off,' radioed Angela. 'Coming through slowly, following on-screen. All units! Form a convoy. Heading south towards you, Danny.'

'Understood,' from Danny.

The morning wore on as Maguire's surveillance team followed the two suspects south down the M6 motorway. Using the tracker device, the distance between the target vehicle and the surveillance convoy was considerable, but never too far away to lose control.

Sitting at Tail End Charlie, listening to the commentary on the net, Maguire eventually realised he was losing touch with the convoy. Checking his rear-view mirror, he pulled out into the offside lane and squeezed the Mazda's accelerator. The lane he had chosen was clear and he soon hit one hundred miles an hour as he closed with his colleagues. On a downhill section in the countryside, Maguire topped one hundred and twenty miles an hour before he saw the convoy ahead of him.

He checked the mirror and in that split second of head movement a deer jumped the central reservation from the northbound carriageway into Maguire's path.

Slamming the brakes and simultaneously swerving to miss colliding with the animal, Maguire felt the Mazda skid awkwardly to the offside. The barrier beckoned until he released the brakes and then swung the steering wheel into and then out of the skid as he fought for control.

The deer pranced across the southbound carriageway and up the embankment out of sight.

Moments later, pulling up on the hard shoulder, Maguire came to a standstill, dropped his forehead onto the steering wheel, and denied the heart attack he felt might follow.

Heaving, he wound the window down and took in some deep breaths. Glancing over his shoulder, he saw the deer standing defiantly in a field adjoining the motorway. It had an arrogant stance and a head that stared right back at Maguire.

Shaking his head, the surveillance commander fired the Mazda and joined the carriageway as he strove to remain in contact with the operation.

Never again, he thought. Never again.

As they travelled through Lancashire, the team monitored the direction their target was headed in. Eventually, Maguire hit the buttons on his mobile and made a call.

'Merseyside Police! How can we help?' came the reply.

'Serious Crime Squad,' requested Maguire.

Meanwhile, back in Kendal, the Saloon was in full flow. Two popular males of unknown origin were still seeking work, drinking for England, and – by now – part of an unofficial pool league that ensured their continued presence. Rod and Barney were becoming part of the woodwork and would often disappear into a corner to take a call on a mobile 'phone or make a call relevant to a job offer of some kind or other.

Even the licensee took a liking to them.

'Two lagers, boys?' shouted the usually grumpy George Rooney. Overweight with a beer belly hanging over his trouser belt, Rooney had already poured the beers for the two undercover detectives when he remarked, 'I'll put them on the slate and you can square up later.'

Such was the repartee that had developed over recent times, Rod replied, 'Yes, please. The slate it is, or do you want a game of pool for double or quits?'

'No!' chuckled Rooney. 'I want you to pay off what you owe before you go.'

'Ahh!' worried Rod. 'No job! I am but a poor man, sir.'

'On the dole and ripping everyone off on the pool table,' smiled Rooney. 'Have you ever thought about selling insurance from door to door? You guys would make a fortune.'

'Not if it's raining,' interrupted Barney. 'We're looking for inside jobs or sunshine jobs, George. By the way, a tenner and I'll do your windows for you.'

'No chance!' laughed Rooney. 'You'd just be a pain?'

'A windowpane?' challenged Barney. 'By the way, did you hear the one about the Englishman, the Irishman and the Scotsman?'

'No,' replied Rooney eager to listen.

'Me neither,' offered Barney removing two pints of lager from the bar. 'But if I do, you'll be first to know, George.'

'Away with you,' snapped Rooney. 'You're wanted on the table.'

Barney turned, slid a pint of lager onto a table close to Rod, and then placed his own on their table. He chalked his cue whilst waiting for Rod.

Standing in the entrance to an empty booth, Rod held a mobile 'phone in one hand and a newspaper in the other. With the 'phone cocked to his ear and his eye on the folded inside page of the newspaper, Rod quietly voiced, 'Morning, it's Rod. Put the usual on the following, please.' There was a slight pause before Rod continued, 'Yes! A pound each way on horses three, four, five and seven on the first race.' Pausing again, Rod offered a smile at the unsuspecting George behind the bar before continuing. 'I'll pay tax. Can you debit my account, please? Yes, how's the going? Good! They'll be off soon.'

Moments later, Rod collected his drink and joined Barney at their table.

'All on?' queried Barney.

'Yep! No problem. Do you want to break?'

'Why not,' replied Barney chalking his cue.

George Rooney leaned on the bar and listened to the two detectives talking.

'How was the bookie this morning?' inquired Barney.

'Fine! We won twenty quid yesterday. I told him to leave it on the account. We're a hundred quid up on the week, so far.'

'Great!' responded Barney. 'It's your table.'

Rod settled to make his first shot when Rooney remarked, 'And that doesn't include what you've fleeced my customers for.'

'Always complaining, George,' insinuated Rod. 'Do you know another pub in town with a pool table?'

'I wouldn't tell you if I did,' replied Rooney.

'Then stop complaining,' advised Rod. 'And notch up a drink for yourself on our tab.'

'I'll have a double vodka and coke,' ventured Rooney.

'Just my luck,' snapped Rod. 'I thought you would.'

Bill Ashworth stood up, vacated the table in the corner booth, and approached the licensee. Aged forty-two, tall, skinny and wearing jeans and a long grey sweater, he rapped the bar with his knuckles and said, 'George! A round of sandwiches for four. Make it snappy. We'll be off soon.'

'No problem,' replied Rooney. 'Right away. I'll bring them over.'

Barney noticed that Rooney wrote the order on a blank piece of paper before passing it through the hatch to the kitchen staff. He then opened a black notebook which was underneath the bar. Rooney scribbled in the book and then leaned over to whisper to Bill Ashworth.

The sandwiches appeared and were served directly to Ashworth's table.

No money changed hands, thought Barney. And Rooney has an obvious habit of jumping to attention every time one of the team's targets interact with him. Interesting, thought Barney. Remarkably interesting! Presumably, the book is a tab for the gang, I wonder.

In the Forward Control Point above the bakery opposite the Saloon, Stan Holliday put down the 'phone and ticked off a list before ringing Chief Superintendent Elliott in the main office.

'Chief Superintendent!' answered Elliott.

'Morning, sir,' ventured Stan. 'I have the following runners and riders gathered and ready to leave.'

'Go on,' suggested Elliott. 'We're ready.'

'Tango Zeros Three, Four, Five and Seven are sat in the corner booth in the Saloon. We have a potential maximum of four surveillance opportunities if they are all tasked and set off shortly. The general thought is they are all waiting for Tango Zero Eight to give them their final instructions.'

'Are you mind reading Rod and Barney?' probed Elliott.

'No! I'm the bookie they ring whenever they need to,' explained Stan. 'If they say put a tenner on horse number five in the next race, I know that means that Tango Zero Five is inside the pub under surveillance by them both.'

'You've been watching too many detective films,' chucked Elliott.

'Wait one,' suggested Stan as he looked out of the window, engaged a huge pair of binoculars, and added, 'Just arrived! Bobby Nelson and Smudger Murray – Two and Eight – are now on the plot, sir.'

'Got that, Stan,' replied Elliott. 'We'll take it from here. Just report the movements out, the direction of travel, and we'll pick it up from there.'

'Noted! Understood,' from Stan.

Elliott turned to Jim Latimer and said, 'We've got Maguire and his Red Alpha surveillance team out early doors following Jones and McArdle, and the rest of the players all gathered for the off. Looks like a busy day ahead.'

'Well, they'll either sit and talk or Nelson will give the final details of their routes and they'll all be off within the hour.'

'Collecting or delivering?' queried Elliott.

'Anyone's guess,' replied Jim. 'Let them run? Yes?'

'Let them run free but followed,' ordered Elliott. 'We're in the process of building a significant conspiracy case against the gang as well as various offences that are down to individuals on the periphery. Keep building, Jim. I want photographs of the targets coming out of the Saloon.'

'Done! Full-time surveillance video deployed,' replied Jim.

'As well as photos of the targets getting into the vehicles, routes, photographs at the arrival point, and photographs and details of everyone they visit either delivering, collecting or whatever. I want those historic daily statements from Rod and Barney identifying and proving association on the file and continued to the last day of the operation.'

'Collated every day, sir,' replied Jim. 'Or to be precise, when sober, if you know what I mean.'

Elliott chuckled, 'Mmm. The defence will have a good poke at that one, but we'll cross that bridge when we come to it. Rooney, the licensee! Is he money laundering or part of the conspiracy? Keep on him and knock up a surveillance job on him. Where does he bank? When? I want his financial dealings and his tax returns investigated. No-one can run a pub like that and not know what's going on.'

'On my list, sir,' replied Jim.

'Keep focused, Jim. One day, we're going to end up with so many in the traps that it's only a question of time before the bubble bursts and the floodgates open. Work with one of your sergeants, if you can, and come up with a list of good interviewers for me. I'm thinking of bringing a couple of lead interviewers into the squad so that I can brief them on the job ahead. They can dissect the evidence so far and be ready to go when the job goes down. I'm not throwing them in cold. I want them fully briefed and up to date. If they've got questions that they want answering set up a meeting and we'll progress it from there. I don't want to lose this case because of something we missed.'

'My sergeants tell me everything is going well so far, sir,' replied Jim. 'I'd use Robbo, Brian and Lilly as interviewers. I'll prepare copy files for them. I'm just pleased we've got the Regional Crime Squads involved. You never know where we're going to end up.'

'And yourself?' inquired Elliott.

'I'm covering the northern route out of Kendal towards Carlisle,' explained Jim. 'One of the team will be picking me up shortly.'

'Good!' ventured Elliott. 'I wonder how Maguire is getting on?'

The two detectives approached a map on the wall and Jim traced his finger from Kendal to Forton Services on the M6, and then south deeper into Lancashire.

In the Saloon, Bobby Nelson had sat with his men, given them routes and addresses, and watched them go.

Once outside the pub, Stan Holliday had photographed them on the cameras and passed each target onto a separate surveillance team. Foot surveillance officers moved in, identified the relevant vehicles that were being used by the suspects to travel in, and then joined their team as a significant surveillance operation took off. The most difficult part of the pick-up for the teams was latching onto the targets as they left town. Most went north or south whilst others went east. No-one travelled west and the pick-up relied entirely on the teams spotting a target vehicle leaving Kendal once a foot surveillance officer had reported the 'off', and the direction of travel.

Luck? Or judgement? That day the team enjoyed a one hundred per cent lift off. Probably because they knew the roads like the back of their hand.

Inside the Saloon, the clack of pool balls continued as the lounge bar grew quieter when the gang members left. Only Bobby Nelson and Smudger Murray remained but the pair left once they had finished their lunch.

Again, Rod and Barney noticed that no money changed hands and the details were recorded in Rooney's book beneath the bar.

The game ended. Barney nodded to Rod who made his way to the bar where he ordered more drinks from the barmaid.

'Gloria! Two more lagers please and one for yourself. You just had your hair done?'

'How did you guess?' replied Gloria stroking her dark brown hair before reaching for two clean glasses.

'Habit,' chuckled Rod. 'My older sister is a hairdresser, so I've been brought up on the smell of fresh shampoo and conditioner as well as the fluffiness of well-kept curly hair.'

'Oh my God,' laughed Gloria. 'Are you sure she's a hairdresser? Your description makes me think she might be a coal miner.'

'Can I borrow a pen for a second,' shouted Barney from further along the bar. Barney reached over the bar and pointed.

'Help yourself,' remarked Gloria.

'Don't interrupt, Barney,' yelled Rod. 'I'm trying to get a job as a hairdresser.'

'That'll be the day,' returned Barney. 'You haven't even got a comb.'

Quickly reaching over the bar, the detective saw a pen lying on top of Rooney's book. He snaffled both articles and made his way to the toilets. Once alone, Barney flicked through the book and realised that every order recorded in the pages had been made by gang members and no-one else. Each gang member had their section. Page by page, Barney read through

Rooney's notes. Eventually, he backtracked to the point where the pages had been scored by a pen which made an X on the page from corner to corner. Barney surmised that the X was an indication that all the orders to that point had been paid. He based this opinion in the knowledge that pages in the notebook since the beginning of the month still did not bear the X mark. Someone clears the account for all these people at the end of the month only, thought Barney. Adding up the previous month's pages, Barney reckoned the total of the expenditure of the eight persons recorded therein – Tango Zero One to Tango Zero Eight – was in the region of £7,500 per month.

Astonished at his find, Barney pocketed the book and decided to return it to the bar.

Note to self, he thought. When search warrants are executed remember to seize this from behind the bar. Taking it now will only lead to a witch hunt amongst the gang and within the bar staff. Rooney might panic or become suspicious if it goes missing. It indicates that the entire gang know each other, are connected, and are associated with the bar and George Rooney. If the Chief Superintendent is out to prove a conspiracy, then this is another piece of the jigsaw that proves regular association. But what drives Rooney to allow them to run up such a huge bill? Okay, he's going to get his money every month from the gang, but he surely has a ton of other bills to pay as well. What else is there to connect Rooney to the gang?

The sound of a creaking metal door invaded Barney's ears. He moved to the toilet window which was ajar and peeped out. There, in the rear yard of the Saloon, he watched George Rooney open a garage door and enter the detached building. The sound of a barrel scraping and rolling on the concrete floor inspired Barney to move closer to the window.

Rooney rolled a keg out of the garage and remarked, 'Here's the first.'

Smudger Murray and Bobby Nelson appeared in Barney's limited vision. They lifted the keg and placed it into the rear of a Transit van that Barney had not seen before.

Rooney returned to the garage and reappeared with another keg which was also lifted into the back of the Transit.

Barney stood his ground, managed to get a good view through the slightly open window, and watched the three men load the Transit van with six kegs.

Full kegs of beer, wondered Barney? Or empty kegs? Either way, those kegs have got something inside them. One man can haul an empty keg that size and lift it into the van. Those kegs needed two men to lift them.

There was a metallic click when a thin chain was passed through the rear door handles and a padlocked closed.

That seals it, thought Barney. You wouldn't lock a van containing empty kegs. There's something of value inside the rear compartment of the van. Money? Hard cash?

Every day, Rod and I watch the comings and goings in the corner booth, but we don't know and cannot see what goes on in there, thought Barney. We can only identify the players moving in and out of the plot. Are they doing visits to take orders and deliver cash payment from their various sorties into the countryside to the gang leaders? Or are the kegs filled with drugs, thought Barney. It wouldn't take much to remove the bung from the top of the keg and fill it with something else. No, drugs can't be right. The mystery man – Wayne – is alleged to be involved in importing drugs so if the briefing, and intelligence reports used to formulate the brief, are correct, they can't be moving kegs of drugs from the pub outhouse to the suppliers. Half a dozen kegs could carry millions of pounds worth of uncut heroin, for example, thought Barney. Or are they moving counterfeit cash around? Our briefing notes mentioned counterfeit cash but there's never been any sign of funny money in the Saloon. This needs to be bottomed out, he thought.

Rooney slammed shut the garage door, locked it, and made towards his private quarters.

An engine burst into life and Smudger and Bobby reversed the transit out of the cramped yard and into the street which led towards one of the main arterial highways relevant to the town.

Barney rushed into the bar, returned the notebook and pen to its original place, and shouted to Rod, 'Back in five minutes. I need to make a call. We might have a job interview soon.'

Initially confused, Rod nodded his understanding but wore a mask of confusion at Barney's sudden departure. Part of him wanted to shout, 'What's going on,' another part of him told him to stand fast and stick to the brief.

'Got any pickled eggs?' inquired Rod.

The barmaid replied, 'Only for amateur barbers.'

She turned to a shelf behind the optics and reached for a jar as the front door closed behind Barney.

Stan Holliday caught sight of Barney through his binoculars as soon as the detective set foot outside the Saloon. He stood up and reached for his 'phone unsurprised that an incoming call was from the very detective he was watching walking along the footpath at the front of the Saloon.

'Back yard, Stan,' snapped Barney. 'A dark grey Transit van driven by Smudger. Passenger is Bobby Nelson. The two men loaded the van with six beer kegs and then padlocked the back door. They reversed into the main traffic flow. Direction of travel not known! I'll say the kegs contain either drugs or cash. Not beer. This needs bottomed out. Rooney has his finger in the pie. This might go towards proving it or otherwise.'

'Got that,' replied Stan. 'Good shout! Leave it with me.'

Barney stepped into a doorway, closed his 'phone, and thought his end of day intelligence report might be a little longer than usual, and certainly more interesting for the readers.

Stan checked his map of who was assigned to cover which area. He engaged the wireless system. and radioed, 'Trafford One! Respond!'

'Trafford One receiving,' came the reply.

'Deploy to the rear of the Saloon Bar and locate a Grey Transit van leaving the premises by the back lane.'

'I'm on it now,' from Trafford One. 'I'm located as instructed in the car park by the river. The vehicle is reversing out of the yard and waiting to enter the traffic flow. It's held by heavy traffic. Do you want the registration number?'

'Yes! Yes!' from Stan.

'Stand by.'

Brilliant, thought Stan as he recorded a registration number. Just what we need.

Detective Constable Mark Kenyon of the Regional Crime Squad, Manchester Branch, was the rider of a black BMW 750cc motorcycle with the surveillance handle Trafford One. Mark watched a Grey Transit van negotiate the traffic and travel south. He fastened his helmet, donned his gloves, and radioed, 'Trafford One has the target following at one hundred yards plus south towards the A65 – A6 junction in Aynam Road. There's no deviation. Stand by! Nearside lane of two. The target has taken the A65 south towards the M6 motorway. Instructions please!'

'Follow and await further instructions,' replied Stan who picked up a telephone and rang Chief Superintendent Elliott. 'Sir, we have an unexpected development regarding a van load of beer kegs being moved by the gang out of Kendal. The vehicle is registered to the licensee, George Rooney, but he's not driving it. He appears to have loaned the van to Smudger Murray and Bobby Nelson.'

Elliott listened to Stan's tale and replied, 'Interesting! Might be dumping rubbish or might lead us somewhere. Keep me posted. Meanwhile, if the van leaves Kendal, divert the Manchester officers from their static positions and tell them to follow the Transit. No-one moves empty kegs when the brewery collect them every week. Stick with it.'

'Done!' snapped Stan closing the 'phone down.

'Trafford One,' radioed Stan. 'Current location?'

'A65 south from Kendal. Oxenholme to the nearside! Natland to the offside. Speed five zero. No deviation.'

'I have that,' replied Stan who then checked his team display and began diverting others to assist the detective.

'Trafford One, continue surveillance. Trafford team travelling to assist you. Understood?'

'All received,' replied Trafford One. 'No deviation, one hundred yards plus behind. Visibility is good. Halfpenny Corner approaching the village of Endmoor on the A65.'

The motorcyclist continued to broadcast developments as Stan threaded a new surveillance team together.

'Through Endmoor,' radioed Trafford one.

A couple of minutes later a new voice burst onto the net when a voice declared, 'This is Trafford Two. I have the eyeball at Farleton Interchange. The subject has taken the M6 south towards Lancaster. Trafford One adopt Tail End Charlie, I have control.'

'Trafford One acknowledged. Moving into back up position awaiting convoy coming through.'

Stan updated his map of the teams, noted they were all variously travelling north, east, west, and south, and then emailed the Chief Superintendent with an update of everything that had occurred in the last few hours.

In the Saloon, Barney strolled to the bar, collected his pint, and asked the barmaid for two sets of darts.

'Game on?' inquired Rod.

'You can say that again,' replied Barney. 'Bullseye?'

'Five hundred and one?' suggested Rod. 'Nearest to the bull starts?'

Both detectives moved to the darts board to begin their game. It was as if they had learnt a new art form by using a skilful play on words. Now they closed together with a set of darts each as Barney casually took his time to update his colleague.

'I'd rather be involved than playing darts,' suggested Barney.

'There's always another day,' replied Rod. 'I wonder where everyone is now?'

~

11

An hour later, that day.
Merseyside

Maguire and his surveillance team – Red Alpha - were down the M6, through Preston, Penwortham, Tarleton, Southport, and Formby, and headed for Crosby. They were on the outskirts of Liverpool when the Merseyside Serious Crime Squad squawked their presence on the multi-channel encrypted surveillance radio.

The convoy was now two teams deep as they entered Crosby.

'Merseyside Boss Car calling Cumbria convoy commander,' over the radio.

Maguire replied, 'Red Alpha One and team moving through Crosby towards a housing estate. Stand by for location update.'

'Merseyside Boss Car, I am callsign Mersey One. Confirm the target vehicle is a dark blue Volvo estate.'

'Confirmed!' reported Maguire.

'It has just travelled right across my bows at the crossroads. I have an eyeball. Peel off.'

'Wilco,' from Maguire.

Never worked with them before, thought Maguire. I sure as hell hope I can trust them otherwise I've just made the biggest mistake in my career to date. Damn this job, it's all about trust.

'Mersey One to Mersey's team. Stop! Stop! Stop! The target has pulled up outside the premises of a known local target to Merseyside. Mersey Two, three and four, deploy foot surveillance. Mersey five come through and activate video on the target location.'

'Mersey Five to Mersey One,' on the net. 'Confirm the subject vehicle and occupants are visiting our squad target coded Ice Cube? I say again, are we plotting at the Ice Cube address?'

'Confirmed,' from Mersey One. 'Video coverage, please. Foot officers to plot the interior. Look out for associates to Ice Cube. Acknowledge.'

The airwaves were full of surveillance talk before the Merseyside Commander radioed, 'Mersey One to Red Alpha One, deploy to the lay-by opposite the church. Understood?'

'Will do,' replied Maguire. 'Cumbria unit break off and take refreshment. Maintain radio contact.'

About five minutes later, Maguire found himself shaking hands with Detective Inspector Andy Bryant who was head of the Merseyside Serious Crime Surveillance Squad, Callsign Mersey One. Of average height and build, Andy wore a cap that hid a mop of unkempt dark brown hair as well as a grey top and denim jeans. The detective also spoke in a strong scouse accent.

Leaning against the rear of his car, Maguire listened to Andy explain what had happened.

'Good shout, Maguire! Stan Holliday faxed me details of the operation,' revealed the Merseyside man who adjusted his earpiece as he listened to the commentary from the team. 'Your Tangos have stopped outside the home of one of our target criminals. How did you know they were coming to the Liverpool area?'

'I didn't,' replied Maguire. 'When we entered Lancashire, I telephoned their HQ as a matter of courtesy in case we needed a swift contact with them. When our target turned off for Southport, I reckoned they were headed into Scouse land.'

'You mean Everton land.'

'No, I mean Anfield land,' replied Maguire with a wry smile. 'I'm a Liverpool supporter.'

'Well, that's us off to a good start,' chuckled Andy. 'Red or blue and you turn out to be red. I'm an Evertonian.'

'Yes, but I wear the blue,' voiced Maguire.

Andy Bryant shook his head and inquired, 'Any problems on the way down or are you still clean?'

'Pretty sure they don't know we've been following them,' explained Maguire,

'Okay! That's good to know!'

'Why? What's the story at this Ice Cube address?' queried Maguire.

'Ice Cube is the licensee of the local pub and has long been suspected by us of being involved in the drugs business. Have your people just delivered a car loaded with class A drugs to that pub?'

'Pub!' snapped Maguire. 'You mean you've plotted up on our targets who have gone into a pub where your target lives. Did I hear you right?'

'Yep! You sure did. Ice Cube lives in a pub. He's the licensee of the Lantern. Now we have them surrounded like rats in a trap and the common denominators are pubs and drugs. This is a great opportunity for us. It looks like your targets may be doing business with ours. Have they just dropped a delivery right into their laps? We have them bang to rights. I'll ring Headquarters, lock down the area, close the roads, get a warrant, and hit them within the next hour. It must be Christmas.'

'No!' snapped Maguire. 'It's not Christmas and this isn't a present from a Liverpool supporter to an Everton supporter. I say sit tight and watch what happens. We're building a conspiracy case, not a case for one strike and you're out. Sorry, but that's a step too far for me.'

'But we have them there,' challenged Andy. 'I'm the DI and you're a DC still wet behind the ears. Are you annoyed because they're ripe for picking and it's not on your patch? They're ours for the taking and I'll take command.'

'It's my case. The buck stops with me,' challenged Maguire. 'In an hour we could be with this lot headed back north into Yorkshire, Durham or who knows where. You won't be with us then, will you? The target always sets the pace. Not us. I'm ground commander and surveillance commander and I'm not wet behind the ears. Just damp! I suggest you're playing a guessing game,' argued Maguire.

'Really?' argued Andy.

'Your guess as to what is happening is as good as mine,' proposed Maguire. 'I'll deploy a couple of my officers and have them walk around the back of the pub. The Lantern, you said. Well, let's see if it lights the way for me. I'd like to know whereabouts the Volvo is and what the occupants are doing. If you've got a problem with me speak with your Head of CID. I'm sure he'll know my boss's number. It's a club you know.'

'Okay! Okay!' snapped Andy. 'Just testing. I wanted to see if you were having a day out by the seaside with the boys or were really onto something. Point taken. It's your surveillance team. It's my patch. Now, let's move on and get the job done.'

'Fine!' replied Maguire. 'Indeed, excellent! And some of my boys are girls.'

Andy squared his cap away again and held his hand up for a moment and replied, 'Same here.' He stepped away, engaged his radio, and waited for a reply.

Folding his arms, Maguire remained settled as he leaned against his vehicle.

'Sit tight, Maguire. I'll have answers for you shortly. Just remember this is not your turf.'

Maguire nodded but did not reply.

'How strong is the case, the intelligence, your gut feeling? Why are you planning not to take them down today?' contended Andy.

'We're building a complex case and they are part of it,' explained Maguire. 'Can I ask what involvement your Ice Cube has in the drugs world?'

'Major distribution in the North West,' revealed Andy.

'Street level?' probed Maguire.

'That depends on who you talk to and who talks to us,' replied Andy. 'The intelligence we have comes and goes like daybreak. Three times we've raided the place following tip-offs and three times we've walked away with our tail between our legs.'

'The cupboard was bare?' suggested Maguire.

'Correct!' nodded Andy. 'We could sit all day and all night and pop off the odd street dealer coming and going, and we have in the past, but our objective has always been to climb the ladder to get at the top people. If the intelligence is right, then the pub is a hub of activity concerning drugs. Our problem is that knowing and proving are two different things. We're convinced it's a focal point for ordering from the main suppliers in the area. A face to face meeting is more secure than a telephone call. Some of our informants have told us it's a communications network. Everything is arranged here but nothing ever arrives here. Does that make sense to you?'

'Yes, it does,' revealed Maguire. 'Our place is similar. Clean as a whistle if you're searching for drugs but connected in some way to a big supplier. It's a mystery to us if the truth is told.'

'They've got it sewn tight,' explained Andy. 'Have you tried a 'phone tap?'

'Yes! Nothing to report,' admitted Maguire. 'And we don't want to deploy covert cameras inside. It's cleaned daily and too risky given that it's one of the biggest bars in town. Why blow a good job when time is on our side? Am I right in thinking you've put foot soldiers inside The Lantern?'

'Yes, I have,' replied the Scouser. 'I'm expecting an update shortly. That's why I'm holding the 'phone to my ear waiting for a reply.'

'Yeah! Sorry! Maybe we should start again?'

'Too late! Look, Maguire, the pub has three different bars and a room just for darts, dominoes, snooker, and pool. I think there's even a skittle table there. Anyway, it's one of the biggest venues in the area and holds about one thousand people when it's full. My team in there are not from around here but they are regular visitors. I reckon they'll come back with a list of names of people they know in there but that's about all.'

'In the bars, you say?'

'Yes, why?' probed Andy.

Maguire studied the ground, eyed his scuffed shoes, and then replied, 'I wonder.'

'About what?' queried Andy.

'Does the name Richard Arthur Wayne ring any bells?' probed Maguire.

'No! I recall an enquiry from Cumbria recently about a Wayne but the one we have a file on is half a page long. Name only, not even an address. He's not in the game here as far as we know.'

'Interesting,' offered Maguire. 'Do you have a photograph of him?'

'No! Why?'

'I think it's the name of the man in charge of this racket,' declared Maguire.

'Based on what evidence?' probed Andy.

'Intelligence only at this stage,' replied Maguire.

'For what it's worth, the licensee here is called Walter King. He's Wally to everyone who knows him.'

'I take it he's Ice Cube,' inquired Maguire.

'That's right. So-called because he's as cool as a cucumber,' explained Andy. 'Excuse me a moment.'

Stepping away slightly, Andy pressed his earpiece a little tighter, listened, and then said, 'Well, would you believe it! One of my ladies is in the lounge bar. She's got an eyeball on Wally, the Ice Cube, and he's sat in his usual position near the front window.'

'Who with?' inquired Maguire.

'Your two targets,' revealed Andy who was still listening to the radio commentary in his earpiece. 'They're having a drink and they've ordered a meal. My lady has just been joined by a male member of our team. Looks like they've settled in for the afternoon.'

'Has your video man captured a picture of the three of them together?'

Andy held his hand for a moment, listened to the radio transmissions, and replied, 'Yes! They have them on camera from outside and under visible contact from inside.'

'Anyone unusual in there?' probed Maguire. 'Do you have a gathering of locals or just three guys sat in the corner eating and drinking?'

'Nothing unusual to report,' remarked Andy. 'What's on your mind?'

'The local library!' revealed Maguire. 'Directions please.'

'About two hundred yards away,' pointed Andy. 'Walking distance! What do you need a book for?'

'The electoral roll for Crosby,' replied Maguire.

Nodding, but then shaking his head, Andy Bryant pointed to a building further down the road and said, 'Good luck with that then. Keep in radio contact.'

Acknowledging the information, Maguire touched base with his team on the radio and learnt they were all eating on the hoof. Not a bad idea, he thought, and promptly joined them for food and a telephone update from Stan Holliday. He soon found out they weren't the only surveillance team working that had come out of Kendal that day and asked Stan to keep him posted about the movement of the van from the rear of the Saloon.

Shortly thereafter, he parked his squad car near the library and found the reference area. Asking for a copy of the electoral register, Maguire accepted one large tome, found a vacant table, and began to leaf through the book for information.

Page by page, Maguire searched for the name Richard Arthur Wayne. There was no trace, and he returned the register to the reception desk.

'Did you find what you were looking for?' inquired the receptionist.

'No!' replied Maguire. 'It's just an old friend I'm trying to trace. I thought he might still live in Crosby but I've no address for him.'

'Have you thought about going through the local newspaper archives?' suggested the receptionist. 'They're all on micro-fiche now but there's a free viewing machine over there if you're interested.'

'I didn't think of that, thank you,' replied Maguire. 'I'll give it a go.'

Maguire sat down and activated the screen. He quickly found the Crosby Herald and began flicking the mechanism on the control pad. With one hand he continued to activate the machine and scanned the records whilst, with the other, he unwrapped a toffee and popped it into his mouth.

The bag of toffees did not last long and by the time Maguire reached the last one, he was growing tired of searching for the suspect's name.

Suddenly, it was there.

Zooming in on the article, Maguire read how the driver of an articulated heavy goods wagon had followed the satellite navigation system in his vehicle and ended up in the wrong street. The driver had stopped, realised his mistake, and then reversed out of the street and back onto the main road. In so doing, the trailer unit of the wagon collided with a wall that bordered a house. Reading on, Maguire noted the address in Lower Warren Road, Crosby. More importantly, and excitedly, Maguire realised that the house belonged to one Richard Arthur Wayne. The news article was nine years old which explained why the image of Richard Arthur Wayne was not as clear as he would have liked. Nevertheless, Wayne's photograph was on the inside pages of the Crosby Herald and showed a tall slender man standing with his left foot resting on a wall that bordered the front garden of his residence. Wayne looked angry and annoyed at the accidental damage that had been done to the brickwork.

Maguire printed off the article and photograph.

Skipping to the electoral register once more, Maguire flicked through to Lower Warren Road and noted the name of the present occupants to be John Alfred Laidlaw and Katherine Anne Laidlaw. He scribbled the details down in his notebook, thanked the receptionist, and made his way out of the library.

Five minutes later, Maguire parked outside the Laidlaw house in Lower Warren Road. At first, he wondered if he should approach the people living in the house. Were they friends of Wayne? Did they know him and were they part of the complicated conspiracy the police were investigating? Or should he do nothing and see where the current surveillance operation would take them, and what they might learn from their escapade?

Damn it, thought Maguire. I've come this far. Do it!

Maguire knocked on the door and told the occupants he was looking for an old school chum by the name of Ricky Wayne whom he had not seen for over twenty years. Eager to assist, the present occupants told Maguire that they had bought the house from Richard Arthur Wayne some eight years ago. He was a single man whom they only met a couple of times during the process of house purchase. They knew nothing of the news article that Maguire showed them, but they confirmed that the man in the photograph was the man they had bought the house from.

'Do you know where he lives now?' asked Maguire.

'No!' explained Mr Laidlaw, the householder. 'You could ask them in the pub up beside the park. He used to work there as I recall.'

'The Lantern?' probed Maguire.

'Yes, that's the one,' came the reply.

'Was he the licensee?' probed Maguire.

'Oh no! He was a barman,' explained Mr Laidlaw. 'A chap called Wally something or other is the licensee there now. To be honest, we seldom go to the pub. Not our scene. Anyway, your school pal told us he was going to live down south somewhere. Yes, that's right. London, I think it was. He had a French girlfriend if I remember right. Can't remember her name.'

'You've been a big help, Mr and Mrs Laidlaw,' explained Maguire. 'Which estate agent acted for you. I'll give them a ring. They might still have a record of the sale.'

'Cooper, Pratt and Higgins Estate Agents,' replied Mrs Laidlaw.

Armed with more details, Maguire bid farewell, got back into his car, and telephoned the estate agents. He introduced himself properly, told them he was engaged in a criminal enquiry and asked his questions. Luckily, there was still a record of the property transaction. Wayne had left Crosby following the sale of his house in Lower Warren Street and had moved to London. However, as the estate agent explained, their subsequent letters to Wayne had all been returned. They had lost contact once the property had been registered correctly and all the finances were sorted out. The address given was a derelict block of flats in East London. It was an accommodation address and had since been demolished to make way for new housing development in the area.

Maguire had identified Wayne but was no nearer to locating his address.

Engaging his mobile, Maguire 'phoned Chief Superintendent Elliott and updated him as to his latest discovery concerning the mystery man that was Wayne.

The Cumbrian detective fired the engine and drove back to the surveillance plot where he learnt from Andy's team that Jawbone and Colin had entered a garage at the rear of the Lantern pub where, with the assistance of the licensee, Wally, a single beer keg was hoisted into the rear of the Volvo estate. Wally covered the keg with a grey blanket, secured the garage, and re-entered the pub.

'Fuel up,' ordered Maguire. 'Tyres, oil, petrol, diesel, whatever. Quick as you can while the locals have got the watch.'

As the team queued to refuel, Maguire flicked through the pages of a road atlas and tried to get to grips with the road system that enveloped the region.

Half an hour went by before Wally emerged from the rear door of the Lantern. He was carrying a dark brown holdall which he threw into the rear compartment. He took a seat behind the driver and passenger. The engine fired. They were on the move again.

The Volvo containing the three targets casually drove out of the private area of the Lantern, entered the estate roads of Crosby, and made towards the M58. A short time later near Wigan, the vehicle, followed by two surveillance teams, joined the M6 motorway and travelled south.

An hour and a half later, Maguire took a 'phone call from Stan Holliday and learnt that the Manchester surveillance team using the callsign Trafford were following Bobby Nelson and Smudger Murray south on the M6. A quick look at the map quickly switched Maguire onto the fact that everyone was travelling in the same direction and were separated only by a mile or two. Three surveillance teams made up of officers from Cumbria, Merseyside and Manchester were now engaged on the operation.

Maguire requested a new encrypted surveillance channel and 'phoned the commanders when to change to the new channel.

For a moment it seemed ludicrous twenty officers from three surveillance teams were following five suspects who were in two vehicles on the same motorway. The surveillance vehicles consisted of two motorbikes, a black taxi, a minibus, and a squad of variously coloured saloon cars. Yet none of the surveillance teams was at full strength because Maguire and company knew that the job was stretched out across the country on a piece of elastic that was in danger of snapping at any moment.

Somewhere in the convoy, Carol drove her Berlingo which felt hot and stuffy. She reached across to the controls intent on switching off the heater. It was at that precise moment she felt the bump-bump of the vehicle tyres as they crossed the cats eyes that separated the southbound carriageway from the hard shoulder.

Tired, she yawned, unaware that her vehicle was gradually drifting further to the nearside and a steep embankment that held only terror for the unwary.

A wagon driver blared his horn.

Carol's head shot up. Realising that she was inches from disaster, she swung the van back onto the main carriageway, wound the window down, and waved the lorry driver through as she returned to the living.

Delving into the dashboard, Carol pulled out an energy bar and a squeezy drink as she regained her composure and snatched a bite to eat. Fatigue was setting in.

In a vacant room at police headquarters, Penrith, Detective Chief Superintendent Elliott, and Detective Sergeant Stan Holliday stood handing out briefing packages and jobs to be done as a squad of detectives filtered in and finalised the completion of a fully manned incident room. The operation had grown so quickly that it had caught everyone off guard. Hastily put together, an array of computers now formed a local network whilst two standalone computers gave access to authorised personnel to the intelligence systems for the north-west of England. Each desk was equipped with a telephone and staff dealing with enquiries as they came into being.

The image of Richard Arthur Wayne was pinned in the centre of a whiteboard. Beneath his image, the surveillance code Tango Zero Zero was written next to his name. Radiating from Wayne's photograph several arrows pointed to images of the other gang members variously referred to as Tango Zero One to Tango Zero Eight. Each relevant surveillance code was written next to a name.

Stan approached the board and added a photograph of Walter 'Wally' King who had been credited with the code Tango Zero Nine.

Elliott looked over Stan's shoulder and said, 'More photographs on their way by fax from various forces where other sightings and connections have been made. I sure hope we don't run out of staff.'

Pointing to a map on the wall, Stan suggested, 'We're stretched to breaking point, sir. We've got Jim Latimer's team in Edinburgh feeding photographs and information to us, another team in Glasgow, one in Newcastle, one on Sheffield, and one in Leeds. They're all sending us images of new people that our targets are meeting. It's always a pub, a licensee, a connection to a pub, and a beer keg or two. The squad here are working on positively identifying these new suspects from the information we are receiving from the surveillance teams. We're checking photographs, addresses, vehicle registration, known associates, and everything you can imagine. The drum is well and truly being turned'

'Good! Exactly what we need!'

'Then we've got Maguire, the Trafford team from Manchester, and the Mersey team from Merseyside all on the M6 headed south towards Birmingham,' sighed Stan. 'God knows where they will end up.'

'Birmingham?' queried Elliott

'Possibly,' admitted Stan. 'Maybe London, who knows?'

'Practically, Stan, what's the biggest problem facing the surveillance teams? Particularly Maguire and Mark Kenyon from the Manchester team.'

'Running out of fuel,' replied Stan. 'Followed by fatigue. It's not just driving a car. It's about keeping the brain being alive to anything that might suddenly happen. Even when you're parked up, you're still listening to the radio, and still engaged. We've halved the teams everywhere so that we can cover all the targets. As a result, the coverage is good, but fewer vehicles mean they have more to do and once they leave the motorway systems it will be harder for them to keep an eye on their targets. I just hope they manage to keep their tanks topped up.'

'Suggestions?'

'Activate more surveillance teams from selected Regional Crime Squads.'

'The Midlands, the North East and the South seem to be the obvious ones,' stated Elliott.

'Do we have a choice?' remarked Stan.

'Leave that with me,' replied Elliott. 'I'll call the Air Support Wing too. Surely we can snaffle a helicopter from somewhere to help in the surveillance.'

'Let's hope so,' nodded Stan.

'Correct me if I'm wrong, my friend,' suggested Elliott. 'But am I right in thinking every member of the gang that we know of is out of Kendal and on business somewhere in the UK?'

'Yes, for the first and only time that we've known of since the beginning of our surveillance operation,' replied Stan.

'They're certainly not delivering drugs,' proposed the Chief of Detectives as he considered the problem before him. 'Lager or real ale?'

'Stolen property, I'd say,' revealed Stan. 'Thinking back to the Sapphire reports, the informant was involved in jewellery thefts. We just might be following a ton of stolen gold and silver from a score of burglaries by gang members and their associates. It's a new can of worms.'

'Or trinkets,' chuckled Elliott.

'Could be counterfeit cash,' suggested Stan. 'That's one of the other things Sapphire mentioned. Come to think of it, that was his last run. Funny money to Glasgow.'

'Absolutely!' replied Elliott. 'I think you hit the nail on the head, Stan. I'd say they were moving counterfeit cash and stolen jewellery from gang collection points to a location where everything is accepted, re-sold, melted down, or exported out of the UK. Look at the map. This gang is all over the place collecting beer kegs. The surveillance teams are picking up on the targets visiting licensees all over the country. If each licensee is giving them a keg of jewellery or funny money instead of beer, then a whole can of worms is about to explode onto the carpet. And it's happening right before our eyes. Thinking back to the beginning, I recall an intelligence report from Sapphire. It was one of many submitted by Maguire. One of their first meetings resulted in a report which stated that Sapphire thought the gang numbered forty to fifty although the source was only switched on to a dozen or so local members. It's beginning to look like Sapphire was right from day one.'

'I think you've just got your conspiracy,' suggested Stan. 'Every licensee mentioned by the surveillance teams is being looked into in this incident room. Criminal records, personal history, employment history, intelligence database history, anything, whatever! They're hard at work on the 'phones. Same with car numbers. Who owns what and for how long? Vehicle history relevant to previous owners. The story is building all the time, sir. We've already discovered that a car once owned by Walter King from the Lantern is now in the possession of a licensee from Newcastle who recently loaded a beer keg into one of the vehicles belonging to the gang we're following. Right now, that might not seem important, but it proves historic contact and is a tiny piece of evidence in a great big plot. Everyone involved seems to know everyone else. It's a conspiracy alright, but only if those kegs hold jewellery and counterfeit currency.'

'I am seldom wrong,' chuckled Elliott. 'It just feels right, Stan. I think I need to speak to the Chief Constable and upgrade our operation even further. I'd like him to speak to other Chiefs and tell them our Indians might be encroaching on their patch. The other thing going through my mind is the money. How long has this been going on? How much counterfeit cash is involved? Enough to unsettle the true value of the pound. I don't know but the Treasury Department in London will, and they might need to be appraised of this. I think we've moved away from the normality of localised policing to another level. If this isn't challenged and dealt with, our currency value might drop like a stone overnight. There could be a million pounds worth of funny money in circulation for all we know.'

'Too much for me to take in, sir,' replied Stan. 'You make the call. I'll put the kettle on and find a bottle of brandy. I sure as hell need one because I know sweet nothing about funny money and the value of the pound. That reminds me.'

'What?' queried Elliott.

'Economics! Well, not so much economics and the value of the pound. More about me needing to buy a lottery ticket for the weekend. I'd like to be a millionaire if possible.'

Shaking his head, Elliott laughed and replied, 'Save the brandy! Put the kettle on, Stan. Oh, that reminds me too. Where are Barney and Rod?'

'In respite care, sir. I gave them two days off. Alcoholic poisoning!'

The Chief Superintendent burst out laughing and said, 'So be it. Do they know how important that sighting of the van being loaded with kegs was?'

'Not yet,' replied Stan. 'Let's hope the kegs aren't empty. If they are, we'll look like real numpties.'

The two men moved to the map on the wall where a set of markers radiated out from the Saloon in Kendal to points north, south, and east. The runners and riders were out and about, but this time the jockeys were hard on their heels.

'Red Alpha One reports meeting in progress,' radioed Maguire. 'We have five Tangos on the car park of Hilton Park Services. Two in a grey Transit van and three in a blue Volvo estate. Trafford team refuel, please. Mersey team hang back. Mersey One take the eyeball on the first movement. Cumbria team put your footmen out and cover the restaurant area of the services before they get in there. All teams confirm deployment on Channel Four Six. Channel Four Six is the designated channel for this operation from now on. Stand by.... Stand by.... Maguire with the eyeball, all five Tangos are making their way into the service area on foot. Mersey team take the movement away when needed. Trafford team disperse from the refuelling point once completed. Send three vehicles south on the M6 and precede the suspect vehicles. These Tangos must need fuel by now. Maintain radio contact.'

The next hour was uneventful but confirmed Maguire's belief that the five suspects had a brief meeting over a hot drink in the café and then refuelled before heading south. From relevant silence, surveillance speak dominated the encrypted surveillance channel.

'Trafford One with a reverse eyeball. Seven zero miles per hour with a clear view of the targets to my rear. One hundred and fifty yards behind. M6 southbound. No deviation at the turn off for Walsall. All units acknowledge with convoy position.'

The team responded as the route carved its way between Walsall and Wolverhampton as it headed towards Birmingham.

'Trafford One with a reverse eyeball. Traffic ahead is building significantly suggest Trafford One peels off at the next interchange.'

'Mersey One got that. I am your back up ready to take over. Surveillance commander acknowledge?'

'Red Alpha One is Tail End Charlie three miles behind the eyeball,' from Maguire. 'Acknowledged.'

Moments later, Andy voiced, 'Mersey One has the eyeball. Southbound seven zero miles an hour. The middle lane of three. No deviation.'

The convoy acknowledged as the entourage by-passed Birmingham and headed south on the M6 towards Northampton.

Happy to remain at Tail End Charlie, Maguire listened to the radio and maintained contact with the crew whilst using the handsfree mobile 'phone facility fitted to his vehicle. A call to the mini Incident Room in Penrith informed him that the gang had collected other beer kegs in various parts of the country. In vehicles driven by the gang, the kegs were being taken south towards London. There were two main routes in use, the A1 and the M6.

'Sounds like Rod and Barney may well have connected Rooney to the team,' suggested Maguire. 'Funny books behind the bar and his beer kegs into a van driven by them. Good stuff! The case is building all the time. Anyone called Wayne involved?'

'No! No-one of that name. Your information on him from Crosby remains the lead intelligence.'

'Any information as to what is in the kegs?' asked Maguire.

'Counterfeit cash or stolen jewellery,' came the reply.

'Where did that come from?' probed Maguire.

'The Chief Superintendent! He's worked it all out.'

'I disagree,' replied Maguire. 'I'm sure it's hard cash.'

There was distortion on the 'phone before Chief Superintendent Elliott butted into the conversation and challenged Maguire with, 'What makes you say that?'

'It stands to reason,' argued Maguire. 'Counterfeit cash is more likely to come out of London as opposed to multiple locations situated all over the country. And as for jewellery, well.'

'Well what?' probed Elliott. 'Before you answer, bear in mind that every known gang member is involved today. They're all out. It's game on in a big way. Go on! I'm listening to your argument, Maguire.'

'It's not an argument, sir,' responded Maguire. 'I understand why you've plumped for dud cash and jewellery. That's how it all started with Sapphire. But I don't see hundreds of jewellery thefts every day of the week and there's no sign of dud money hitting our streets in a big way. I think the gang spends its time collecting money every month or so for one big buy. Possibly tens of thousands of pounds, maybe more. A quarter of a million? I don't know but it's collected nationwide. The money is collected from the middlemen, the licensees and regional suppliers who never touch the drugs - they just handle the money – then the cash is delivered to wherever the buy takes place.'

'It would be so much easier to electronically transfer the money to the seller,' contended Elliott. 'Why run around the country with a car full of money when the tap of a button on your keypad will transfer funds from one end of the country to anywhere in the world?'

'Because it leaves a digital trail,' proposed Maguire. 'Just like a mobile 'phone does. If you were moving the money and thought you might be under suspicion then the last thing you would want to do is to leave an electronic map of the where the money came from and where it was going to. Think about it. One reason this man Wayne has remained in the background all these years is that there is only one telephone trace to him on a mobile 'phone from years back. He has no electronic traces anywhere. Don't you see, sir?'

'I'm listening, Les.'

Continuing, Maguire added, 'This gang has been at it so long that they are used to the old-fashioned ways of using hard cash. Me? I'd open a false bank account and do exactly what you've described but once I'm caught, I've no way out. The digital trail at the bank, CCTV, and a mobile 'phone record will deliver me into the hands of the police. I'd say the gang wasn't old-fashioned. They've just moved around in a circle where once it was the norm. Everyone changed but they decided to stick with the old ways. It was working for them so why alter a proven method? I suggest they didn't create this network in a month or two. It's taken them years and, to be precise, what we've seen so far is a bunch of amateur local hoods who made good. The man at the top is the brains who created this network. He's the one who has watched it grow, worked it all out, and decided to stay with the hard cash model. I'd say he was an authoritarian dictator who has an iron grip on his organisation and has the wherewithal to control it from afar. He uses the local hoods as enforcement officers and pays them well for their trouble and their silence. It's the modern way of doing business in the drugs world. The way forward for us is to penetrate their weakness and we can. This gang had been at it so long, they've become almost blasé about how they operate. They consider they're untouchable and undetectable because they've never been taken down. The gang has been right under our noses for years but never massively come to light because Kendal is their base. They do their business from a pub that is dwarfed by many others in the bigger cities, and they've never pushed their product too much in Kendal in case of being fingered. Their boss, this Wayne character, has it all nicely packaged up the way he wants and the way they are used too. The Saloon is so out of the way and trouble-free that it seldom comes to notice. Somewhere in the past, there's a link between Kendal and Wayne but we are nowhere near finding it at the moment. This gang has been at it so long that they've become complacent. That's the weakness we need to exploit. Complacency! We're onto them not because of our expertise but because they've been rumbled by one of their own and a whole can of worms has been spilt all over the carpet.'

'You finished yet, Les?' inquired the Chief Superintendent. 'Or still rambling on in lecture mode?'

'Not quite finished, sir. If you don't mind?' replied Maguire.

Elliott did not reply.

Pushing on, Maguire continued with, 'I think we're headed for London and I want an armed surveillance unit to join us. Whether or not those kegs are laden with jewellery, counterfeit notes, or hard cash, the value is considerable. At the end of the road, I expect to be confronted by someone who doesn't want to come clean. Do you think the gang is taking all this gear down to a little old man sitting in his greenhouse? No, millions are at stake, either way, you look at it because it's been going on for a long time. That means armed protection for the money when it arrives at wherever it's going to. It's no longer a follow and gain evidence for a conspiracy case, Mr Elliott. And it's not a one strike and you're out job anymore. These Tangos are going to take us right into the mouth of the crocodile and our people need protection when we get there and before the jaws snap shut. If the bullets start flying, how do you think my unarmed surveillance teams should respond, sir?'

'I'll get back to you, Maguire,' snapped Elliott.

The 'phone went dead.

Maguire soon realised they had left the M6 and had entered the M1. He closed his call down, made ground on the surveillance convoy, and began to move through the team as he sought to adopt a position closer to the action. Halfway through the convoy, he reduced his speed from ninety miles an hour and slid into a space in front of Bernie.

Hours later, the retinue took the M25, crossed the Queen Elizabeth II Bridge at Dartford and headed into Kent. As the team by-passed London, Maguire's mobile rang.

'One of the Met's armed surveillance unit should be joining you shortly,' advised Chief Superintendent Elliott. 'Callsign Sabre! They are fully briefed. Take care.'

'Will do and thank you,' replied Maguire.

Despite continually changing positions in the convoy, the three teams were tiring following the long drive. Traffic was heavy and as they joined the M2 and headed towards Canterbury, there was little change in the volume of traffic.

Where the hell are we going, wondered Maguire.

'Sabre One making ground from Dartford,' rattled across the airwaves.

'Trafford One has eyeball. Welcome to the party. All five Tangos remain in the same two vehicles following each other.'

'Sabre One at Tail End Charlie. For the information of all units, the air support wing is with us. Callsign India Nine-Nine.'

Before Maguire could reply, the crew in the police helicopter broke radio silence and said, 'India Nine-Nine is above you trying to locate your two Victors. We have an articulated vehicle in sight. The load is covered with a bright orange tarpaulin. Can the eyeball assist at this time? Are the two Victors ahead of the orange sheeting or behind it. Position of Tangos please.'

'Trafford One to India Nine-Nine advance two miles further south of the orange sheeted wagon. We overtook that vehicle a short time ago. You're almost with us. Both Victors are in the centre lane overtaking slower moving traffic.'

During the next five minutes, ground to air networking managed to lock the helicopter onto both the van and the

Volvo estate. The surveillance convoy pulled back from the follow and listened to the helicopter above radioing updates as they moved closer to the south coast. Eventually, the M2 evolved into the A2 and the traffic flow eased slightly.

Things can't get any better, thought Maguire. Trackers deployed on both suspect vehicles, mobile 'phones covered, four surveillance teams and a helicopter. What do we do if they catch the ferry at Dover? Stop, go with them, or 'phone home for advice? Either way, will the ferry be big enough for all of us? What could possibly go wrong at sea?

There was a storm at sea.

They were out of Cartagena, away from Colombia and the Caribbean Sea, and across the North Atlantic Ocean headed for The English Channel and an onward destination to Calais in France. Six thousand three hundred and forty-two nautical miles was the length of the journey to be undertaken. This equated to seven thousand two hundred and ninety-eight land miles in the UK. It was a long way to go and a storm here and there on the route was not the best way to spend a life on the ocean wave.

Captain Jeronimo Garcia stood in the bridge, studied the rising waves ahead of the vessel, and, unafraid, steered directly into the fray.

On the deck before him, and in the cargo hold beneath him, over two hundred and fifty container units held tight as the Atlantic heaved up and down like a bucking bronco.

'Wild one today,' remarked a crew member.

'The Bay of Biscay is notorious for its rough seas and violent storms. Thank God it is behind us and we are in the English Channel. We are north-west of Brest in France and well ahead of schedule. All is well. We will make it. The worst is behind us. Steady as she goes.'

'Aye! Aye! Captain. Steady as she goes.'

The container ship ploughed on through the roaring waves.

~

12

Folkestone – Dover
That day
Kent

Road signs came into view for Dover and the suspects left the motorway system and headed into town.

To the relief of Maguire, the police helicopter reported that both the van and the Volvo had ignored the road down to the harbour and were headed in the direction of Folkestone.

A short time later, the two suspect vehicles turned into an industrial estate and weaved their way towards a collection of warehouses. There was no-one behind the suspects at the time. Both the tracker car driven by Angela and the helicopter above had good coverage of the suspect vehicles.

'All units! Stop! Stop! Stop!' ordered Maguire. 'Clear the highway. Sabre team come through and take closer order.'

'Sabre One wilco. Closing, ETA five minutes.'

'India Nine-Nine reports video coverage ongoing. We see five vehicles parked outside a building on the industrial estate. Stand by for registration numbers...'

The numbers were passed. Maguire noted the details and 'phoned Stan.

'India Nine-Nine reports no bodies with these vehicles. They've gone into the building which is a warehouse lying at the end of the estate next to a field and the countryside. Stand by for details of the exact location.'

'Angela, Red Alpha Five has one of the vehicles on the tracker. Location of the stop is under investigation on my system too. Stand by for details.'

Tired, confused, bombarded with self-imposed questions and puzzles, Maguire grabbed his surveillance map and pinpointed his precise location in the tome-sized atlas of the UK. He seized the opportunity to activate his throat mic and instructed, 'All units, I say again. Stop! Stop! Stop! Give the air to Red Alpha Five and India Nine-Nine.'

'Red Alpha Five has the target on the tracker,' radioed Angela.

'India Nine-Nine copied.'

'Move into covert positions,' from Maguire. 'Clear the highway for all traffic.' He leafed through to the correct page on his mapping system and instructed, 'All team commanders make for rendezvous at page 36 map reference Yankee Three One Nine. Wasteland off the highway at the last roundabout. All units, time to confer. Take five. Hold covert positions out of sight of the highway and remain in radio contact.'

'Skiddaw One to Red Alpha One.'

Maguire instantly recognised the voice of DI Jim Latimer, the head of Cumbria's Force Surveillance Squad and replied, 'Go ahead!'

'We're coming through the plot and circling the site. We have an eyeball on Tango Zero Four who is headed for the same site as the rest of the suspects. I intend to deploy one CROPS officer to the vicinity rear of the target premises in the countryside area. Do you copy?'

Relief swam through Maguire's mind at the news that the experienced and much respected DI Jim Latimer had arrived at the scene having followed one of their suspects from Scotland. Suddenly he had an officer of equal rank to the others with him. His self-confidence grew a foot.

Trying hard not to sound over-enthusiastic, Maguire replied, 'Copied, Skiddaw One! Have you travelled from Edinburgh?'

'Yes! Yes!' came the reply. 'No speech from Skiddaw. CROPS deployment underway.'

Maguire accepted from Jim that he needed to keep quiet as he was engaged in what might be construed as a dangerous operation on the industrial estate. He also knew that CROPS was an acronym for Covert Rural Observation Post and presumed the surveillance team had entered the industrial estate overtly and were in the course of deploying a CROPS officer.

Jim Latimer casually drove into the industrial estate, took a left, and then began to drive around the edge of the estate. He knew he was away from the warehouse that was now at the centre of the operation, but he also knew how valuable a CROPS officer might prove in the circumstances.

'End of the road ahead, Bob,' mouthed Jim. 'I see a hedgerow and fields. We're two hundred yards at least from the rear of the warehouse. Are you ready?'

'On five,' replied Bob. 'You count.'

Jim Latimer reduced speed, took a lower gear, and began to turn to his right to travel parallel to a hedgerow that bordered the estate.

'Five... Four... Three...'

As the car began its slow turn, Bob eased himself across the rear passenger seat and unlocked the nearside passenger door.

'Two...'

Bob opened the door and heaved himself into position as the vehicle reduced speed still further and reached the right angle of its turn.

'One...'

Bob rolled out of the rear passenger seat of the surveillance car, hit the tarmac, and immediately rolled again into the hedgerow.

Jim Latimer increased his speed slightly, finished cornering, and then accelerated down the road and out of the estate. If anyone had been watching, they would not have seen the swift and adroit manoeuvre from the CROPS officer, Detective Constable Bob Martin.

As Jim Latimer departed the estate the slimly built CROPS man, draped in a grey-green camouflage cloak, dragged himself through the hedgerow from the estate and found himself in the green fields of Kent. He padded himself down, checked his monocular and tiny camera were intact and gathered his mind for a moment. Then he hugged the ground, lifted an ear, and heard only the sound of Jim's car gradually leaving the estate. Bob waited a few minutes to allow his hearing to adjust. He'd been in the rear of the squad car long enough to have his hearing unsettled. Blending his senses into the outside world was as important as blending his appearance into the surroundings. Eventually, Bob moved closer to the hedge. From his position, he could see the warehouse. It appeared deserted but he knew from the radio network that the vehicles were parked outside only because their drivers were inside.

Using the ditch next to the hedgerow, Bob Martin made his timely, camouflaged, and stealthy approach to the warehouse. It was as if a part of the field was moving surreptitiously along the side of the hedge. When he reached the best vantage point, the camouflaged man would bury himself deep inside the hedgerow and watch. He would be unseen.

The police helicopter was circling above the industrial estate at an altitude of about two thousand feet. Inside the cockpit, there was a pilot, a navigator, and an air observer. It was the observer who manned the air to ground camera system, thermal image seeker and surveillance radio whilst the rest of the crew concentrated on flight control.

'India Nine-Nine to Red Alpha One,' voiced the air observer. 'Sending a video and still images to your mobile. Stand by.'

Maguire checked his 'phone as a BMW motorbike arrived at his location. It was Trafford One ridden by Mark Kenyon from the Manchester team. He was joined a few minutes later by Andy Bryant from Liverpool and Terry Calder from the Sabre One Met firearms unit. Last to arrive was a smiling Jim Latimer who shook Maguire's hand and said, 'Listen out for Cuckoo One. CROPS deployed.'

'Brilliant,' replied Maguire. 'That will be a big help, Jim. It's your command now that you're here. Just tell me what you want me to do.'

'Carry on!' remarked Jim. 'Just crack on, Les. Alexander the Great has instructed me to let you have your head. I'll speak if I must. It's your case. Make it.'

'Who is Alexander the Great?' inquired the man from Merseyside.

'No worries,' winked Jim. 'My problem, not yours.'

Surprised, nodding, Maguire took a deep breath and made sure his earpiece was well connected to the radio network.

Clustered together, Maguire shared the images from the helicopter as the surveillance commanders held a conference on the next steps to take. As the planning continued, a succession of surveillance convoys swept into the Dover area at an alarming rate.

A collection of buses, taxis, estate cars, motorbikes, blacked-out vans, and ordinary vans trundled towards the Folkestone area and an industrial estate under both aerial and ground surveillance.

Channel four-six was alive with transmissions when the target vehicles travelled to a warehouse on the estate whilst their followers were held back to await instructions. More target vehicles arrived. More surveillance traffic drove through and gradually surrounded the area as a helicopter transmitted the gathering to the officers below.

Fifteen minutes elapsed before Maguire addressed the team with, 'Okay! Just to inform you that Kent police have been informed of our location and the ongoing operation. I expect they'll send a senior detective to meet us shortly. It's their patch. Now, you've seen the aerial videos from India along with the still images. We've also scrutinised the maps, so we know exactly where we are in relation to the industrial estate.' Maguire pointed at the map and said, 'The tracker signal confirms one of our target vehicles is parked outside this warehouse which appears to be the size of an airport hangar.'

'About fifty feet by forty feet or thereabouts,' suggested Terry Calder, as he adjusted his weapons belt. 'Looking at the video from the helicopter it's a sizeable building but unlike an airport hangar, it doesn't have big wide doors. The main doors remind me of a domestic double garage door. This is the main entry point, I suggest. I also see two side doors. There's nothing at the rear where it adjoins a field into the countryside. The other thing I see is the windows above the front doors. They look like office windows and that suggests to me there is a second floor to the building which we can't see. It might, on the other hand, only be a mezzanine floor that does not extend the full width or length of the building.'

'You got enough personnel onboard?' inquired Mark Kenyon. 'Some of my people are trained in firearms although they aren't carrying now.'

'That depends on whether we choose to mount a raid on the premises or wait for them all to come out again. Are we going to arrest them and, if so, for what? How many have we clocked going in there?'

'We've nine of our suspects on the plot,' explained Maguire. 'And a CROPS officer moving into position. As it stands now, Smudger Murray and Bobby Nelson arrived in a Transit van. Jawbone Jones, Colin McArdle and Wally King arrived in a Volvo estate. Our other suspects are Tiny Philpotts, Jeffrey Jackson, Bill Ashworth, and Jed Atkinson. All four of them travelled out from Kendal and went elsewhere to pick up beer kegs and people we presume to be licensees or their riders escorting the kegs. Also, there are ten other suspects in five vehicles. They were all seen collecting beer kegs from licensed premises when they were visited by Philpotts and company. I'm afraid we're still firming up on these identities. Some of them are new to us. In all, we have twenty-three suspects in that warehouse with their vehicles outside and close on forty detectives in the various surveillance convoys. That includes the armed officers from the Met.'

'Some party,' suggested Andy.

'Did anyone bring a cake?' inquired Mark.

'Not enough bodies,' announced Terry. 'If they all have access to firearms or a weapon of some kind, then we need more people. Every one of your suspects has an escort which means the load must be valuable. What do you think they're carrying that's so unique that they bring it down here with an escort in the passenger seat?'

'Cash, I believe,' replied Maguire.

'You believe but you don't know,' challenged Terry Calder. 'Have you ever thought that it might just be bad beer?'

'Which you would take back to the brewery,' proposed Maguire. 'I don't see a brewery on the industrial estate. Do you?'

'Fair point,' came the reply.

'But the truth is we don't know what's in the beer kegs,' remarked Andy. 'A guessing game, as you say. No disrespect but it's a long drive for a day out by the seaside. What have they done that is arrestable and we can prove?'

'Money laundering!' revealed Maguire.

'Conspiracy!' added Jim Latimer.

The sound of an approaching car engine denied any further conversation when a grey Mercedes saloon car pulled onto the wasteland. The driver wound his window down and asked, 'Looks like I found the right place. I'm looking for a Mr Maguire?'

'That's me,' replied the Cumbrian detective stepping forward. 'And you are?'

'Detective Inspector Jack Henderson, Dover CID. My boss told me I had to come to the party. Sorry, I'm late but your Stan Holliday emailed me the operational order so I'm up to speed on the start of things, but not the current situation. What the hell are you all doing on my patch? No-one invited you.'

Henderson opened the car door, laughed, and shook Maguire's hand as he remarked, 'Introduce me! Who's who?'

Maguire did the honours and updated DI Henderson as the newcomer quickly got to grips with the current situation.

'So, it's a bunch of drug dealers who have travelled from the north, stopped here, there and everywhere else, to collect who knows what from who knows who and then brought it here for who knows why?' proposed Henderson.

'Precisely!' remarked Maguire. 'Got it in one.'

'Simple then,' proposed Henderson. 'All we have to do is… err…What's in the kegs?'

There was a mixed reaction of laughter, applause, and shaking heads before a scouse accent penetrated the air with, 'That's the million-pound question, Jack. We've all asked the same question. The answer is guesswork. Drugs! Jewellery! Counterfeit banknotes! Cash! Body parts?'

'I'm told it's your case, Maguire,' challenged Henderson. 'So, the way I read things is that it's your decision unless you have a boss from Cumbria with you who is going to tell me otherwise.'

No-one replied. Jim Latimer remained tight-lipped and winked at Maguire.

'In which case, it's my patch so if the elements of your argument don't add up, I'll withdraw support and you'll be on your own. Understand?'

'I do,' nodded Maguire.

'Good! Now that we understand each other, what do you think is in the kegs?'

'Money!' replied Maguire. 'No disrespect to everyone but none of us know what is in the kegs. We're all in this together because we want it to be money for a drugs buy. That's why you're still here. You all want it to be money, but you're obsessed with evidence as opposed to gut feeling.'

Henderson nodded and said, 'It's a go from me. In some way, it's criminality in action. Let's get to the bottom of it. The only way we'll find that out is by opening the kegs, and that means hitting the warehouse.'

There was a sigh of relief from Maguire when he recognised a voice of support.

Then there was a quiet whistle in Maguire's earpiece when a voice came across the airwaves and said, 'Cuckoo One to Red Alpha One, permission.'

'Go ahead,' replied Maguire raising his hand to silence the group.

On the industrial estate, there was the slightest of movements from a hedgerow situated about fifty yards from the target warehouse when Bob Martin activated his throat mic. Looking through his monocular, Bob radioed, 'Multiple Tangos have emerged from the warehouse and have approached their Victors. Stand by!'

'Shit!' sounded Terry Calder within the group. 'I need to get back to my team.'

'Wait!' instructed Maguire. 'Listen!'

'Cuckoo One with the eyeball. Multiple Tangos are at their Victors and removing beer kegs. Wait! Stand by!'

Maguire stood with his hand raised and said, 'Wait! Listen! Something is going on!'

The group shuffled nervously suddenly derailed by the unexpected movement. They all thought the same. Were the gang moving on? Should they not be with their surveillance teams?

'Cuckoo One with the eyeball. They're taking the kegs inside the warehouse. No movement from the vehicles at all. The Victors remain immobile. One…. Three…. Five…. Wait, still counting…. All kegs now inside the warehouse. Doors closed! No more movement. Over!'

'India Nine-Nine confirms aerial video coverage duplicates report from Cuckoo One,' from the helicopter

'All received,' replied Maguire. 'Maintain watch.'

At a detached bungalow in Levens, a village a few miles south of Kendal, a gloved hand manhandled a short jemmy and attacked a rear door. The windowpane in the door rattled for a moment and the burglar immediately stopped. He did not want the glass to break and only needed to manipulate the lock area of the door. He tried again, forced the door ajar, and then entered the dwelling.

The burglar moved quickly through the house ignoring most of the rooms. It was as if he knew exactly where to look. He wasted no time.

In the hallway, beneath the stairs, the intruder found the safe, turned it around, and applied a longer and stronger jemmy to the rear corner of the metal box. It was leverage he sort from the jemmy, not strength. Like many household safes, the fronts and sides were thick, chunky, and substantial, but they all had two things in common. Firstly, the front of the safe displayed a complex lock that required the insertion of the correct numbers into the device. The correct numbers activated a set of tumblers that fell into the place and allowed the safe to be opened. The housebreaker knew how to force a criminal entry into the building but did not know the correct sequence of numbers to insert into the digital lock to open it. Secondly, the rear of the safe was thinner, often riveted to an interior framework, and was the weakest part of the entire structure.

The rear panel bulged. The front of the safe remained robust. He tried again. This time he inserted the edge of the jemmy deeper into the corner of the rear panelling, manipulated the jemmy, and threw all his weight behind his labours as he wriggled the blunt-edged jemmy into the corner. He'd chosen the broad blunt blade because he knew that a diamond-edged sharp blade would leave a clear impression on the metal. Not so the blunt blade when used correctly.

The rear of the safe gave way slightly, opened, and allowed the thief to infiltrate the cabinet.

Eager fingers delved inside, withdrew a dark coloured hardback book, and then laid it down on the floor. The invader removed a mobile 'phone from his inside coat pocket and began photographing each page of the book. Licking his finger, he turned over a page, took a photograph, flicked to the next page, and continued until he had photographed the entire book. The intruder then returned the book to the safe and replaced the rear panelling, tapped the fixtures back into place with the hindside of the jemmy, and then positioned the safe in precisely the same location as it had been when he had first attacked it. From the front, it looked as if the safe had not been touched. The owner would only know the safe had been tampered with if he turned it around and closely examined the rear of the safe. It was unlikely that the owner would realise his book had been removed from the safe, photographed, and returned intact.

The burglar withdrew and made good his escape.

Climbing onto a pedal cycle, the travelling criminal casually pedalled away without a care in the world. Yet the inside pocket of his three-quarter-length coat carried an ordinary mobile 'phone with a camera facility and no more. The photographs proved the content of one of the most valuable assets in the whole of Cumbria.

On the outskirts of Dover, Bob Martin was still part of the hedge when India Nine-Nine reported they would have to withdraw from the operation to refuel. Shortly thereafter, the skies above were bare. India Nine-Nine was gone from the scene.

'It's a great time to go in,' suggested Jack Henderson. 'I could rustle up some reserves from Dover, Folkestone, Ashford and Canterbury and hit the warehouse in an hour or so's time. We can apply for a search warrant if you wish but I believe that a delay in obtaining that warrant might defeat the ends of justice because the evidence inside the beer kegs might be destroyed or removed if we leave it too long.'

'We're within the law,' proposed Jim Latimer. 'It might take all day to find a magistrate.'

'Agreed!' replied Jack. 'On the other hand, what do we gain by raiding the warehouse? I'd say they were emptying the beer kegs now so we've plenty of time to bring the reinforcements in. They might be on the road again in an hour. What do you think?'

'Do it,' replied Maguire. 'Start the ball rolling and no more. Let's use that hour to get closer to the warehouse. We can position some of our teams on the industrial estate itself, surround the area, bring some uniform cars into the outskirts in preparation, and get a feeling for the landscape.'

'India Nine-Nine might be back with us by then unless they get called somewhere else,' suggested Jim.

'Okay!' decided Maguire. 'As it stands, we will hit the warehouse when the reserves arrive. Just before we strike, we'll close the entrances to the estate down and prevent any escape. Terry, can I suggest you put the plan together regarding the actual entry to the warehouse. You're the firearm's team commander and you'll be first in.'

'The Sabre team will deploy to the estate right away and use the time to decide how we're going to secure the warehouse,' proposed Terry. 'I'll reconnoitre the target. We can strike it hard and fast with a rapid entry or we can sit it out and let them come out one by one. The problem is if they all leave at the same time, we could be snookered. If you can bring some armed officers from your patch, Jack, that would be a big help. The Sabre team will execute the raid supported by a Kent team of armed officers manning the perimeter. Everyone else can encircle the show so that we have two perimeters in action. Does that make sense?'

Jack Henderson was already on his mobile 'phone to his boss. He nodded and stuck his thumb up as the conversation with his supervisor continued.

Maguire glanced at Jim Latimer and asked, 'What do you think? What have we missed?'

'Breakfast, lunch and afternoon tea at the very least,' chuckled Jim. 'And confirmation of aerial support from India Nine-Nine. I'll make a call. I know they're refuelling but if they get tied up, then I'll ask for a reserve to be deployed. It's a big area to cover and if one or more make a break for it when we hit them, we might just lose a few.'

'Okay, Jim, Thanks!' remarked Maguire. 'Stay in radio contact but disperse. Return to your teams and listen out for Sabre One. Terry, put your people in the estate and bring the Mersey team in to scatter but take closer order to the warehouse. The other teams can encircle the plot as discussed.'

There was an acceptance of the way forward before radio silence was broken.

'Cuckoo One to Red Alpha One,' broke the airwaves.

'Go ahead,' replied Maguire.

'Tango Zero One and Tango Zero Eight are out of the warehouse. They are each carrying a hefty looking suitcase. Both suitcases are grey. They're into the Volvo estate. The suitcases are in the rear luggage compartment. The warehouse doors have closed behind them. Stand by!'

'Scatter,' ordered Maguire to the team commanders. 'My team will take this movement. Jack, will you join us. Jim, can you take control here? I have a feeling whatever was in the kegs is now in the suitcase and it's not going far.'

'Will do,' replied Jim as Jack Henderson stole into the passenger seat of Maguire's car. 'You've got Bobby Nelson and Jawbone Jones moving. Take them.'

'Red Alpha One to all teams, stand by for movement. All teams switch to personal channels for orders from your team commanders. Red Alpha One will take the next movement.'

There was a brief silence from the airwaves before Bob Martin broke in with, 'Cuckoo One has the eyeball on the Volvo. The two tangos are on the move travelling away from the warehouse towards the main Dover to Folkestone road. Stand by.'

Whilst the surveillance teams quickly regrouped, Bob felt the tightness of the camouflage cloak around him slacken slightly as moved into a better position where his view would be improved. There was only a slight movement in the dark green hedgerow when Bob continued, 'Cuckoo One has the eyeball. The Volvo has turned left towards Dover.'

'I have them on the Tracker,' reported Angela. 'I am engaged. Towards Dover.'

'They'll cross our bows any minute,' remarked Maguire before radioing. 'Red Alpha team engage. Give them plenty of room. Angela!'

'Angela has them on the tracker. They are approaching the roundabout. Allow then to run free. Stand by.'

The team fired their engines and listened to Angela as she followed the Volvo's journey on the tracking device. It was the same car they had followed from Cumbria and it was still

Jawbone Jones that was driving. The development for the team was that the passenger was Bobby Nelson, and he was thought to be the main man in the Kendal area.

'Red Alpha Five is towards Dover on the A20,' radioed Angela firing her BMW. 'Capel-le-Ferne on the offside. No deviation. I am one mile behind the subject.'

'Where are they headed?' asked Maguire as he gunned his Vauxhall into the convoy.

'I could guess,' replied Jack Henderson. 'But I might be wrong.'

'Red Alpha Five has the eyeball. The targets are approaching a flyover, Stand by!'

'They're heading for Dover alright,' remarked Henderson. 'By the Folkestone road or the coast road. That is the question.'

'And the answer is?' chuckled Maguire.

'Red Alpha Five,' radioed Angela. 'Subject vehicle remains on the A20 taking the coast road towards the port of Dover. I am one mile behind the vehicle. Fifty miles per hour.'

Sitting in the passenger seat, Henderson tapped the digits on his mobile and said, 'I'm turning the office out and sending them to the port. Pound to a penny says they're heading for the harbour.'

'What makes you think that?'

'The tide is in,' replied Henderson. 'I wonder what else is in.'

'Red Alpha Five with the eyeball,' radioed Angela. 'Take closer order. The subject is heading for the town and reducing speed in heavy traffic. Come through.'

As the team responded, Angela continued to monitor the suspect's journey on the tracking device, but she was aware that the vehicle might be more difficult to follow in the conurbation, as opposed to the countryside.

The surveillance convoy gained ground and sped past Angela as the target vehicle entered Dover via the coast road and made for the docks.

The coast road into Dover, and the highway and byways that surrounded the harbour, were festooned with bars, clubs, cafes, restaurants, and an array of terraced hotels and boarding houses that catered for every need and every wallet. There was even a swimming pool and a leisure centre situated on the approach to the harbour.

From a room on an upper level of a hotel overlooking the seaboard, a man in his mid-thirties manned a row of high-tech static tripod-mounted binoculars linked to an online video facility capable of supervised global communication. From his position, he covered the area from the cruise terminal to the inner harbour, the outer harbour, and the quay where the Dover Port control was situated. For practical purposes, the cameras covered the western arm of the harbour to the eastern arm and everything in between.

On a nearby table, a technologically superior wireless scanner hummed quietly in the background constantly searching for radio transmissions from the immediate operational area.

There were no photographs on the blank walls of the hotel room. Just a couple of standardized pictures on the wall. The pictures were in every room and every branded hotel in the country. Nice, but irrelevant to the camera operator and his assistant who handed him a mug of coffee.

'Time!' said Ruth. 'I'll take over. Take five.'

'Thanks! My eyes are done and need a rest,' chuckled Josh. 'Nothing from the radio scanner and there are three ships in the dock. Three gangplanks, and no change. No movement. The middle one is ours. It's the smaller of the three container ships. If my observations are correct, it's next for unloading. The container crane is gradually moving along the dockside. It should begin unloading ours soon.'

'Anyone used the gangplank yet?' probed Ruth as she took over and positioned herself for an up to date view on the target.

'Nope! Well, other than some of the crew disembarking and someone from Port Control boarding. If our man is already on that ship, then he hasn't come into view yet.'

Engaging a set of binoculars, Ruth flicked away a curl of dark brown hair that kept dropping onto her eyelid. She smoothed her denim jeans and remarked, 'I don't expect to find him on the ship, Josh. Just my own belief. Not unless we missed him and... Well, what do you know? Is this him?'

Josh returned to the binoculars immediately, swivelled the device on the tripod, and zoomed into the target at the harbour.

'You sure?' he asked. 'I don't see him.'

'The taxi! The white taxi,' advised Ruth. 'He's just got out of the vehicle. Rear nearside passenger door! I'm running the registration number. Wait one.'

As Ruth engaged her mobile 'phone, Josh began taking photographs and replied, 'He's lost weight. Or rather, he doesn't look as bulky as the historic 'photos suggest. He's out of the taxi and is approaching the gangplank. The taxi is moving off.'

'They were the best photos MI6 had at the time,' explained Ruth. 'That's what they gave us to work with. I've written the vehicle number down here. The boss's team will determine where the taxi came from.'

'Local 'phone number on the side of the taxi,' replied Josh. 'I'm not even sure it's the man we're looking for. It's like him but I'm not convinced it is the target. The video is rolling by the way. The switches are on the side of the binoculars. The yellow coloured one. You do know how to work these contraptions properly, don't you?'

'Of course,' replied Ruth. 'I twiddle with them when needs must.'

'Twiddle with them when needs must!' gasped Josh. 'Let me show you how the system works. They're all on the same circuit. You've forgotten.'

Josh returned to the binoculars and pointed at the various activation switches thereon.

'Thanks,' voiced Ruth. 'At times, I'm all fingers and thumbs.'

Josh shook his head, looked through another pair of binoculars, and replied, 'Do you know what bothers me most about this job?'

'No! What?' explored Ruth.

'What if the target arrives in Calais and then gets the ferry to Dover?'

'We have the ferry covered from here, don't we?' inquired Ruth.

'Yes,' replied Josh. 'We can pick it up with the surveillance gear quite clearly if he shows. Don't forget, there's always Border Force scrutinising those leaving the ferry.'

'Impossible to stop everyone,' replied Ruth. 'Selective intelligence-led searches are the order of the day. It's a complicated game at the ferry terminal.'

'Keep watching,' suggested Ruth. 'We've got a long way to go yet.'

'Anything from the French?'

'No!' declared Ruth. 'Just that the ship we're interested in is flagged to Panama but works out of Colombia with a mixed Mexican and Colombian crew. I'm told it saves the owner money by employing people at a lower rate of pay than would be expected in their own country. I think French Intelligence are annoyed they've got the port of embarkation but not the port of arrival. Here or Calais? I suppose we'll find out soon enough.'

'But the players we're interested in are still the same,' proposed Josh.

'Oh yes,' smiled Ruth. 'The mystery man will arrive in either Dover or Calais. It just might be our lucky day. Tell you what, I need to make a 'phone call. What's that one you spotted doing now?'

'Walking up the gangplank,' announced Josh. 'But there's no show yet.'

'Target acquired?'

'Not sure!' revealed Josh. 'The guy is like the man in the photograph, but I don't know for certain if it's him or not. I'd have to say no if pushed. Interesting though.'

'What is?' probed Ruth.

'He's arrived minutes before the container crane has reached the ship. Deliberate or coincidence?'

'Time will tell. Drink your coffee.'

Bobby Nelson and Jawbone Jones continued their drive into Dover, hugged the coast road, and eventually neared the Port of Dover complex. They headed into a hotel car park close to the security exit and pulled up facing the harbour area where three container ships were berthed ready for unloading.

One of the ships flew the Spanish flag, another the flag of Holland, and the third flew the flag of Panama. It was the ship from Panama that was the focus of their attention.

'Is that the ship?' inquired Jawbone. 'No sign of the man.'

'I don't know but if it is, he'll turn up when he's happy,' replied Bobby. 'Wayne is probably watching us now. He's not stupid and he loves the money. He'll show when he's ready.'

'What do we do in the meantime?' asked Jawbone.

'Relax and wait. He'll be looking over our shoulder to make sure we're not being followed for one thing.'

'But he won't want to stay there too long unless Customs and Excise come along and do a rummage search,' suggested Jawbone.

'Relax! He might be on the ferry. It all depends where the ship carrying the goods landed,' argued Bobby. 'We're as clean as a whistle and he'll show when he's ready and not before. Park up and enjoy the view. Look, there's boats, sea, and more boats, more sea and…'

'Okay! Okay!' snapped Jawbone. 'We'll wait. I just want him to get on with it. That's all. This has taken months to put together. It's the biggest lift we've ever been involved in and it needs to be done with as soon as possible.'

'Wayne once told me it all started years ago in Northern Ireland,' explained Bobby. 'His first buy was from a Belfast dealer he met in Kilkeel. He told me he brought the gear over in a fishing trawler instead of the Stranraer-Larne ferry. He brought two kilos! Yeah! He started with two kilos of pre-cut heroin. Look at him now. Way to go or what?'

'I'm not looking at him now because I don't know whether he's arriving by ferry from Calais or by container ship from Colombia! Damn it!'

'Steady on,' replied Bobby. 'It's the captain of the ship that makes the decision. They were originally bound for Calais but if the weather in the Channel turns bad, they might have to put into Dover. Then again, there's always Dunkirk.'

'Or Folkestone?'

'I doubt it.'

'While we're talking about Wayne,' proposed Jawbone. 'Where's he living now?'

Bobby looked straight ahead and did not speak.

'Bobby!' challenged Jawbone. 'Ricky! Where does Ricky Wayne live?'

'Dover! I presume.'

'Bollocks!' growled Jawbone. 'I remember he once lived in an apartment at Murley Moss in Kendal. That was years ago when all this began. He moved, got a job as a barman at the Lantern and pulled both rackets together. Then it took off and you tell me you don't know where Ricky lives. Well, my so-called friend, I don't believe you because I was present about a year ago when you 'phoned Ricky Wayne about a buy. Do you remember because I sure as hell do?'

'He prefers to be called Wayne, not Ricky.'

'I don't give a damn what he prefers to be called,' growled Jawbone. 'Get Prince Charming on the 'phone. Find out where he is and get him down here. Let's get this done.'

Bobby Nelson felt a trickle of perspiration run down his spine because he did not like talking about Wayne. Nevertheless, he glanced at Jawbone and offered, 'Alright! I hear you. I'd say he has a penthouse in London somewhere.

Maybe somewhere in Kent, I don't know. If the truth is told, we only see him once or twice a year subject to how the business is going. He's on a pinnacle of his own making and wants us to think we are with him all the way.'

'I bet we're not his only customers anymore, are we?'

'No! We never have been. It's something he's worked on and dragged us behind him because he doesn't want to let go.'

'Why?' probed Jawbone.

'Because we were the first. We're the longest serving never been caught out mob from sunny Cumbria. Remember? We're more enduring and resilient than the rest and still free to tell the tale. Not that we ever would but I think Wayne values us because we've never let him down. We've always paid the money upfront, got the customers lined up for him, and us, and never breached his security policy.'

'Security policy?' challenged Jawbone. 'You're having a laugh. That's me and my threat to destroy anyone who steps out of line. It's called muscle, frightening the shit out of people, and making them cringe in fear at the very mention of the gang. That's the security policy. What the hell does he think it is?'

'Making sure we're not being followed by the police or rival gangs every day of the week,' offered Bobby. 'That's usually my telephone lecture whenever I line up the next buy with him. It's not just us. It's everyone else involved. He's at pains to make sure the police don't latch onto us and he'll stop at nothing to keep rivals away from us. We sometimes forget he's got contacts all over the place. Do you see that ship there?'

'Yeah, I see it.'

'It's out of Colombia. That says all you need to know about Ricky Wayne,' revealed Bobby. 'He's got the best associates going, manages to smuggle whatever into the country, keeps his ear to the ground via all his contacts, and spends his business days making sure he's not being followed by the cops.'

Jawbone reversed the Volvo into a vacant parking place on the hotel car park. He snatched the handbrake, switched the engine off, and said, 'Followed! Are you telling me that Wayne thinks we are followed everywhere? Is he for real or what?'

'No!' challenged Bobby Nelson. 'He's built this business up over the years by reminding us to exercise security when necessary. How do you think we've got away with it for so long?'

'Yeah, you're right. I forgot,' from Jawbone.

'You mean you forgot about security on the way down?' probed Bobby. 'All that cash hidden in the beer kegs and you didn't check to see if you were followed out of Kendal? Tell me, I'm mistaken and you're an idiot.'

Staring directly ahead, through the windscreen, Jawbone rasped, 'We got here, didn't we? It's watertight. We're the only ones who know about the kegs. They are the best safety deposit boxes on the planet.'

'That wasn't the question,' denounced Bobby. 'Answer the question, Jawbone.'

'And you never once looked in the rear mirror?' challenged Jawbone.

Bobby Nelson reached into the glove compartment and removed two handguns before replying, 'No! You're right. We've been clean for so long it's not a problem anymore. It's the same old routine and it has become a habit. But I understand Wayne's logic. Don't take anything for granted. Here, take this and stick it in the back of your belt. It's loaded.'

Accepting the handgun, Jawbone eased forward and pushed the weapon into his trouser belt at the small of his back.

Simultaneously, Bobby slid his firearm into the left-hand side of his torso, reached down the length of his lower limb, and said, 'I'm also carrying in my ankle holster. I take it you are?'

'It's the only time we ever need them,' remarked Jawbone.

'Simple really,' proposed Bobby. 'A nice easy drive down the motorway, one collection only this time, back to the motorway nice and easy, and all is done. Don't draw attention to yourself and you won't get stopped by the police.'

'But you mentioned rivals,' argued Jawbone. 'By that, I suppose you mean people trying to muscle into our patch.'

'We've never had a problem yet, Jawbone. That's because things are kept in house and no one runs around blabbing their mouth off. Here!'

Bobby handed over a pair of binoculars, removed another from the glove compartment, and gestured to his partner to start using them.

'Why?'

'Because if the man is watching us, let's show him that we are switched on and are looking for the followers. You know what I mean.'

'Do me a favour, Bobby,' implored Jawbone. 'Just ring him and tell him we're ready to make the payment.'

'He'll ring us when he's ready and not before,' replied Bobby. 'I don't even know where he is but what I do know is that he said he would meet us this afternoon in this car park where the exchange would take place. I'd expect him within the hour if that. We're here, Jawbone, so is the money, and we'll just sit and wait. Understood?'

'Okay! Okay! I need some fresh air. I'll take a walk. I'm always nervous just before the lift.'

'No, you won't,' insisted Bobby reaching for his handgun. 'I don't want to use this. There's are a million pound in hard cash in those two suitcases and you want to go for a walk and leave me with the money? Why do you think we're carrying guns? Have you flipped? Where's your mind right now, you idiot!'

'Alright! Alright!' snapped Jawbone. 'I hear you! I hear you! I'll scan the quayside. You do the seafront.'

Edgy, perhaps a little nervous as the exchange approached, the two men began to reconnoitre the area with their binoculars as a red coloured container crane slowly drew closer to the ship. Onboard the vessel lay over two hundred

containers all bound for various destinations throughout the
UK.

~

13

The English Channel
A short time later
Dover

Nearing the white cliffs of Dover, approaching the harbour walls, the ferry from Calais was in the final stages of its run into the port. The vessel was laden with foot passengers, heavy goods vehicles, and dozens of light vans and saloon cars.

On the access roads to the port, countless heavy goods vehicles converged on the harbour area ready to join the queue at the security entrance and carry out the offloading procedures. A gang of stevedores gradually moved from one part of the dock to another as the ship-to-shore container crane moved along the quayside and unloaded the container ships. A dockside grab rope was grasped by three of the stevedores as the team began to secure the operation with a variety of thick ropes that were used to stabilise the unloading operation on one of the vessels.

On the coast road into Dover, Maguire's convoy was still active.
'Red Alpha Five can advise that the targets have stopped in the vicinity of a hotel close to the outer harbour at Dover Port. No eyeball but the tracker trace is static.'
'All received,' replied Maguire. 'I wonder if they're waiting for someone. Danny and Bernie, come through and plot for a take-off. Peter, Angela, and Carol hold and cover a reciprocal movement. All acknowledge.'

As Maguire's team manoeuvred into position and exchanged radio transmissions, a man and woman in a hotel overlooking the harbour picked up the radio transmissions on a secure MI5 wireless tracking device.
'Encrypted transmissions!' cried a shocked Ruth.

'Police or military?' probed Josh. 'Or the enemy?'

Ruth snatched the scanner, dialled into the national police network, and began working through the channels before she replied, 'Channel forty-six! It's the national police surveillance channel and it's only used for nationwide multi surveillance team operations. Not local or regional jaunts. We can listen to them, but we can't transmit to them. Josh! We've got opposition.'

'Rivals! Where are they?' asked Josh.

Listening to the radio conversations, Ruth replied, 'In the hotel corridor.'

'You're joking.'

'Yes! I am,' chuckled Ruth. 'They may as well be. I'd say they're within a mile of us.'

'Could it be Border Force?'

'No! Different wireless system!'

Picking up her mobile 'phone, Ruth tapped in a number and said, 'Rafferty! Where are you? We have infiltrators you should be aware of.'

'Halfway between Folkestone and Dover with the rest of the team,' came the reply. 'What's happening?'

'Can you deal with an immediate problem or are you tied up?' inquired Ruth.

'Yes! Fire away,' instructed Rafferty.

'We're tuned into the national police surveillance channel. We're monitoring channel forty-six. Looks like we have a police surveillance team working our plot. Rafferty, they're in danger of stepping on our toes. They are that close. Listening to their transmissions, they're watching the port for something or someone.'

'Explain,' ordered Rafferty.

'We're both looking at the same ship from Colombia and three of their cars have just driven straight through our plot and parked near the ferry drop. Not for me to judge, Rafferty, but we're chasing international terrorists and the shipment of arms whilst they might be looking for a wanted person or an insignificant drugs bust. Someone might get hurt if it goes down today.'

'I'll be with you shortly.'

Ending the call, Ruth walked to the window, listened to the conversation on the scanner, and declared, 'The boss is on his way.'

'Good! I wonder if the police are following a tip-off about a shipment of arms. Is it possible they might be working on the same target as us?'

'I doubt it, but you never know. We'll find out later today, I expect,' replied Ruth. 'Look! That container crane is on-site and is swivelling across into position above the cargo hold.'

'Alternatively,' proposed Josh. 'Is it the police we're listening to or a criminal gang who've bought into high tech encrypted wireless communications? You never know these days. Anything goes.'

'Maybe we're listening to a gang of crooks about to rob another gang of crooks,' frowned Ruth.

'By the end of the day, someone is going to walk away with a thousand firearms and enough ammunition to start a war if the tip-off is correct?' remarked Josh. 'We'd better be a mile away when this goes down.'

'And a bit more for safety's sake,' suggested Ruth.

Rafferty began by 'phoning the office and receiving an update from his French liaison officer. Ringing Kent police headquarters, then Dover CID, and then Penrith police headquarters, the Head of the MI5 surveillance unit slowly unravelled the events of the day and realised numerous police surveillance squads were about to invade their plot at Dover Port and possibly destroy the operation of which he was responsible for. British Intelligence was close to a major strike against international criminality and a terrorist organisation. The police had to be stopped in their tracks. Right now, or they would bungle things.

The nation's 'phone lines were alive with chaos and mayhem when Rafferty inquired of those in command if the MI5 plot had been breached by other surveillance teams from different police organisations. Either that or a very advanced mobile crime gang was in play and appeared to be on the verge of destroying a five-day operation. Working against terrorism with MI6, explained Rafferty, MI5 had received a tip from them that an arms shipment was bound for a Channel port. The source of the tip-off was French Intelligence who had instructed the French Navy to locate a container ship travelling from Colombia. The favourite locations were Calais and Dunkirk, but the ship's name was not known. The port of Cartagena was likely to be the starting point in the ship's journey, but its exact destination was unknown. Dover could not be discounted. It was a possibility. The hurried deployment of officers to the port was actioned and several container ships were immediately put under the eye of MI5 operatives as the British Government were appraised of the situation.

The dilemma for all came into focus. Was a tip-off from the French that originated in a South American country true or false? If it were false, how would they know unless they took positive steps? If the information was true, how should they handle the situation? Were the arms on board the vessel loaded or unloaded? Were they hidden in the cargo load or within the structure of the vessel itself? Who should search the ship? Customs and Excise, the police, the SAS, or Uncle Tom Cobbly and all? Should the police abandon the area and give way to MI5 on the strength of the evidence lying on the table?

More calls to the French were made but nothing further was learnt.

There were plenty of questions for those in charge to ask, but not so many answers forthcoming in the haze of confusion that slowly enveloped the situation. It wasn't the first time that surveillance units had crossed paths in the complex and lengthy operations that often took place throughout the UK.

Rising to the challenge, Rafferty let it be known that he was aware that a man using the name Richard Arthur Wayne was on the 'watch list' of French Intelligence. It was believed he had manoeuvred himself into a position whereby he was able to adopt multiple identities. He was something of a mystery to investigators. But who was to take primacy at ground level in the UK, and who would make that decision? That was the question that needed to be answered.

Rafferty nodded to the driver of the Porsche Cayenne he was travelling in and gestured for him to increase his speed whilst he continued using the 'phone.

A short time later, Bernard Rafferty and Les Maguire met each other for the first time on a layby near the security control at Dover harbour. They shook hands and shared details of the current situation before the two men exchanged photographs of the main target – Wayne. As they mulled over the situation, they listened to the radio commentaries from the surveillance teams.

'I take it you have primacy in this matter,' inquired Maguire.

'I would say yes,' replied Rafferty. 'Mainly because we are senior representatives of Her Majesty's Government but then I suppose the police will play the same card.'

'Bit like the Royal Navy preceding the Army and the Air Force because they are the oldest of the three services. Spies originated long before the police. Maybe we can work something out that will satisfy both our needs on the ground without involving those above.'

'Talking to you and Chief Superintendent Elliott in Penrith,' revealed Rafferty. 'I'm not so sure we should take primacy now. You've got evidence about conspiracy and we're acting upon a tip-off.'

'You mean an MI6 source that you can't tell me about, but you believe will be right because he or she has come up trumps before?' challenged Maguire.

'I can neither confirm nor deny that assertion from yourself,' replied Rafferty. 'But you seem to be on my wavelength. My problem is that the matter began somewhere in France. According to French Intelligence, this man Wayne has contacts with a Colombian crime syndicate who are shipping him a large consignment of firearms and ammunition which he, in turn, will presumably pass into criminal hands.'

'Or the hands of terrorists?' queried Maguire.

'Could be,' replied Rafferty.

'And?' ventured Maguire. 'What else?'

'That's about it,' explained Rafferty. 'Our hands are tied somewhat because the information is routed through the French into MI6 and then to ourselves. I don't know how much of it is diluted before it arrives with us. On the other hand, that might be the entire intelligence snippet. The French are playing the cards close to their chest – they always do – whilst MI6 is reminding us that we are responsible for matters on our turf, not them. They've nothing useful from their man in Cartagena, for example.'

'It sounds like a right pickle,' proposed Maguire.

'That's a good way of putting it,' replied Rafferty. 'All I will say is that the French might not be masters of intelligence protocol, but they are usually right. I think there might be something in it but whether it's here, Calais or Dunkirk remains to be seen.'

'And we've both got the same photograph of Wayne by the look of it,' suggested Maguire. 'Richard Arthur Wayne, Lower Warren Road, Crosby. He's a former barman at the Lantern pub. Did you pick that up from the Crosby Chronicle? It's an old photograph.'

'Yes! It was on our database. It's an old one, as you say. Our operatives have a possible sighting of the subject boarding the ship via the main gangplank earlier today. I asked if they were sure and the reply came back that they are unsure because of the age of the photograph they have.'

'I see,' replied Maguire. 'How long has he been of interest to you?'

'Since the French tipped us off.'

'Excuse my ignorance,' remarked Maguire. 'Where is Cartagena?'

'It's Colombia's busiest port on the edge of the Caribbean Sea,' explained Rafferty.

'I see,' replied Maguire. 'Well, one thing's for sure, you want guns. I want drugs. We both want Wayne.'

'What do you have in mind, Les?'

'I'm relevantly new to the game in comparison with you,' explained Maguire. 'But one thing I have learnt is that we don't run the surveillance. The target does. When the target moves, we react. When the target remains dormant, so do we. The surveillance squad is only active when the target is moving. If Wayne walks down the gangplank of a container ship with an AK 47 slung across his shoulder, a Smith and Wesson in a holster, and a hand grenade between his teeth then he's yours. If he turns up in Dover and does an exchange with the two men we're watching, then he's ours. If he doesn't show, one of us has been rumbled or he's changed the game plan. He's the architect of whatever is happening. You see, Bernie...'

'Rafferty!'

'Sorry, Rafferty,' continued Maguires. 'I believe our two suspects have brought a lot of money down here so they can pay him in hard cash for the drugs he's imported. Standing here looking at those ships by the quayside I'd say Wayne was involved in the importation of drugs using a container vessel. There's only a couple of hundred container units on each ship to search. We could camp out for a week while someone roots through them all. The harbour will be clogged for weeks. That doesn't mean the tip-off about the guns is wrong. It's what we can see that counts. We can work together and work it all out as it happens. On the plus side, I have an armed plainclothes surveillance unit situated up the road and half of Kent Constabulary's firearms unit on the way to provide a hard perimeter at the warehouse where the dealers are waiting for the cut to be made. That tells me the gang at the warehouse are waiting for the delivery to that location once payment here has been made. Does that sound good to you or am I lost in the land of the cuckoos?'

'It sounds good enough to join forces with you and watch the ball roll,' revealed Rafferty. 'You've got more to go on than us at the moment. How flexible are you, Les?'

'I'll bend any which way I can to get a result for us,' replied Maguire.

'In that case, how about I join you in your car and we watch developments?'

'That's a done deal,' replied Maguire.

'I suggest we watch the suspects we currently have, look out for Wayne either leaving the ship or coming off a ferry and keep a record of every vehicle involved. We can run the details through various databases later.'

'Let's do just that,' decided Maguire. 'Why do you think he might be on a ferry from France?'

'Because of the imprecise nature of our intelligence,' explained Rafferty. 'I'm just covering all the bases.'

Maguire nodded his understanding.

An agreement reached the two teams were merged on the communication network before the watch recommenced. And watch they did as the cranes began removing the containers from the deck and the cargo hold of the ship from Colombia.

The containers were placed onto the rear of a brigade of heavy goods vehicles. The carrying vehicle then drove along the quayside to the Security and Customs area where they were stopped and checked. Documents were examined and a search of the vehicle might take place. Vehicles selected for extensive searches were filtered into a special search lane where technology was used to examine the load. The technology was such that it could now detect a heartbeat from inside a container. In addition, an X-ray facility existed whereby the operator could examine the interior of the container courtesy of the technology now being used. Sniffer dogs were also on hand to add to the daily battle against smugglers and illegals. Once searches, checks and documentation were completed, the wagons were out of the port complex and into the county of Kent.

The problem for the watchers was that the heavy goods vehicles that were queuing to leave the quayside via the security complex were all well known to the port authorities. They were regulars who had been searched time and time again. That did not mean they would always be above suspicion. It did mean that nothing out of place was in play today.

At the ferry terminal, there was a controlled rush to leave the vessel when foot passengers began to make their way into the port area. Simultaneously, vans, cars and leisure vehicles all took their turn to gradually disembark and head inland.

In the security area, uniformed personnel stopped several vehicles to speak to the occupants. Occasionally, some vehicles were routed into a separate lane where more complex searches similar to those that related to container vehicles were carried out. Here, sniffer dogs trained to detect drugs were on show and at work.

One such vehicle was a large white campervan driven by a man in his early forties. He was accompanied by a dark-haired woman of a similar age. They drove to the front of the queue where a uniformed officer from the Border Force stopped them and politely asked some basic questions.

'Good day, sir. Where are you travelling from, may I ask?'

'Paris,' replied the driver. 'Just a short weekend break for me and my wife. We're back at work tomorrow, but it was nice to get away.'

'You're English then, a holidaymaker?'

'That's right,' replied the driver who immediately handed over his driving licence and passport without being asked. 'My wife is French. We visited her parents for the day. Paris! Do you know it at all? It's a beautiful city.'

The examining officer ignored the question, inspected the documents presented to him, and then said to the passenger, 'French! Do you have a passport too?'

'Yes,' she replied rummaging in her handbag. 'My passport. I'm his wife.'

The Border Force officer took the woman's passport and said, 'One moment, please.'

A CCTV system continued to operate when the officer took the travel documents into a kiosk, scanned the documents beneath a verification device, and then returned them to the couple.

'Your names, if you please, sir?'

'A Mr George Wood and a Mrs Veronique Wood,' proposed the driver.

The officer glanced over the driver's shoulder into the rear of the vehicle and said, 'Nothing to declare?'

'Just the next rain shower on its way,' replied George Wood.

'Indeed!' replied the officer returning the two passports. 'Have a nice day. Thank you.'

Gesturing the couple through the checking area, the officer retreated slightly when the driver of the motorhome selected first gear and drove on with a cursory wave.

The officer beckoned the next vehicle forward, waited for the driver of a white van to wind his window down, and repeated the conversation he had just undertaken with Mr and Mrs Wood. Except this time, something wasn't quite right, and he gestured the van into a separate lane for a more detailed examination.

Minutes later, Mr and Mrs George Wood emerged from the port complex onto the open road and drove a short distance to a hotel. Once in the hotel grounds, George Wood turned to his wife and said, 'We're here. Nice and easy, Veronique. No worries?'

'Bien entendu,' she replied. 'Pas de problème.'

'There they are,' nodded George. 'In the Volvo as instructed. Sit tight whilst I do a circuit or two. I want to be sure we're safe.'

The surveillance team noted another vehicle had entered the hotel car park. It was a motorhome occupied by a man and woman in their forties.

In the Volvo estate, Bobby nudged Jawbone and said, 'He's here.'

'Where?'

'In the motorhome by the looks of it. There's two of them. Sit tight. He's on a drive-by.'

Exhaling loudly, Jawbone muttered, 'About bloody time. Are you ready?'

'Not yet,' replied Bobby. 'Wait until he parks. You know what to do?'

'The same as last time,' replied Jawbone.

The motorhome toured the car park twice apparently looking for a convenient space before reversing into a vacant spot. The vehicle remained stationary with its engine running and its windscreen wipers occasionally spoiling the driver's view as it combatted the commencement of a slight drizzle.

'London Bridge Three calling. Ruth has an eye on a suspicious vehicle in the hotel car park,' from the MI5 team on the net. 'Can anyone from the Red Alpha team look? I have a cream coloured motorhome that has circled the car park on two occasions before parking opposite your Volvo target. There are about fifty yards between them.'

'Noted,' from Maguire. 'Red Alpha Three - Bernie, can you assist?'

'On my way, stand by,' radioed Bernie.

The surveillance officer fired the Renault engine and drove from his location near the ferry terminal security complex to the car park. On driving into the area, Bernie headed directly to the entrance, got out of the car, and entered the hotel. His Renault was parked equidistance between the Volvo and the motorhome.

Once inside the foyer, Bernie radioed, 'Red Alpha Three! There's only one motorhome in the car park. Male in the driver's seat, female in the passenger seat. They've only just come off the ferry. That vehicle passed me a short time ago once it had been cleared by the Border Force.'

'Noted,' from Maguire. 'Can you get an eyeball?'

'Yes! Yes!' replied Bernie who took a seat near the window.

A waiter sauntered over to the plainclothes officer and asked, 'Can I help you, sir. Are you staying at the hotel?'

'No, I'm not,' replied Bernie. 'I'm waiting for some friends. I hope it's alright. They're booked in for the night, I understand. Would it be possible to order coffee whilst I wait?'

'Of course, sir,' replied the waiter. 'Black or white standard or would you like to see the hotel's extensive selection?'

'A cafetiere would be great. Black, if you please. No sugar! Perhaps a scone as well? No jam just butter.'

'No problem,' replied the waiter. 'Today's newspapers are on the side there if you need them.'

'Many thanks,' replied Bernie.

The waiter scribbled the order on his pad before retreating.

Bernie turned back to the window, engaged his throat mic, and radioed, 'Red Alpha Three is in position. Good eyeball on the motorhome. One male in the driver's seat resembles the target Tango Zero Zero, Black top. Primary operational target is not yet a positive sighting. I say again possible sighting of Tango Zero Zero but not confirmed at this stage. The passenger is a female, same age range, dark-haired. Lemon coloured top. She's a beauty by the way. The situation is static. No change.'

'Noted,' from Maguire who turned to his passenger and asked, 'Two days on surveillance and Bernie is still looking out for good looking females. Ah well! Jack, Rafferty, what do you think? It looks promising.'

'Ruth is too far away from the Volvo to make a better sighting,' suggested Rafferty. 'And I don't think your man inside the hotel can make the Volvo. I'd put someone else in, if possible. As for Bernie and his love of the female form, well, that's' your problem.'

Nodding in agreement, chuckling, Maguire radioed, 'Red Alpha Four - Peter, can you take a static eyeball on the Volvo. We might need you there for a while. Not sure!'

'On foot only,' replied Peter. 'Wait one!'

The surveillance net hummed quietly with covert commentary as the team moved closer to try and obtain a better view of what was going on.

In the Volvo, Jawbone glanced at Robert and said, 'How long?'

'Soon,' replied Bobby. 'He'll switch the engine off. That's the signal.'

Parking his car about fifty yards from the entrance to the hotel car park, Peter snatched a newspaper from the glove compartment and got out of the squad car. He locked the vehicle and then walked to the hotel where he found the garden area which was situated at the front of the complex and served to present the hotel in a good light. Several hotel guests were mingling in the area, chatting, and enjoying the ambience.

Peter took a seat on a wooden bench with a metal backdrop and loudly rattled his newspaper free. He wasn't trying to hide. There was no need. He wanted to be able to see what was going on and sometimes being so obvious was often an indication to the other side that you couldn't possibly be a watcher pretending to read a newspaper. Such people hid from sight, didn't they? Peter thought he would sit tight and move away to join the hotel guests when he was ready.

It started to rain.

Damn it, thought Peter as the first splodge of rainwater battered the front page and smudged the ink. What next?

Richard Arthur Wayne alias George Wood alias umpteen other names, according to his passport collection, switched off the motorhome's ignition, watched the windscreen wipers berth in their usual position, and glanced at Veronique with the words, 'Let's go.'

Wayne left the key in the ignition and set down from the vehicle the same time as Veronique.

Fifty yards away, Bobby nudged Jawbone and said, 'We're on.'

The two men got out of the Volvo, left the keys in the ignition and strolled towards Wayne and Veronique as a cluster of hotel guests ran across the car park in front of them intent on making the hotel bar before the heavens opened.

'Bernie has an eyeball on the couple from the motorhome. They are out of the vehicle and walking towards the Volvo. Stand by.'

'Peter has the eyeball on the two Tangos from the Volvo. They are out of the Volvo and walking towards the other couple. Stand by.'

The surveillance net was alive with whispered acknowledgements as the main players approached each other on a hotel car park on the edge of the Port of Dover.

'It's a meet,' suggested Maguire to Jack and Rafferty.

'Stop, go or take them both out of the game now?' queried DI Henderson. 'I say let it run.'

'Agreed,' from Rafferty.

'Stand by for contact between all players,' radioed Bernie. 'Do you see them, Peter?'

'Yes! Yes!' from behind a soggy newspaper.

Rising to his feet, Peter folded the newspaper, pushed it into a nearby waste bin, and joined the rest of the hotel guests scurrying across the car park towards the hotel entrance. He knew he had to join them, despite his initial thoughts, or stick out like a sore thumb as a man reading a newspaper in the pouring rain.

Wayne nodded as he closed with Bobby and quietly mouthed, 'See you soon.'

Nodding in reply, Bobby and Jawbone by-passed Veronique and Wayne as they headed towards the motorhome.

Bernie took a ten-pound note from his wallet, placed it on a saucer near the cafetiere, and made for the doorway. Engaging his throat mic, he radioed, 'It's a miss. Bernie has an eyeball on all four and it's a miss. They've by-passed each other. No meeting! Repeat! No meeting!'

In Maguire's car, Jack murmured, 'It's on. The exchange is going down right before our eyes.'

'They're swopping vehicles,' proposed Maguire. 'They've left the keys in the ignition and they're swopping vehicles.'

'London Bridge One are you getting this, Ruth?' on the net from Rafferty.

'Yes! Yes! Video rolling,' replied Ruth.

Shaking his head, Rafferty remarked, 'What the hell is going on? The guns! Where are the guns? If the money is in the Volvo, then either the guns or the drugs are in the motorhome.'

'The ship!' replied Maguire. 'Ship or motorhome, and what about the Volvo. Which?'

As the rain fell gently on the tarmac, Bobby reached the motorhome, climbed in, smiled at Jawbone who clambered into the passenger seat, and said, 'We're off.'

Bobby fired the engine at precisely the same time that Wayne and Veronique made the Volvo. The couple rummaged in the estate area and unzipped two suitcases. Satisfied, they zipped the bags up again, got into the Volvo, and fired the engine.

'Exchange of vehicles complete,' from Bernie on the net.

'Confirmed,' from Peter.

'Copied,' from Ruth.

'Jeez! Now what?' voiced Maguire.

'Who's going where?' asked Jack. 'It's anyone's guess.'

Maguire fired the engine and radioed, 'Red Alpha One to all units! We want Wayne, but we'll go with both vehicles. The Red Alpha team will form on the motorhome. All other teams form on the Volvo.'

'Nice one,' declared Rafferty.

The net overflowed with acknowledgements as the motorhome drove past Les Maguire, Rafferty, and Jack Henderson.

In a scene resembling the dashing white sergeant on a ballroom dance floor, half of the surveillance teams latched onto the Volvo whilst the other half followed the motorhome.

Moments later, the two vehicles were out of the port complex with the Volvo heading into Dover town and the motorhome travelling towards Folkestone and the warehouse where the gang was gathered awaiting its arrival.

Maguire 'phoned DI Jim Latimer, updated him as to events at the port, and then said, 'I'm on the Volvo that I believe contains Wayne and the money, Jim. The motorhome is headed back your way where I think the drugs will be shared out. Take command, please. If you agree, we'll take out the Volvo and I'll get back to you right away. The London Bridge team have the ship covered but London Bridge One is riding shotgun with Jack and I.'

'Noted,' replied Jim. 'Tell me when and where you hit the Volvo. Stay in touch. I want to know what you find. What you find will determine whether we go in hard, soft, or somewhere in the middle. I'm going to sit and watch as long as I can here. Understood?'

'Yes,' replied Maguire. 'Good luck!'

'And you!' from Jim.

Maguire engaged the net and radioed, 'This is Red Alpha One to all teams. Overall command now rests with Skiddaw One. Units on the Volvo listen out for forthcoming details when we take it out. All units on the motorhome take your lead from Skiddaw One.'

More acknowledgements flitted across the net as the surveillance team leaders adjusted to the new regime and thought processes taking place.

It was an unexpected problem, thought Maguire. The problem of multiple teams from different areas with different leaders all striving to get a grip on the movement of the targets, and their officers. Such things were commonplace when several teams were on the same plot or working in tandem.

'It just shows you that no matter however you plan these things, the target always makes the running,' announced Maguire. 'When the targets split, it doesn't make the job any easier.'

'I hope Jim keeps them watertight at the warehouse,' remarked Jack.

'I just hope I've made the right decision,' explained Maguire. 'We've got six surveillance teams on the job – Trafford, Red Alpha, Sovereign, Mersey, Skiddaw and Sabre – and we're not yet in control.'

'You've said it before,' stated Jack. 'The target makes the running and everyone else chases around like headless chickens trying to follow.'

'If they don't turn into the industrial complex and just keep going into Folkestone, I'm going to feel a right fool,' revealed Maguire.'

'Sit tight and listen in,' advised Rafferty. 'How do you propose to stop the Volvo? If it's clean, then we're up the creek without a paddle.'

Chuckling, Jack Henderson suggested, 'What's the worst thing that can happen? I'll tell you. The motorhome drives right past the industrial estate, hits Folkestone, and takes the Channel Tunnel at Cheriton. Any bets?'

'Jack!' challenged Maguire. 'Your locals, please. We need a couple of Armed Response Vehicles.'

'Already on it,' from Jack Henderson who engaged his mobile.

Maguire's team made their plans as the Volvo estate car took the northern route skirting Dover onto the A2 road to Canterbury.

Meanwhile, on the industrial estate, embedded in a hedgerow watching the warehouse, Bob Martin engaged his mic and radioed, 'Cuckoo One has an eyeball on the motorhome approaching the warehouse. Stand by!'

Jim Latimer breathed a sigh of relief. He acknowledged the signal and radioed, 'All units take up covert support positions on the estate as recently discussed and stand by for updates. Listen out for Cuckoo One who has the eyeball.'

'Cuckoo One has the eyeball on the motorhome and it's coming to a stop outside the warehouse. Stand by.' Bob brushed away a fly that was attacking his face and then cleared some foliage out of the way. His line of vision was slightly impaired, but he radioed an update with, 'The warehouse doors are opening. Multiple Tangos emerging on foot from the warehouse. The motorhome has stopped. The two occupants are tampering with the internal part of the roof system above them. Stand by!'

Some of the teams pulled into the nearside of the road and listened. Others cruised into car park areas at some of the business premises on the estate. The engines were switched off as they all listened to a man with a radio transmitter hidden in the hedgerow no more than fifty yards from the target.

'The warehouse doors have opened wider,' from Cuckoo One on the surveillance net. 'The motorhome is being driven into the warehouse. Everyone is smiling. I see laughter but I can't hear it. Handshakes outside! Hey! Some of them are now dressed in dark overalls as if they were car fitters. Stand by!' A fly died in a hedgerow following a swipe from a camouflaged hand. 'The motorhome is now inside the building. The doors have closed behind it. No Tangos are in view. No movement. Cuckoo One has the eyeball on the target premises where it is now all quiet. No change.'

'Skiddaw One, all received,' from Jim. 'All units hold tight. Sabre One report deployment and location.'

'Sabre One to Skiddaw One,' radioed Terry Calder. 'Plotted and ready. We are one minute from the target and in position. Standing by.'

'I have that,' replied Jim.

Behind a disused building, hidden from view, next to two black unliveried personnel carriers, Terry and the rest of his team were now fully booted and suited. They were armed and masked wearing protective headgear and bulletproof vests as well as jeans, tee shirts and an array of casual clothing.

A finger slid along the trigger guard of a Heckler and Koch submachine guard as the owner relaxed his mind by chewing gum. The officer next to him adjusted her vest and allowed her hand to rest on the handle of her Gloch handgun. The team were briefed, prepared, and ready to go.

Come on Maguire, thought Latimer. We've got them just where we want them. Don't let me down.

Jim Latimer checked his wristwatch and radioed, 'Sabre hold positions. All other units prepare to move to perimeter markers and await instructions.'

The acknowledgements filtered across the net as Jim Latimer signalled to two uniform officers from Kent to remain at the estate entrance and get ready to lock down the entrance when required.

Glancing at his 'phone, Jim checked for missed messages but saw only a blank screen.

Where are you, Les? Where are you? thought Jim.

~

14

The A2
Dover - Canterbury

Mark Kenyon was out in front of the convoy on his BMW motorcycle. Positioned about four hundred yards behind Wayne's Volvo with three cars for cover, Callsign Trafford One was half a mile ahead of the rest of the convoy who were racing to keep up at sixty miles per hour.

The road was a single lane carriageway out of Dover headed for Canterbury. The traffic was medium. It was enough to cause a problem if the Volvo suddenly changed route and journeyed down a narrow country lane but Maguire had convinced himself that the occupants thought themselves to be virtually home free and headed into a world of never-ending luxury and wealth thanks to a greedy desire for financial power from whatever source came into play.

The Volvo increased its speed to seventy miles an hour as Trafford One held its position and talked in India Nine-Nine to the correct location.

In the skies above Kent, a pilot began a circling motion as he locked onto the target and concentrated on his flight path. Next to him a navigator plotted the course, listened to air traffic on their net, and tapped the screen where the fuel level read high. In the rear seat, a surveillance officer zoomed into the road system, located the Volvo, and engaged the video system.

'India Nine-Nine has you Trafford One back off,' on the net.

Mark closed the throttle down and dropped back whilst the rest of the convoy closed ranks and two black high-powered saloon cars joined the rear of the surveillance.

The net burst into life with, 'Medway One to Red Alpha One, we're with you. Callsigns Medway One and Two containing six armed plainclothes officers ready to assist. Armed response in attendance.'

'Thank you, all received,' remarked Maguire who then engaged the net with, 'Red Alpha One to all units, take closer order and stand by for vehicle strike. Make ground! Make ground! Closer order, please. Prepare for a change in control.'

As the net filled with acknowledgement, Maguire radioed, 'All units, stand by. All units Medway One has control. On your mark Medway One.'

'Medway One has that,' replied the Kent leader.

'Do they know what to do?' inquired Rafferty.

'Oh yes,' replied Jack Henderson. 'We've had a telephone conversation. It will happen when they're close enough and on song.'

'Absolutely,' replied Maguire. 'It's their patch and they know the story.' Maguire engaged the net with, 'Stand by for Trigger action. Medway One has control.'

'Well, that's pretty simple then,' chuckled Rafferty. 'I'll just keep my head down for the next five minutes.'

'Might be longer,' replied Maguire. 'The team will need to pick the time and place.'

The surveillance team began to gradually close together as the two dark saloon cars worked their way through the convoy whenever oncoming traffic allowed them.

Music played softly from a stereo in the centre of the Volvo's dashboard as Veronique checked her hairstyle in the mirror of the dropdown passenger visor.

Wayne allowed his hand to rest on the gear stick whilst the other held the steering wheel. Casual, unruffled by the exchange with Bobby and Jawbone, Wayne held the Volvo at seventy miles an hour and said, 'Canterbury ahead. How would you like to visit the cathedral, Veronique?'

'How would you like to just bypass Canterbury altogether and get us straight into the city?' replied Veronique with a slightly discernible French accent. 'The sooner we deposit this money with your wealth management people the better.'

'I've told you before, Veronique. It's a private bank, not a wealth management system. Where did you get that idea from?'

'Yes! Yes, you have. I forgot. My memory is not as good as yours. It has taken me long enough to learn the English language properly never mind work out the intricacies of the organisation. There's a lot of money to hide, Ricky. The hard part must be burying it somewhere. Or is it invested?'

'Both!' replied Wayne. 'Which is why our trip to London is a one drop banking slot by arrangement with Manuel, my financial director,' replied Wayne. 'To the banking authorities, we're agents of a company based in Colombia dealing in the research and production of military robotics. Did you know Colombia was the first to produce a heart pacemaker?'

'Non, Je n'ai pas,' replied an astonished Veronique. 'I thought they just produced cocaine.'

Wayne smiled and said, 'Fortunately, the country is highly advanced in relation to some of its medical research. It's also involved in research into military robotics. It's leading the rest of the world, so I decided a few years ago to invest there because it's up and coming and bound to grow. Such an investment also answers a dozen questions if I'm ever asked to explain how I made so much money in a relatively short time. The industry is booming.'

'Is a false company a good avenue to launder money?' inquired Veronique. 'Or is it a magnet for the authorities to check you out?'

'Manuel has things sorted out in that respect,' revealed Wayne. 'Everything is going fine and has done for years. False companies manufacture false invoices and pay each other as they move money around.'

'Ah! Manuel! Your friend from Panama. So that is what the pair of you were talking about that time you introduced me to him.'

'He insisted on meeting you,' revealed Wayne. 'The same man wanted to meet Bobby and Jawbone, but I drew the line at that. My soulmate, yes. The gang, no.'

'What does he get out of this?' ventured Veronique.

Drumming his fingers on the steering wheel, Wayne replied, 'Do you want to know?'

'Yes, please.'

'Manuel is the banker. He'll take twenty-five per cent and the rest of the money will magically appear in at least twenty-odd accounts under our control. Our friends in Moscow are well-chosen and have good links with Manuel. This, my dearest young lady, is the end of the line for me. We are now made for life. Retirement beckons.'

'You will never retire, Ricky,' proposed Veronique.

'A long holiday for a while then. That might be a better idea.'

'You will be bored within the first month,' proposed Veronique. 'You love the action. You are the James Bond of the criminal world. Even I am not sure what your real name is, and we've been together for over six years now.'

'Ricky!' explained Wayne.

'George on the ferry!' laughed Veronique. 'It was Jeremy at the airport last month in Paris. I wonder what will be next.'

'Simon,' chuckled Wayne. 'Maybe Sean. I'll be Irish for a while, so I will.'

'You won't stop until you are too old to count the euros,' grinned Veronique.

'Pounds!' admonished Wayne. 'Euros! Dollars! Other currencies that have a long-term upward trend. Anything goes if it buys and sells. The fact is Manuel will spread the money out across multiple sectors converting pounds along the way into several varying currencies from the dollar in America to the rouble in Russia. That's why his twenty-five per cent isn't a problem.'

'The rouble? But you are not a communist.'

'Only when it comes to money,' revealed Wayne. 'And Russia ditched communism at the end of the Cold War. Our money is safe with my Moscow friends.'

'All that money going to the bank,' mentioned Veronique. 'What happens if the bank starts to ask questions about the amount of money going into the account.'

'Technically,' explained Wayne. 'They would submit a suspicious activity report to the banking authorities but as they would submit that report through their banking chain first, it would arrive on Manuel's desk. End of the journey.'

'So, if we did not have Manuel on our side, they could catch us at the bank.'

'Not immediately, No! Maybe in a week or so. I wouldn't worry about that side of the business, Veronique. Manuel works with Moscow to spread our fortune all over the world.'

'Taking a cut everywhere?' proposed Veronique.

'Yes,' admitted Wayne with a chuckle. 'A cut to the launderers that is offset because the money is safe and will be making interest wherever it is. Neither Panama nor Russia will rip us off. They know there's more where this came from.'

'Are your friends from Moscow escorting us to the bank?'

Glancing at Veronique, Wayne replied, 'Of course not, what makes you say that?'

Studying the dropdown mirror in the visor, Veronique remarked, 'I noticed two cars at the port terminal when we arrived. They were parked close together. One of them was a blue Renault and I'm sure that it's behind us now. Why are they behind us? Are they following us or are they your friends?'

Wayne glanced in his rear-view mirror and said, 'I see it. Yes, I remember it too. It was in the hotel car park shortly before we did the exchange. The Renault?'

'Yes, the Renault,' admitted Veronique. 'Is it the police?'

High in the skies, a helicopter observer radioed, 'India Nine-Nine to ground units. Clear road ahead approximately two miles.'

'Medway One has that,' voiced on the net. 'Team, report Positions!

'Red Alpha Three has the eyeball,' from Bernie.

'Red Alpha One is in two,' from Maguire.

The helicopter descended slightly as the surveillance officers reported their exact positions in the convoy whilst the armed officers in the Kent cars committed the positions to their brain and cleared the safety catches on their weapon.

Reducing speed, Wayne offered space to overtake for the cars following him, but no-one overtook the Volvo as he weighed the situation up.

'I doubt it's the police, Veronique,' replied Wayne. 'They could have stopped us at the ferry terminal if they'd wanted to. Why would they follow us this far?'

'If it's not the police then it might be another gang,' suggested Veronique. 'You always said people had to be careful and make sure no-one else infiltrated the group. Maybe they have.'

Changing down a gear, Wayne began to accelerate again and replied, 'That makes more sense than it being the police. What does the driver look like?'

Checking mirrors, Veronique then twisted around to look out of the rear window before replying, 'I can't tell. It's the car I recognise not the driver.'

Nodding, deciding, Wayne remarked, 'Hold tight.'

To the rear of the Volvo, the surveillance convoy grew restless but as the traffic flow lessened a long straight came into view. It was clear. There was no oncoming traffic.

'India Nine-Nine reports the road is clear ahead for one mile,' from the helicopter.

'Medway One and Two are coming through,' sounded on the net followed by, 'Trigger! Trigger! Trigger! All teams stand by. Prepare to strike!'

As Kent's armed plainclothes squad rushed to overtake Wayne's Volvo, the rest of the surveillance team drew closer to the Volvo.

'It's a hard stop,' ventured Maguire. 'Fingers crossed.'

'I'm ready,' replied Jack.

Medway One accelerated hard, drew level with the Volvo, and began to overtake it whilst Medway Two pulled out and locked onto the boot of Medway One.

Simultaneously, Bernie, in his blue Renault, accelerated and inched towards the rear of the Volvo. The police plan was clear to see from the helicopter above. They intended to stop the Volvo's progress by blocking it at the front, side, and rear, and then gradually reducing speed to bring it to a standstill. Given that the nearside of the road was just grass verge, and nothing more, the Volvo had no place to escape. The police would force the Volvo off the road if necessary and then move into an armed arrest phase.

'They're coming for us,' yelled Wayne. 'Gang attack! That damn brother of yours has sold us down the river.'

'Strike! Strike! Strike!' radioed Medway One.

Mayhem on the A2 witnessed Medway One swerving into the path of Wayne's Volvo at the same time as Medway Two clung to his partner's rear bumper and moved to the nearside to end up inches from the Volvo's driver's door. Bernie, in the Renault, brushed the Volvo's rear bumper when Wayne hit the brakes and realised his options were virtually diminishing by the second.

'It's the police,' screamed Veronique. 'They've got those black and white diced caps on.'

'Maybe! Maybe not!' growled Wayne.

Glancing at his attackers, Wayne saw the headgear with its black and white band, the word police on a bulletproof vest, and the barrel of a weapon pointing towards him from the rear passenger seat of a black saloon car. The vehicle was alongside him, overtook him, and was then in front of him as the cars engaged in a dance of death that would surely end with one or more on the grass verge.

Feet on the accelerator pedal danced with feet on the brake pedal and a hand on the gear stick.

The melee continued along the A2 as a helicopter videoed proceedings from above and the rest of the surveillance convoy closed ranks ready to move in for the kill.

The hounds had cornered the fox, but the fox was still fighting.

Wayne slammed the accelerator hard down, collided with Medway One and tried to force his way through the slight gap he had created. Medway Two closed the space between them, nudged the Volvo back into place, and then swung to the nearside trying to force Wayne onto the grass verge.

Bernie held his nerve, swung his steering wheel to the right, collided with the offside rear of the Volvo, and slammed the accelerator to the floor hoping to push the Volvo onto the grass verge and out of the game.

It was what the British police called a Tpac manoeuvre followed by an American style PIT manoeuvre which originated in the Fairfax County Police Department of Virginia, America. PIT is an acronym for 'pursuit immobilization technique.'

Half a mile further down the road, with all the vehicles now doing less than thirty miles an hour, Wayne snatched a view of a five-barred gate on the offside of the road. A second later, he hit the brakes, stopped the Volvo, and reversed into Bernie's Renault as Medway One and Medway Two moved on slightly.

Bernie lurched forward, felt the seat belt restrain him, but saw the Renault's bonnet explode high in front of him with the force of the impact. The steering column slammed into Bernie's chest and temporarily put him out of the game.

A gap appeared to Wayne's offside.

Wayne rammed the gear stick into first, slung the steering to his right, and raced through the space towards the wooden gate that bordered the farmer's field.

Medway One swung to the offside. Medway Two swung to the nearside. The road ahead was blocked when

Maguire and the nearest cars in the surveillance convoy rushed forward to close the gap and prevent the Volvo from escaping.

'He's going to turn around,' yelled Rafferty

Determined, Wayne gripped the steering wheel like a man possessed and headed towards the gate. The Volvo bounced over the offside grass verge, smashed through the wooden gate, and headed into the green fields of Kent.

The farmer driving a tractor in the middle of the field turned to watch as a Volvo hurtled across the meadow, followed by Maguire's Mazda, Danny's Ford Focus, and Mark on a BMW motorbike that slithered in the wet grass before he managed to steer it back onto the road.

Medway One and Medway Two regained the highway, accelerated along the A2, and listened to India Nine-Nine on the net when the observer radioed, 'Five hundred yards ahead, take a right into a narrow lane. The Volvo is headed that way. Cut him off.'

The two saloon cars followed instructions as the helicopter swept low in pursuit of the Volvo whilst Maguire and Danny bumped and bounced over the rough terrain of the meadow.

A pipe in the farmer's mouth fell to the floor of the tractor as the Volvo screamed past churning muck from its rear wheels and covering the tractor's cab with a deluge of mud.

Screaming in fear, Veronique clung to a roof strap in the passenger seat and hung on tight as the car leapt up and down on the uneven ground.

Wayne glanced in the mirror and realised there was more than just two black cars and a blue Renault chasing him. He headed for another five-barred gate.

Medway One and Two were down the narrow lane looking through gaps in the hedgerow, following the Volvo's journey, still in the game with a helicopter above advising them on the net of the scene from above.

The Volvo crashed through another gate, swung wildly to the right with its backend swinging from one side to another as Wayne propelled the vehicle down the lane at breakneck speed.

Dead end! Cul-de-sac!

The lane tapered when the tarmac ran out and turned into a gravel-strewn track which evolved into a grassy pathway leading to a farmyard and nowhere else.

India Nine-Nine descended to an altitude of about fifty feet above the ground and dominated the lane as it held its position and slowly, but steadily, challenged the approaching Volvo.

Wayne braked, slid to a halt, opened the driver's door, and ran towards the farm.

Veronique was still screaming when the first armed detective from Medway One pulled her from the Volvo, flattened her to the ground, and applied the handcuffs.

Medway Two discharged its three detectives who set off in immediate pursuit of Wayne.

The hustle and bustle of a bullet-proof vest rubbing against the denim shirt of an individual carrying a lethal carbine and a short-muzzled pistol in a holster next to his denim jeans could be heard. There was a skidding trainer when Wayne met the farmyard and the excrement of a herd of dairy cows. He slithered to the ground unable to keep his feet. Then there was a pointed threat from a law enforcement weapon in the face of the mystery man of crime when the officers from Medway Two eventually overhauled Wayne, cornered him, took him to the ground, and handcuffed him.

The Red Alpha team arrived in a hurried cluster of excitement. Some came bouncing over the meadow, others tore down the narrow lane to assist.

Maguire stepped from his Mazda, beckoned the arresting officers and Wayne over to the Volvo, and opened the luggage area of the estate to see two grey suitcases.

Introducing himself to Wayne and Veronique, Maguire proposed, 'Yours?'

There was no reply from Wayne. Veronique shuffled nervously.

Opening the first suitcase, Maguire cast his eyes over piles of money. Wads of banknotes had been carefully held together with elastic bands, placed into small transparent plastic bags, and then neatly laid out to fill the entire case.

There was a gush of both surprise and relief from the assembled detectives.

Wayne tried to wriggle free, but the Medway team held him tight.

Lying on top of the money, Maguire found a loaded handgun which he pointed at saying, 'For your protection, Wayne?'

A look of surprise crossed Wayne's face.

'Oh yes, I know who you are, Wayne,' ventured Maguire. 'Or should I address you as Richard Arthur Wayne?'

Maguire opened the second suitcase and found the same. Row upon row of parcelled banknotes filled the case, and a handgun lay on top of the money.

'And yours again?' probed Maguire as he looked directly into Wayne's eyes.

'It's my money,' replied Wayne confidently. 'I'm on my way to the bank with it. I've done nothing wrong.'

'How much is here?' probed Maguire gesturing to the contents of both suitcases.

'Twenty-five million pounds!' replied Wayne.

'All that money and there's no record of a Richard Arthur Wayne holding a firearms certificate,' declared Maguire. 'Is it counterfeit? It won't take long to find out once we get it under a microscope?'

'No! It's straight cash,' replied Wayne.

'From drug dealing?' suggested Maguire.

Wayne looked at the money and then Maguire before replying, 'It's never too late to do a deal, is it?'

'What do you mean?' inquired Maguire.

'Help yourself. Split the cash. My freedom in exchange for one suitcase.'

'Why not both?' challenged Maguire.

'Come on! Think about it,' proposed Wayne with a forced but twisted smile. 'There's only a handful of you here. Who's to know? Take the money, leave me a bundle, and walk away richer than you will ever be working for the police.'

'No thanks!' replied Maguire.

'Both suitcases then,' pleaded Wayne.

Maguire shook his head, formally cautioned both Wayne and Veronique, and said, 'I'm seizing this money under the Proceeds of Crime Act as I believe it is the proceeds of crime. I'm also arresting you on suspicion of conspiracy to launder money and being in unlawful possession of firearms.'

'You just lost some easy money,' replied Wayne.

'And you just lost your liberty,' declared Maguire

'Don't forget the bribery, Les,' proposed Jack Henderson. 'Yeah! Bribery too, pal.'

In the skies above, an observer radioed, 'Two in custody in the area near Woolage village just off the A2, Dover-Canterbury road. This aerial incident is closed. Attending Dover industrial estate to support the ongoing operation. Documentation to follow.'

Maguire engaged the net with, 'All received. The Medway team will secure both prisoners and the Red Alpha team will carry out a more detailed search of the Volvo in their possession. All units will rendezvous in the farmyard at the end of the lane. The prisoners will be taken to Dover police station and a uniform response patrol has been requested to attend the location to provide community support where appropriate. Do not speak to the media or the local population. The operation is not yet finished. Expedite requirements.'

Acknowledgements filled the net whilst Maguire glanced at Jack and Rafferty and said, 'What do you think?'

'I've never met a millionaire before,' chuckled Jack. 'If memory serves me well twenty-five million quid will buy you a ton of uncut heroin or cocaine.'

'When cut that would turn you around a hundred million pounds at street value,' proposed Rafferty. 'If its drugs, of course, and not guns.'

'That's unbelievable,' remarked Jack. 'Now we need to finish it.'

'He came off the ferry,' ventured Rafferty. 'Then they swopped vehicles. He's got the money so presumably whatever those two had is still in the motorhome. Either way, I need to speak to the French.'

'And I need to 'phone Jim Latimer,' replied Maguire.

Moments later, on the industrial estate, Jim answered his 'phone and said, 'Les! Any luck?' Jim listened to Maguire's report, smiled, and replied, 'Thanks! They were armed, you say, but not carrying on the body. Two loaded firearms. It's plan B here then. Thank you. Spot on. We're going in very shortly. Wish us luck.'

Jim ended the call, and then 'phoned Terry Calder. He updated him as to the recovery of the money and the two guns recovered from the suitcases. Jim then engaged the net with, 'Skiddaw One to the Kent unit.'

'Medway Foxtrot One receiving,' on the net.

'Move to perimeter cordons as discussed,' instructed Jim. 'Await contact from India Nine-Nine. The Sabre team will take closer order as we move towards a trigger situation. All other units prepare to lockdown.'

Adrenalin pumped through the veins as car engines burst into life and moved from their covert positions into the open. Unarmed officers would cordon off the estate with their vehicles, whilst plainclothes officers donned police caps as headgear, and bulletproof vests bearing the word 'POLICE'. Armed uniform officers from Kent had arrived earlier, as planned, and were now close to providing a further inner cordon designed to prevent escape.

Bob Martin was no longer in the hedgerow. It had taken him over an hour to carefully escape the clutches of the thorny fly-infested row of shrubbery that denoted the extremity of the industrial estate. Now he was in a shallow ditch and had crept on his belly over twenty yards closer. The warmth and comfort of his full-length camouflage jacket were appreciated. The garment served as trousers and top, enjoyed good thermal qualities and was both watertight, waterproof, and storm-proof. Pulling the head unit still closer to his skin, he removed a periscope device from a thigh pocket and raised it slightly above ground level. Swivelling the periscope, Bob realised he had a much better view of the warehouse from his current position. Only the hedgerow lay behind him and he felt he had more room to tense and slacken his muscles in the ditch than in the hedge. He knew it was important for him to keep his body active by slight muscles movements that would maintain steady blood flow through his body.

Holding the periscope an inch higher, Bob focused closely on the building ahead.

Meanwhile, Terry Calder recounted the last briefing to his officers opening with, 'It's plan B. Plan A and C are ditched. We go with plan B.'

A safety catch was removed. A shoulder holster readjusted, and a pair of skin-tight leather gloves were smoothed to the wrist.

'India Nine-Nine is on the plot,' from a helicopter in the sky. 'Video rolling.'

'Skiddaw One,' from Jim Latimer. 'All units report current positions.'

More commentary from the net as Jim worked out in his mind where everyone was and confirmed the estate roads were locked down.

'Cuckoo One report,' from Jim.

'Cuckoo One has the eyeball on the warehouse. All Tango Victors still on site. I have movement at the front windows above the front entrance. Several unidentified figures. They are too murky to identify. The windows need to be washed. Has anyone got a sponge? Otherwise, no change.'

'Skiddaw One to all units. Sabre One has control.'

'Sabre One, I have control,' radioed Terry in acknowledgement. 'We are moving towards position Sabre Strike One.'

Terry's Sabre spearhead unit stealthily approached the warehouse on foot whilst the others waited just out of sight of the building in their vehicles.

'Cuckoo One has movement at the side door,' from Bob in the ditch. 'I have an eyeball on Tango Zero Three and Tango Zero Four. They are smoking and drinking. Tea or coffee presumably. One unidentified figure in the upstairs windows.'

'I have that,' from Sabre One. 'Are they armed with visible weapons?'

'None seen,' from Cuckoo One.

Terry led his team on foot. They crouched down behind one of the vehicles parked outside the warehouse. Gesturing with his hands and fingers, Terry indicated what would happen shortly and then engaged the net with, 'Cuckoo One, current situation.'

A tired man, hot and sweaty, but now with an excellent view of the side door replied, 'No Change. Two Tangos at the open side door drinking and smoking. Looks like they're having a break from whatever. The side door is slightly ajar. I can hear voices from within and can see several figures inside the warehouse at ground level. They all seem to be working on something on a table inside. Can't see them anymore. Further! No movement from front office windows on the second floor. Cuckoo One over.'

'Sabre One, I have that. India Nine-Nine current please.'

'India Nine-Nine has a video in play. Multiple Victors parked in front of the warehouse. Your perimeter cordon is now in place and has been consolidated by the deployment of armed uniform officers to your interior cordon. Target is surrounded on all four sides. Looks good from here, Sabre One.'

'Thank you, I have that. Cuckoo! Can you give me a green light?' from Sabre One.

Bob stole another inch with the periscope, took a wider and longer view, and replied, 'It's a go from me.'

'India Nine-Nine?'

'It's a go from me.'

'I have that,' from Terry. 'Sabre One will move to Sabre Strike One.'

Turning to the five officers behind him, Terry said, 'Ready?'

There was a nod from the team and sudden alertness that invaded the atmosphere.

'Let's go.'

The six men from the Sabre team suddenly broke cover and rushed towards the front of the warehouse where they hit the wall hard, flattened out, and then immediately dropped to their knees.

'Cuckoo One reports no change.'

'Sabre One, I have that. Sabre One on my mark. Sabre Strike Two.'

On Sabre Strike Two, the remains of the Sabre unit fired their engines and headed at speed to the front of the warehouse where they blocked off the suspect vehicles thus preventing any escape in a motor vehicle. Rushing to the front doors, they took up positions close to the entrance.

Simultaneously, Terry Calder led his six-man team down the side of the warehouse to a side door where Tiny Philpotts and Jeffrey Jackson were men stood talking, smoking cigarettes, and drinking from pot mugs. Both men were blissfully unaware of either the surveillance officer watching them from a nearby ditch or the spearhead now rushing towards them.

Sprinting down the side of the warehouse the spearhead team used elements of surprise and speed to ram Philpotts and Jackson against the wall where they held them tight.

Levelling a firearm into the eyesight of both prisoners, the armed officer stated, 'Enough! Don't even twitch.'

The side door stood ajar. Only the mumble of chatter interspersed with laughter could be heard.

Snatching a stun grenade from his weapons belt, Terry brazenly kicked the side door wide open and threw the missile into the building. Within seconds, two more projectiles exploded inside the warehouse allowing the masked Terry and one other to enter unseen.

'Sabre One Strike One has entered,' on the net.

At the front of the warehouse, an explosives officer surreptitiously placed devices at each of the door hinges. He waved everyone to safety, activated the devices electronically, and watched them blow up into the air and out into the car park.

The Sabre team poured in through the front door.

'Sabre One, Strike Three,' on the net.

Moments later, 'Sabre One Strike Three has entered.'

The inner perimeter cordon consisting of firearms officers from Kent Constabulary rose from their covert positions and began to close on the building. One contingent climbed over a low-level wooden fence in the field adjoining the estate. Finding their feet, they rushed to help the Sabre team secure Philpotts and Jackson at the side door.

A foot accidentally kicked over a pot mug. A cigarette fell from a curled and nervous mouth to the ground. There was a slight struggle when Philpotts finally realised what was taking place. It had all happened so fast. A body thudded hard against the brick wall and a click confirmed the locking of a pair of handcuffs. There was a grunt or two when bodies were taken to the ground.

Inside the warehouse, panic ensued when Terry shouted, 'Armed police. Stand still!'

The order was drowned out when two more stun grenades exploded in the middle of the warehouse and threw the gang into total disarray.

Dropping to the ground, Bobby Nelson covered his ears with his hands in sudden desperation.

As the smoke began to clear, the Sabre team took stock of the beer kegs that had been placed in a rectangular configuration inside the building. Once emptied, the kegs had been strategically placed in a rectangle so that they could support layers of laminate tabletops at which people had been working. The tabletops were conjoined into a sizeable set of workstations. On the floor beside some of the tables, other kegs were in various stages of being emptied. Several bungs had been removed from the kegs and left lying on the floor nearby. Every time a keg was emptied it was used as a leg for the next table. On each tabletop, there were bags of white powder each weighing about two kilos.

It was heroin or cocaine, thought Terry Calder. Possibly talcum powder here and there because the colour of talcum powder was not dissimilar to the drugs involved and was the favourite cutting element in the reduction of uncut heroin to street market heroin The bags resembled the size and shape of a two-kilo sugar bag except some of them had been cut in half and others into quarters. The once empty warehouse was now a factory for breaking down the huge supply of illegal drugs into smaller packages for the assembled dealers, runners, and riders.

Terry had seen it all before in various parts of the Metropolitan area, except this was the biggest factory he had ever seen, and it was situated in a temporary 'one day only' facility that beggared belief. It was how the dealers turned a twenty-five million pounds drug deal into a hundred million pounds enterprise. The drug was bought uncut at the lower price and then repeatedly cut again with the addition of talcum powder and similarly coloured soft substances. The strength was diluted during the process but the quantity available to sell and make a profit grew according to the number of cuts made.

In the centre of the warehouse sat the motorhome.

From where Terry stood, he could easily see that the vehicle's roof had been removed and was lying on the floor beside the vehicle. He decided that it didn't take a genius to work out where the drugs had been hidden.

In the far corner, there was another table which had been erected on top of more kegs. It was strewn with jewellery of all types. There were rings, necklaces, earrings, several tiaras, wristwatches, brooches, tie pins, cufflinks, and just about every item of jewellery that you could think of. Made from diamonds, emeralds, rubies, sapphires, tanzanite, peridot, garnets, pearls, platinum, gold and silver, the value was astounding.

Terry immediately suspected it was stolen property.

Jim Latimer appeared at the open front door with a loudspeaker and addressed the assembly with, 'Armed police! Stand still! Hands in the air! Now!'

Walking forward, dominating the ground, Jim used the loud-hailer again ordering, 'Everyone! Hands in the air! We are the police. You are all under arrest! Hands! Let me see your hands!'

Deafened by stun grenades, now confused, and disorientated with smoke still drifting through the air, the gang members were in various stages of buoyancy. Several immediately held their hands up whilst others were shocked to the core and either stood like statues or lay on the ground upon which they had fallen when the grenades had exploded. A few seemed unruffled, unperturbed, ready for anything.

The detectives moved in and covered each other as they set about handcuffing the gang.

A quick count by Jim led him to believe there were close on fifty males to arrest and secure.

'Skiddaw One has control,' he radioed. 'We are making arrests. All units close in to assist, please. Being prisoner vans and photographers to the front doors.'

As the net filled with more commentary, Jawbone Jones stood alone on the mezzanine second floor that butted out partially into the main body of the warehouse. The makeshift floor was directly above the front doors and overlooked the car park below. The level gave access to two unused offices where he had been when the raid took place.

Jawbone looked out of the front window, saw more plainclothes police arriving in numbers, and considered climbing out of the window to the ground below. Two seconds later, he'd worked out it was a leg-breaker, far too high, and too dangerous.

Three livered police vans approached the warehouse with blue lights flashing and sirens sounding.

There was a creak on the staircase behind Jawbone which caused him to spin around on his heels.

'Hands!' shouted the armed officer. 'Hands up! No messing.'

Jawbone froze.

'Turn around,' ordered the detective. 'Place your hands behind your head and kneel onto both knees.'

Harnessing no intention of surrendering, Jawbone set off headfirst towards the officer. Bundling the detective over, Jawbone rolled down the staircase with him as he grappled for the officer's handgun.

The gun went one way and the detective's radio system went the other as the two men landed on the ground floor at the bottom of the stairs with a loud clatter.

Jawbone released the gun from his ankle holster and knelt by the officer. He held the gun to the detective's head as a group of detectives rushed to help their colleague.

'Get back!' screamed Jawbone. 'Everyone back or he gets it.'

Blood seeped from the officer's forehead where he had knocked against the metal steps.

'I mean it,' threatened Jawbone. 'No more handcuffs! I want a car and he's coming with me.'

There was an exchange of glances from one to another in the police line. This wasn't written down in plans A, B or C, thought Terry Calder.

'We all want cars,' yelled Jawbone. 'Yes! Let them go. Get your car keys, boys and whatever you can carry. Take the handcuffs off! Do it now or I'll kill this man. No problem. It's him or me and right now he's my ticket out of here or he's a dead man. Make your mind up.'

'Whoa!' yelled Jim. 'Easy now! No-one is going to hurt you. Just put the gun down and...'

Jawbone lifted his gun and aimed at Jim. His finger reached to the trigger.

The sound of two rapid gunshots plunged everyone into a state of shock when a man wearing a soil-covered camouflage outfit stood at the side door and fired his Glock 19 directly at Jawbone.

The two bullets entered Jawbone's skull above the nose and slammed him back into the staircase he had recently fallen from. His handgun slipped from his grasp. His mouth opened and then he slid ungraciously to the floor.

Jawbone Jones died almost immediately.

Bob Martin stepped forward. A thin line of wet slimy mud followed him, trailed from his soiled footwear, and painted a bizarre zigzag picture on the floor behind him.

Holstering his gun, Bob voiced, 'My radio went down. No-one heard me when the stun grenades exploded. I saw him upstairs at the window. I tried to tell everyone.'

'Okay!' replied Jim immediately recognising that Bob Martin was exhausted, 'It's okay, Bob. Just relax. It's all over.'

Nodding in agreement, Bob Martin replied, 'Cuckoo One! I'm all done here. All done.'

An eternity of silence seemed to pass before Jim Latimer resumed control and said, 'Get them secured. Handcuffs! Come on! Let's have them.'

~

15

Twenty-four hours later
Calais.

'By the way, is your man, Bob Martin, alright now?' inquired Maguire.

'Yes,' replied Jim. 'And you're forgetting, Les, he's not my man. He's our man and a member of the Cumbria surveillance squad.'

'Yes, of course,' nodded Maguire. 'I understand he's suspended now. Is that normal? He didn't do anything wrong from what I've been told by those who were there.'

'Unfortunately, he is suspended. Yes!' confirmed Jim. 'He's excluded from duty and is currently resting in a hotel in Canterbury before we all go home. Standard operating procedure dictates events. There'll be an enquiry and I expect him to be fully exonerated in time. I've made a witness statement in which I describe how he probably saved an officer's life even though he had to take Jawbone Jones's to do so. I expect to get roasted for deploying a CROPS officer for too long a period. Probably by people who've no idea what either a surveillance operation or a CROPS officer is.'

'I can see you are annoyed,' suggested Maguire.

'Only with the system of bureaucracy,' frowned Jim. 'I'll be putting Bob Martin forward for a commendation at the very least. It's just that sometimes I think the system prefers dead heroes to live ones.'

'Gentlemen!' intruded Jack Henderson. 'It's my pleasure to treat you to a pint of beer as a gesture of congratulations following yesterday's operation. What a great result. Lots of arrests, a ton of drugs taken off the streets, twenty-five million pounds in cash, a dozen firearms from the gang in the warehouse, and a free trip to Calais on the ferry with thanks to our friend Rafferty.'

'You are so kind,' replied Rafferty. 'But whilst my service is happy with the outcome for yourselves, we are saddened to learn that it seems our friends in France have been let down by one of their agents.'

Dispensing drinks from a tray, Jack declared, 'Oh! I didn't think you could speak of such things being from MI5 and all that.'

'I can't,' confirmed Rafferty. 'It must be the wind you heard, not me. I'd appreciate it if you kindly considered that this is just a leisure trip across the Channel at the expense of my service. Our sortie into France is little more than a day out in the country designed to build bridges, extend loyalties, and create contacts on behalf of the service.'

'And your real reason is?' chuckled Jim.

'To take you to the docks in Calais to show you what happens next, and then for a trip in the countryside towards Paris. We'll be visiting a wine tasting establishment. It's all taken care of. We'll meet some friends there all being well. I hope you enjoy the day. For myself, I'm still searching for guns.'

'Many thanks! We'll drink to that,' laughed Maguire taking a large drink from a pint of lager. 'Wow! I needed that. What a nice cold drink this is. I could get used to it. Where are my sunglasses? Suntan lotion? Anyone! This reminds me of life before Dover. Whose round is it?'

'Yours on the way back,' chuckled Jim clinking glasses with everyone. 'You'd best be fit for later because Alexander the Great and Stan the Man travelled overnight to assist in the operation following the raid yesterday. They'll liaise with the other forces and make sure the file is put together properly. You know what the boss is like. He'll turn everything over whilst he's looking for mistakes, making suggestions, and putting things in order.'

'Oh!' from a stunned Maguire. 'Are we in trouble?'

'No! He's delighted but he's arranged for a team of Cumbrian detectives to interview some of the gang members. We've got people up north who've been studying the file and waiting for this opportunity for quite a while now. He's not going to let this slip through his fingers and although the case may well be dealt with down south, he's determined that the right questions are put and the right evidence is produced, recognised, and consolidated in the case file.'

Maguire nodded in satisfaction, but the MI5 man asked, 'Who on earth is Alexander the Great?'

'Our Chief of Detectives,' replied Maguire. 'A local legend in our neck of the woods.'

'Oh, yes! I spoke to him on the 'phone, of course. So, he's putting the file of evidence together? Or rather, the sergeant Stan the Man will be?'

'Not quite,' explained Jim. 'He's working with the other surveillance team leaders to make sure all the relevant documentation and evidence is in the pot, surveillance logs, forensics, fingerprints, DNA, ballistics, everything. I'm sure he and the Chief of Detectives in Kent will get their heads together and unite a team to process the legal side of things.'

'Good!' replied Rafferty. 'Shall we look out of the viewing window? We don't always get a leisurely opportunity to cross the Channel every day.'

Rafferty led Maguire, Jim, and Jack to an area on the ferry where they watched the white cliffs of Dover disappear and the French coast appear. Within the hour, the ferry had docked in Calais and the four men disembarked, all slightly better for the smooth passage of a relaxed alcoholic beverage or two.

A grey Peugeot minibus pulled up in front of the men. Rafferty gestured for them to enter and the vehicle set off. A short time later, Rafferty led the others to part of the dock where several police vehicles and plain saloon cars were parked. The area was cordoned off and under armed guard. The vehicle paused at the entrance when an officer challenged it, glanced at a document produced by the driver, and then instantly waved them through.

The entourage was yards away from the gangplank of a sea-going vessel that towered above them.

'You seem to have influence even in France,' suggested Maguire.

'Just friends,' explained Rafferty in a matter of fact manner.

'Is this the ship that brought the drugs from South America?' inquired Maguire.

'Yes!' replied Rafferty. 'Unfortunately, I recently learnt that the French lost an hour before they realised our target ship had landed in Calais and not Dunkirk.'

'Dunkirk?' queried Maguire.

'The French wrongly presumed that Dunkirk would be more attractive to the Colombians than Calais, so they plotted up in Dunkirk. As it is, the vessel arrived at Calais during the night, was met by pilot boats as usual, and upon docking was visited by the Port Authority and the local Immigration Unit.'

'How did Wayne come into possession of his shipment?' inquired Maguire.

'We're working on that,' replied Rafferty. 'Or rather, the French are. CCTV shows several crew members walking down the gangplank on arrival. Each carrying a couple of suitcases or holdalls. They bundle their personal belongings into a minibus and then toddle back up the gangplank.'

'It was that easy?' queried Jim.

'I'm not sure, but I don't think so,' replied Rafferty. 'I've put forward my theory has to how it happened.'

'Go on! We're all ears.'

'The ship arrived at night,' explained Rafferty. 'It was dark. The vessel lay off the harbour for a while before a pilot was requested, notified, and went out to escort it in. If you were delivering an illegal consignment it's not beyond the realms of possibility to meet a smaller seagoing yacht or speedboat, offload the shipment, and carry on as normal into the port.'

'That would make you think a speedboat would then cross the Channel and land the catch at Dover or somewhere on the coast,' argued Maguire.

'Precisely!' nodded Rafferty. 'Except Wayne trundled across on the ferry in a motor home in which a ton of drugs was hidden. That's why we need to keep an open mind and why this side of things are still under investigation by the

French. I take it Wayne will be questioned as to how he came into possession of the drugs?'

'Oh yes,' admitted Jim. 'Most definitely. Thank you for the heads up, Rafferty.'

'My pleasure. By the way, you were certainly right when you tagged Wayne with the title 'Mystery Man'. Because he certainly is. One thing more,' continued Rafferty. 'I think that only the captain of the ship knew where they would land. I just wish they'd docked at Dover and it had been ours. We'd still be there, and I'd still be looking for my guns. I'm beginning to think the intelligence story isn't quite what we thought it was.'

'What can we do to help?' inquired Jim Latimer.

'Watch part of a Colombian drugs cartel being dismantled,' suggested Rafferty pointing to the vessel. 'My people are working closely with the French authorities. The ship in the dock is a container vessel laden with two hundred and seventy-five containers. It was registered in Panama, but it sailed out of Cartagena, in Colombia, and into the Caribbean Sea. It crossed the North Atlantic Ocean and arrived in Calais six thousand three hundred and forty-two nautical miles later.'

'Shadowed by the French presumably?' inquired Jack.

'No!' replied Rafferty. 'It was nearing the Bay of Biscay when we got to know that the French had been tipped off by a source in Colombia. It wasn't until it docked that we were on it. Guns, it was said. We got drugs instead. No matter.'

'It's not over yet,' suggested Jack.

'You're right,' smiled Rafferty pointing to the gangplank. 'The man being led down the gangplank by the Gendarmerie is Captain Jeronimo Garcia.'

'Do you know him?' asked Jim.

'No, but of him, yes,' nodded Rafferty. 'He's been of interest to colleagues in Portugal, Italy, Spain and France for some years now. Garcia has been arrested on three previous occasions and walked free each time, without being charged, purely because we've never been able to place enough evidence against him. You guys know as well as I that knowing and proving are two different things.'

'Did you try to turn him?' probed Maguire. 'You know. Offer him a deal he could not resist?'

Jim Latimer turned sharply on Maguire and felt his jaw drop when the words in his head refused to come out.

'I wish,' replied Rafferty. 'The problem is that he's the cousin of Garcia the Great who heads one of the cartels in Villavicencio, just south of the capital, Bogota. There's a ring of iron around him when he's not at sea.'

'I hope he's not related to Alexander the Great,' frowned Jim.

'Not as far as I know,' laughed Rafferty.

'If we can tie Wayne to the ferry from Calais, and then log him on the Calais dock system, it will be a big help.'

'If we can forensically compare anything found in the ship to the drug's packaging that we've recovered in the motor home, that will help also,' suggested Jim. 'It's all to play for and we do have the original packages under lock and key.'

'The other factor in play is that one of those arrested - one of the gang – might just want to turn Queen's evidence in return for a lesser sentence and spill the beans as far as they can. As you say, Jim, it's all to play for.'

Nodding Rafferty replied, 'Right now, there are over two hundred and fifty officers from various services deployed in the security and searching of the vessel. It's a long story, gentlemen, but when you have a case file on a ship's captain that had been suspected of drugs and gun-running for the last ten years you eventually reach a time when you just know that you have enough to throw a conspiracy charge at the very least at the individual and know it will stick. Today, with the French, we're going to arrest every member of the crew, search every container on the ship, and interview the pilot, the crew, the ports people, everyone. I'm just waiting for a call. The search is ongoing.'

'I think you might have enough already if we can connect Wayne to the ferry. The CCTV will show him and the motor home if nothing else,' proposed Maguire.

Two officers bundled the handcuffed Captain Garcia along the quayside, placed him in the rear of a patrol car, and set off with its light flashing and siren sounding. They would not stop until the prisoner was at the local police station.

A 'phone rang and whilst everyone checked their pockets, the MI5 man immediately answered his with, 'Rafferty!'

Moments later, Rafferty man closed his 'phone and said, 'That was my deputy on board the ship helping the French. They've just removed a large amount of what looks like heroin from a bulkhead. He reckons there could be as much as ten tons to recover. It was well hidden apparently, but the good news is that another team in the stern area have found over a hundred rifles and handguns along with some ammunition. To quote your friend, I'm all done here, gentlemen.'

The gathering was euphoric and slapped Rafferty on his back with congratulations before Maguire challenged the MI5 man with, 'Just leave us here. We'll find a café or a bar. I think I speak for all of us when I say I know you'll want to be on board in the thick of things.'

'Here! Here!'

Smiling, Rafferty declared, 'Not at all. If you cannot trust your deputy to finish the job, then why employ him in the first place? My team know where I am. Now then, gentlemen, I promised a ride in the country and a glass of wine. Come on. Driver! The wine tasting, please. Time for a ride in the country.'

Maguire and Jim exchanged puzzled glances as they climbed into the Peugeot.

They were even more puzzled when half an hour later, on the Calais to Paris road, the vehicle took a left and drove down a narrow lane towards a hostelry standing alone in the countryside.

'Where are we now?' queried Jack.

'At the home of Richard Arthur Wayne and his wife Veronique,' replied Rafferty. 'Thanks to yourselves, I noted in your case logs that when he was stopped at the ferry terminal in Dover, he gave the name George Wood. I ran that name and his vehicle through the French system. It turned up trumps in that the motor home had been clocked on the motorway CCTV system on numerous occasions in recent months. Always on the Paris – Calais road. Anyway, I picked the most frequent area of sightings and contacted the local Gendarmerie. In turn, they traced the vehicle historically to a particular area courtesy of those CCTV sightings. I asked them to speak with the local Mayor and find out if Wayne owned property in the region.'

'Why not use the land registry?' inquired Maguire.

'Because the system is different in France,' explained Rafferty. 'The owner of a particular property, or parcel of land as the French call it, is recorded in a document called the 'matrice cadastrale'. The local Mayor has access to this and no one else. We sometimes forget that foreign countries have different procedures. I asked one the local Gendarmerie to make enquiries on behalf of my service and French Intelligence.'

'Cheeky!' posed Jack.

'It was, but it was worth it in the end,' admitted Rafferty. 'The Gendarmerie traced Wayne's name to this place. It's called 'La Villa de la liberté.'

'The villa of freedom?' ventured Jim. 'Am I correct?'

'Yes, you are,' nodded Rafferty.

'There has to be an irony of some kind in all this,' suggested Jim. 'Liberty!'

'The Gendarmerie made a cursory visit to these premises on our behalf,' explained Rafferty. 'They spoke with the domestic staff who told them their master and his wife had gone to England for the weekend. I asked if there were any photographs in the house of the master and his wife. Guess what?'

'The gendarmes sent you a photograph of our prisoners Wayne and Veronique,' ventured Jack.

'Correct! The man from Kent has won a coconut. Yes, they found a photograph of them both standing on the cliffs somewhere with the sea in the background,' revealed Rafferty. 'It looks like a selfie. Yes, Jack. You are entirely correct. This is their home in France and I do believe we will find it is their main home since the staff here say they all live locally and have been in full-time employment for Mr and Mrs Wood from London for quite a few years.'

'Potentially, this is a gold mine,' suggested Maguire.

'It is indeed,' added Jim. 'And Wayne isn't the only mystery man on the block is he, Mr Rafferty?'

'The couple run a wine tasting business from here,' smiled Rafferty ignoring the veiled compliment. 'I think we shall partake of their offer. I expect to meet Monsieur le Maire at the premises. Follow me, gentleman.'

'Monsieur le Maire?' queried Maguire.

'The chairman of the local municipal council,' explained Rafferty. 'He has responsibilities for the municipal police amongst other things. The mayor has no authority over the Gendarmerie but as he has been most helpful to us without knowing it. I thought it my duty to meet him personally and thank him for his assistance in this matter.'

'Yes! Yes, of course,' nodded Maguire. 'I agree. Another contact falls into place.'

'You know me too well,' replied Rafferty. 'But this is merely a courtesy to the French authorities and no more.'

As the group followed Rafferty to a nearby building, they walked past an elaborate villa which was situated with two pools that formed a semicircle around the villa. There was also an outdoor gym area littered with gym equipment, outdoor showers, and what seemed to be an artist's retreat of some kind. In addition, an outdoor bar was in situ along with scores of potted plants that provided a colourful display.

'It's a millionaire's paradise,' suggested Maguire.

'The owner needs to explain where the money came from to buy this little lot,' suggested Jim. 'Leisure visit! My mind is working overtime. There's a ton of evidence here, I suspect. Evidence of a luxurious lifestyle for an unemployed man, either in England or France.'

'Red, white, rose, or bubbles,' probed Rafferty. 'This is Edmond. He is the keeper or the premises when Mr Wood is not at home. I do believe you are the butler at times, Edmond.'

'I am,' replied Edmond who promptly shook hands with all assembled. 'This is one of the finest wine tasting areas in this part of France although you will probably know we are many miles from the Loire region where the nearest vineyards are situated. I believe our Mr Wood is in some kind of trouble from what the Gendarmerie say, so I think we should drink a toast to his health before I tell Mr Rafferty the full story of what goes on here. He is a big criminal, yes? At least that is what the gendarme told me.'

'Perhaps,' replied Maguire. 'A glass of Syrah if that is possible.'

A look of bemused engagement rippled along the bar as Edmond selected an appropriate bottle of wine and Maguire settled himself on a barstool.

'Are you here for the duration, Les?' inquired Jim.

'That depends on what my good friend Edmond has to say,' replied Maguire. Turning to Edmond, Maguire asked, 'Why do you speak out now about your Mr Wood but not previously?'

'Monsieur le Maire is involved,' explained Edmond. 'It is important that the people who work here are seen to be honest and helpful, monsieur. Our mayor is an important and powerful man locally. To give him the impression that we are somehow involved in crime with Mr Wood is a bad thing for the future of many of us. We presume our jobs are already lost and we shall be looking for work elsewhere in the municipality quite soon. The mayor may choose to help us or not. He is a landowner and has much influence in the area.'

Maguire nodded and replied, 'I see. Edmond, Mr Wood is in deep trouble. If you can tell us about him it would be most useful to our enquires. We are all detectives from the UK. You have the floor, sir. Please take it because we will need to speak to you formally in due course. For now, I shall thank you for a glass of wine and look forward to what you have to tell us.'

Jim shook his head, studied the ground, and then looked up when Edmond responded.

'I will tell you now,' replied Edmond. 'We are what the English call domestic staff and although he paid us well, he did not treat us well. His wife treated us like scum even though she was once a poor villager from this very area. I can tell you about his friends from all over the world if you wish. Some of them are crazy. Sacre bleu! Crazy!'

Edmond held the wine bottle on the bar and looked into Maguire's eyes.

'A cover!' murmured Maguire. 'I'll get right to the point, Edmond. You run a wine tasting hostelry to attract all the tourists and launder some of Wayne's ill-gotten money. This place is a rendezvous for selected contacts visiting the area from across the globe. They come here to do drugs business under the cover of a wine tasting holiday.'

'To prove,' remarked Rafferty. 'But we are on the same wavelength.'

Ignoring Rafferty, Maguire persisted with, 'Now tell me I'm wrong, Edmond.

A cork was removed, a bottle tipped, a glass filled, and a deeply refreshing drink in the French countryside was tasted by Maguire who nodded in satisfaction and then gestured an open palm to Edmond saying, 'Excellent! Smooth with a long taste on the palate. Now, where were we?'

'The staff have talked about it between themselves,' revealed Edmond. 'I want you to know Mr Detective, that it has been agreed amongst us that I will speak for all of us.'

'I see,' replied Maguire. 'Then who am I to argue with you, Edmond? Please proceed as instructed by your friends.'

'We do not know what Mr Wood has been doing that causes you to visit us,' explained Edmond. 'But my wife is the housekeeper here and she will tell you of the passports that are kept in a safe in the bedroom. Mr Wood's wife called him Ricky. We knew him as George. His guests called him Wayne.

Some of the gardeners heard one of his visitors call Mr Wood Doctor George Eldred. It always troubled us. Mr Wood has many passports from many different countries and uses many different names. We never knew why and did not ask. It is not our place to enquire when we are nothing more than a butler, a housekeeper, a maid, a gardener, or a servant. And then there is Mr Manuel from Panama, of course. He is a regular visitor.'

'Panama?' gasped Jim.

'Presumably, after the Gendarmerie initially visited you, everyone got together and decided to speak up,' continued Maguire. 'I need this to be clear in my mind. Have I got that right, Edmond?'

'Yes! As I said earlier, I speak for everyone working here, Mr English Detective,' revealed Edmond. 'We have done nothing wrong. It is not a wrong thing to do when you follow the orders of the master of the house. It is the strange people that have visited here that has always caused us some confusion and made some mystery. I will tell you of those people because tomorrow I shall have no job. No-one will pay me, and it is the way forward for us all if we are to seek work in the weeks ahead.'

Maguire nodded, beckoned another glass to be placed on the bar, and said, 'Join me, Edmond. Talk to me. Tell me of your life under the regime of Mr George Wood.'

A drink was poured, and a chink of glasses followed.

A convoy of police cars and plain salon cars trickled into the estate as the French began their first formal enquiries. Rafferty introduced himself to Monsieur le Marie and then spoke with colleagues from French Intelligence and the Gendarmerie as a helpful distraction for Maguire and the team. It will all come out in the wash, formally, in due course, thought Rafferty. But right now, it was all to play for, and England were away from home on French soil.

Maguire nodded, smiled, and gestured to Edmond to carry on as he listened intently to the life story of George Wood alias Richard Arthur Wayne, alias Doctor George Eldred alias several more, as he was known to the household staff with whom he had spent many recent years.

~

16

The Sportsman Inn
Heads Lane, Carlisle
Mid-afternoon
Ten days later.

By arrangement on the telephone, Chris Cobb strolled into the Sportsman Inn, reached the bar, and then gazed into the mirror behind the optics as he scrutinised the gathering of customers who frequented the establishment whenever they were in the town centre.

The Inn dated back to the early eighteenth century and was built on the site of the Blackfriars Convent. Over the years, it has been known as the White Ox, the Lowther Arms, Guy Earl of Warwick (1797), the Rose & Thistle, and the Golden Quoit (1848). The pub had been the Sportsman Inn since the mid-nineteenth century. Realistically, it was always referred to by its customers as 'The Sportsman'. Situated in Heads Lane, near the junction with Blackfriars Street, the Inn was more or less adjacent to the burial ground of St Cuthbert's Church and was now famous for its midday lunches and evening entertainment ranging from quiz nights to Karaoke.

Today it was a chosen meeting place.

Scanning reflections in the mirror, Cobb caught sight of Maguire sitting in a quiet corner of the pub.

Nodding, the detective moved a newspaper from one side of the table to another and took a drink from a pint of lager. It was the signal that all was well. As Cobb approached with a pint of beer, Maguire began chuckling.

Cobb took a seat next to him, and asked, 'What's so funny?'

'Your coat,' replied Maguire. 'Is that the only one you have?'

'Why! What's it got to do with you what I wear?'

'It's the only one I've ever seen you in,' stated Maguire. 'If we were outside, I'd see you coming a mile away. Three-quarter length coat, collar up, hands in pockets! You never change, Chris!'

'I can't afford a new coat,' growled Cobb. 'Anyway! What's that got to do with it? Where the hell have you been?'

'On holiday in France!'

'Ha-Ha!' laughed Cobb. 'It's all over the newspapers.'

Maguire turned the newspaper on the table over and displayed the front page saying, 'You can say that again. Did we miss anything?'

'Nope,' ventured Cobb. 'Not a one as far as I know. And I'll let you into a secret. I'm free. I feel like I've just dropped a ton of worries from my back and I can breathe again. What about you?'

'Tired,' replied Maguire. 'Just tired. We've never stopped.'

'Is that a complaint?'

'No! It's because of a good result,' declared Maguire. 'By the way, I've ordered two ploughman's lunches. I hope that's okay because they have just arrived.'

A waitress appeared and served two light lunches from the tray before returning to the serving hatch for the next order.

'Are you well? Any problems?' inquired Maguire.

'I take it I'm in the clear?' asked Cobb dissecting a piece of cheese. 'I've been waiting for a knock on the door, but it never happened.'

'Because you weren't directly involved,' explained Maguire. 'No-one is coming for you from my mob. I want to be sure there's no residue of the gang roaming about the street who've worked out who the leak might have been. Do you feel safe?'

'Totally! Everyone has disappeared. I heard Rooney got locked up as well so the pub in Kendal is closed. It's all boarded up and for sale.'

'I see!' replied Maguire. 'Tell me what your plans are?'

'Tell me what yours are?' insisted Cobb. 'Who was been charged with what? Will they all go to prison? How long will they get? I need to know these things.'

Nodding, toying with his meal for a moment, Maguire replied, 'We've charged more than sixty-five people with various offences ranging from conspiracy to import drugs, conspiracy to import illegal firearms, conspiracy to supply drugs, being in possession of illegal drugs, illegal possession of firearms and ammunition, money laundering. Hey, all kinds of stuff.'

'How long will they get?'

'The majority can expect long prison sentences of between five and twenty years,' revealed Maguire. 'Others, perhaps less, but then they are people you have never met and know nothing about you. Just residue arrests along the way really.'

'I understand you,' nodded Cobb. 'I'll just need to keep out of the prison system then and I'll be alright.'

'Yes! Why do you say that? Are you thinking of a long-term career in crime, by any chance?'

'No! I'm looking for a job, that's all. Having a record doesn't help. No-one wants to know and I've not much money now that the gang is locked up. There's no money coming in.'

'Oh!' remarked Maguire. 'I think I can help you there. Ever been to Ullswater?'

Cobb ignored the question for a moment, tucked into his meal, and eventually said, 'No! I've heard about it but never been there.'

'Seriously?' probed Maguire.

'Yes! Seriously,' replied Cobb.

The two men continued their lunch, engaged in small talk, and then pushed the plates away and relaxed.

'That was good. Thank you!' ventured Cobb.

'You deserve more,' replied Maguire. 'I've got you a job in a hotel on the shores of Ullswater working as a kitchen porter. Twelve hours a day! Five days a week! Live free on the premises, and three meals a day. Interested?'

'Kitchen porter?' queried Cobb.

'Pot washing, cleaning, carrying, general dogsbody until you get yourself on your feet and used to life outside the gang.'

'How did you spring that for me?' inquired Cobb.

'A contact owns the hotel.'

'And you live nearby,' suggested Cobb.

'What makes you think that?'

'Well! Do you?'

Maguire drained his glass but did not reply.

'Les! You know everything about me, and I know nothing about you. I don't even know if Les Maguire is your right name.'

'It's the name I used in the court case against you,' reminded Maguire.

'Married or single?'

'Single?'

'Gay presumably then?'

Maguire scowled.

'Age?'

'Mid-twenties!'

'Home address?'

'No fixed abode,' declared Maguire.

'Favourite pub in the city?'

'This one.'

'Car?'

'Bike! Three-wheeler with a bell on the handlebars!'

'You're a liar and a control freak,' argued Cobb.

'Correct,' admitted Maguire.

'And you're giving nothing away.'

'Correct again! Two in a row,' replied Maguire. 'Look, Chris. I should tell you that I've got a new job. My papers came through yesterday. I'll be moving away soon. Just transferring out of here.'

'Still in the police?'

'Yes!'

'Where to?' demanded Cobb.

'You don't need to know, Chris. You have a life to lead and you don't need me in it anymore. Walk away. I'm sorry, but we're all done here. That's what you wanted right at the start and that's where we are now.'

'A 'phone number then?'

'No!'

'Are you sure?' pleaded Cobb.

'I'm sure,' replied Maguire. 'Now if you've finished this interrogation, let's get a breath of fresh air outside.'

Maguire eased himself from behind the table, paid the bill at the bar, and then gestured that Cobb should follow him.

Outside, in the fading light, Maguire strolled into Blackfriars Street before turning into a pathway leading to the church. Pausing for a moment, the detective turned to Cobb and said, 'Take the job. You might not like it but it's a start. You'll get a proper wage and a roof over your head. I think we're done now, Chris. We both knew it would come to this one day.'

Cobb pursed his lips, nodded in agreement, and sat on the wall looking into the churchyard.

'Okay! I'll give it a go.'

'Good!' replied Maguire removing a package from his jacket. 'As promised, this is your bank book. All the money you've earned working for us.'

'For you,' interrupted Cobb. 'I never worked for the police. I worked for you because you were the only one who wanted to know the real story of my life.'

'Thank you,' agreed Maguire handing the bank book over. 'The account is with a local bank, in your name, and only you can withdraw money from it. Do you remember signing the papers shortly after all this started?'

Cobb accepted the book, flicked over the pages, and felt his mouth drop.

'Happy?' queried Maguire.

'Not half,' replied Cobb. 'That will buy me a new car to drive to Ullswater with.'

'And the rest,' suggested Maguire. 'Not for me to say but I suggest you use public transport to get there and keep the cash in the bank until you need it.'

Cobb nodded and said, 'It's great but I made more money running drugs and stuff for the gang.'

'You wanted the gang removed,' argued Maguire. 'It's been completely dismantled. Now, who's complaining? Just remember, you always ran the risk of being arrested. How long do you think you had to go before that happened again? If you hadn't moved onto our side, you'd be doing time somewhere by now. You know that so please don't tell me otherwise. From the start, it was all about getting you out of the gang.'

'True! I got out just in time.'

'In the back of the bank book you'll find some loose papers,' explained Maguire. 'They contain all the information you need, and the relevant forms you require, to change your name by deed poll in the years ahead.'

'Oh! Yes, I thought that was the last resort if things went wrong,' challenged Cobb.

'You're right,' replied Maguire. 'But I somehow don't see you washing pots on the shores of Ullswater in ten years. Not if you get your mind together, get away from the gang crime culture, keep yourself to yourself, and stay out of trouble. Are you on my wavelength, Chris?'

'Ahead of you,' nodded Cobb. 'I've got something for you too.'

'What?' inquired Maguire.

'This,' replied Cobb producing a book from his coat pocket. 'It's a photo album.'

'Photographs?' queried Maguire. 'What photos?'

Cobb did not reply but watched Maguire casually flick through the album before coming to rest on one of the pages.

'Jeez! Are these what I think they are?' remarked Maguire. 'Those numbers look like sort codes and bank accounts. Names! Some of the names are foreign. What the hell is this, Chris?'

'The gang's finance records,' revealed Cobb.

'Where did you get them from?' demanded an astonished Maguire.

'They fell out of a safe in a house owned by Bobby Nelson. Someone photographed them. It's just a series of numbers, that's all.'

'What do they mean?' inquired Maguire.

'Do you know anything about money laundering when it comes to moving a ton of money?' probed Cobb.

'Enough to get by, I would say, Chris, but I don't understand this,' revealed Maguire. 'It looks like a route to an unknown place via various map references.

'The first set of numbers is Wayne's master account,' explained Cobb. 'The rest of the numbers are a route to the very last number. Think of this type of money laundering like it was a raincloud moving across the planet. Every hundred miles or so, it drops a rain shower somewhere. But for rain read money.'

'Okay!' replied Maguire. 'I got that. Do I need an umbrella?'

'No!' frowned Cobb. 'Just the sleazy old leather jacket you usually wear. It'll keep you dry.'

'Ouch!'

'It's like this,' explained Cobb. 'Some foreigner from South America shifts the money from that account through over forty different accounts situated in various banks across the globe. Most of the banks are in America because the financial laws over there are weak in comparison with other countries. The numbers in the book are the bank account numbers. The names match the bank account numbers. When the South American in the bank launders Wayne's money, he takes a cut, and it goes into his account. See photograph three. The rest of the money is transmitted through the global banking system like lightning. It's in and out of false business accounts until it starts to take on a look of innocence. You'll find leads to what they call 'shell companies.' These are companies that are properly set up with directors and financial controllers, but they don't have an operating base where you can go and knock on the door. They don't employ people to work. It's an empty shell.'

'I've heard about them,' replied Maguire.

'It takes you guys ages to prove a company doesn't exist but only minutes to create one and move money around in its accounts,' explained Cobb. 'Within minutes the cash is moved through different preordained accounts until it arrives in Wayne's clean account. Ordinarily, it would take months to follow the transmissions because the electronic system is a flashlight. The flashlight is money. The cash is in one account for one minute and then another for a minute and then another. It moves so fast that you might never unravel the route of transmissions. The South American set this up. I don't know who he is but it took him months to manufacture it and only minutes to move money around the globe from one dirty bank account into a good clean bank account forty or fifty electronic transmissions later. The photographs show you the numbers of the accounts and the route. They're not 'phone numbers although some people might think so.

Manuel from Panama, I'll bet, thought Maguire who then said, 'I know some who would think they were 'phone numbers. I thought Bobby lived in Kendal.'

'He does,' confirmed Cobb. 'Until he was locked up. Bobby has a rented house on the Kirkbarrow estate. These are from his own house in Levens, just outside Kendal. He's also got houses in Milnthorpe, Staveley, Bowness on Windermere, and Ambleside. He's a property tycoon who feigns poverty whilst being quite rich. Not a bad place to hide your money, Les. In property!'

'Okay, but tell me how on earth did they end up in Bobby Nelson's house?'

'Bobby's sister is Wayne's wife. Veronique!'

Stunned for a moment, Maguire glanced at the photographs and then looked directly into Cobb's eyes before asking, 'How long have you known about this?'

'A while,' admitted Cobb. 'I worked out that Bobby always had more money than the others. He took long holidays abroad and went to see his sister. She was born in France. I never knew where Bobby was born. They have the same parents both of whom died some years ago. One day I had nothing to do so I went browsing when Bobby was on holiday in France. The finance book was in a desk drawer then. I looked at it, didn't know what it was, put it back, and forgot about it. Then you came along and got me thinking about all kinds of things, I realised what the book was for. I went back for it when they were on their way to Dover and you were following them. I photographed the contents and put it back in the safe. No damage! No theft! A break in without a break if you see what I mean. I photographed it for you.'

Maguire studied the album and shook his head in disbelief.

'It never happened. I was never there, or here,' suggested Cobb. 'You might be dreaming. Understand?'

Nodding, Maguire said, 'All this time and now I wonder who is running who? You're good with numbers, aren't you?'

'I'll be better pot washing,' replied Cobb. 'Look, it's time to go. I'll take the job. I'll be there on Monday as promised. I'll do my best but can't say I'll stay there.'

'I'm pleased to hear it,' replied Maguire.

'We're finished,' proposed Cobb. 'Thank you for all you have done for me.'

'Before you go,' replied Maguire. 'You dropped this a while back.'

Cobb watched as Maguire reached inside a pocket and spilt the contents of a package onto a space on the wall between them.

Two ingots and a pendant attached to a silver chain lay on the sandstone.

'Yours, I believe,' challenged Maguire.

A hint of a tear in the corner of Cobb's eye emerged but was quickly wiped away and the words, 'So it is,' were heard. 'I wondered where I'd dropped it.'

'You know where you dropped it and so do I, Chris. If I hadn't pocketed it, and you hadn't dropped it, we'd have never met in the way that we have over the last year or so.'

'Yeah! I've missed the chain.'

'Do me a favour,' pleaded Maguire.

'Of course, anything,' replied Cobb taking the chain into this possession.

'Don't drop it again.'

Cobb studied the chain and muttered, 'Memories,' before reaching behind his neck and securing the chain. 'It belongs there, around my neck.'

'Good luck!' offered Maguire.

'You too,' voiced Cobb.

'What was my code name?'

'You never had one,' lied Maguire. 'Goodbye!'

Chris Cobb stood up, left the churchyard, and began to walk down St Cuthbert's Lane.

'But you were a gem,' murmured Maguire. 'A pure gem!'

Cobb disappeared into the twilight as he walked away. He did not look back

The two men planned never to meet again.

That night Les Maguire jogged casually to the foot of the hill, met his coach, Stan Holliday, and ran all the way to the summit in precisely twenty-seven minutes.

Objective achieved, thought Maguire. A three-mile hill climb in record time without a stop on the way. I feel great.

Stan approached Maguire, saw that the younger man was now much more experienced in the ways of the job, and in the practice of running up hills.

Clasping a hand on Maguire's shoulder, Stan announced, 'Well done, Les. I always knew you had it in you. Same time tomorrow?'

Nodding, Maguire replied, 'Ever played tennis, Stan?'

Stan threw his leg over the bike, engaged the pedals, and began his journey downhill shouting, 'No! I'd need a good coach.'

Maguire stood with his hands on his hips and allowed a special grin to crease his face before he took his first step into the descent.

Winter had given way to Spring and summer was close. It would soon be time to hit the tennis court where he hoped to play in the club mixed doubles championship.

It was time to find a lady in his life, thought Maguire. One who plays tennis.

~

17

Twelve years later
An Office
Somewhere in England

'I want everyone plotted up by nine o'clock tomorrow morning,' instructed Maguire. 'Commit the map to memory and know it like the back of your hand because once the target shows, he'll park the vehicle and proceed on foot for the rest of the day. And he won't be carrying a map, and neither will you. It's a square mile plot. Learn it! You'll need plenty of change for telephone kiosks, cafes, tube stations, buses, the usual. Eat on the hoof when you can. Just remember, the target runs the show until we move in because he's satisfied the criteria for evidence. If the informant is correct, the target will check, check, and check again to make sure he's not being followed. Then he'll collect the gun from a litter bin around the corner from the bank. Once he's got the weapon, he'll make for the bank. I am informed that the weapon will be loaded with six rounds. Here,' Maguire rapped a pointer on the map, 'is where we'll take him out. On the bank's doorstep. His previous convictions suggest he would be more than happy to discharge the firearm at anyone who gets in his way. Be aware that two plain-clothed armed officers will be situated inside the bank from the word go to deal with any problems that may occur. But we're not going to lose him, are we?'

'No!' groaned the gathering.

'Exactly!' continued Maguire. 'That's not going to happen. I want him with one foot on the bank's doorstep. I don't want any future court confused that he was carrying a gun for a friend. Nope! He's going to use the gun to rob the bank. We're going to intervene and take him to the ground before he takes the gun out of his trouser waistband because he's just the type to use it on a cashier and I don't want to run it that far. Remember, Bill is keeping the surveillance log and it will be part of the evidence. Evidence is when the target parks three hundred yards from the bank and then spends the next two hours dry cleaning himself making sure he isn't being followed before going to the bank that was always a hundred yards away. A good result will put the target away for close on ten years.'

'Bus pass?' queried a young lady on the front row to the amusement of the assembly. 'Do I need a bus pass?'

'You're too young, Irene,' laughed Maguire. 'Keep trying.'

The door opened and a middle-aged woman stuck her head into the room and shouted, 'Mr Maguire! A telephone call for you. Line four!'

'Thanks,' replied Maguire moving to a desk in the corner of the room.

'You're welcome,' replied the lady.

Maguire lifted the 'phone and punched the button on the display. He covered the mouthpiece with his free hand and said, 'Check the map. Tell me what you think of the plan, and I'll be back with you in a moment.'

There was a mumble of agreement before the detective engaged the 'phone with, 'Maguire!'

'Hi, Les. How are you?'

'Speak up, please. I can't hear you. Say again!'

'It's me. The drainpipe man!'

Maguire's mind spun into turmoil for a moment when he recognised the voice and replied, 'Say again. Who are you?'

'Cobb! Chris Cobb!'

'Well, I never,' replied Maguire. 'Where are you, and how are you?'

'Oh, here and there. I'm well, thanks. How about you?'

Maguire sat down at the desk, wiped his brow, and replied, 'Fine! Who gave you my number?'

'That doesn't matter,' replied Cobb. 'I started a few days ago with a call to your old office in Penrith. I followed the route, dug about a bit, saw your name in the papers. I got to you, didn't I? What more do you want?'

'A double brandy now. It's been so long.'

'I want to tell you something?' offered Cobb.

'What? Like you did years ago? Please don't tell me you're back in trouble again?'

'No! I have something for you. Have you got a minute? I'll briefly go through it with you?'

One of the team interrupted Maguire with, 'Guvnor! We're ready for you.'

Maguire gestured his understanding and then said to Cobb, 'Okay, give me a taste or, rather, give me a clue. Three words?'

'I can give you three letters,' revealed Cobb.

'Try me!'

'P.K.K.'

'Is that a delight?' probed Maguire.

'A Turkish one,' replied Cobb.

'You jest?' suggested Maguire who knew immediately that Cobb was onto something.

'When did I ever tell you jokes?'

'Okay, understood,' ventured Maguire. 'Enough for now because now is not a good time. Have you got a pen and paper?'

'I have,' replied Cobb.

'Then ring me on the following number at eight o'clock tonight. Understood?'

Cobb scribbled the 'phone number down and replied, 'Eight! Will do.'

'Is it hot, warm or cold?' inquired Maguire.

'I've no idea,' voiced Cobb. 'But it's recent. It's a clean lift. It's safe, and it's right up your street. Les, things have changed. I'm working in financial services, married, two kids, three-bedroom semi in the suburbs and a member of the local golf club, although I don't play for love nor money. Boring game but influential people. I fell over this. I think in the right hands it's potentially lifesaving.'

'No drainpipes involved?'

'None!'

'How about stuff that fell out of a safe?' probed Maguire.

'I own the safe,' replied Cobb.

'Eight o'clock tonight,' declared Maguire. 'Don't be late.'

'I won't be late. Make sure you're not.'

The call ended with Maguire slightly astonished at the unexpected telephone call. He hit the digits and made another call.

'Is that you, Rafferty?' queried Maguire.

'It is. How are you, Les?'

'I'm good. Where will you be at eight o'clock tonight?'

'Why? Where do you want me to be?'

'With me listening to a voice from an old friend who has a story to tell.'

'What about?'

'The PKK!'

'Who's the storyteller?' inquired Rafferty.

'Sapphire!'

'My office seven-thirty?'

'See you then.'

Nodding to himself, wondering what treasures Cobb had to release, Maguire returned to his conference, concluded the briefing, and later that night listened to what Cobb had to say. He arranged for a face to face meeting with Cobb. Rafferty would be present throughout.

Three days later, Euston railway station was its usual teeming self with people from all over the nation, and beyond, either catching a train, leaving a train, switching trains, or waiting for someone to arrive from a train.

Maguire stood on the marble concourse and waited for Cobb to arrive from an east coast route. It wasn't long before Cobb arrived with an overnight bag over his shoulder. He lugged a black suitcase.

'Heavy!' exploded Cobb when he dropped the suitcase at Maguire's feet.

'Stopping long?' inquired Maguire.

'It's yours now,' replied Cobb. 'Not mine anymore. How are you, Les?'

'Pleased to see you again,' smiled Maguire. 'How long, eight, ten years?'

'Twelve actually.'

'My God! You've put a bit of beef on but otherwise, you look great,' suggested Maguire.

'You don't look so bad yourself,' ventured Cobb. 'Your hair is much longer though, and I see you've got a newer looking leather jacket.'

'You too,' chuckled Maguire. 'I told you pot washing would change your life.'

'It did,' nodded Cobb.

'I'd like to introduce you to a friend of mine,' revealed Maguire. 'His name is Mr Bernard Edwards and he's a member of the Security Service.'

'MI5?'

'Yes! There's a car waiting for us outside. Come on!'

Slightly puzzled, Cobb walked beside Maguire as the detective hoisted Cobb's suitcase off the ground and carried it to the car park where Rafferty opened the boot and helped Maguire place the suitcase inside.

'This is Mr Edwards,' announced Maguire introducing Rafferty to Cobb. 'His work involves counter-terrorism, and his duty is to safeguard national security.'

'Wow!' replied Cobb. 'You've gone up in the world, Les. A spy! I've never met a spy before.'

Cobb and Rafferty, alias Mr Edwards, shook hands before Rafferty replied, 'That may be the case, Mr Cobb, but Mr Maguire here tells me you were a spy a long time ago. Welcome to my world. Jump in. We're going to a safe place to talk.'

'You mentioned financial services?' voiced Maguire. 'What kind?'

'Bank accounts, insurance, loans, creditors and debtors, stuff like that,' smiled Cobb.

The trio drove to the outskirts of London, parked in a secure location, and entered a detached house where Mr Edwards made his guests comfortable, offered them drinks and nibbles, and then settled down to listen to what Cobb had to say.

A suitcase was brought in from the boot of a car.

In the hours that followed Chris Cobb, alias Sapphire revealed to Maguire and Rafferty how his work had taken him into the Turkish community situated in various places in the United Kingdom where he had offered for sale several financial products tailormade for the community. As the months had gone by, he had learnt of the PKK: a proscribed organisation under the Terrorism Act in the UK and elsewhere. It was otherwise known as the armed wing of the People's Defence Force, which was formerly called the Kurdistan National Liberty Army. It was a dangerous group responsible for various terrorist attacks in Ankara and other parts of Turkey which, since 1984, had engaged in an armed struggle against the Turkish state for cultural and political rights, and self-determination for the Kurds in Turkey. The group was founded in 1978, in the village of Fis, by a group of Kurdish students, led by Abdullah Öcalan. They sought the creation of an independent Marxist–Leninist state in the region. It would be called Kurdistan if it ever existed.

Rafferty was particularly interested because the service was investigating financial donations to the illegal group.

Cobb produced evidence of who was donating what to the illegal organisation. His documents revealed the names, addresses, and bank accounts of the donors as well as the amounts donated. It was an incredible find for Rafferty because it not only consolidated the work of the service but did much to extend it.

Historically, it was known that the first-ever PKK training camp was established in 1982 in the Bekaa Valley, Lebanon, which was then under Syrian control. The PKK at that time had the support of the Palestine Liberation Organisation (PLO) and Syria.

Rafferty studied Cobb's documents, knew that everything that was being said was being heard by a team of eavesdroppers in an adjoining room, and knew that the audience with Cobb and Maguire was being videoed for analysis the following day.

In due course, anti-terrorist officers in the United Kingdom detained members of the PKK and seized their assets in Britain. These financial assets remain frozen. They are valued at millions of pounds.

Six months later, on a grey and daunting day, Les Maguire locked his car in the grounds of a cemetery and walked towards a group of people who were celebrating the life of Christopher Cobb: a married man with a family who was employed as a Financial Director in a well-known international company. His children were in attendance along with many of his friends, colleagues, and workmates.

The minister spoke nice words and prayers were said. Hymns at the graveside were sung.

Maguire stood back, some fifty yards from the gathering, wiped a tear from his eyes and paid a quiet moment of respect to a man he had known and worked with for about twenty years of his life. The detective acknowledged that he knew all about Cobb, but Cobb knew virtually nothing about him.

Now he stood apart, watched the family, and knew it was time to close the file and walk away. He had never loved Cobb. It was not that kind of relationship. It was not based on political correctness, ethnicity targets, or false forced friendship.

It was based purely and simply on necessity from both parties.

Maguire had always admired and respected Cobb for his fortitude, his inner strength, and his determination.

When the cortege had moved off and the grave was abandoned and people-free, Maguire moved out of the shadows and placed a simple pink rose beneath the gravestone.

Maguire turned and walked away. It was the way of the job, of secrecy, of mystery, of stories untold and tales still to tell.

Of protecting the vulnerable. Of trust, and loyalty. And of beginning life as a failure and making something of it along the way. Change for the better!

And of a two-way street called RESPECT.

... SAPPHIRE...

The End.
Nearly...

Author's Notes....

'Sapphire' is based upon, and inspired by, the true story of a man I chose to call 'The Subject', as first mentioned in my autobiography (Strike, Strike, Strike) when it was published a few years ago.

The subject was an individual who became a habitual offender through lack of life chances. He was a clever young man with a sharp brain, a quick tongue, and a love of climbing other people's drainpipes and breaking into various premises.

He left school at the age of 16 never having taken the opportunities available to him. Sadly, he came from a broken home and at one stage began to live rough in barns, local parks, and anywhere he could rest his head. His homeland, for want of a better word, was Penrith, but he drifted between several places because of his Romani lifestyle. He had a criminal's mind, an agile body, and an ability to beguile those around him.

During one burglary, the necklace he usually wore was detached from his body as he climbed a drainpipe. I recovered the necklace into my possession. It would lead to his downfall.

I was called out to another break-in, searched the area, and found him hiding nearby. It was the only time he'd activated the burglar alarm and hadn't escaped before a cordon went down. He'd been slowed down by having to climb down from the roof. Arrested, he was taken to the nick and eventually charged with burglary. In all, when re-introduced to the cherished necklace he had left behind on the roof of a jeweller's shop, he admitted over a dozen rooftop climbing burglaries that he was solely responsible for. He always worked alone.

'Are you interested in helping us?' I asked.

He was. The man had become part of a gang, a culture that was occasionally violent and always centred on criminality. He wasn't even sure he was a fully subscribed member of a culture he knew he was a part of, but never understood why he became part of it.

300

The subject pointed the finger at several local crooks and helped secure several convictions. Then he was sent to prison himself. I asked him to look me up when he got out.

When he did, he had no home, no money, no job, and no hope.

I asked a close contact in the catering trade if he would be interested in helping someone out. To my surprise, my contact agreed, and the subject began to work almost right away as a kitchen porter in a hotel on the shores of Ullswater. He had money in his pocket, three square meals a day, and a roof over his head.

In the years that followed, I took several telephone calls from him as a Detective in Cumbria and then the Regional Crime Squad. We seldom met on those occasions. But by then I knew him very well and just knew that what he told me would be right, and it was.

In particular, he reported upon and helped to dissect various networks in the north-west of England that were supplying drugs directly from a link to a gang engaged in importing drugs from South America. His intelligence was top grade. His safety was a dominant factor.

One such local operation was handed over to the Regional Crime Squad because of its complexity. Eventually, other squads and agencies in England became involved and we took a back seat due to the geographical nature of the enquiry. The trail took the police to Dover, a village outside Calais, and a Colombian drugs cartel. One could only describe the two-year-long operation as a significant example of teamwork.

As arranged, the subject changed his name by deed poll and never came to adverse notice again. Sapphire disappeared into who knows where. His codename was never Sapphire, by the way. But he was a gem.

Many years later, the subject went out of his way to contact me. We had known each other for close on twenty years, were never what you might call friends, but were probably best described as 'business associates.'

He told me he'd stumbled across something vitally important and thought he should pass it on. The subject considered the matter to be potentially lifesaving. More phone calls were made between us and these led to a meeting in London. I was accompanied by an officer from the Security Services whom I had known for many years.

The subject was housed safely in the capital where we spoke to him at length. His information was indeed crucial, gratefully received, and high grade. The content remains classified. When I asked him why he had got in touch he told me that many years earlier I had arranged his first job, removed him from a local gang, and given him a new and better lifestyle. Even if it had all begun with washing pots in a hotel on the shores of a lake. He'd never looked back since then and had never forgotten. Married now, with children, he was living in the south of England, or was it the Midlands, or the south-west? Security is always an issue to address. His annual income and status in his chosen organisation were admirable. The individual had done so very well for himself in a profession which had nothing to do with the catering trade. He had changed his life completely and was a totally different person to the drainpipe climber I had once known.

'We're even now,' he explained. 'It's called respect and honour. I've paid my dues. Thank you! My family and friends know nothing of my past and that is the way it will be. We're all done here. When I walk through the door you will never see me again.'

I didn't.

Some years later I learnt of his death. Sadly, he was taken too young and died from a brain tumour without reaching the age of forty.

RIP my drainpipe climber.

~

Reviews

~

'One of the best thrillers and mystery writers in the United Kingdom today'....

Caleb Pirtle 111, International Bestselling Author of over 60 novels, journalist, travel writer, screenplay writer, and Founder and Editorial Director at Venture Galleries.

*

'Paul Anthony is one of the best Thriller Mystery Writers of our times!'...

Dennis Sheehan, International Bestselling Author of 'Purchased Power', former United States Marine Corps.

*

'When it comes to fiction and poetry you will want to check out this outstanding author. Paul has travelled the journey of publication and is now a proud writer who is well worth discovering.' ... Janet Beasley, Epic Fantasy Author, theatre producer and director - Scenic Nature Photographer, JLB Creatives. Also, Founder/co-author at Journey to Publication

*

'Paul Anthony is a brilliant writer and an outstanding gentleman who goes out of his way to help and look out for others. In his writing, Paul does a wonderful job of portraying the era in which we live with its known and unknown fears. I highly recommend this intelligent and kind gentleman to all.' ...

Jeannie Walker, author of the True Crime Story 'Fighting the Devil', 2011 National Indie Excellence Awards (True Crime Finalist) and 2010 winner of the Silver Medal for Book of the Year True Crime Awards.

*

'To put it simply, Paul tells a bloody good tale. I have all his works and particularly enjoy his narrative style. His characters are totally believable and draw you in. Read. Enjoy'....

John White, Reader and Director at Baldwins Restructuring and Insolvency.

*

'Paul Anthony's skills as a writer are paramount. His novels are well-balanced throughout, all of which hold the reader with both dynamic and creative plots and edge-of-your-seat action alike.

His ability to create realistic and true-to-life characters are a strength lacking in many novelists that pen stories based on true events or real-life experience. He is a fantastic novelist that will have you craving for more! Get his books now...a must-have for all serious readers!'

Nicolas Gordon, Screenwriter - 'Hunted: The enemy within'.

*

'Paul Anthony has been working with the Dyslexia Foundation to develop a digital audio Library, he has been very generous in giving his time and expertise for free. As a long-time fan of Paul's work, it was very altruistic of Paul to allow us to use one of his excellent books. We have recently turned 'The Fragile Peace' into our first audiobook, to be used in an exciting project to engage non-readers into the world of literacy. The foundation has an audiobook club that will be running in Liverpool and Manchester and Paul again has been very generous with his time in agreeing to come and talk to the audiobook club about his book The Fragile Peace. The Foundation and clients are very appreciative of the support of the author Paul Anthony.

Steve O'Brien, C.E.O. Dyslexia Foundation,

*

This guy not only walks the talk, but he also writes it as well. Thrillers don't get any better than this...

Paul Tobin, Author, novelist, and poet.

*

The UK ANTI-TERRORIST HOTLINE

~

If you see or hear something that doesn't sound quite right, don't hesitate. You may feel it's nothing to get excited about but trust your instincts and let the police know.

~

Remember, no piece of information is considered too small or insignificant.

~

If you see something suspicious – tell the police.

~

'Suspicious activity could include someone:
Who has bought or stored large amounts of chemicals, fertilisers, or gas cylinders for no obvious reason…?
Who has bought or hired a vehicle in suspicious circumstances…?
Who holds passports or other documents in different names for no obvious reason…?
Who travels for long periods, but is vague about where they're going…?

~

It's probably nothing, but if you see or hear anything that could be terrorist-related trust your instincts and call the Anti-Terrorist Hotline on 0800 789 321.

~

The UK Anti-Terrorist Hotline
0800 789 321

~

THE END…

Until the next time….

Printed in Great Britain
by Amazon

17872502R00174